Heretics

a love story

Mary Saracino

PEARLSONG PRESS
NASHVILLE, TN

Pearlsong Press
P.O. Box 58065
Nashville, TN 37205
www.pearlsong.com
www.pearlsongpress.com

www.marysaracino.com

Book & cover design by Zelda Pudding

Trade paperback ISBN 9781597190732
Ebook ISBN 9781597190749

ALSO BY MARY SARACINO

The Singing of Swans | *Voices of the Soft-Bellied Warrior* | *Finding Grace No Matter What*

Library of Congress Cataloging-in-Publication Data

Saracino, Mary, 1954–
    Heretics : a love story / Mary Saracino.
        pages cm
    ISBN 978-1-59719-073-2 (trade pbk. : alk. paper) — ISBN 978-1-59719-074-9 (ebook)
    1. Twins—Fiction. 2. Sisters—Fiction. 3. Spiritual healing—Fiction. 4. Christian heretics—Fiction. 5. Priests—Fiction. I. Title.
    PS3569.A65H48 2014
    813'.54—dc23
                                    2014004066

FOR JANE

&

Per mie nonne
Fiora Lazzuri Vergamini e Immacolata Patella Saracino

He drew a circle that shut me out—
Heretic, rebel, a thing to flout.
But Love and I had the wit to win:
We drew a circle that took him in!

EDWIN MARKHAM
(1852–1940)

Chapter 1
The Dream

SHARDANA WOKE WITH A START. The chilling dirge of a howling wolf rang in her ears. Her heart raced. She rubbed her eyes, but was unable to erase the face of the animal that had haunted her dream. In the murky residue that lingered from her night vision, Shardana could still feel the anger that radiated from the wolf's bloody stare. His fangs, sharp as the blade of a shepherd's knife, glinted in the moonlight that bathed the deck of the sea-going vessel. His thick coat bristled along the bony ridge of his spine as he prowled the squeaking wooden planks.

Shardana stared into the darkness of her bedroom, allowing the blackness to calm her. *"Dea Madre!"* she called out. She kicked off her blankets and reached across the mattress to where her husband Basilio should have been—and would have been—had he not spent the night at his shepherd's hut outside the village on this early February night, tending his herd of birthing ewes.

Sweat bathed Shardana's brow, though she didn't wipe away the dampness. She grabbed a shawl to chase away the cold before walking to the kitchen to boil some water to make a medicinal remedy to calm her mind.

She stepped softly through the quiet rooms of the house she shared with her husband, her son-in-law Giovanni, and her granddaughter,

Martina, hoping she wouldn't disturb her granddaughter, fast asleep in the second bedroom. The terrible dream wouldn't relinquish the woman, even though she'd left the world of visions and returned to the more solid realm of the living, a realm that contained walls and a roof, a room with tables and chairs, a stone hearth and the embers of a dying fire.

She shivered and pulled her shawl tighter around her shoulders. The image of the wolf remained vivid in her mind. She saw his cocked, mangy head baying at the moon. She felt the sea waters swell and the boat rock roughly against the onslaught of stony waves. She smelled the salty sea air even though she was hundreds of miles from the sea, living as she did in the hills and upland plateaus of Sardinia's Gennargentu Mountains.

She lit a candle and made her way toward the hearth. Stooping low, she tried to coax the embers into a small flame to boil some water. She gently blew to encourage the fire. A flicker of red took hold. As she poured water into a pot, snippets of the dream revisited her: the wolf's loose tongue hanging from his gaping mouth; his saliva dripping onto the wooden boards of the sea-worn deck; the animal foraging dark corners in search of prey.

Shardana's hands trembled. Her legs shook. She reached for a chair. More images rushed at her: the wolf, baring his teeth, lunging at a pile of coiled rope; the rope spinning and twisting, struggling against the sharp edges of the animal's fangs; the fibrous cord transformed into a snake.

"Madonna!" Shardana prayed, her heart pounding. "How can I make this vision stop?"

The images refused to dissipate. The hissing snake spat at the wolf; the snake writhed and shook her flexed body, then spun twice before muscle and bone evaporated into molting skin. The wolf gnashed and tore at the empty membrane. He raised his snout, narrowed his eyes, opened his jaw and wailed at the dark sky.

Shardana shook her head, trying to jostle the lingering images, hoping to send them back into the nether-realms from which they'd come. She wrapped her arms tightly around her chest, rocking back and forth, back and forth as the frightening images faded. She sighed and rubbed her face, her eyes, the back of her sweaty neck. She considered crossing the small lane that separated her house from her twin sister Sarda's house. She wanted to tell Sarda about the wolf and the snake, ask her for help in deciphering the meaning of the dream, but she decided it was best to wait until later, after the sun had risen and Sarda had begun her day. No need to wake her now.

Shardana focused on finishing her task of making a medicinal infusion. As she placed the pot on a hook over the fire, someone knocked on her door. She cocked her head, listening for a voice at the threshold, hoping the caller would identify himself. Perhaps a villager's child had taken sick or a searing inflammation had disturbed the sleep of some over-worked farmer. Countless times before, Shardana had been awakened in the dead of night to ply her trade. The knock sounded again, more loudly.

An insistent whisper called out, "Shardana! Open up!"

Recognizing her twin sister's voice, Shardana smiled. Of course Sarda would have sensed her discomfort. Hadn't they always been connected in that way, one feeling the other's deepest emotions—pleasant or painful? It had been like this since their childhood, perhaps even before, when they had shared their mother's womb. Others thought it uncanny, the way one twin always knew the other's thoughts, always sensed the other's needs. But this second-sense knowing was second-nature to the sisters. Often there was no need to speak or explain. Words were rarely necessary. Somehow, they just knew.

Shardana reached for the lit candle and walked toward the entryway. With her free hand, she opened the door. Sarda stood before her, wrapped in a shawl to shut out the cold air.

"The wolf and the snake?" Shardana asked.

Her twin sister nodded. "I dreamt it, too."

IN THE EARLY HOURS BEFORE DAWN, Shardana and Sarda discussed the many possible meanings of their shared dream. Perhaps all the newborn lambs would die soon or the ewes' milk would run sour. Perhaps a plague would strike the village, causing their husbands, their children, and their neighbors to become grievously ill—maybe even die. Perhaps the wheat would rot in the fields and the villagers would starve next winter. Or perhaps something else was about to occur in their small hamlet, something dire for which they had neither name nor antidote.

"We have to send Martina up to the sheepfold," Shardana said. "She's got to tell Basilio and the others. Warn them to pour a pail of milk on the ground. They've got to give thanks, return that liquid's blessing to the Earth. If they do, we might be able to prevent any curse from taking hold."

Sarda agreed. "Yes, we'll send her as soon as the sun comes up. We can't be too cautious. Something grave is about to happen. I can feel it in my bones."

"What do you make of the sea?" Shardana asked.

"It could be many things," her sister replied. "Since we live in the mountains far from the shore, maybe it's the watery realms of worry. So many are fretting about the harvest. They fear it'll be meager this year. Hunger is a powerful force. Or maybe the choppy water in the dream is the unsettled soul of a villager, or two. I can think of several who are battling anger and a couple of others whose hearts are cracked open with grief. But the iciness of the seawater and the ferocity of the wolf signal something more ominous."

"*Furat chi benit dae su mare,*" Shardana said. She covered her heart with her hand.

"He who comes from across the sea is a thief," Sarda replied, echoing her sister's concern.

"The serpent in the dream is strong medicine," Shardana said.

"It's a good sign, but we shouldn't be overly optimistic," her sister replied.

"Should we tell the villagers?" Shardana asked.

"Yes, " Sarda said. "But we can't be sure just when the wolf will arrive."

"Or under what sort of guise he'll appear," Shardana added.

"We better prepare," Sarda insisted. "We're *majarzas*. It's our sacred duty to protect our people."

Shardana nodded. Much work lay ahead. The wolf's bite would be fierce—perhaps even rabid. And the twins' magic had to be equally potent to counterbalance whatever terrible circumstances were about to unfold.

Chapter 2
The Voyage to Alghero

ANTONIO ALBÓNDIGA STOOD on the deck of the carrack staring at the gloomy expanse of gray sea. His mood was as agitated as the seawater that slapped the belly of the ship. He was angry that his superiors had sent him on this long, uncomfortable voyage across the Mediterranean, exiling him from Spain, his homeland, so he could atone for his most recent bout of misbehavior. They'd warned him that the reassignment to a parish in Alghero, on the western coast of Sardinia, was the last chance he had to set things right. They'd admonished him to make use of the opportunity to prove his mettle and reaffirm his allegiance. Antonio failed to see any value in the kernel of redemption they'd offered. He felt outraged, persecuted. While he confessed that he had exhibited an error in judgment, he refused to admit that he had disgraced himself. He didn't believe his actions warranted as grave a reprimand as he'd received.

Antonio watched the morning sun streak the sky with layers of orange and red. On this morning of the second day of his seven-day journey, he failed to appreciate the beauty in the sunrise. It only made him homesick for the balcony off his rooms in Seville where he always took his morning meal. Here, on this godforsaken ship, no doting housekeeper knocked on his door, presenting him with a silver tray of breakfast treats. Here, no one cared that he preferred grilled sausages and a sliver of Spanish omelet to a meal of stale bread and moldy cheese.

The damp air chilled him. He pulled his cloak tight against his body and shoved his hands into his pockets. All around him the boat's crewmen worked, mopping the deck, securing knots, observing the sky, monitoring the horizon. Once or twice a sailor would pass by and nod a greeting or even venture to say, "Good morning, *Padre.*" But Antonio would only purse his lips and grunt "Harrumph." Never did his eyes meet theirs, never did he smile or nod or wave an affable greeting. He looked beyond and through the crew members as if they were bothersome children whom he'd rather scold than placate.

Days before, when Antonio had first boarded the ship, he was introduced to the Captain, who'd extended his hand to greet him. "Welcome, *Padre.* We hope your trip is safe and enjoyable. I look forward to dining with you in my quarters tomorrow evening." At this cordial welcome the gloom in Antonio's eyes briefly lifted. "It would be a pleasure, Captain. I have no doubt we will enjoy one another's company. Until then—"

A crewman had carried Antonio's bags to his quarters and set them down near the narrow cot in small room that was to be his home throughout the voyage. When the sailor paused, waiting for a nod of gratitude or some indication that the priest was thankful for his help, Antonio scoffed. "Go now. I have little time to spare for a *peón* like you." The porter left in silence, but soon shared news of his encounter with the other crewmen. "Priests are the worst," he said. "Always looking for us to fill the church's coffers, but never expressing any gratitude of sharing any kind remarks with the likes of us."

Antonio settled into his cabin and rested for an hour before growing bored with the solitude. He longed for a glass of wine and good conversation. Hoping to encounter the Captain, some other ranking officer, or an educated fellow traveler or two, he ventured onto the deck. To his dismay, he found only two other travelers, merchants with dark hair and dark skin. "*Marranos!*" he scoffed. "Why do they insist on infesting every inhabitable corner of the world?! Heretics, every single one of them. They should all burn in hell." When the merchants glanced at him and nodded in greeting he sneered and turned away, pretending to watch the waves swell on the open expanse of sea.

Unable to ease his rising agitation, Antonio nursed it with all the doting care a young mother reserves for her firstborn. The merchants—and others like them—were tainting the blood of true Christians. Why couldn't the bishop and the archbishop see that? Though he had tried his best to help eradicate this blight upon Christendom, his superiors had misunderstood his actions. From the very first day of his service to the diocese, he had believed that the ones who controlled his destiny had been lying in wait to squelch his ambitions. Every misspoken word was charted in some imaginary book of grievances, scored and tallied to be used against him when the time was right. Every task he'd insufficiently fulfilled, every obligation he'd mismanaged, every action mishandled became a smudge on his soul, a sign of his incompetence. He'd convinced himself that his superiors had underestimated his determination and resilience. These were men who'd easily and capriciously dismantle his chances to succeed. He'd lived among them long enough to know that they paid no mind to the careers of underlings, unless they found their lackeys useful in advancing their own interests. Antonio cursed the day he ever entertained the idea of rising in the ranks of such scoundrels.

While Antonio compiled a list of grievances and possible courses of revenge, his bones listened to the lap of the waves against the ship's hull. The rhythmic roll and nudge of the salt water roused long forgotten memories of his mother, Maria, memories tucked away in the recesses of his marrow of when he was a baby and she'd cradled him in her strong arms, nestling his small body against her soft breasts, rocking him to sleep as she hummed a lullaby. Though he was an adult now, and a man whose heart had long been hardened against his mother's tenderness, some outpost in his belly heeded the ebb and flow of the seawater. As the waves rushed forward, then retreated, his ears sucked in the amniotic sound, thirsty for comfort, though his brain disallowed such weakness.

His destination lay in the distance, far across the Mediterranean. The carrack that carried him had set sail from Spain, charting its course for the Bay of Alghero on the western shore of Sardinia, an island that Antonio Albóndiga thought of as unremarkable. The little he knew about Sardinia he'd learned from the tales his father Pablo had told him years before, when Antonio was a youngster eager for stories about the skirmishes and battles that had bloodied the sea waters that separated his homeland from that far-off inhospitable place.

Throughout the long winter nights of his youth Antonio had sat at Pablo's feet, rapt in attention, lapping up every story his father told him about Spain's conquest of Sardinia's backward shepherds. Antonio's imagination was captured by sagas of wars and conquerors. His youthful daydreams had been peopled with real or fictitious (it mattered not to him) tales of kings and generals, pompous popes and their powerful allies, whose ambitious feats and political machinations he wished to emulate. His father's rendition of maritime lore omitted the mundane details about the daily lives of the peasants and the farmers, the soldiers, the wives and mothers and children whose livelihoods were decimated in the aftermath of historical upheavals, and Antonio never thought to ask. He wasn't interested in the human casualties of war. He believed he was destined to live among the kings of time, not grovel beside humble and powerless *peóns*. When he wasn't attending to his studies, he spent a considerable portion of what little free time he had whittling branches into swords and racing over the fields subjugating trees, rocks and animals and claiming them for his imaginary realm.

Spurred on by his father's history lessons, Antonio trapped rabbits and tossed them into makeshift jails he'd built out of twigs and mud. He tried the animals for high treason and hung their trembling bodies from the low branches of olive trees. He hunted feral cats, crying "Kill the heathen Moors! Annihilate the heretical Jews!" as he chased the frightened animals over the fields near his father's house. When he caught the wild cats, he sentenced them to death for crimes against the Holy See and tied stones around their scrawny necks before tossing them into the river.

One afternoon when Antonio was ten, he and his father traveled to a nearby village to buy a round of cheese. There they came upon a mob of angry men taunting a Jewish family who lived near the outdoor market.

"Jesus killers!" the men yelled. "Heretics! You deserve to die!"

The husband and wife huddled together, heads hunched in shame, their arms encircling their son and daughter, shielding them from the mob's ire. In unison the family stepped back, attempting to retreat from the henchmen and escape back into their home, which stood several steps behind them. The men rushed at them, erasing each retreating step. One man spit into the husband's stoic face. Another tossed eggs at the trembling wife. One tore away the daughter's headscarf. Another poked the boy with the blunt end of a stick.

Antonio fixed his eyes upon the Jewish lad, entranced by the boy's defiant gaze. As the mob's cries grew louder, fiercer, the boy's face grew tenser and more despairing. His mouth tightened, then opened wide as he cried out, "Papa!" Antonio shuddered and reached for his own father's hand, but Pablo brushed him away.

A man in the crowd yelled "Death to the heretics!" as he lit a torch and raced toward the family's modest house. He kicked open the door and tossed the torch inside. The home burst into flame. Smoke billowed into the sky; sparks flew. The family pleaded for mercy.

"We will convert!" the father promised. He fell to his knees and cried, "Please don't harm my wife! Please, spare my children!"

Another man grabbed a rope and shouted, "Take them to the trees!"

The crowd encircled the family. The husband kicked and punched, using all his strength, but he was unable to fend off the attackers. The wife bit and screamed, slapping at her captors and howling, but she was unable to stop the onslaught. The daughter and son began to sob. They clenched their fists and swung at the men, hitting the faces and arms, chests and shoulders of the aggressors.

Antonio watched with fascination and dread. He wanted to join the men, sentence the family to death as he'd done to the rabbits and cats he'd captured, but something held him back. He recognized something in that boy no older than himself—something that would not let him revel, as he wanted to, in the horrors he was witnessing. He wanted to rush into the mob and grab the boy, lead him through the back lanes of the village toward the outlying fields, liberating him from the outcome he knew lay ahead.

Two members of the mob grabbed the boy first and dragged him to a nearby tree. They hung a noose around his neck and strung him from the branches. The boy's mother collapsed to the ground. Her inconsolable wailing pierced Antonio's ears.

A shudder shivered through Antonio's body. His stomach began to twist and threaten to heave his breakfast, but he swallowed his fear and focused his gaze on the horrors unfolding before his eyes.

The boy's father reached for his daughter to protect her, but the men pushed him to the dirt and grabbed her hair, dragging her to the tree. They hung her too, as her mother and father pleaded for mercy, their wails of grief shattering the dusty air. "Silence!" the men ordered, but the husband and wife were too bereft to obey. The men stabbed the wife in the heart, then beat the husband senseless before setting their bodies on fire.

"Die, heretics! Die!" Pablo cried out, his voice joining the rousing voices of the mob.

"Die, heretics! Die!" Antonio mimicked. A piercing pain claimed his temples and his mouth contorted as he stared at the swollen, distorted face of the dead Jewish boy.

MEMORIES OF THOSE BOYHOOD DAYS—the hunted animals, the tales of seagoing battles, the vacant eyes of the dead Jewish boy, how his flaccid body swung from the tree branch, the acrid smell of burning flesh and burning houses—were buried deep in Antonio's bones. His mind was forever closed against the horrors he'd witnessed and the terrors he had enjoyed. He preferred to wander through other less taxing childhood memories that did not burden his heart with inexplicable pity and grief, for he couldn't find a way to reconcile his lust for revenge with his love for pleasure and his need for forgiveness for sins he could not confess.

As the cold sea winds chilled his cheeks, Antonio closed his eyes and saw his mother's face—the tears she'd shed when he'd told her he was going to be sent away, the way her hand had stifled her cries when he'd told her the reasons why. "Your father would have intervened on your behalf," she insisted. But Pablo had been dead for nearly eight years, and his influence was as cold as his lifeless body.

On the boat sailing toward Sardinia Antonio stared at the seawater, ruminating and cursing the twist of fate that had led him to his exile. In a few days he would arrive in Alghero, the peninsular port that had once been a trading post for ancient Phoenicians and later a Saracen naval base from which the Moors had launched raids on southern France, the Italic mainland, and other strategic regions throughout the Mediterranean. The thought of being exiled to that city made his tense brow tighten even more, a precursor to an impending migraine.

Antonio briefly considered how his dead father might have reacted to his son's impending plight. "Impertinent asses," Pablo would have said. "Be strong in your convictions, Antonio. Prove them wrong." A brief smile lingered on Antonio's lips. In a low, strong voice he said, "Only a fool would underestimate Pablo Albóndiga's son."

ALTHOUGH ANTONIO ALBÓNDIGA wasn't aware of it, having done little to prepare for his departure other than to pack his few belongings and curse his fate, the city of Alghero had originally been a small fishing hamlet called L'Aleguerium, in honor of the copious sea vegetables washed ashore by the swiftly flowing currents. Like Antonio, that village would fall prey to the precarious whims of time and circumstance, twin, disinterested elements that ushered in one's fate, sealing one's fortune—good or ill.

L'Aleguerium had been home to seafarers, fishers, and harvesters of coral, secured from the reefs that populated the harbor with a seemingly inexhaustible storehouse of wealth. Deep beneath the bay waters, clusters of red-orange coral reached toward the dim surface sunlight. These encrusted casings, tossed away by tiny sea animals, had been hardened by time and tide and sea salt. The reef-bound sea-bottom promised riches to those brave enough to delve into the watery netherworld.

L'Aleguerium was not destined to remain a tiny fishing town; after supporting countless generations of seafaring families, the hamlet outgrew its maritime identity. The sons and daughters of its sea-loving inhabitants began to also make their living from the surrounding landscape. They mined silver, grew grain, harvested sea salt, became merchants of fine jewelry, purveyors of cheese, crafters of breads and pastries, vendors of meats procured from native sheep and wild *cinghiali*, sellers of fresh asparagus, fava beans, greens and herbs teased from the willing soil.

In time, L'Aleguerium came to be known as Alghero—*full of algae*—a descriptive name that failed to evoke the image of glory or riches that its inhabitants envisioned as its rightful future. History lists Alghero's official founding as 1102 Anno Domini. Geography would play an influential role in the city's destiny; the land and the bay shaped Alghero's prospects as a pivotal trading post. Geography also condemned it to be an object of desire, coveted by competing nation states lusting after mercantile power and expanded empire. Many were the heads of state who craved the strategic vantage point promised by this shimmering Sardinian city by the bay.

Nearly five hundred years before Antonio Albóndiga's mother gave birth to him in the remote hills of the Spanish countryside, Saracen Moors had staked out a presence along Sardinia's coastline, using the harbors of port cities as bases from which to launch raids to control trade and extend their empire. For three hundred years the Saracens sailed from Sardinian outposts, stealing food, kidnapping residents, seeking ransoms. When ransoms went unpaid, they shipped their wretched captives back to North Africa to a life of enforced slavery.

Antonio's favorite bedtime stories were the tales his father had told him about the Saracen conquests and the eventual undoing of the Moors. Pablo's eyes would grow wide in anticipation, his breath quickening, as he recounted how Saracen raiders ransacked whole villages, carrying off screaming daughters, slaying strong sons, stealing grain and livestock. "The heathen Moors were intent on eradicating good Christian people," Pablo would insist. "It was necessary for Christian countries to join forces and defeat them."

"Did Christ's people prevail?" Antonio asked, hoping, praying that they had.

"The Saracens' might was seemingly unstoppable," Pablo continued. "But by the beginning of the eleventh century Sardinia had had enough. Its ruling families had grown weary of fending off invaders. They were tired of fighting to preserve their wealth for their heirs."

"How rich were they?" Antonio asked, his eyes glistening with envy.

"So rich that their wealth couldn't be counted," his father explained. "They owned salt and silver mines, fields overflowing with grain. They owned the seas teeming with fish. Their pasturelands were bursting with hearty cattle and robust sheep!"

"Those greedy Saracens were trying to keep it all that for themselves!" Antonio asserted.

"Yes!" his father replied. "But the Sardinians had a plan. The ruling families hated each another far less than they hated Museto, the Saracen Prince of Mogeid-al-Amiri."

Antonio nodded. "So they got together and killed all the Moors? Museto, too?!"

"No. Not quite. But they did the next best thing. They formed an alliance with Genoa and Pisa, two city states on the Italic peninsula who'd been their trading partners for a long, long time."

"And then did they kill all the Saracens?!"

"Enough to take back the island," Pablo explained. "But beware the motives of unproven allies. Of course, the Genovese and the Pisans had their own visions of wealth! You understand. Had you or I been a Pisan or a Genovese, the whole world would've opened to us once we'd taken control of those Tyrrhenian trade routes."

"Would we have piles of golden coins? Chests overflowing with diamonds and rubies?"

"All that and more," his father crowed. "

"What happened next?"

"Well, my son, Sardinia's elite families got stabbed in the back! Life is not often fair. But if fate deals you the right hand, it can be prosperous. The Pisans and the Genovese didn't waste any time. They each took some of the most strategic port cities on the island—the very same ones they'd just wrestled from the Moors."

"So they got very rich and very powerful. And the Saracens were wiped out. End of story!" Antonio crowed.

"Not so fast," his father cautioned. "Always watch your back, Antonio. Someone you think is a friend can turn on you in an instant. Pisa and Genoa became arch-enemies. Each grabbed everything they could get their hands on—salt and silver, farmlands and pasturelands, trading routes and the fishes in the deep blue sea. Avarice? Perhaps. Or perhaps simply good business sense."

"I want to be a businessman!" Antonio announced.

"You have the keen intelligence, my son. And the ambition. Still, God's hand guides each man's destiny. And so it was with the Genoa and Pisa. For many years the power shifted back and forth between them, like a pendulum. Sardinia's ruling families played both ends against the middle, trying to curry favor with whichever city-state held the upper hand.

"Control shifted from one to another. Treaties were signed. And broken. Castles were besieged. Rulers overthrown. Land was transferred and property and rights-to-rule were inherited through royal blood lines. Allegiances wavered. It would have made your head spin,

Antonio. When military might proved ineffective, marriage contracts were proposed. Aristocratic daughters were wed to blue-blooded sons, forming fresh coalitions. By the middle of the thirteenth century protracted arrangements had been sealed. After the dust had settled and the wedded couples had been toasted, Sardinia belonged to the Tuscans!"

"Did the Genovese fight back?!"

"Ha! This is where youth fails you. The pope stepped in and disrupted everything!"

"Why?" Antonio asked.

"There are no such things as religious matters or temporal matters. Only political matters. Obliging a friend, Pope Boniface VIII cast the final deciding die. Complete with a formal ceremony in Rome! The pope named James II of Aragon as seigneur in perpetuity over Sardinia and Corsica, its island neighbor."

"And the Tuscans?"

"They weren't consulted. Neither were the Genovese. Years before, in Sicily, Boniface—when he was still only a cardinal—had forged a friendship with King James II. Maybe they shared a supper of roasted lamb and rice seasoned with saffron, a bottle of dry red wine; perhaps they navigated the muddy waters of their ambitions, anchoring their aspirations into a burgeoning bond. The alliance proved fruitful for the king. Years later, when the cardinal became the pope, he tossed a generous bone to the Spanish king. Boniface dusted off some five-hundred-year-old document—a deed of gift from Louis the Pious, the third son of Charlemagne. It didn't matter—to the pope or to the king—that the document was of questionable origin. He was the pope! He could do whatever he wanted. In the blink of an eye, Sardinia belonged to the Spanish. And that, my son, is how Spain came to own that godforsaken nub of rock in the Mediterranean."

Each night Antonio's dreams were filled with the heroic tales his father had told him. In the morning he would awaken, clutching the handle of his hand-fashioned wooden sword. Before he ate breakfast he would pray to be strong and brave enough to emulate the men who fought to rescue Sardinia from the heathen Moors and claim the island for his beloved country Spain. Later that day, more wild cats and rabbits would succumb to his desire to be a good and faithful soldier in

Christ's army.

Antonio's mother, Maria, tried to dissuade her husband from planting seeds of warfare and bloodshed into the mind of her youngest, most cherished son. She'd seen Antonio torture the wild creatures, witnessed the gleeful sneer upon his face as he executed them. She worried that his actions were more than mere child's play. She noticed that he often had to take to his bed with a migraine after one of his torturous escapades in the fields. On nights when Pablo was too tired or too disinterested to entertain Antonio with tales of mayhem and violence, Maria offered stories of her own. She spun tales of noble knights rescuing beautiful maidens. She shared folklore renditions of talking trees and sly foxes outwitting humble farmers and war-weary soldiers. Antonio's mood would sour and he would complain that his mother's stories were for simple-minded girls, not heroic Christian boys with a duty to fulfill.

At night after Antonio had gone to bed, Maria would plead with her husband, "Use your influence. Find a way to get Antonio an education. Perhaps the priesthood. I will not have him be a soldier and die a bloody death in some distant country!"

Less disturbed by Antonio's affection for bloody battles and military might, Pablo would shake his head and reply, "He's a healthy boy. And boys are virile and fierce. What good could he do as a priest?"

"Plenty!" Maria had insisted. "He is smart and ambitious. He could be a peaceable shepherd, like Christ Our Lord."

"You don't know your own son, Maria. He's more lion than lamb. More soldier than shepherd. Let him be. God will take care of the rest."

Maria would not be deterred. Every day she lit vigil candles at the altar of the Madonna, beseeching Our Lady to ask Her son, Jesus, to have pity on a mother's heart and spare her sweet Antonio.

MORE THAN ONE HUNDRED YEARS before Antonio Albóndiga was born in the countryside outside Valencia, the Spanish claimed the island that would one day become the place of his exile. As a grown man Antonio had forgotten all but the slimmest of details of that conquest once related with fervor by his father. It took King James II of Aragon twenty-six years to raise enough funds to send an armed fleet to claim Sardinia and establish a Spanish presence there. Half of the monies that filled the Spanish coffers and funded the king's military take-over were generously provided by none other than his mitered friend, Pope Boniface VIII.

In 1353, over a century before Antonio Albóndiga set eyes on the brilliant blue waters of the Bay of Alghero, a Spanish fleet entered the harbor. The ships' imposing banners—a Catalan crown encircling four red pillars, floating above a band of blue, inscribed with fierce red birds—angered Alghero's residents. They revolted, killing the Catalan commanding officer. Spain sent twelve thousand soldiers and one hundred galleys to quell the uprising.

Blood was wasted. Lives were lost. Peace remained elusive.

When a treaty was finally drawn up, the pact forced Alghero's inhabitants—the men, women and children of Sardinian birth, and the second, third and fourth generation Genovese born on Sardinian soil—to abandon their homes, their shops, and their livelihoods. Under penalty of death, all non-Spanish citizens were ousted from the city. The prohibition spawned rebellion. Under cover of darkness the displaced sneaked back inside the city's gates, raiding shops, burning buildings, wreaking havoc upon the conquering Aragonese. Though valiant, the former residents' fierce attempts to regain control of their city proved futile. Catalan sovereignty endured.

ON THE THIRD EVENING of Antonio's sea voyage to Alghero, the captain invited him to share a meal.

"Welcome to my table, *Padre*. I hope you find the supper to your liking."

Antonio's eyes widened when he saw the platter of fish and fava beans, and two bottles of red wine. "I have no doubt I will savor every bite and every sip, Captain."

"Please sit. And enjoy."

Antonio filled his plate and ate with gusto. He cleared his plate, then filled it again. He emptied and refilled his wineglass.

"How is it that you came to be on my ship, *Padre?*"

"I'm on an important—though secret—mission, sent by none other than the Archbishop of Seville! Without going into details, suffice it to say that I'm to ensure that the Catholics of Alghero adhere to the tenets of their faith."

"I'm sure you'll find that quite challenging, *Padre.*"

"Why? Are they all heathens, straying from the fold?"

"Not all of them. Of course. But the history of the city leads me to assume that a fair amount of them are, shall we say, less than pious. Even though they're mostly Spanish through and through. You might find some comforting similarities between your new city and Seville."

Antonio scoffed. "Nonsense! One is an uncivilized outpost and the other a thriving metropolis."

"Perhaps, *Padre.* But you might be surprised at what you'll find when you step foot in that bustling city on the bay. Our beloved Spain has ruled Alghero for over a century. It's practically more Spanish than Seville."

"Impossible!" Antonio scoffed before draining his glass of wine and refilling it.

"Well, of course that wasn't true at first. Alghero's residents didn't succumb without their fair share of bloody battles. But it didn't take long for the Spanish king to order Aragonese-Catalan officials and families of high standing to emigrate to Alghero. Soon, fancy castles fell into Aragonese hands. Villas were appropriated, land holdings were seized. And the yellow Catalan flag fluttered in the sea breezes. Within twenty years important families from Barcelona, Valencia, and Mallorca joined the Catalan settlers. Eventually Spaniards of lesser nobility arrived and the city was resettled with immigrants, all loyal to the throne of Aragon.

"Those Spanish transplants enjoyed the easy access to fine fabrics from Tuscany and Flanders and sumptuous foods from all over the Mediterranean. But the native Sardinians didn't fare as well. Being an island and all, they were used to dealing with conquerors. And to them, one vanquisher was indistinguishable from another. Romans. Moors. Pisans. Genovese. Spanish. The way they saw it, a foreign hand is an alien hand that only robs them of their bounty and their birthright."

"But surely," Antonio insisted, "they could see the benefits that would come from being part of the Spanish empire. The culture. The food. The religious and political might."

"Let's just say they didn't quite rejoice about any of it. Or give up so easily. It took nearly two decades for Spain to silence the insurgency. There were midnight raids and other acts of rebellion. So the Spanish king ordered more Spaniards to immigrate and, in time, the Spanish loyalists infiltrated every cobblestone road and byway, every *piazza* and shop, all the stone churches in the city. Catalan became the language of commerce, respectability, and power."

"And for that they should be grateful!"

"Ah, I thought you would've been a more astute observer of human nature, *Padre*. What was also usurped was the Sardinian Sardo, the *lingua prima* that had once danced upon the tongues of the island's native inhabitants. All that was intrinsically innate to the city—the vowels and consonants of its mother tongue, the fine *pecorino* sheep's milk cheeses, the eerie, melancholy tones of its triple-piped *launeddas*—had been banished. The town was fully clothed in Aragon customs and traditions. The Sardinians must have felt violated, don't you think, *Padre*? And angry. And you know nothing good can come of that now, don't you?"

"I see nothing wrong with civilizing brutes and bores," Antonio retorted. "Sometimes people have to be saved in spite of themselves."

THE CAPTAIN INVITED ANTONIO to dine with him one more evening before he grew tired of the priest's pedantic opinions and his myopic vision of humanity. Throughout the rest of the long voyage, Antonio was left to entertain himself through what felt like endless days and nights. He spent most of his time alone in his small, cramped quarters, avoiding contact with the merchants he'd seen on the first day at sea.

Twice during the remaining days of the voyage he craved fresh air and ventured out onto the deck, glancing with disinterest at the open sea. Each time a stiff wind slapped his uncovered head, spraying his face with salty droplets of water. His gray-green eyes mirrored the color of the waves that roared across the open expanse of sea. His thin brown hair flew about the crown of his head, buffeted by the steady stream of air that wafted around his cold ears. A chill shivered up his spine, and he shuddered before pulling his long, black cloak tighter cross his shoulders and hurrying back to his quarters.

Antonio hated the sea. He despised its salty sting, its odious scent, its impetuous disturbances. He longed to be on high ground, to stand on top of a mountain or on a hillside green with treetops and vegetation and to look at the bright blue sky, drinking in its cloudless splendor.

Though Antonio wouldn't have admitted it to others, he was a man of stone and earth. His great-grandfather, Marco, had been a farm worker, tilling the hillsides outside of Valencia, tending the olive trees and, afterwards, pressing their green flesh into sweet-scented, rich oil. By a fluke of kindness the man who owned the estate upon which Antonio's great-grandfather worked had died without an heir. The landowner had left the estate and all its holdings to Marco Albóndiga. Marco, who loved the olive trees as dearly as he loved his sons and daughters, had taught Antonio's grandfather, Jose, to tenderly tend the olive grove and supervise the pruners and pickers who now worked for the landowning Albóndiga family. Jose also oversaw the family's sheep-fold and lemon groves. Marco and Jose were compassionate bosses, having known first-hand the boot-heel of cruelty at the hands of others. They treated their farmhands and shepherds well, and in time their reputation as equitable employers earned them the trust and the loyal, hard labor of their workers.

Antonio's father, Pablo, was sent to school and learned to read and write, for his family recognized that he didn't share his grandfather's affinity for the trees, nor his father's patience with the sheep and the laborers. Pablo was a man of ambitions, a self-styled aristocrat with no bloodlines to afford him the status or stature that came with noble titles and land holdings. He became a magistrate, serving the court of a local duke, a man who made it possible for Antonio to enter seminary and, to Antonio's mother's relief, become a priest. Everyone in the Albóndiga family held high hopes that someday Pablo's son would wear a bishop's miter, or maybe even the red robes of a cardinal. Even after Antonio was ordained a priest, his mother kneeled before the Madonna's altar begging for the Mother of God to intercede so that Antonio would put his considerable gifts to good use in saving the souls of sinners.

Antonio's mother's fervent wish was that her son would not succumb to the greed of politicians or the death-wishes of military men. She thought his severe headaches were a sign from God that her beloved Antonio was not fulfilling his spiritual duties. She still feared that Antonio had been hardened by the military tales her husband had long ago instilled in him. She knew her son's hands were stained with the blood of countless cats and rabbits that had been sacrificed to his misguided dreams of power and conquest. She also feared his heart had been stained by the way Pablo's temper sometimes erupted, causing him to lash out and strike her. Several times Pablo's fist had hit Antonio as he stepped between Pablo and Maria, trying to shield his mother from his father's outbursts. She'd sobbed then, for herself and her son, knowing she could not protect either of them from the inexplicable rage that sometimes exploded from deep inside her husband. She hoped and prayed that her son would not follow in Pablo's footsteps. She pleaded with God, believing that if Antonio was permitted to wear a cardinal's red robes, his soul might be spared the damnation of a life lived only to sow hatred, instill fear, and dishonor others.

Antonio preferred to forget that he was the great-grandson of a humble fieldworker. He was on an intimate basis with power, having long lusted after it and all he believed it could provide. He understood a man's need to control his fate, dictate the outcome of his future. Hadn't his great-grandfather Marco proven that to be true? Hadn't Marco seized fate by the throat and strangled poverty, banishing it from the destiny of his heirs? Hadn't he been loyal to his own betterment, the single-minded urge to rise above his lowly beginnings to make something more of himself, his legacy? Marco had proven that loyalty to one's fate was all the comfort a man could hold fast to at the end of his life. It was true that Antonio's grandfather, Jose, had often relayed stories to his grandson about Marco and his beloved olive trees, but Antonio's mind had translated these tales into chronicles of rising above and surpassing the shame of poverty and servitude. He held no reverence for the passionate connection that tethered his great-grandfather to a life lived in service to olives and sheep and humans. That was folly to Antonio, merely a romanticized memory served up by his grandfather Jose, who needed the comfort of lies to chase away the chill left by the loss of his father, Marco.

Antonio understood the pangs of disloyalty, the steep requirements of fidelity at all costs. He was no stranger to bribes or avarice. He accepted that humans were frail and weak, easily caught between their desire for good and their desire for self-gratification. Life had taught him that the flesh was immeasurably more pleasing than the spirit, but not as readily forgiving. He had imbibed in abundant quantities of red wine and indulged his palate in platefuls of rich tortes, roasted meats, savory pies, freshly made bread, succulent paella, even as the people of his parish, whom he'd been called to serve, starved outside the windows of his dining room. Holy water might save their souls, but their bodies were doomed to decay for want of a crust of bread. Had *Padre* Albóndiga given one-tenth of his daily meal allotment to fill the bellies of his parishioners, no child in his congregation would've gone hungry.

Still for all Antonio's many faults, gluttony was not his most grievous offense. The *padre* was arrogant and vain, loyal to no one and nothing except his own interests. He'd lost the kindhearted generosity that had endeared his great-grandfather Marco to others and that had secured the Albóndiga family's exit out of poverty. Antonio had lost the determination and strength of character to place others before all else, a trait possessed by his grandfather Jose. And he'd lost the common sense so important to his father, Pablo, that had enabled him to choose his alliances with care, meting out his loyalty only to those who could secure his children their rightful place in the prominent sectors of society.

Antonio's aspirations had included marrying the beautiful daughter of a local count, but his father finally abided by his wife's wishes and decided it best that his son take on the duties of a priest. In truth, Antonio might have made a splendid pirate—in the ruthless pursuit of gold and gems, sending to the plank anyone who tried to undermine his authority, tossing back a swill of grog as the poor fellow toppled foot over head into the murky mouth of the sea. Any poor fellow who crossed Antonio's path the day after a night of excessive merriment, during which he'd dream of courting princesses and their fortunes, might end up pushed to the cobblestone street or slapped across the mouth with a sudden outburst of Antonio's considerable outrage—outbursts often fueled by insufferable migraines that plagued him from time to time, especially when he felt overwhelmed by stress.

To those who'd endlessly refill his wine glass or re-stock his larder with fine sweets and the finest of meats, Antonio was a true and loyal friend. Had the encounter in the dark alleyway after a night of drunken revelry two months before been less messy, Albóndiga wouldn't have found himself on the sea-going vessel bound for Sardinia. His lapse in judgment would've been dismissed as a frightful mistake, an unfortunate incident, instead of grounds for arrest and perhaps a trial. In a civilized society the authorities couldn't refuse to exact punishment when one's dinner knife was plunged into the thigh of the illegitimate son of a *vizconde,* a viscount who was the distant cousin of the Archbishop of Seville.

The other mishap, in which Antonio's frightful migraines had caused him to vomit on the visiting cardinal, could have been more easily forgiven, even overlooked, had it not followed shortly on the heels of the incident with the *vizconde's* illegitimate son.

Albóndiga's superiors were relieved that the man Antonio had harmed wasn't the legal heir to the *vizconde's* estate and fortune. Rumors abounded that the mother of the man Antonio had injured was a gypsy who'd given birth nine months after she'd read the *vizconde's* palm. It was Antonio's great fortune that the man he'd knifed was an illegitimate commoner, though the blood that ran through the man's veins was, in part, royal. To Antonio, and many others, the man's gypsy lineage branded him an outsider, a worthless malcontent, less valuable than the rats that scavenged the dirty alleyways.

The lowliness of the victim's status provided the church authorities with some latitude in discerning how best to proceed with handing down Antonio's punishment. They were less inclined to turn Antonio over to governmental authorities, and they knew the civil authorities wouldn't force their hand in this matter. If they could handle the situation internally, they could avert attention from the unfortunate incident and avoid disgracing the office of the bishop for whom Albóndiga worked. A scandal it was not; a blemish on the respectability of the Holy See it was.

Antonio's ties to his distant cousin Juan de San Martin, the son of Antonio's mother's third cousin, would also prove useful in lessening the severity of his punishment. Juan worked for Tomas de Torquemada, the Grand Inquisitor appointed by King Ferdinand and Queen Isabella. This enabled Antonio's superiors to make a strong case that the unfortunate incident was a religious matter and should be handled by diocesan officials, for the *vizconde's* illegitimate half-gypsy son qualified as an undesirable heretic—removing the need for civil charges. The civil authorities acquiesced once the archbishop convinced them that he would personally see that Antonio would be reprimanded. He was eager to be rid of Antonio. Time and time again, the priest's errant behavior and demeanor had proven to be unseemly and unpredictable. The archbishop reasoned that exile to Sardinia would suffice. The step-sister city Alghero would be as dire a jail cell as any Spanish dungeon.

After Antonio learned of his impending exile, he sent a letter to his distant cousin, Juan, asking him to intercede and prevent his deportation. "I pledge my service to your Holy Cause," Antonio had vowed. Antonio would never know if his letter arrived safely or if Juan approached the archbishop on Antonio's behalf. The archbishop's orders were swiftly executed. Within days, Antonio was on the ship to Sardinia.

AFTER BEING SNUBBED by the captain, who had ignored Antonio's repeated requests to dine with him again, the priest skulked in his quarters, spending hours laying on his bed, brooding and concocting ways to get a message to his cousin Juan. "More than anyone else, he will understand!"

He recalled the times when he had dined with his cousin and how, after a satisfying meal, he had leaned forward in his chair, glass of red wine in hand, eyes intent on Juan's animated face, listening with rapt attention as his cousin denounced the sins of the Christian heretics, the Moorish *moriscos* and the Hebrew *marrano*. Both men despised Jews and Muslims—even those who'd professed to have turned away from their ungodly religious ways and rites to embrace the salvation of Christ. Antonio looked on gleefully as his cousin ranted about the need to torture, maim, even kill the turncoat Jews and Moors—those *conversos*—who had professed the Catholic faith in name only, going through the motions in public while reverting to their traditional, illicit practices behind the closed doors of their heathen homes.

ON THE LAST DAY of the long voyage to Alghero, Antonio left the stuffy confines of his quarters to stroll the ship's deck. The afternoon light was fading and the fresh sea air cleared his lungs, though it did nothing to unclutter his mind. Antonio's heart ached with the desire for vengeance. His mouth filled with bile, which he pushed to the edges of his pursed lips before spitting it into the sea. It was then that his mind finally and completely squelched the insistent hope harbored in his body.

In the marrow that coursed through his bones, a small part of him still believed that the sea and the sky, the earth and the air were vast enough to contain all paradoxes and ease his troubled heart. Though long buried and nearly forgotten, those cellular outposts knew there was no need for keeping score or counting sins; no need to categorize people as Jewish or Muslim, Catholic or heretic. Had he been able to decipher the humming in his bones he would have understood what it was trying to tell him: whatever Mystery had created the world and all its peoples simply didn't care about such petty differences. Grace awaited everyone. All God's children—even malcontents like him— were worthy and whole, saved and sanctified.

In that unconscious moment of pondering, Antonio Albóndiga turned away from the orange sunset that blanketed the edges of the darkening sea. He pulled his cloak around his tense body, pushed his stiff hands beneath the woolen garment, and scowled. He vowed to the wind-eroded planks that he'd return to Spain one day. Soon, the demerits against him would be erased without question. He'd exact revenge—if not against the ones who'd exiled him, then against the ones most hated by those who'd banished him: the Hebrews, the Moors, the gypsies, the witches, and other heretics who clung to their evil ways. By doing so, his reputation would be restored and his position reinstated. Until then he would continue to send letters to his cousin Juan, seeking his counsel and aid, asking him to intervene.

Antonio imagined a time—it might take a month or a year or more—when the Archbishop of Alghero would absolve him from all wrong-doing and sign the edict that would end his unjust exile. Then he would board another godforsaken boat and return to his homeland. He'd ask Juan to secure a position for him with Tomas de Torquemada. Then, he knew, his name would live on in history as one of the many fierce warriors of God who dared to purify and sanctify the blood of nonbelievers. He would become the great leader he believed he was destined to be, the man his clouded mind crowned with unearned glory. If it took the rest of his life he'd be vindicated.

As the sea winds grew calmer and the first stars of the night sky shone down upon him, Antonio clenched his fists, determined that someone would pay for this most dire humiliation, his most wretched exile. Of that he was certain.

Chapter 3
La Madre Vecchia

THE IDENTICAL TWIN SISTERS were born in Orune, a small village nestled in the high granite plateaus of the Barbagia, the wild interior region of Sardinia north of the Gennargentu Mountains. The villagers called their rugged hills "the towers of the wind." While life in the mountains was often difficult, the daily challenges of making a living were softened by the natural beauty that surrounded them.

The countryside overflowed with oak and cork trees, alder, yew and juniper. Wild pigs, wild horses, untamed deer and mouflon roamed the land; golden eagles, griffons, falcons, kites, vultures and sparrows reigned over the sky. Each spring bright wildflowers carpeted the hillsides and pasturelands; each summer lavender, thyme, myrtle and rosemary fragranced the air. Everywhere lush oleander bushes painted the landscape with brilliant color.

Like their *ayaya*, their beloved grandmother, Maredda, and their mother, Augustina, Shardana and Sarda had deep-set eyes, dark as a moonless night sky. Their hair was dark brown; their skin had the rich caramel hue of an acorn. Both women stood barely five feet tall, although every man, woman and child in the village would have sworn they were at least six feet tall because of the commanding presence they exuded. Their hips and shoulders were broad, making their stout, strong bodies all the more useful for the arduous tasks assigned to them as the village's healers in which day after day, month after month, year after year they climbed the hillsides and stooped low to harvest medicinal herbs. Their square jaws reflected their steely determination; their flat, broad noses and full lips revealed an uncommon beauty. Their hearts were as fiercely indomitable and as enduring as the holm oaks that populated the dense forests surrounding their village. The sisters were inseparable, and everyone in Orune knew not to come between them. Never did a day pass without the women sharing a meal, a conversation, or a consultation about one of their patients.

Still, spoken words were not always necessary between them. They had a way of communicating that relied neither on vowels nor consonants. Both valued silence and cherished the wisdom that often came with it. Sometimes a gesture sufficed. Other times a twitch of the eye transmitted all that needed stating. Like all the other inhabitants of the Barbagia, their speech was parceled out sparingly and judiciously. In those isolated mountains, words were considered the rope that bound the oxen to the plow. Never were sentences spoken in haste or wasted on nonsense. Words contained powerful magic; they could kill a person or they could sustain him. They reasoned that it was better to communicate with actions. How one behaved towards another human being or animal spoke more loudly than a chorus of angels, more eloquently than pages of words fashioned into leather-bound books.

There were some in Orune who swore the twin sisters could read one another's thoughts, although both women denied it. Their healing skills were known far and wide—in their village and beyond in the valleys across the mountain passes. Both had married well, choosing men of deep compassion and uncommon sagacity. Both had given birth to one daughter and one son. Both had demonstrated a gift for healing at a very young age.

When Sarda was five years old, she mended the broken wing of a sparrow after the bird had fallen from the branch of an olive tree, the victim of the impeccable aim and exuberant arm of a young neighbor boy and his sturdy stone. At that same age Shardana had concocted a salve to heal the cut in her mother's finger after a kitchen knife she had been using to slice some *pecorino sardo* cheese missed its mark. Pleased with the initiative and skill shown by both of her granddaughters,

Maredda announced, "I have found my apprentices! When it's my time to die, I can do so peacefully knowing my *majarza* lineage will go on."

Though none of the other residents of Orune were privy to the secret ways of *majarzas*, all were blessed by the depth of knowledge the twins possessed. They trusted the sisters to administer the right balm for a wound, the right concoction to ease an ache, the perfect prescription to mend an ailing heart or a broken bone. For countless generations the people of the Barbagia had honored their *majarzas*. No one ever spoke a word of anger against the village healers; no one ever unleashed an unkind thought or action upon their families. The *majarzas* were as essential to the villagers' lives as air and food and water. The healers attended births and steadfastly cared for the living and the dying. They nurtured the sick, dispensing good humor along with doses of good medicine. Without them no one would have health, no home would enjoy prosperity, no heart would know peace.

A few months after the twin sisters dreamt about the sea wolf, Shardana and her granddaughter Martina went to the woods outside of their small village to pick the early spring plants and harvest bark from the oak trees. The winter had been long and Shardana needed to restock her apothecary. The healer and her apprentice had been walking for hours, stooping to the ground to hear the plants singing, waiting for the plants to invite the healers to pluck their leaves or stems, unearth their roots and place them in their baskets.

The spring sun warmed Shardana's face, and the gentle breeze was a welcome relief as she engaged in her strenuous task. Her once sturdy back ached from bending low to the ground to gather the medicines of her trade. Upon her head she wore the traditional headdress of her village, a black woolen scarf tied in a tight knot beneath her chin. Her white blouse was damp with sweat, and she hitched her long red woolen skirt above her knees to invite the cool air to refresh her legs.

Older and less agile than her sixteen-year-old assistant, Shardana moved more slowly and the hard work caused her to tire more quickly than her granddaughter. She paused to take a breath and rest by the holm oak.

"*Madre Vecchia*, Old Mother," she said. "Thank you for letting me lean against your sturdy body."

"Sit for a while, *Ayaya*," Martina said. "I'll keep foraging."

"Remember what I've taught you. Only pick the plants that give you permission to do so."

"Yes. Yes. Don't worry. Enjoy your visit with the Old Mother."

Shardana rested her head against the sturdy tree trunk and watched her granddaughter stroll deeper into the forest, cradling her herb-collecting basket in her arms. Martina reminded Shardana of Grazia, her daughter and Martina's mother. Grazia had died ten years before, when Martina was six. To quell the stinging tears that began to rise, Shardana closed her eyes and let the spring breeze calm her. The softness of the wind reminded her of Maredda and the loving way she used to touch Shardana's shoulder just before kissing her forehead.

"Oh, *Ayaya* Maredda. I miss you the most in the springtime when we come to harvest the first of the new green shoots. I remember how you and me and Sarda would always stop and rest at the Mother Tree—such a faithful guardian, as you always said She would be. I've tried so hard to be true to your teachings, to teach Grazia, and now Martina, all the things you taught me. But I miss Grazia—every day I think of her, and now Martina has grown to be a young woman and there is still so much left for her to learn, so many things I've yet to tell her. The Mother Tree and Her magic have helped me, just as you said it would. But sometimes I fear Martina's path will lead her elsewhere—I wish you were still alive to help me instill in her all the things a young woman needs to know to grow strong. Sarda and I do what we can, but—without Grazia—I can only do so much—and well, you know, my heart is less fierce that it used to be."

A crow cawed, and Shardana glanced up at the bird, perched on one of the low branches of the Old Mother Tree. "Is that you, Maredda? Or could it be Grazia?"

LIKE SO MANY TREES in the primeval forest, the Old Mother Tree towered above Shardana, surpassing her by nearly sixty feet. A weathered being of gnarled, dark gray bark and toothy, evergreen leaves, the Mother Tree had survived countless summers of searing heat. It had lived through chilly autumns when the orange moon shone upon its ample canopy, and it had withstood fierce winters of biting wind and icy snow. It had welcomed wet springs with heavy rains, which had compelled it to shed its tenacious leaves, like tears, to the forest floor.

This ancient, unyielding oak was the oldest tree in the forest. More than a thousand years before, a smooth acorn, adorned with a brown, fine-scaled cap, had split its hard cupule and anchored a tiny shoot into the soil. Slowly the sprouting nut had burrowed eager roots into the ground, claiming this corner of the forest. From there, over time, a seedling emerged and, eventually, a tender black trunk, rough and patterned. Its fragile limbs sprouted leaves, single-lobed and smooth, unfurling toward the blistering Sardinian sun. As the sapling grew, its bark ceded the blackness of youth to the dark-green-grey of maturity. Its limbs grew stronger, gracefully reaching toward the sky with steadfast purpose. Dark brown acorns nestled among the clusters of tapered foliage, their long hard cups ripening before tumbling to the ground, assisted in their journey by wind and rain, birds and bees. The being's white sapwood matured to a heartwood of dark brown, firm and durable, beloved by all the people who inhabited the Barbagia.

The Old Mother Tree's bole measured thirty feet in diameter. Its highest limbs stretched sixty feet toward the heavens. The Old Tree had endured the onslaught of time to claim sovereignty in the forest outside Orune. Countless generations of women and men had whispered their secrets into her massive trunk; many more would do so long after Shardana had died and her loved ones had planted her body in the ground nearby. This Tree served as both doctor and high priestess to the inhabitants of Shardana's village. Shepherds, farmers, bakers, basketmakers, cobblers, children, even foraging *cinghiali* found comfort in a brief visit to *La Madre Vecchia*. The smallest moment spent under her healing shade was enough to sweeten the most bitter of sorrows.

Like *La Madre Vecchia*, the other holm oaks were slow to grow. Each tree matured through years of changing seasons, withstanding the precarious whims of weather to populate the forests throughout the region. The holm oak's wood gradually ripened into timber of nearly indestructible hardness, and the people of the Barbagia prized this species for its grain and texture and for the rich color it procured after polishing. The holm oak bore its priceless utility with equal amounts of modesty and majesty. Though the Old Mother Tree would remain inviolate, the people of the region would transform the wood from the other holm oaks into casks and barrels, cabinets and coffins, tables and chairs. In this way the trees became intertwined with every facet of human life, making of themselves constant companions and compatriots.

UNDER MAREDDA'S TUTELAGE, Shardana and Sarda became accomplished healers. Sarda was a generalist, tending to the health and well-being of her townspeople from cradle to tomb. She'd mastered the art of curing of all kinds of illnesses—acute or chronic, big or small. Her herbal remedies healed children of influenza and fever. She eased the aching bodies of fathers and mothers with joint and muscle inflammation. Villagers with troubled minds found renewed strength and clarity after undergoing a course of her medicinals. From time to time Sarda's potions were unable to save a weakened spirit or cure a battered body, and one of her patients would die. On those days she wept as deeply as the grieving family.

Like her sister, Shardana was known for her healing skills, but what she loved most was to tend to the village's pregnant and birthing women and their unborn children. For many years, before the fateful incident that ended her desire to be the town's midwife, Shardana's wide, sturdy palms had gently caught the crowning heads of every child born in Orune. She called them "my children" even though she hadn't physically given birth to them, for she'd cared for their physical needs from the time of their conception until the time their mothers nursed them at their breasts and rocked them to sleep. Many a young mother in labor would cry out to Shardana, calling her *bis-mama*, twice-mother. Never did a mother begrudge Shardana that honorific title. Shardana had stopped the hemorrhaging of hundreds of birthing women hovering on the edge of death. Using her herbal potions, she'd coaxed them back to the land of the living. Without Shardana's potent doctoring, many of Orune's children would have sucked at ghostly nipples, aching for the sweet taste of their dead mother's wasted milk.

While some birthing mothers sailed through their labor without incident, others were dogged by the sharp pain that seized their wombs as they pushed and strained to release their infants. Fatigue would break them, and the greedy hands of Death would claim their souls. On those times when the babies were snatched away before their lungs had suckled the air of life, Shardana's heart trembled even as her hands and face remained calm and comforting. She believed that her first duty was to gently ferry grieving mothers over the waters of loss, when their hearts were severely splintered and they could find no reason for why fate had been so cruel.

On the night of the full moon, in the year 1475, Shardana's beloved daughter Grazia lay in bed writhing in pain, pleading with her mother to stop the searing ache that raced across her swollen belly. Across the lane Grazia's husband, Giovanni, waited with six-year-old Martina, trying to distract his daughter with a doll her *ayaya* had made out of reeds and sheep's wool. Although the young girl could hear her mother's screams, Giovanni did his best to soothe the youngster, even as fear raced through his own heart.

"Mama?" Martina said, her mouth quivering.

"She's alright," Giovanni said. "She's giving you a baby sister or maybe a baby brother. It hurts sometimes. But don't worry. *Ayaya* Shardana is with her."

Silently, he prayed that Grazia would live through the night.

From the start, Grazia's pregnancy had been difficult. But Sarda and Shardana had been able to use their remedies to circumvent the cramping and spotting and the other early signs of a possible miscarriage. Under their care Grazia had managed to weather the physical hardships that had befallen her during her pregnancy, so by the ninth month they all had high hopes that the delivery would be easy and smooth. Even so, every night as she fell asleep something nagged at Shardana, although she refused to admit it to anyone—even Sarda—or to indulge it.

One morning at dawn Grazia's water broke and her labor began in earnest. Shardana worked swiftly and with great intention, her sister Sarda diligently assisting her. They made a potion to ease the pain, but Grazia continued to moan loudly. Shardana's heart tightened as her daughter cried out, "Mama! Help me! *Dea Madre* have mercy on me!"

The healers tried soothing balms and herbal infusions, but nothing they did alleviated Grazia's mounting discomfort. By late evening the heavy bleeding came. Shardana's face paled. Her hands began to tremble. She wanted to walk away, leave Grazia in the care of Sarda's steadier hands, but she couldn't. She prayed, "Death, don't you dare take my daughter!" The thought of getting up each day without hearing her daughter's melodic voice, seeing her loving face, was unthinkable. How could she survive if Grazia were no longer alive? And how could sweet Martina ever be happy again without her mother's love? Who would guide the young girl as she grew? Who would care for her in the ways that only a mother could?

Shardana cursed and tried to strike a bargain. "Take me, instead! Let Grazia and her unborn child live."

Through the long night, Shardana and Sarda worked to circumvent the outcome both knew was inevitable. Their hands were swollen with exertion and stained with Grazia's blood. Grazia continued to fail; her strength waned until her breathing grew weak and shallow. Shardana massaged her daughter's swollen belly, trying to coax the baby to join the living, but she was unable to deliver the infant, who clung to his mother's womb with unexpected fierceness. At the stroke of midnight an owl screeched from the rooftop across the alleyway. Shardana's legs collapsed and she howled. She slumped over her dying daughter's body and wept. Sarda tugged at her sister's arms, trying to pull her away from Grazia's flaccid body, but Shardana would not yield. Sarda watched in helpless horror as her twin wailed and her niece Grazia slipped away.

For hours Shardana cradled her daughter's lifeless body in her blood-stained arms, until she collapsed in fatigue. No touch from Sarda's hand could comfort her. No kind word of shared grief could ease the unbearable pain that pierced her.

As the early morning light began to tinge the edges of the bedroom window, Shardana screamed: "No! No! No!"

How could the sun dare to rise? How could the day presume to begin without her daughter alive and well and beside her?

Three days later, on a sunny midsummer's afternoon, Shardana and her kin buried Grazia and her unborn son on a hillside, beside the sacred spring that ran near the ancient water temple, *Su Tempiesu*. No priest officiated at the funeral, for the town had none. Decades before, the windows had been boarded up on *La Chiesa di Nostra Signora Nera*, Orune's one-and-only church. The lock upon its door was rusty from disuse. No one in the village cared. Those in Orune who were Christians—like Basilio, his brother Constantino, and Grazia's husband Giovanni—had taken to visiting the water temple to pray to their God and His Holy Mother; before the village's Catholic Church had fallen into disrepair and been permanently closed, the townspeople had removed its statue of *Nostra Signora Nera* and taken care to place Her in a sacred spot where She could be duly venerated and cared for.

The townsfolk loved their Black Madonna, clothed in a red dress bedecked with brilliant yellow stars. A golden coronet rested upon her head, crowning her long black hair. The beautiful statue was said to have been carved out of holm oak wood by none other than St. Luke. To honor Her, the devoted villagers had built a shrine in an alcove in a grotto carved out of granite not far from the water temple. In a procession filled with music and overflowing with bouquets of fresh flowers, they had carried Her from the musty church to *Su Tempiesu*.

Some residents of the village—like Shardana and Sarda—followed more ancient spiritual ways; they believed the Divine resided in the living waters of the Earth, in the vibrant rustling of the ancient oak trees, in the granite mountains and hillsides. For them, the sacred spring at *Su Tempiesu* was already imbued with the breath of God; they felt no need to venerate statues, but they accepted *Nostra Signora Nera* as a reflection of the Mystery that lived in every being—Christian or not. In Her, they saw the power and might they recognized in the Old Mother Oak Tree, *La Madre Vecchia*; the very same Soul that dwelled within their mothers and *ayayas*, their fathers and grandfathers, their sisters and brothers; the same essence that lived within the Earth and in all the creatures upon it.

When Grazia died, Shardana, Basilio and Giovanni agreed that *Su Tempiesu* was a fitting resting place to bury her and her baby. The area was holy to each of them in their own ways.

As a girl, Grazia had straddled both worlds: the realms of her mother's ancient devotion to the Divine Mystery that resided in all beings and the realms of her father's veneration to the Catholic Jesus and his mother, the Black Madonna. Grazia had passed these beliefs on to Martina. In their short time together, Grazia had taught her daughter how to discern temporal things with a spiritual eye. It was a way of seeing that Grazia shared with her brother Isidoro and her cousins Anna-Bella and Brontu. They melded the traditions of their foremothers and forefathers with the customs brought to the region centuries before by the Christians. They venerated the Black Madonna, and none of the more traditional Catholics in the village considered this odd or blasphemous, although in truth, few of the townspeople practiced the Catholic faith, at least the way it was taught to the faithful in Rome.

On the day of Grazia's funeral, near *Su Tempiesu* and the statue of

Nostra Signora Nera, the women of Orune stood by the gravesite and lifted their voices in lamentation. Together, these *attitadoras* intoned their chant of bereavement, paying tribute to the fallen daughter's virtues. The women sang their *attitidu,* their dirge, to honor Grazia's parents, Shardana and Basilio, and all their kin, living and dead. They sang of the great deeds the young mother would have performed if Death hadn't untimely snatched her from the arms of life. They sang of the ways Grazia's living had blessed her mother and father, her brother, her husband, and her daughter. As the voices of the *attitadoras* rose, a flock of crows took leave of the treetops, flying into the overcast sky, aggrieved to learn of the passing of the young and promising *majarza.* A pair of griffons soared in the sky above the circle of mourners.

As Grazia and her unborn son were laid to rest in the ground, Giovanni stood solemnly beside his mother-in-law and father-in-law. Without crying, he stared into the deep pit of dirt that would soon swallow his beloved wife's cold body. He stood motionless, unable to uproot himself from the weary soil. He couldn't look skyward at the griffons or the circling crows—he could barely hear their cries of comfort, for he couldn't foresee a future without Grazia.

Martina kicked the dirt at her feet and held her father's hand. "When is Mama going to wake up and climb out of the soil?"

Her six-year-old granddaughter's soft voice made Shardana's knees buckle. She collapsed into Basilio's arms. Sarda swooned; her husband Constantino caught her before her face hit in the dirt. Anna-Bella rushed to her mother's side, and Brontu helped his father support his mother's limp body. Grazia's brother, Isidoro, rubbed his hands and then his eyes, unable to ease his suffering. He wondered if his mother would ever heal from the unbearable grief. He knew his heart would always ache, remembering his sister's dark eyes, her kind laughter.

AFTER GRAZIA'S DEATH Shardana refused to midwife another baby, not even years later when Sarda's daughter-in-law, Viviana, had her first child. After Grazia's funeral Giovanni and Martina moved into Shardana and Basilio's home, and both grandparents helped their son-in-law raise his daughter. Isidoro moved into Giovanni and Grazia's house, in hopes that he'd one day marry and fill its rooms with healthy babies. Several years later, when Isidoro married Teresina, Shardana allowed herself to briefly surrender to a glimmer of joy.

Ten years later, after wildflowers had taken up residence near Grazia's burial site and bees began to linger, collecting fragrant pollen, Shardana was still unable to midwife the births of the women of Orune. While Shardana grieved the loss of her daughter, Sarda was left to tend to the village's birthing women and usher their newborns into the waiting arms of Orune. During the difficult years of Shardana's grieving, when she was unable to help her twin with any of their healing duties, Sarda also maintained her regular practice, caring for all the town's young and old residents.

For many years Sarda was a midwife to Shardana's grief, nursing her through the labor pains of letting go. It proved to be Sarda's most difficult assignment.

The additional *majarza* duties began to take their toll on Sarda, even though her daughter Anna-Bella helped her by interviewing patients when they first arrived at Sarda's home. Anna-Bella asked them questions to determine their ailment so that her mother could properly diagnose and treat them. Anna-Bella was a caring and capable assistant, but she was not a trained healer. She couldn't fill the void left by Shardana's absence. During those years, an uneasy silence lingered between the twin sisters.

At night they continued to share meals together as was their custom, but they barely spoke to one another. Sarda would fill a plate of food for her twin and Constantino would place it on the table in front of Shardana.

When Constantino asked his wife about her day she would frown and say only, "It was busy. Very full."

Anna-Bella would nod. "Yes, so many villagers came to see us today. I hardly had time to tend to the bees. But we do what we have to do. The bees understand."

At family gatherings when the shepherds returned to the village from their *tanca,* Sarda found comfort in their laughter and their stories of the sheepfold, although Shardana rarely smiled as she listened to their tales.

When Isidoro asked, "Mama, how have you been?" Shardana would shrug her shoulders and sigh.

Martina tried to cheer her grandmother, without success. "*Ayaya,* sing me a song like you used to."

But Shardana would shoo the child away without saying a word.

It would take years before Shardana was able to begin to slowly emerge from the dark well into which she had fallen. Sarda prayed to be released from her growing resentment even as she prayed for Shardana to be delivered from the darkness that claimed her.

Two years after Grazia's death, Shardana was able to help her twin sister *majarza* in small ways on days when she was able to rouse herself out of bed and find the strength to mix a potion or listen to a patient relate the reason for his visit. Within three years of Grazia's death Shardana was able to go into the forest to harvest the medicinal herbs Sarda needed. In that way she slowly began to ease some of the burdens that her sister was forced to shoulder.

Five years after Grazia's death, Shardana woke one morning and walked across the lane to her sister's house. Entering the main room, she announced, "I'm ready."

Sarda nodded and handed her sister an apron. "Better put this on before the patients start knocking on my door."

Although Shardana never again presided at a birth, she began to attend to the needs of the sick villagers when they came to her door, dispensing medicines to alleviate colds and coughs, to cure dysentery and gout, and all the many other maladies that afflicted them. By then Martina was eleven, old enough to begin her apprenticeship, so Shardana began to teach her the ways of the *majarzas*.

WHEN MARTINA RETURNED from collecting medicinal herbs in other parts of the forest, she sat by the Old Mother Tree and held her *ayaya*'s hand. "The plants were very generous today. The Mother Tree must have sung to them before we arrived."

Shardana nodded and offered a small smile. Martina's eternal optimism was so much like Grazia's—both were always so quick to attribute a good harvest to the Mother Tree's ability to sing to the plants. "We have much to be thankful for," Shardana replied. "The Tree has always been so good to us. Do you remember the stories?"

"The ones Maredda taught you? The ones you taught to me?"

"Yes. And to your mother—Oh, I remember how Maredda would enchant us by the fireside on long winter nights. When I was younger than you are now. I can still hear her—the way she would nearly whisper the tales so softly, so reverentially—and yet her voice would fill the room. She'd always begin by saying, 'Through the ages, the holm oak has served as sanctuary and temple to pilgrims who encountered the Divine Mystery in its towering limbs and sturdy base.' As we fixed our eyes upon her, Maredda would continue, satisfied that she had our rapt attention."

"Did she sound the way you always sound when you tell me the stories?" Martina asked. "When you tell these tales, I picture you as a high priestess preaching to her young novices: 'Sacred, holy groves of oaks emerged from the dark, rich soil in lands far and near, across many continents. The ancients revered the oak above all other trees. We have always believed that the oak, more than any other trees, possessed the strength, wisdom and all-seeing eyes of the One Great Spirit. For millennia, humans have honored groves of oaks for their powers of prophecy. Legends of the oak have always been passed from fathers and mothers to children and grandchildren, whispered into ears, tender or old — just as I am telling you today.'"

"And do you fall asleep when I share these stories with you?"

"No, *Ayaya*. I sometimes close my eyes, but it's so I can imagine in my mind what you're saying. My favorite is the part about the two black doves that journeyed from Thebes. How one of the beautiful black birds flew to Libya and the other sailed on the wind to Greece to roost at the foot of Mt. Tomarus. Each dove rested on an oak limb and dispensed its oracular wisdom to all who could interpret the meaning encoded in their cooing."

"Ah yes," Shardana said. "The black doves sang and the local people listened, divining the future through the music of the birds' sacred messages. The black doves of Libya and Mt. Tomarus instilled their wisdom in other birds, too, and sent them to nest in other oak branches around the world, enchanting forests in every country, captivating the hearts of people, animals, and plants. This is how the oak became a sentinel of strength. Its sturdy body has always provided stability and protected the deer, the foxes, the birds, humans, and other creatures great and small—all the many and varied beings that reside in and near the forestlands in which the oaks flourish."

Shardana used to recite the legends every chance she got, whether by the fireside during long winter evenings, over a bowl of soup in her kitchen on crisp autumn afternoons, or by the river on warm spring and summer days as she refreshed her tired feet in the cool water after she, Sarda—and Grazia, when her daughter was still alive—had combed the forests and hillsides, harvesting plants and herbs and roots. Like Maredda, Shardana's passion for this recitation was as boundless as her dedication to remembering the ways of her kin, their stories, and their magic.

Shardana's grandfather and father were always eager to share their own stories about the oak's powers. She and her twin would often sit beside their grandfather as he carved wooden sheep and other animals from the oak twigs, making toys for them to play with. His agile fingers handled the knife, paring away snippets of bark to unveil a tiny sheep's nose or ear, a tiny bird's wingspan. As he worked he would say, "The oak was the first tree created by God. *La Dea Madre,* God the Mother, the original Womb of All Life. Not the other God, the one the priests would like you to believe in."

At supper on nights when Shardana's father wasn't up in the sheep-fold tending his flock, he offered thanks to this Mother God, whispering Her name reverentially, bowing his head slightly, closing his eyes before he picked up a spoon to eat his soup. "We owe much to Her and Her beneficent Trees," her father would say. "We humans are merely acorns, shed from Her sturdy branches. Rooting ourselves in the soil of our towns, doing as best as we can to sprout shoots and grow big, strong, tall enough to please Her. After our mother's breast milk, the Tree's acorns are the first fruits to fill our bellies, nourish our bodies."

Though Shardana's father and mother, her grandfather, and her *ayaya* Maredda were long dead, their words forever lived in her mind and in her heart. With a pang of urgency Shardana turned to Martina and said, "Remember, always, that you come from strong and resilient people. Remember, always, that we people of the Barbagia call the oak *Regina della Foresta*, Queen of the Forest. When you honor and protect the trees, they protect you. That's why we sometimes mark a circle on the girth of a furrowed trunk, bisecting the design into four equal parts, invoking the elements of Earth, Air, Fire and Water."

"Yes, I know, *Ayaya*. I see those markings on the trees every time we enter the forest."

"Those are sacred signs, Martina. Not meant to scar or harm the Trees, but to remind us that we are part of the cycles of the seasons, part of all living things. To thank us for remembering, the Trees share their acorns, bark, leaves, and branches with us. In ancient times, the priest-esses and others charged with tending undying fires for food and heat fueled their flames with holm oak acorns. Those with sorcerer's powers crafted their magic wands from the topmost branches of these mighty trees. Those who are healers—like you and me and Sarda—harvest the oak's spring bark and autumn fruit to make our medicines. I hope you always remember that we do not own the trees or the forests, or the waters or the sky or the ground or the animals and plants that live among us. We are kin to them, not kings and queens imposing our power over them."

EVEN AS YOUNG GIRLS, Shardana and Sarda loved to visit the Old Mother Tree. Some days their grandparents or their parents went with them. Other times, freed to explore the hillsides and forests on their own, the sisters would go singly or together and sit beneath the Tree's shady bough to rest or to cry, sometimes to laugh, always to confide their innermost secret thoughts with the knobby being of rutted bark and smooth leaves. In autumn they'd be sure to collect the long, nar-row acorns, scooping them into their handwoven baskets to carry them home to their mother, who'd grind them into flour which she'd use to bake bread. The twins would always set aside several handfuls for Maredda's medicines, too.

On this early spring day when Shardana scoured the forest with her sixteen-year-old granddaughter, the heavy rains of March had come and gone, washing winter from the hillsides. Shardana was no longer a child. She was nearly fifty, a busy *majarza*, a married woman, an *ayaya* and mother of two, but still something youthful—perhaps even hope-ful—compelled her to visit the Old Tree several times each week, no matter what the season. She felt Maredda's spirit in every tree and ev-ery herb in the holm oak forest, even though her *ayaya* had been dead for twenty-five years. Grazia's spirit was there, too. Shardana knew the danger of letting herself linger too long in that familiar anguish; she knew she wouldn't be able to loosen the jaws of the demon that always threatened to devour her if she indulged her grief.

Shardana inhaled the fragrant aromas of the plentiful wildflowers and herbs. The sweet scent of spring always made her feel giddy, and the aromas temporarily dispelled some of the crippling sadness that had seized her.

She glanced at Martina. "It's time to continue your lesson."

Shardana and Martina's trip to the woods had begun early that morning with the selection of medicinal plants and seasonal wildflowers, but by afternoon their focus shifted to harvesting bark from the tree trunks. It was easier to relieve the oak of its gnarled skin in springtime, before the leaf buds opened and the trees' sap flowed again. The healer and her apprentice continued their work, humming and smiling at the occasional pollen-laden bee as it buzzed past them, heading home to a wild hive nearby. Shardana's husband, Basilio, and their son, Isidoro, would make use of the furrowed tree epidermis, rich in tannin, to cure sheepskin hides when they made leather for their family's shoes and satchels. Shardana and the other women of the village would infuse the collected bark with small amounts of copperas to make a purplish dye for the sheared wool they spun into yarn to knit and weave cloth for their clothing and their household linens. Should a brown dye be preferred, the women mixed alum with the bark instead. When a black pigment was preferred, they would infuse the oak bark with the salt of iron. To coax a yellow color the bark was mixed with salt of tin.

"Spring bark is best for concocting antiseptic potions," Shardana instructed her granddaughter. "First we gather bark from the young trees, then dry it in the sun before extracting the medicine. It's bitter-tasting but slightly aromatic. What do we do with it after it's fully dried?"

"We chop it and store it in your apothecary," Martina said. "When someone comes to see us and they're all achy, we measure an ounce, put it in a quart of water to boil. After the mixture thickens, we give them a pint of the potent medicine with instructions on how to use it."

"Remember when the baker knocked on our door complaining of a sore throat? How did we help him?"

"You gave him some of the potion and told him to gargle with it several times a day."

"Yes. And when your father complained of bleeding gums and piles?"

"We gave him some of the same stuff."

"Exactly. And when your grandfather got frostbite last winter while tending his sheep at the sheepfold, I added some to a hot bath. Cured him."

"When Great-Uncle Constantino had hemorrhoids, you gave it to him to use as a hot compress."

"And when the cobbler's son had chronic diarrhea, it cured that as well."

"When old man Carlos was confined to bed for a long time, you sprinkled the powder on his bed sheets to ease his bedsores."

"You're learning well and quickly, Martina."

"Just like Mama did?"

Shardana's chest tightened. She turned away so her granddaughter wouldn't see how her words had knocked the air out of her lungs. She reached into her pocket and ran her sturdy fingers over the small piece of rough bark she'd placed there earlier that morning, after she'd dressed herself in preparation for the day. As was her custom, this talisman served to protect her from harm and provide safe passage as she roamed the forests and hillsides. She felt tired from their work in the woods. The sun was beginning its march westward. She knew they mustn't linger too much longer.

Finally able to catch her breath, Shardana said, "Come, Martina. It's time to go home. Your grandfather will be waiting for his supper. He promised to join us tonight. Said he could leave the *tanca* in Isidoro's care for two days. Not nearly enough time for me to enjoy his company, but I've learned to be content with what he can give. The sheep need him as much as we do."

The sweet song of a sparrow, perched high in the holm oak tree, filled the late afternoon air. Shardana gathered her basket of bark and herbs, then stood for a moment gazing at the hills of granite peppered with forests dense with oak, cork and chestnut. Her heart grew lighter as she looked out upon the long rows of vineyards, the groves of pear trees in the orchards, the hillocks of flowering macchia. Hedges of rosemary and thyme, outcroppings of rock roses, arbutus trees bursting with red berries, black-berried myrtle filled her line of sight. She inhaled the aroma of violets and heather and thought about the musky flavor of the still unseen wild mushrooms upon which the wild boar would feast in the autumn. Roasted boar had been Grazia's favorite supper, and now Martina always asked for it at festival time.

The bleating of grazing sheep across the fields reached Shardana's ears. Basilio's dark eyes flashed before her own. Her shepherd husband would be wondering what was keeping her so long in the forest. An oak leaf flittered through the air, resting in her upturned palm. A good omen, she knew, one that promised luck and prosperity. She set the leaf upon the forest floor, unfastened her woolen scarf, tucked it into her herb basket, and headed down the hill, Martina racing ahead of her towards their village.

On the way back home Shardana thought about making her hungry husband his favorite *pane frattau*. Every time she prepared that simple combination of flat shepherd's *carasau* bread soaked in tomato sauce he sprinkled it with hearty *pecorino* made from the milk given by his own sheep. Then she'd set a fried egg on top, one laid that morning by her precious, productive hens, and Basilio would eat it with the eagerness of a child savoring a slice of cake.

After supper she'd visit Sarda, like she did every night. Her twin and her twin's husband, Constantino, lived in the small stone house directly across the lane from Shardana and her husband. She'd run a finger over some of the old acorns that she and Sarda had placed on each of their window ledges to guard against evil and protect their houses and their inhabitants from lightning strikes and other pernicious visitors. Her day in the woods had stirred up bittersweet memories, and she needed to remember the comfort and safety the oak trees provided, whether she was in the forest or the village. Together in the waning twilight hours, the sisters would talk as they picked through the young bark and the spring shoots that Shardana and Martina had gathered earlier that day. She would tell her twin how well Martina did that day; how each week their apprentice was getting better at listening to the plants and deciphering which leaves to pick, which to forgo. She would tell her how her legs and back weren't as strong as they used to be, and how grateful she was that they had Martina to pass their knowledge on to. She would tell Sarda how the scent of the newly greening leaves and plants reminded her of their *ayaya* and the times they used to help Maredda harvest the herbs. But she would not say that she sensed Grazia in every nook and corner of the forest. Even though Sarda had nursed Shardana through her sorrow and would have allowed her sister room to feel her sadness, Shardana didn't want to share that private memory of Grazia with anyone.

Still, she knew that sitting at her sister's kitchen table as the sun set would help her feel content to be alive, unafraid of whatever the future might bring.

Chapter 4
The Alliance

A BRILLIANT BLUE SKY GREETED the ship carrying Antonio Albóndiga as it entered the harbor of Alghero. A pair of golden eagles circled the high, steep sandstone cliffs facing the bay before drawing closer to the ship's mast.

The sea breeze smelled of juniper and salt, which displeased Antonio. The damp air penetrated his lungs, making it difficult for him to breathe without great effort. He wheezed and coughed as the ship's crew busily finalized its preparations for disembarking. The noise and bustle of their labor annoyed him. He counted the minutes until he could step foot on dry land. His breakfast of hard bread and moldy cheese hadn't settled well, and the insistent rocking of the harbor waters soured his stomach. The endless ebb and flow of the waves irritated him, roused his ire until he felt trapped by the relentless motion and could take no more comfort in the tug and pull of the harbor waters than he would of a room full of screeching, runny-nosed urchins.

The stark landscape of gulf waters and precipices nudged against hills covered in purple violets and pink rockroses. Beyond the tan hills rose the green tops of towering trees. Antonio glanced impatiently at the view, then fixed his eyes on the point of land at the far end of the harbor, counting the minutes until his feet would touch the cobblestone streets. His eyes strayed once toward the outline of parapets and battlements, the fortressed walls that surrounded the city that was to be his new home.

He did not notice the magnificent golden eagles; he failed to register their welcome. He'd lost his boyhood wonder and appreciation for the natural world, when he'd spent time roaming the oil groves of his grandfather's estate or hunting rabbits in the fields behind his father's house, stopping to toss stones into the river that ran through the property. As a grown man he viewed the natural world through a different lens. Nature's usefulness lay only in how easily it yielded its resources to provide materials to ensure comforts for his life. A tree's value lay not in its sturdy roots to hold erosion at bay, or in its lush canopy's ability to provide shade and shelter. Its worth resided solely in the hardness of its wood, its serviceability that rendered it into a boat or a chair, a bed or a table. A stone was good only for building a wall, a fence, or a church.

When at last the ship moored and he was beckoned to enter the small boat that would deliver him to land, a weak smile crossed his tense lips. The sailor mistook his expression for friendliness, a mood the seaman had not witnessed in the long voyage across the Mediterranean. The crewman smiled back, offering "Good morning, *Padre*." Antonio's eyes narrowed, and the slight upturn of his lips twisted first into a frown, then into a scowl.

The choppy harbor waters did little to lighten Antonio's frame of mind. His hopes rose and fell with the waves and, in spite of himself, he fell to praying. "Holy Jesus, bring me safely to land and let me be done with this." He glanced at the bay water, thinly skimmed with green algae, and sighed. He longed for a bottle of red wine and a lunch of roasted lamb and rosemary-scented fava beans. He had little faith that such civilized delicacies were possible in this dreaded Sardinian outpost. Before he'd set sail a friend in Seville had assured him that Alghero was thoroughly Spanish and he wouldn't have to endure the savagery of Sardinian culture, with its boorish food and uncouth ways, and the ship's captain had corroborated that as well, but Antonio hadn't believed either one of them.

When at last Antonio stepped upon the wooden pier, he steadied his sea-wobbly legs. The boatman who'd ferried him to shore cheerfully bid him goodbye. "Be careful, *Padre*. And good luck to ya."

Without a word of gratitude for the sailor's simple kindness, the priest collected the bag that held his belongings and turned toward the plaza. The area near the pier hummed with activity, though Antonio failed to notice the red and blue fishing boats or the fishermen gathered near the docks. His ears didn't register the call of voices, the laughter of friendship, the ringing of bells from a church steeple in the center of town. His nose, however, did capture the stench of decaying manure, deposited in the road by workhorses lugging carts. He held his breath until his lungs burned. When forced to exhale, the first intake of air that greeted his nose contained the aroma of bread baking in ovens at a shop near the water's edge, and that pleased him.

In the nearby market, fish vendors hawked fresh sea bass, merca—the region's gray mullet—*l'aragosta* and *polpagliara*—the small octopus that was especially pleasing when simmered in a spicy sauce—as well as eels and many other varieties of fish caught earlier that morning. "It's the freshest in all of Alghero!" the fishmongers called. "Look, the gills are still breathing!"

Women purchasing vegetables from the greengrocers haggled over prices. "Too much! For this? I've seen more inviting fava beans in my pantry, two days old!" Basketmakers, cloth-weavers, and cobblers showed their handcrafted wares to passersby. "The best in Alghero! Look at the artistry!"

Antonio strolled past the hubbub without stopping. He walked away from the smells and din, and headed toward the *Torre dell'Espero Reial*, the Tower of Royal Ambition. He'd been instructed to go there and wait for a church emissary who would meet him and escort him to his small suite of rooms near the *Chiesa di San Francesco*. At that church he would begin his new life of service, administering to the Catholic souls of the Aragonese transplants who inhabited Alghero.

He walked toward the appointed spot oblivious to everything around him, thinking about the grand greeting that awaited him. He presumed the bishop had sent one of his important assistants to welcome him to his new assignment. He believed that nothing less would do. He strolled past the enduring monuments to Spain's victory—tall, thick stone walls that encased the city's core like a chestnut burr, protecting the tender seed from harm. Here and there trees lined the narrow streets and byways as they had in his beloved Spain. A pang of sadness crept into his heart, but he squelched it, choosing instead to swat at a pesky fly that buzzed about his face, landing on his nose. The sun shone on his uncovered head, and he began to sweat profusely, although the steady northwest wind cooled him more quickly than he'd anticipated, for which he displayed an uncharacteristic sense of gratitude.

At the *Torre dell'Espero Reial* a young man dressed in a plain brown cleric's robe greeted Antonio. "*Padre* Albóndiga, so pleased to meet you. I'm *Padre* Diego Quintanto."

The priest extended his hand, but Antonio did not reach out to meet the welcome.

"And I am hungry and tired," Antonio snapped.

The diocese had sent an underling—and one without a cart or a horse to carry Antonio or his bag. Clearly this Quintanto fellow was not a member of the bishop's entourage. Antonio managed to suppress a sneer, but he refused to be cordial or even civil to this inconsequential lackey of a priest, a man who'd most likely only been ordained less than a year ago.

"Of course," the younger man replied. "Your journey has been long and arduous. The rectory isn't far from here. A meal awaits us there."

"Let's be on our way," the older priest ordered.

The men walked briskly through the streets, lined with shops selling jewelry, bread, vegetables, fish, and kitchen utensils and other household goods. Every now and then the priests would pass a tiny plaza, randomly situated off the main thoroughfare as if the stones with which it had been constructed had been left by accident after tumbling haphazardly from a passing stone mason's cart. Stone archways bridged the wider streets, linking one side to another, creating a false sense of congeniality that belied the city's history of hostile foreigner takeovers.

"Quite lovely, our fair city. Isn't it?" *Padre* Quintanto asked. "We call it Barcelloneta."

Antonio glanced first at the shop windows, then at the archways, then back at his companion. "I've seen lovelier."

The young priest pursed his lips, but didn't reply. He didn't care for the older man's sour attitude, but it was nonetheless his duty to attend to Albóndiga, and he would do it with humility and respect. That was God's way, Quintanto told himself. Christ would do nothing less. And the bishop had warned him that *Padre* Albóndiga might be a bit surly.

Or perhaps it was just that the elder priest was tired after his long sea journey. Either way, Quintanto tried to make the best of it and not succumb to the elder priest's bad mood.

"Ah, we're here at last," the young priest noted.

"At last, indeed," Antonio huffed. He momentarily glanced at the octagonal church tower, built from the same sand-colored stone used to construct so many of the other buildings he'd failed to notice since his arrival in this city of his exile.

"*San Francesco,*" Quintanto said, proudly pointing to the stone statue set in a niche in the alcove above the church's entry way. "He welcomes you home."

Antonio shrugged and frowned. He cared little for St. Francis, a man born of wealth and privilege who had abandoned his fortunes to live in poverty and tend to the needs of the world's castaways.

Quintanto opened the side door that led to the priests' quarters, releasing the aroma of fried fish into the dusty street air. Antonio's nostrils flared. His stomach growled in anticipation. For a brief moment a sliver of teeth shone through his clenched lips, suggesting appreciation, or at least relief.

"Our cook's very talented," Quintanto assured Albóndiga. "She knows how to satisfy a hungry man's appetite. Even if he's a priest!"

The younger man laughed. Antonio nodded and smiled, his orneriness temporarily disabled by his stomach's longing for the promised meal.

Encouraged by the sudden and unexpected display of cheerfulness, Quintanto replied, "Let me show you the rest of the house, and then I can take you to your private quarters. We'll dine after you've had a chance to rest."

Quintanto led Antonio down the hallway. "On the left is the library."

He opened the door to a small room containing one wall of shelves stuffed with volumes of books. By the window stood a single desk upon which stood an oil lamp and an old Bible.

"I trust you'll find everything you need in here to prepare your sermons, *Padre.*"

Antonio glanced quickly at the bookshelves and the meager furnishings. The room was less than half the size of the library at the rectory in Seville where he'd lived for four years.

"We're quite proud of our collection," Quintanto said, gesturing towards the bookshelves. "We've amassed work from most of the renowned theologians in Europe. We even have the collected works of St. Augustine."

"Does this so-called library contain a copy of the *Malleus Maleficarum?*" Antonio's eyes widened. The corners of his lips turned slightly upward.

"No, not yet. But the archbishop has been pondering whether he'll add it to his personal library."

"When do you expect that might happen?"

"I wouldn't presume to know, *Padre*. However, Pope Innocent VIII has endorsed the book, also called *The Hammer of the Witches,* and Archbishop Orozco has some family ties to several of the friars in Germany who are members of the Dominican Order."

"Heinrich Kramer? Jacob Sprenger? Or both?"

"Perhaps. I'm not certain about that. So you're familiar with the work of these two friars?

"Yes. My cousin is an assistant for Tomás de Torquemada."

"Oh, I see." Quintanto glanced out the window to avoid Antonio's intense stare.

"And you? Are you committed to purifying the blood of heathens as well, *Padre* Quintanto?"

"I've only been a priest for six months, *Padre* Albóndiga. I leave such serious matters to other, more capable hands. Shall we continue with our tour of the house?" Quintanto offered a cursory smile as he gestured toward the hallway.

Antonio glanced at the younger priest's face, trying to discern if he might become a potential ally in his plan to return to Spain, or if Quintanto was someone who might impede his attempts to restore his reputation and continue his mission to rid his beloved Church of heretics. Quintanto's face revealed nothing of his thoughts or his aspirations. The younger priest turned and walked toward the door. Antonio followed him out of the library.

"Here's the sitting room." Quintanto pointed to a different door on the opposite side of the hallway. "This is where you'll meet with parishioners when they come for your counsel. We don't have a separate office yet, but we hope to one day, when we raise enough funds to build

HERETICS: A LOVE STORY

a bigger rectory. Until then, this will have to suffice."

The small room was furnished with two armchairs, a small sofa, and two end tables. A crucifix, framed paintings of Saint Francis and Saint Claire, and a portrait of Pope Innocent VIII adorned the walls. The only natural light came from one narrow window on the north side of the room.

"It's a bit cozy," Quintanto said. "But our parishioners enjoy visiting."

"How often do they come?" Antonio replied.

"Every Sunday after Mass, people gather for thirty minutes or so to socialize. For pressing matters they must make appointments, which are usually held on Tuesday evenings and Friday evenings, after confession.

"Every week?" Antonio asked. "There must be a lot of pressing matters."

"Yes, the saving of souls is arduous work, as you well know, *Padre*."

"Indeed," Antonio replied. He worried there wouldn't be enough time in such a busy schedule for him to leave the rectory and the church and accomplish the work he was intent on pursuing. He considered it his higher calling, much more important than hearing the confessions of lowly parishioners. Until he was more certain of where Quintanto stood on the subject of eradicating heresy, he needed enough freedom from his parishioner duties to forge bonds with influential people in the community who could become his allies.

"The dining room is down the hall to the left. But first let me show you to your rooms."

ANTONIO'S QUARTERS were unadorned, yet serviceable. One room contained a small wooden desk, two oil lamps, several rows of empty book shelves, writing utensils, and a window overlooking a central courtyard that contained a garden of roses, lilies, shrubs, and two small olive trees. The second room contained a narrow bed and a wooden bedstand upon which rested a second oil lamp and a Bible. Nearby, a smaller table held a wash basin and a pitcher. By the door stood a small armoire, which he was to use to stow his personal belongings. A crucifix hung above the bed.

Antonio pursed his lips as he glanced at the head of the dying Jesus, lowered in pain, his eyes closed in anguish, his right side pierced and bleeding, his hands and feet nailed to the cross, a crown of thorns piercing his temples. He set his bag on the bed and walked toward the wash basin to cleanse his hands and wipe his face.

"I'll leave you to your preparations," Quintanto said. "Please join me in the dining room when you're ready."

THE REPAST PLEASED Antonio. It was a meal the likes of which his mouth hadn't savored since he'd left Spain weeks before. The rectory's cook, *Senora* de Leon, a woman whose family had emigrated to Alghero centuries before from Spain, brought trays full of succulent food to the table, smiling at him each time she placed a morsel on his plate. "Eat, *Padre*. Your voyage was long. You must be hungry for a real, sustaining meal."

Antonio barely looked at the woman, whose dark eyes and skin and plain housedress revealed that she was not a descendent of one of the wealthier set of Spanish immigrants that had come to the island generations before. While she was fluent in Spanish, her dialect was peppered with strange words the priest could not understand.

"Sometimes she slips into Sardo," Quintanto explained. "The native tongue of the island's original inhabitants. She must have picked it up from one of her neighbors. She lives on the outskirts of the Spanish sections of the city. We keep her on here because no one cooks better than her. And she's good at keeping secrets."

Antonio relished the dishes she laid before him, the small meat pies, savory and seasoned with thyme, enclosed in a delicate pastry shell. His tongue lingered on the soup of broth and rice, sweetened with the slightest hint of saffron. Although he was a man who hated the sea and all its watery depths, he eagerly swallowed the fish, a filet of red mullet sautéed in olive oil, garlic and onions. He drank goblets of dry red wine, his dour mood easing with every sip.

Unfortunately, the dinner conversation Antonio had with Quintanto was not as satisfying.

"*Padre* Albóndiga, tomorrow we can go back to the harbor, and I'll introduce you to some of our parishioners who are street vendors there."

"I have no interest in meeting them. That can wait until Mass on

57

Sunday."

"But—they'll be expecting a visit from you. Every new priest—"

"No. I have more pressing matters to attend to. It's best they—and you—realize that quickly. When am I to meet with Bishop Sanchez?"

"He can't see you until next week. I've already scheduled an appointment for you. Until then, you'll be holding office hours this week and you'll hear confessions on Friday."

"Next week is not soon enough. It's imperative that I not wait to see the bishop. I've got important business to discuss with him. And, yes, on Friday, I'll hear confessions. But I will not be meeting anyone in that dreadfully small room you call an office. If they want to talk to me, they can do so in the church."

"But it's not private there, in the pews, out in the open."

"It'll have to suffice. If they have something secretive to tell me, they can do it in the confessional booth. But that's of no concern to you. I expect you to contact the bishop and get me in to see him tomorrow afternoon. The next day at the very latest."

"The bishop is a very busy man, *Padre.*"

"And so am I, Quintanto. If Sanchez won't make time, then get me an appointment with Archbishop Orozco."

"I'll see what I can do, *Padre.*" The younger priest turned his gaze to the dishes and silverware cluttering the table top. He pursed his lips, avoiding eye contact with Antonio.

"Now," Antonio barked, "where is *Senora* de Leon? My plate is empty. And so is my glass of wine."

After having consumed his fill of the thoroughly satisfying welcome dinner, Antonio feigned exhaustion from his long sea journey, said goodnight to Quintanto, and retired to his quarters. The conversation at dinner had bored him, and he wanted to avoid the requisite idle chitchat that too often followed a meal when a man of his stature dined with a lower ranking priest. He wanted to ensure that Quintanto would not grow accustomed to spending time with him outside of their working hours. Although Antonio knew he couldn't avoid dining with Quintanto, he couldn't bear the thought of spending even half an hour with his assistant, a man he mistook as dull and unworldly.

IT DIDN'T TAKE LONG for Antonio to decipher the political machinations of Alghero. He was a master at sensing when to divulge information, when to withhold, whom to shun, whom to ply with loyalty to ensure future assistance when favors were needed. Within a week of his arrival Antonio had met with Archbishop Andres Orozco and had been invited to dine with him and an assortment of bishops and priests—Bishop Sanchez among them. Within two weeks of his arrival the archbishop had introduced him to many of Alghero's important citizens. At a party at the home of one of the city's dignitaries he'd met the magistrate, *Senor* Frederico Bautista, and his wife, Juliana. He'd also attended the baptismal party of the firstborn son of an influential nobleman, Count Alonzo Carmago.

Alghero suited Antonio in ways he hadn't expected. While the city retained the airs of a typical Spanish trading center—complete with the Catalan propensity for hospitality, generosity and the love of leisure and revelry—the city's social rules and obligations were less mired in centuries of the staunchly embedded customs and restrictions that flourished in his Spanish homeland and which typically inhibited the rise of a man of his class and standing. Antonio surmised that the less strident adherence to Spanish tradition was in part due to the influence of the Sardinians, even though the emigrant Aragonese had made every attempt to eradicate the island's native customs.

Those few Sardinians whom Antonio had met since his arrival—the shopkeepers and street cleaners he encountered during his daily visits to local *cafés* for a glass of wine and conversation with his new elite friends—were amiable and tolerable. They appeared to be fiercely loyal to the Aragonese noblemen and civic leaders, even though they also demonstrated a fierce and unapologetic propensity for independence. They possessed an understated strength that surfaced when confronted with a challenge that others of less fortitude and self-worth might find insurmountable. And that, Antonio found, could prove to be useful should he need an advocate from the ranks of the native-born Sardinians.

ANTONIO'S DAYS were filled with the mundane tasks of administering to the needs of the parishioners of the *Chiesa di San Francesco*. He recorded births and deaths, baptized infants, blessed the sick, administered last rites to the dying, heard confessions, and said Mass. While the daily demands of his flock rarely made his life miserable, he found fulfilling his clerical obligations to be unbearable, even though Quintanto had proven to be a capable assistant. Never a day passed that Antonio didn't assign some portion of his diocesan duties to the younger priest so he could be free to pursue his favorite pastime, which was to sip cognac at a café with his friends and discuss the burning issues of the times in which he lived.

Antonio preferred a life in which others, like Quintanto, hustled about catering to his every whim and fancy. He thought it a woeful mistake of fate that he hadn't been born a nobleman. He longed for servants to fill his bath, ready his horse, prepare his meals, drive his carriage, and tend to the grounds of his opulent estate. Of course he had *Senora* de Leon to cook his meals and clean his rooms, wash his clothes and attend to every household necessity, but her mood was often irksome, if not downright surly, and she failed to defer to him in matters of opinion when hers differed from his. When minor spats arose between them, such as when he'd asked for rice baked with saffron and she'd served him unseasoned barley, she'd storm out of the dining room muttering some cross-pollinated version of Catalan and Sardinian Sardo, clanging pots and pans in the kitchen until the din gave Antonio a severe headache. What riled him most was that he held no power to release her from employment. She was hired by Bishop Sanchez, and even though Antonio was now friendly with the bishop, he alone could fire the rectory's housekeeper.

Antonio always hurried through dinner, avoiding Quintanto's nightly invitations for conversation and a glass of wine. Every evening he made his way through the city streets to a small café, where he talked until the wee hours of the morning with Magistrate Bautista and Count Carmago. From time to time Archbishop Orozco joined them as well.

After a long night of wine and revelry with his cohorts Antonio sometimes overslept, waking late and delaying the daily 8:30 a.m. Mass until 10. He often missed appointments, then blamed Quintanto for mishandling his schedule. He flirted with the young women of his parish, allowing his hand to linger a bit too long on their scented shoulders or brush away an errant strand of their girlish hair. But he suffered no consequences for his actions. Even the archbishop was rumored to have a mistress. Often the young women whom Antonio had singled out as objects of his affection would blush and share a shy smile before moving beyond his reach. During festivals he spent more time in the streets, making merry with the town's citizens, than in preparing to process through the roadways leading the cavalcade of men who shouldered the tabernacle carrying the statue of the honored saint. No one complained, not even Quintanto. Although Antonio Albóndiga hadn't been in Alghero long, his connections with the city's powerful elite ran deep.

As his time in the city lengthened and his contacts with the prominent ruling families expanded, Antonio began to express his ideas more freely, although he was always careful to choose like-minded allies when he engaged in discussions about topics, like heresy, that some found distasteful or too inflammatory. To his delight and surprise, Archbishop Andres Orozco shared his abiding passion for eradicating that more vile of religious plagues. Antonio soon discovered that Orozco had been a childhood friend of Tomás de Torquemada, the Inquisitor-General of Spain's King Ferdinand and Queen Isabella.

The archbishop failed to inform Antonio that it had been over a decade since he'd been in contact with de Torquemada. He thought it prudent to wait until he had a better sense of the priest and his alliances with the tribunals in Seville.

Orozco and the inquisitor had parted ways long before de Torquemada had risen to national notoriety. The deterioration of their friendship had nothing to do with any disapproval of the Grand Inquisitor's need to purge Spain of its heretics. On that point the two men shared a common vision. Orozco simply preferred measures that were less harsh than those employed by his former friend and ally. While the archbishop found it difficult to champion de Torquemada's methods, he never denounced the inquisitor, publicly or privately. Torture, public burnings and beheadings unsettled the archbishop. Orozco's temperament was more suited to conversion. Turning synagogues into Catholic churches could be equally potent in curing the pox of heresy. He reasoned that if the Jews could no longer worship as they had for centuries, the source of their spiritual strength would wane and, eventually, die.

To curry favor with the archbishop, Antonio revealed his own inquisitional alliances while enjoying a glass of wine one evening. Albóndiga boasted, "My cousin Juan de San Martin is a Dominican monk. He's one of de Torquemada's assistants."

Orozco returned the comment with a slight smile and replied, "Your pedigree is better than I'd suspected, Antonio."

Antonio found another ally in Count Carmago. Years before, Carmago's cousin had lost a good sum of money conducting business with a merchant in Granada who was a Moor. "It's not right that heathen Muslims, not Spanish Catholics, hold the economic cards in Granada," the count had insisted. "It is our homeland! We should profit from its wealth!"

As a fierce believer in the one true Apostolic God, Christ Jesus, Count Carmago adamantly disapproved of his father's Muslim ties. Although the elder Carmago often traveled to Granada to do business with the richest of the Moors, Alonzo Carmago distanced himself from his father's affiliations. The count disliked Jews as well, although he never admitted that he felt a slight leniency toward them. Jesus had been Hebrew, after all.

Like the count, Archbishop Orozco had severed past ties to people he viewed as heretics. Early in his cleric career Orozco had been a priest in Barcelona, the capital of the Crown of Aragon, where he'd made the acquaintance of many rabbis who lived in the city's *Juderia*. As Orozco rose through the Catholic ranks, he began to sever his connections to the Barcelona colleagues whom he feared would impede his advancement. His heart hardened against the rabbis—hardened, too, against anyone else who was not Catholic. It was a matter of practicality for Orozco. He had no hope of wearing a cardinal's red hat if he allowed friendship to soften his adherence to the prevailing sentiments of his times. He was fond of saying, "The *limpieza de sangre*—the cleanliness of blood—must be enforced. To insure the success of wholesale purification, we must insist that each and every heretic convert to Christianity."

If the Jews and the Moors would be baptized as Catholics, all the better. If not, there was little Orozco could do to alter their fate. Those who refused to yield would be forced to suffer dire consequences.

Antonio enjoyed his burgeoning friendships with these men, whom he felt were his intellectual and political equals. He admired their zeal and envied their connections. The count, the archbishop, and even the magistrate, Frederico Bautista, exacted a high price for loyalty and exhibited little tolerance for people they deemed inferior. Antonio mistook their snobbery and elitism for sophisticated charm. Insularity and arrogance were traits he shared with them.

Over a glass of wine at the café one afternoon, Count Carmago educated Antonio on the finer details of Alghero's history, and how its fortresses and towers served to purge the city of unwanted non-Christian outsiders.

"No doubt you've seen our city's beautiful sandstone walls, its massive towers, its sturdy bulwarks," the count said. "Long ago the city's early Aragonese inhabitants decided who could and couldn't live inside Alghero's gates. Only citizens whose allegiance to Spain was verifiable and uncompromising were permitted to reside within the city. There's the *Torre dell'Espero Reial*—the Tower of Royal Ambition—which speaks to the strength of Spain's monarchy, and of course the *Torre dos Hebreus*, the Jewish gate. Non-residents—Jews and Moors and those few remaining native Sardinians—are only allowed to enter the city during daylight hours so they can conduct business or work for an Aragonese establishment. But each and every evening they must leave the city by sunset. At dusk, our fearless sentinels proclaim, *"Foras los Sards,* 'Sardinians out!' as the gate closes behind their sorry asses. Best of all, any undesirables caught disobeying are tossed over the wall!"

"I have no patience for heathens," Antonio said. "They're ignorant! Arrogant in their refusal to accept their long-prophesized messiah—even when he walked among them. But you know, I hate the *conversos* even more! They hide behind the mask of Catholicism only to relapse at home. Behind their closed doors and locked shutters, they practice their evil Jewish or Muslim ways. *Conversos* are only fit for the fires of hell or the vilest of rat-infested dungeons."

Raising their wine goblets, the count and the magistrate said in unison. "Here, here, Antonio!"

The deep-seated hatred that lived in their hearts had festered in countless Spanish Catholics for decades. The fires of intolerance were fanned by none other than King Ferdinand. Ferdinand was not the first, nor the last, to incite fear in the people who inhabited his realm. That antagonism was first sowed by the early Church fathers who sought to purify their Christian lineage from associations with the likes of King David, Solomon, and Abraham. For centuries the tide of hatred against the Jews—and the Moors—had pummeled the shores of the countries bordering the Mediterranean Sea.

The stories that Antonio learned from his cousin Juan cast this centuries-old persecution and its perpetrators into the starring role of knightly vindicators, not marauding militants hell-bent on waging an unwinnable war with legions of faithful foot soldiers. Their triumphant tales contained no sign of contrition, no evidence of remorse or regret. They reminded Antonio of the stories of war and conquest his father, Pablo, had told him long ago when he was a boy. His loyalty to the cause began then as well, when he'd witnessed the murder of a Jewish family the day he and his father had gone to buy a round of cheese in a nearby town.

His allegiance to the holy war that sought to purify the blood of Christianity continued after he was ordained. When his duties permitted he would visit Juan and they would empty bottles of red wine as they talked about all that had been done and all that continued to be done to rid Spain of heresy. Antonio was especially fond of the stories about zealous Catholic clerics who used their Sunday pulpits to admonish Jews for crucifying Christ.

Tales of torture and bloodletting thrilled both cousins. Juan loved to talk about the fourteenth century Spanish archdeacon in Seville who'd bellowed from his pulpit, "We must purge our city of its filthy Jews!" Each time, to re-enact the story Juan would stand, arm raised in indignation, and mimic the long-dead Spaniard's strident roar.

"Why did so many try to silence him?" Antonio asked. "He had such true vision."

"Yes, and he persevered even when so many others didn't approve. Instead of giving up, he emboldened his congregation. On Ash Wednesday his faithful followers took to the streets and returned to the *Juderia!*"

"I hope they burned every filthy Jewish house in the district," Antonio crowed before refilling his empty wine glass.

"Well, the police intervened," Juan lamented. "And arrested and flogged some of the Christians. Unfortunately, the district wasn't completely destroyed."

"What a pity," Antonio said.

"Yes. But the archdeacon couldn't be stopped," Juan continued. "In June of that year the *Juderia* was attacked again. They slaughtered hundreds. Injured countless more."

Antonio cheered. "God's justice finally prevailed!"

"The survivors either fled Seville or converted to Christianity," Juan said.

"A living and breathing New Christian is only slightly better than a dead Jew," Antonio said. "But I suppose it's impossible to eradicate them all."

ANTONIO AND HIS FRIENDS would adamantly deny it, but the Christian Spaniards owed a great debt to their Jewish countrymen. A century before Antonio was born Spain was one of the wealthiest nations in the Mediterranean, in large part due to its Jewish merchants. Still, far too many Christians felt no such gratitude. Spain is a Catholic country! The nation's riches should fall into the hands of true Catholics!

Every mangy cat must have its mouse to chase and kill. And so a deadly game ensued. To the Spaniards seeking wealth and clout the looting of Jewish homes and businesses became a necessity, and a pall began to settle over the kingdom. The persecutions grew more rabid and more violent. Often lives and property were taken and reputations were ruined. Conversion became a sensible alternative for the sons and daughters of Yahweh.

As the ranks of the *conversos* grew, so did the number of Spaniards who scoffed at the thought that Jews and Muslims could suddenly be transformed into true Christians.

"The only real Catholics are those who are baptized at birth," Juan insisted.

Rumors whistled down the narrow lanes of Seville. Reports surfaced that *conversos* were wearing their Catholic faith as if it were a cloak they could use to shield themselves from inclement weather.

"Every Friday they put on clean shirts," Juan said. "Do they really think we can't see that they're celebrating the Sabbath?"

"And they still refuse to eat roasted pork," Antonio complained. "They can't be true Catholics."

"Even worse, they refuse to say *Gloria* after reciting a psalm," Juan added.

"They don't fool me!" Antonio said.

Antonio and Juan saw heresy in every minor deed or action. Nothing but absolute compliance to Catholic doctrine would appease the cousins. Proof of unorthodoxy—whether verifiable or not—was readily and easily proffered. Neighbor spied on neighbor; every eye was a suspecting eye.

In Seville, Antonio had personally informed Church authorities about the suspicious behaviors of twenty of his own parishioners. His actions inspired others to do so as well.

One night during Holy Week a young man from Antonio's parish was out for a stroll. He happened to pass by a storefront where a group of Jews and *conversos* were sitting around a table engaged in an activity he didn't recognize. His eye caught a glint of something metallic, a menorah—or so he thought—and he shouted "Blasphemy!" before running to report the gathering to Antonio. Word spread quickly. Within half an hour a crowd gathered, torches in hand, ready to burn the building to the ground. But the local magistrate stepped in. "I know these men. They're good, god-fearing Christians. Go home. Leave them alone."

The atmosphere of suspicion and subterfuge suited Antonio. Having distanced himself from his great-grandfather's peasant beginnings, he'd successfully erased the stigma of poverty. He was no longer a lowly outsider. Through luck or fate or perhaps the hand of God Almighty, he'd risen from the dusty clay of his childhood and been reborn a man with a modicum of authority—though in truth his influence and power were limited, constrained by his meager status as a parish priest. He longed to be a hidalgo, a member of the gentleman's class, although no royal blood flowed through his veins and he would never amass wealth as a baron of commerce. The best hope for his future lay in the slim possibility that he would one day wear a bishop's miter and oversee a diocese of devout Catholic souls.

ANTONIO'S FERVOR FLOURISHED, ignited by the words and actions of his nation's king and queen.

King Ferdinand set out to eliminate the threats Jews posed to his royal sovereignty, even though a loyal court astrologer, a Jew named Pedro de la Caballeria, had arranged for him to marry Isabella of Castile, a union that merged the two most powerful states of Spain. To make that happen Ferdinand's father had borrowed a large sum of money from Jewish lenders, but died before the debt could be repaid. Ferdinand needed a fail-safe solution. Condemning the Jewish note-holders would wipe clean the debt he'd inherited.

While Queen Isabella's zeal was stoked by her devout Catholicism, Ferdinand's concerns were more practical. But first he had to persuade Pope Sixtus IV that it was a good idea to set up Inquisitional tribunals throughout all of Spain. For years the pope refused to grant Ferdinand's request. Eventually fate smiled favorably on the king. Twice the pope found himself in need of the king's military might—once he asked Ferdinand to protect the kingdom of Sicily, and once he requested that he send his navy to protect the southern Italian port of Otranto after the Turkish sultan had unleashed several thousand janissaries into the countryside to pillage and wreak havoc. The Turkish rampage continued unchecked for three days. That protection was paid for with a papal blessing of the king's inquisitional plans. Freed to confiscate property, Ferdinand's treasury soon overflowed with wealth stolen from Spanish Jews, Muslims and *conversos*.

FERDINAND'S PIOUS QUEEN had ascended to the throne under the motto "One country, one rule, one faith." Emboldened by her own rhetoric and goaded by her close advisor, Tomás de Torquemada, Isabella pledged to eliminate heresy if she was crowned the Queen of Spain.

Before de Torquemada served Isabella, he'd led an unremarkable life as a Dominican monk, a member of a religious order known as *Domini canes,* the Hounds of the Lord. It was there that he'd met Antonio's cousin Juan. Although de Torquemada and Juan were never close friends, they shared the desire to help the queen uphold her vow.

A decade after Isabella married Ferdinand, the rulers appointed de Torquemada as the Grand Inquisitor of Castile and Aragon. In time their tribunals infiltrated every corner of the country. De Torquemada's enemies called him a wrathful, murderous man. Juan, and others who thought of him as a humble servant of Christ Jesus, praised him.

"He's the Hammer of Heretics, the Light of Spain, and the Honor of his Order," Juan would often crow.

JUAN HAD HEARD RUMORS that some of the branches of Tomás de Torquemada's family tree bore *converso* fruit, but he dismissed such blather as attempts by de Torquemada's enemies to taint his reputation and undermine his growing authority. "His blood line is as pure as any real and true Catholic's," Juan insisted.

Antonio admired de Torquemada's ability to ferret out heresy in every godforsaken corner of the kingdom. Using elaborate networks of spies and secret police, the Grand Inquisitor hunted and captured his prey. A master interrogator, de Torquemada used whatever means necessary to extract confessions. The persecuted were hung by their arms, their joints stretched and pulled until they could no longer bear the pain. De Torquemada's henchmen poured buckets of water down the gullets of accused men and women until their lungs and bellies burst, flooding the floor with their confessions. Who cared if the rantings that sprang from the mouths of tortured souls were verifiably true? During the first dozen years of this reign of terror, more than 3,000 *conversos* were brought to trial. Those who refused to testify against the accused were arrested. More than 700 souls were tied to the stake and burned. The rampage to purify Spain was unstoppable.

Caught in the spell, Antonio kept a daily log, which he called "Reclaiming Spain for God." He chronicled the slaughter, delineating the dates and cities, the numbers of people maimed, tortured, and killed, the coffers seized, the lives ruined. He made detailed lists of the feasts that followed an *auto-da-fé* when the noblemen and their wives, the civil authorities, and the honored churchmen retired to banquet halls to celebrate, enjoying a lavish meal, quenching their thirsts with casks of fine wines. Antonio's mouth watered thinking about the cheeses and breads, the roasted lamb and the tender asparagus, the sweet cakes for dessert.

When Juan was away on official Inquisitional business, he sent Antonio weekly letters detailing the whys, whens, and wherefores of the tribunals. By candlelight, alone at night in his quarters, Antonio would read his cousin's tightly written words. His eyes raced across the pages, his heart pounded, his legs twitched, so anxious was he to rush to Juan's side and help in this most Holy Cause.

What good could he be in Seville? Here he could only participate in a riot every now and then—torch a house, push a *converso* to the cobblestone streets and step on his fallen body, perhaps throw stones at the astonished faces of women and children. He longed to be appointed to a tribunal, sit at the right hand of the illustrious de Torquemada, mastermind of the Inquisition. He longed to sit beside the gentry at an *auto-da-fé* and watch the wretched heathens writhe, then dine extravagantly afterwards, savoring the delicious victory.

Before he fell asleep Antonio would close his eyes and envision the long line of heretics clad in yellow robes, carrying unlit candles made from yellow wax. He'd see the conical hats they wore; he'd recite the lists of anti-Christian sins painted on their headwear. And he would fall into a deep slumber knowing that the world had witnessed their shame.

Antonio thought the *auto-da-fé* a singular stroke of brilliance. What better way to test the faith of the accused than to subject them to a public Act of Faith by parading them through the streets? The central square was the perfect place in which to pelt them with shame—a shame they brought upon themselves, in their wanton refusal to accept Christ as their Savior. They deserved to stand for hours under the blazing sun or the harsh, icy winds, eviscerated by the fervent eyes of ecclesiastic and civil authorities. They deserved to tremble as their sentences were read aloud. Antonio would grow agitated when he thought of their vile lies, their blatant disavowal of all that was right and good and true. His temples would begin to throb and a migraine would overtake him, forcing him to lie in bed for days with a cool cloth over his eyes, trying to extinguish the fire that raced through his head.

Antonio met with the Bishop of Seville to express his desire to assist in the Holy War. "The blood of Christianity must be cleansed!" Antonio asserted.

The bishop dismissed his request. "You have confessions to hear, *Padre*. It's best you set your mind on saving the souls within your own parish. Leave the Jews and the Muslims for other more capable hands."

Angry, Antonio decided to send a letter to Juan to tell him of the bishop's curt reply. He seethed as he returned to the rectory. There he muttered to the walls, the floor, the window sills, "They can't prevent me from serving the wishes of the Crown! If it takes a meeting with Tomás de Torquemada himself, or Her Majesty the Queen, I'll help rid Seville of its heathen vermin."

There would be no appointment, no audience with Isabella, no conversation with Tomás de Torquemada. Within a week of Antonio's ardent proclamation to the bishop he was ousted from Seville and shipped off to Sardinia. Had he known during the sea voyage to Alghero that his plans to faithfully serve his king would find renewed hope in the hearts and minds of his new friends, he might have felt less conflicted about his exile, more eager to embrace the city on the bay that awaited his fervent convictions.

IN ALGHERO ANTONIO met with his friends, Archbishop Orozco and Count Carmago, once a week at the home of the magistrate Frederico Bautista to dine on their favorite meal, fish stew and roasted wild boar or tender suckling pig. Sometimes they feasted on rice mixed with olive oil, mixed with shavings of dried and hardened mullet eggs. They downed countless glasses of fine red wine. They wiped the grease from their faces before walking to a nearby café for dessert, more wine, and conversation. As the trio strolled under the watchful gaze of the moon and the stars, Antonio planted seeds of sedition.

One balmy evening in Alghero, Antonio shared a letter about the *auto-da-fé* that he'd received from his cousin Juan. He felt anguished that his exile from Spain had left him unable to participate in these forced public confessions of faith. Antonio's eyes raced over the page. His heart pounded as he read his cousin's words aloud to his friends.

"The gatherings are full of splendid fervor. Dukes, counts, barons, and other men of noble birth arrived dressed in their finest clothing. Ladies of high social status accompanied them, clothed in gowns to rival the most elegant of balls. Archbishops and bishops were there, too. And two cardinals. Priests and monks from every Catholic order stood by. Anticipation ignited the air as they all waited to witness the workings of the Tribunal. Of course the streets were lined with common citizens, too, men, women and children of more humble birth. They must be made to watch the dire end that comes to those who turn away from the One Truth Faith."

Antonio paused to order another bottle of wine.

"Go on," Bautista urged. "What happened next?"

"The day began with the usual parade of penitents. The men were stripped naked to the waist, the women were prodded along in their gowns of shame. The heathens were led through the streets, the soles of their shoeless feet chafed raw by the rough pavement stones. One by one the sinners approached the inquisitor's throne. One by one they fell to their bony knees and proclaimed their sins before recanting them, loudly, so everyone in the crowd could hear. Then they were beaten until their bodies were bloodied and bent. When they were nearly ready to take their last breath, they were sentenced to walk through the streets for the next six Fridays, going from church to church. Only in this way can they sufficiently be redeemed from the bondage of their sins against the Holy Catholic Church."

"And what becomes of those who refused to repent their heresy?" Bautista asked.

"Death," Antonio said. "The only fate they deserve. The henchmen bind the hands of those pitiful monsters before tying them to a pole and dragging them to the stake. For some, the punishment is swift. The soldiers hang them right then and there or cut off their heads before burning them at the stake. The more defiant ones face a more fitting death. Sometimes their hair is lit and a fiery halo envelopes their faces; then their clothing is tarred and torched and they become engulfed by the fiery tongues of hell. To seal their coffin, the wood below the stake is lit and they ride to their grave on the Devil's howling tongue!"

"The punishment fits the crime," Carmago said.

"Indeed," Bautista agreed.

"Just last week, I received another letter from my cousin Juan," Antonio continued. "He tells me that de Torquemada has instituted the public burning of books. And of course the heretics who read them."

"Ah, yes," Carmago said. "There's something of pageantry about such a public ceremony of sentencing. Keeps the scoundrels in line, that's for certain. If not burning, or beheading, then confinement to dungeons, and where necessary, physical persuasion, if you understand my meaning. Instruments that prod and poke to encourage confession and conversion. These are the things that are required to rid the world of heretics."

"I heard he's trying to expel all Jews from Spain," Archbishop Orozco stated. "I wish he'd do the same with the Moors. Send them all back to wherever it is they came from. Useless filth."

"Marranos!" Antonio cackled. "Pigs. Better to roast them on a spit and serve them as slop to the swine."

The men laughed. Their banter grew louder as they emptied the wine bottle, filling their glasses and their gullets.

"Is it true that they're arranging for tribunals in Aragon, Catalonia and Valencia?" Bautista asked.

"Yes," the archbishop attested. "And they're overseen by inquisitors with ties to the civil authorities, not the pope."

"Oh, to smell the stench of burning flesh," Antonio slurred.

"To see the flames singeing the pages of sixteen thousand heathen books!" Carmago seethed.

"And to confiscate their estates and worldly goods!" the archbishop said, gleefully rubbing a small handful of coins between his palms.

"And assert the power of civic duty in service to the purification of Spain's hereditary Catholics," Bautista crowed.

"While we eradicate the Jews and the Moors, let's not overlook the witches and their sorry lot," Antonio asserted. "Death to the pagan whores!"

The men lifted their wine glasses and smiled, toasting the achievement of de Torquemada. They slapped one another's backs, congratulating each other for their relentless dedication to the purity of their Catholic faith. When the last dregs of wine had been swallowed, they retired to their homes and a night of sound, dreamless sleep.

In their beds, dead to the world, they failed to hear the wailing cries of the murdered and disenfranchised, failed to heed the dirge that echoed against the walls of majestic cities, that bounced off the wooden doors of cathedrals and the cobblestones of village squares. Their slumbering ears failed to hear the woeful howl for restitution that reverberated throughout the countryside over fields of grain and hilltops of granite, over oceans of salty seawater and beaches smeared with bloodied sand.

Chapter 5
The Shepherds

BASILIO SAVORED THE COOLING TOUCH of soil against his legs, the certainty of the ground that cradled his weight as he shifted from time to time, settling into the task at hand. He glanced at the juniper bush beside him and inhaled slowly, deeply, bathing his lungs in the sweet-spicy aroma that emanated from the evergreen. Behind him stood his *pinnette*, the round, thatched roof hut in which he slept during the nights he stayed with his flock of sheep instead of returning to the village to be with his wife, Shardana, and their granddaughter Martina. Above him songbirds roosted on tree limbs, warbling at the morning sky. Basilio listened contentedly to the chirping as he plaited horse hair, fashioning it into a rope. His son-in-law, Giovanni, planned to give the sturdy woven tether to his brother, Malthinu, a farmer who lived in a mountain town on the other side of the valley. Basilio's horsehair ropes were strong and durable—and prized by many people in the towns and villages throughout the region. Malthinu would use the gift to fashion a yoke for his oxen.

As Basilio focused on his work, his beloved collie, Mutos, sat beside him. Though the dog's eyes were open and his ears alert, he was content to rest close to his master and watch the sheep feed on grass and wild herbs. Inches away a speckled lizard slept on a sun-soaked rock, unafraid of the man or his dog.

The clear February morning sky held a bright sun that, while pleasant, promised to send more invigorating rays by noontime to scorch the shepherd's head. By late afternoon the blue dome of heaven would deepen to a light mauve, turning violet before shimmering to bronze at the first blush of evening. Later, when the sun set, a blood-red sky! On this early morning, as Basilio wove the horsehair rope and finished his breakfast of bread and cheese, he paused from time to time to savor the cloudless expanse of the heavens, which to him resembled the sea, although in his fifty years of life on the island of Sardinia he had never seen the sea, never stepped foot on the beaches—sandy or rocky—that hugged the shoreline.

Basilio's mind wandered as his fingers worked the coarse threads of horse hair. He gazed at the rolling green pastures dotted with granite rocks. Here and there the patchwork fields were interspersed with asphodel, the plant so integral to the basket-weaving craft of his older brother, Constantino. Both men had grown up tending sheep in the hillsides with their father, Arturo. After Arturo's death, the brothers had taken over the care and feeding of the three hundred small, yet hardy, members of the flock that comprised their family's sheepfold *tanca* until Constantino's arthritic knees and his weakened heart confined him to the village. For a time Constantino had worked as a carpenter, crafting sturdy tables and shelves from holm oak limbs and logs. But one day he became entranced as he watched his daughter Anna-Bella weaving a basket from asphodel. He set down his carpenter tools and stood beside her. "Teach me," he said.

"This is women's work," she replied.

"And when I have mastered it," Constantino asserted, "it will become men's work, too. The basket doesn't care if the artist's hand belongs to a man or a woman."

Anna-Bella chuckled and made room for her father on the bench. As a tender of the bees that inhabited the wild hives and a harvester of their sweet honey, she understood that work was best accomplished when done communally. Many eager hands made tasks more pleasant and more readily accomplished.

In short time Constantino became a master basketmaker, and although he missed working beside his brother in the sheepfold, he found great pleasure in weaving round, sturdy vessels out of native plant materials. From time to time he also still crafted tables and other household goods out of holm oak and sold them to villagers or traded them for things he and his family needed, like pots and pans, shoes, or tools.

SARDINIAN SHEEP are as resilient and robust as the shepherds who watch over them. Basilio's ewes and rams withstood harsh winters and drought-parched summers in which the stingy sky often withheld rain for six months or more. The ewes grazed on hillsides dense with fragrant herbs and in wild pastures of grass connected by ancient footpaths, and they yielded ample milk that Basilio and the other shepherds transformed into *pecorino sardo*. While many were adept at cheesemaking, Basilio's son, Isidoro, and Constantino's son, Brontu, were especially gifted.

The cousins crafted their cheese in stone hut outbuildings attached to brushwood milking enclosures that they'd built by hand. Sometimes they'd season the mixture with peppercorns, sometimes saffron; other times they'd toss in rosemary or lavender, harvested from the hillsides. Always their mothers, Shardana and Sarda, anticipated the days when their sons returned from the sheepfold, arriving in town with cheese wheels loaded on the backs of their mules. The women were always the first to sample the latest batch of *pecorino*. They marveled at the concoctions their sons had crafted, and their mouths would salivate, anticipating how the cheese would melt sweetly on their tongues. It gave the men great joy to see their mothers' broad smiles when they returned from the hills bearing gifts of sheep's cheese.

Ewe's milk was not the only precious commodity offered by the sheep to the men who cared for them. The animals' thick fleece, sheared each June, provided precious wool, which the village women spun into thread and wove into fabric to create clothing for their husbands, their sons and daughters, and themselves. Occasionally, to grace a celebratory wedding table or a festival gathering, the shepherds would slaughter a lamb. Before the animal was sacrificed, the shepherds would kneel and say a prayer of praise and thanksgiving for the life they were about to take. Only then could they feel released by the animal to share the delicious, grass-sweetened meat with their relatives and friends.

Basilio set aside his rope-braiding task to cut a piece of *pecorino* with his *sa resolza*, his prized pocketknife. Above all the other tools he used to ply his trade, Basilio most valued his *sa resolza*. He loved its sturdy handle, carved from a bone-hard ram's horn. He loved the way the sharp edge of its blade shone in the sunlight. As he sliced into the cheese, he admired the knife's shiny point, tipped at the topmost edge like a myrtle leaf. He bit into one corner of the *pecorino*, then tossed the rest to Mutos. The dog swallowed it whole, then gratefully licked the shepherd's fingers. Thoughts of Shardana drifted into Basilio's mind. He sensed that his wife felt upset. It worried him that it would be days before he would be able to return home to help shoulder whatever troubles burdened her.

He recalled the protracted years of grief after their daughter Grazia died. His precious daughter, a young wife and mother, had been snatched by Death before she was twenty-two. For years Basilio's wife had been unable to shake the terrible sadness from her bones. Often she'd spend her days walking the forests, visiting the Old Mother Oak Tree, sitting beside it, drawing comfort. Sometimes she'd take the longer trek to the pasturelands and arrive at his *tanca*, bringing a bunch of figs as an excuse for her visit. Without her customary smile she'd hand him the fruit, then stare out over the hillsides, tears running down her cheeks. While the dark emptiness that had claimed his wife's spirit slowly eased, it never fully relinquished. Over time, from time to time, joy agreed to return to Shardana's weary face, but it lingered only for brief moments. A part of Shardana had been buried with Grazia the day they'd covered their daughter's dead body with dirt. Even now, ten years after Grazia's passing, on certain days without cause or reason Shardana would take to the hills to weep alone, comforted only by the towering limbs of the Great Old Oak.

Lately something lay heavily on Shardana's heart, although Basilio knew it wasn't the residue of grief that gnawed at her. His wife had mentioned a dream without offering details. He couldn't imagine what kind of night vision could cause her to fret so, though he trusted the power of her intuition. The morning after she dreamt it, she'd sent their granddaughter Martina up to the *tanca* to tell him to pour a pail of ewe's milk on the ground. Martina had warned, "*Ayaya* was very certain. Something ominous is ahead. Be sure to give the Earth a thorough soaking of the sheep's precious liquid. We'll need all the blessings and protection it can offer us."

He'd done as they'd requested, but that was months ago. There was still no sign of whatever troubling thing Shardana had sensed. Maybe the milk's protection had sufficed. Or maybe, just maybe, whatever it was that was about to descend upon the village hadn't yet arrived. He sent a silent prayer to the undulating hills asking that his wife be able to find the strength she needed to endure whatever disquietude she now felt, whatever challenges she and the village were meant to face. Until his return to town she'd have her sister, Sarda, to rely on, and that truth comforted him greatly.

Basilio squinted into the morning sun and smiled as if greeting an old friend. He rested his eyes upon the hills that lay beyond the perimeter of his sheepfold. He felt a kinship with the land that provided a livelihood for him and his family. This wordless affinity was a kind of brotherliness, as tangible and eternal as a human bloodline. The air and soil flowed in his veins, the spring waters coursed through his marrow; the mountains and high plains powered his body as surely as sinew and muscle. He never tired of seeing the green rows of tamarisk and thickets of thyme and arbutus nudged against vast stretches of high plains and rocky plateaus. Behind him, to his right, the fields blazed with pink oleanders, honeysuckle, sweet peas, lilac mallows, and dog roses interspersed with low scrub, wild fig trees, and hedges of rosemary, mint and lavender. To his left groves of oak and chestnut trees flourished among outcroppings of hazelnut bushes. He inhaled deeply as his eyes beheld the macchia, its coarse, beautiful tapestry woven together with heather, rosemary, thyme, rock roses, red-berried arbutus trees, black-berried myrtles, and juniper bushes.

Across the field, low stone walls demarcated the edges of Basilio's *tanca*. His mountainous pastureland contained everything his heart could hold: his sheepfold, his shepherd's hut, his milking shed and his son, Isidoro, standing affably beside Giovanni, and Constantino's son, Brontu. The three younger men were busy coaxing twenty ewes away from a patch of wild thyme and thistles; that morning the ewes preferred to linger over breakfast, enjoying the morning sun rather than being herded into the milking shed.

Basilio sucked a bellyful of mountain air into his contented lungs.

Life was beautiful and generous, and he began to sing a shepherd's song he'd been singing ever since he was a boy and used to race over the pasturelands behind his father, running through the thickets with glee, unleashing the exuberance that rushed through his body.

Basilio felt fortunate to share his livelihood with his son, his son-in-law, and his nephew, three souls who loved the high lands outside Orune as much as did he. Basilio and Constantino had decided that the sheepfold they'd inherited from their father, and had once tended together, was to be shared equally among Isidoro, Brontu and Giovanni. Though they owned little in the way of earthly goods, they would bequeath the sheep and the *tanca* to this next generation of shepherds. And the thought of that gave great peace of mind to both of the brothers. While the sheepfold did not grant great wealth, it afforded a good life, when the seasons cooperated and the milk ran plentiful, the fleece thickened, yielding abundant wool, and the sheep procreated, replenishing their flock.

Although the three younger men were not brothers, they shared the affection of brothers, and they all enjoyed the company of the elder shepherd, old Basilio. By day he was a wise and patient teacher, instructing them in the ways of their trade. By night he was quick to join in their leisure. When Isidoro and Brontu played their triple-reed *launeddas* flutes, Basilio settled in beside them. Young and old, their hearts embraced the melancholy tune that wafted from the beloved instrument of their homeland. All four sang as they warmed themselves by the small fire in the center of their *pinnette*, reciting songs as ancient as the wind.

The shepherds' fire pit was more precious than gold. It served as a camp stove to heat a bit of soup, if they were fortunate to have any. It served, also, to ward away the chill, for the spring evenings retained more than a bit of winter's bite. There, inside the shepherd's hut, the men would sing and sip a bit of *mirto*, if they hadn't already emptied the bottle of liquor they'd brought back from their last excursion to the village. When fatigue finally claimed their limbs, they set their rush mats on the hut's dirt floor, covered themselves with sheepskin fleeces, and fell asleep.

Though a shepherd's life was strenuous, it gave each of them a singular satisfaction to work among the animals, in the lusty arms of the hillside, with nature's unpredictable temperament and its insatiable demand for courage, fortitude and beauty. They learned to read the slightest changes in the sky, a shift in the winds, the smell of impending rain, the whisper of a storm rumbling over the mountain ridges. Lightning was their deadliest foe, and so they keened their eyes toward the heavens, translating nearly imperceptible signals sent from above to warn them to take cover.

The bleating of lambs, the tinkling of sheep's bells, and the clomping of hooves over rocky terrain were music to their souls. The scent of wooly lanolin mingling with heather, wild tarragon, and lavender filled them with serenity. Even the aroma of sheep shit and urine did nothing to alter their affection for the work that filled their days and often their nights. The lilting melody of a distant flute, emanating from another shepherd's stone hut across the hillsides, set their eyes to smiling and their lips to whistling. Their lives were arduous and oftentimes lonesome, for it wasn't uncommon for the men to traverse the pasturelands for months at a time with their flocks, not returning to their families in the village. Still, a life full of satisfying labor suited these men.

Every morning Isidoro milked the ewes, collecting the warm liquid in oak casks. After setting some aside for their lunch, Brontu and Giovanni toted the reserves to the hut, where, later, they'd turn the milk into cheese. The men enjoyed toting rounds of *pecorino* back to their homes on those rare Saturdays when they were able to make their way to the village. They proudly shared their bounty with their wives, their mothers, their sisters, and Constantino, who would gather around the table—every man, woman and child—savoring the pungent cheese. They'd comment on the batch's distinctive flavor. Usually their mothers were able to discern if the ewes had feasted more on heather than on thyme or if the animals had chosen, instead, to munch on grass, rock roses or rosemary.

IN THE AUTUMN, the fieldworkers in the heaths below the shepherd's grazing lands would burn thickets of thyme and thistles to break up their acreage, preparing the ground so they could sow wheat, barley and rye. On those days the air would be perfumed with smoke rising from the herbs' charred skins, and later, if the autumn rains came, the scent of mushrooms would rouse the *cinghiali,* compelling them to root through the forests in search of a satisfying meal of fresh fungi. But autumn was still many months away. Summer, too. Spring had just wrestled winter from the sky. The air was fragrant with tender wild-flowers and buzzing with bees. The snow on the mountaintops had just begun to recede, emptying its ice-cold runoff into serpentine streams. The sheep romped friskily over the hillsides, baaing at one another and at their shepherd tenders. The ewes would soon birth their young, and the cycle of life would begin again.

Spring was Basilio's favorite season. Though February was not often spring-like in warmth it was the season of birthing lambs, and so the people of the Barbagia saw its connection to rebirth and declared it the demise of winter and the resurgence of all that was vital and alive. During this season Basilio slept in his *pinnette* many nights, seeing to the pregnant ewes in his flock. In the spring he and Isidoro, Giovanni, and Brontu were only able to return to the village once a week, on Saturday evening. He often dreamed of his wife standing in the doorway of their small house in Orune laughing, her brow loosened with mirth as it had been when Grazie had been a baby. On those nights he'd wake with a start in the coldness of his shepherd's hut, comforted only by the bleating of the ewes in the pen nearby. In the dark he'd count the days until he could once more return to town and settle his eyes upon his wife's face.

The ritual of returning to the village seasoned the lives of every shepherd in the Barbagia. In groups of threes and fours, five or more, or on their own, the men descended from the hills. The dirt roads home were dotted with tired travelers, sweaty from their work on the mountainsides. This exodus of shepherds trudged through fields and over makeshift paths to return to their families and their village homes. They entrusted their sheep to the hands of an overseer so they could enjoy an evening, or two, with their wives and their daughters, their sons too young to join them in the hills, their friends and neighbors who kept to the confines of town tending stores, hoeing gardens, making shoes, sewing clothes, baking bread, sweeping steps, and living the life of those anchored to cobblestoned streets rather than to stony crags.

Anticipation quickened in the steps of each of the returning shepherds as they arrived at the outskirts of their village. Their hearts eased as they eyed the rows of stone cottages, some whitewashed, others retaining the grey of the granite from which they'd been made. The entryways of some of the homes were festooned with benches made of stone where the townswomen would rest for a breath of morning air, sit to craft baskets, or spend an hour or two clearing soil and debris from the roots of herbs and vegetables freshly harvested from their gardens. Here and there groupings of stone benches were aggregated before the vestibules of several homes, serving as a common courtyard where neighbors gathered to visit on days when the sun was kind enough to hide behind the clouds and rein in its relentless heat.

As the returning shepherds strolled through the cobblestone lanes, reacquainting their feet with manmade pathways, they were warmly greeted by the local women who were busy scooping water into pails at the well in the center of the *piazza* and by men who lived and worked in town as shopkeepers, bakers or blacksmiths.

"Hey, Brontu," one called out. "Have your ewes birthed yet?"

"No," the shepherd called back. "Early next week, we suspect."

"May your flock increase tenfold," the women replied.

The shepherds smiled and nodded, appreciative of the greetings, but they didn't tarry. Each held their sights on home. Brontu was eager to see his wife, Viviana, and kiss his sweet daughter, Leda. Basilio sought out his beloved Shardana. Isidoro anticipated the soft smile of his wife, Teresina, and the big embrace of their young son, Donatello. Giovanni looked forward to seeing his daughter, Martina. Each would be welcomed with a nod, a smile, and a nudge to take a bath—for they smelled of dank soil, sour milk, lanolin, and sheep dung, and they were in dire need of removing the grit and sweat they'd accumulated from living among the sheep.

After washing up and changing his clothes, Brontu would call to his wife and daughter, "Time to go to see *Ayaya* Sarda and *Ayaya* Shardana!" Then he, Viviana and Leda would stop by his parents' home before accompanying his sister Anna-Bella, and Sarda and Constantino, to Basilio and Shardana's home. There they would share a simple meal of soup and bread with their kin. Isidoro, Teresina and Donatello would join them, too, sitting at Shardana's table right next to Giovanni and Martina. At this table made from sturdy holm oak, Basilio presided like a shepherd king beside his formidable village queen, Shardana.

Holding out a round of *semi-stagionato pecorino*, Isidoro and Brontu would present their mothers with their gift of freshly made cheese, bowing their heads in deference, satisfied smiles claiming their faces.

"From ram and ewe to man and woman!" Sarda would say, reverentially lifting a cheese round into the air as if it were a Catholic communion wafer.

"The cycle continues," Shardana would crow, biting into a thumb-sized slice of *pecorino*.

The shepherds would laugh and the mothers would kiss their sons' faces, happy to have them back home, safe under their roofs, warmed in the tight embrace of their arms.

Together this gathering of shepherds and healers would give thanks for the Earth and its bounty, the mountain and its pasturelands. The herders would tell tales of their days under the sun, their nights beneath the stars. The women and Constantino would share stories of the comings and goings of those who remained in town, their conversation easy and warm.

As they ate, Constantino always asked about the sheep. Were they healthy? Had the ewes' pregnancies progressed? Were the rams battling one another, vying for supremacy? Was the milk abundant? The shepherds patiently answered all his queries, sensing Constantino's lingering need to entwine his life with their labor and remain as close to the sheepfold as was possible for a man whose health restricted him, day after day, to the stone stoop outside his front door, making baskets instead of herding sheep.

Sarda and Shardana ladled steaming fava bean and cabbage soup into the men's bowls. Viviana and Teresina dispensed baskets of thick bread. Anna-Bella and Martina sliced slabs of *stagionato pecorino sardo* from the rounds of cheese the shepherds had brought from their pasturelands months before, cutting into a wheel that'd been aging to perfection. Its crust was dark brown, its flesh as golden as straw. Later, the twin healers would cut a nugget of cheese and tuck it into their skirt pockets, should they or one of their patients find themselves hungry and in need of a bite. "Cheese makes you strong," the villagers always said, savoring the hearty *pecorino*. Whether healthy or ill, no day passed without munching on a morsel of that vital food.

Martina always sat beside her father, Giovanni, touching his fingers from time to time, happy to have him home again, if only for a short while. "Once the lambs are born," she announced, "I'll come to the *tanca* and name them all!"

"Me, too!" Donatello chimed in.

"Me, too—me, too," Leda added, not wanting to be left out of the fun.

The grownups laughed and agreed that Martina, indeed, was the one to undertake such a task, for her mother, Grazia, had bestowed names upon the animals every spring when she'd been a small girl. Though she laughed with the rest of them, Shardana discretely wiped away a tear, eager to disguise the sudden upswell of grief. Sarda kissed the top of Martina's head, thick with black curls. "You alone shall be the anointer of the lambs!" she proclaimed.

After dinner Constantino uncorked a bottle of *mirto*, the potent liqueur he'd distilled from myrtle berries and juniper. He passed the bottle to the men, who each poured some of the liquid into a glass and swallowed it. Anna-Bella and Viviana cleared away the dirty dishes, then joined the others at the table, telling stories of all that had happened in the village while the shepherds had been away toiling in the hills.

"The shoemaker's daughter gave birth to a healthy baby boy," Sarda announced.

Shardana added, "The baker finally proposed to the cartmaker's widow. And the carpenter's daughter paid for her herbal remedies with four jars of golden honey."

"And they accepted the gift even though they didn't need any honey," Martina added. "We already have Anna-Bella's bees."

"We take what people are able to give," Sarda asserted. "To do otherwise would only shame them."

When all the tales were told and all the *mirto* consumed the yawning began, and so did the leave-taking. Sarda and her family stepped into the night air, heading back to their cottages and their beds. Isidoro, Teresina, and their son headed home as well. Giovanni and Martina bid goodnight to Shardana and Basilio. Everyone fell fast asleep.

The following evening, supper took place at Sarda's home. As they'd done the previous night, both families gathered to share a meal. That evening they feasted on sausages, barley, and field greens. All too soon Monday morning would arrive and the shepherds would return to their *tancas*. All too soon they'd rise before the Monday sun to restock their provision bags with *pane carasau*, the unleavened flat bread that was their main sustenance. They'd grab a pot of ricotta cheese and a bottle of *mirto*. They'd steal a goodbye kiss before crossing their thresholds and trekking back to their sheepfold.

Viviana and Teresina would linger at their doorsteps watching as Brontu and Isidoro greeted Basilio and Giovanni. The women would steal one last look at their husbands before turning back inside to check on their young children, still asleep in their beds. The day, with all its work, called to them. They had cloth to weave, baskets to make, gardens to till, eggs to collect. Their morning would be full of the duties and tasks of motherhood and homemaking that anchored them to the village and made their cottages a refuge for their shepherd husbands. Anna-Bella would soon attend to the wild bee hives, harvesting honey for medicine and food. Sarda and Shardana would open their doors to villages in need of healing. Martina would assist them.

Before the morning sun had time to tint the clouds a rosy pink the shepherds headed away from their families, down the lane toward the *piazza*, retracing the steps that had brought them home just two short days before. Back through the village streets they'd walk in silence, their minds shifting from memories of kitchen tables and warm beds to thoughts of milking huts and lumpy bed mats.

Up and up the shepherds would walk, over stony hillsides, through fields of fragrant flowers and thorny brush, alongside forests of juniper and oak, beside creeks cold with rushing water. Up and up they'd trek, making their way back to their *tancas* and their sheep, back to their days of windy sky and expansive land, back to their nights of campfires and bittersweet music, back to their rock-hard ground and their humble sheds, their songs of living in the outdoors, their stories of beautiful women and silent men, of the children who brought them joy, of the fathers and mothers who sustained them, of the mountains that sheltered them through storms of rain or snow, until, once more, their duties permitted them to leave their flocks and return to the warm, waiting arms of their families in the village.

Chapter 6
Antonio's Plan

ANTONIO TRIED FOR HOURS TO CONVINCE his companions that his plan was foolproof.

"We must convene a group of true Christians and purge Alghero of its *conversos*. We must institute a cleansing that'll rival the glorious night of terrible burning in Seville back in 1391."

Antonio's gray-green eyes darkened in his pale face. Spittle gathered in the corners of his tight mouth as he planted seeds of insurrection in the hearts of Count Carmago and the magistrate, Frederico Bautista. With each puff of his expectant breath the candle flame flickered, its glowing center reflecting the horrors of hell.

"There's no need to be worried about being reprimanded," he assured. "The archbishop won't bring any sanctions against us. He's our friend and ally! The civil authorities won't bring any charges, if we can reach the God-fearing among them. *Senor* Bautista, your connections can be of great use on that account."

"While I agree about the need to sanctify Christianity and verify the piety of alleged Christian souls," Alonzo Carmago insisted, "we have to proceed with extreme caution. There are no Jews residing within Alghero's walls, Antonio. The laws ensure that they leave at dusk. They can't return until the gates reopen in the morning."

"Yes," Bautista added, "while admirable, your plan is unnecessary, dear *Padre*. What's to be gained from organizing a rebellion against people who aren't even residents of our city? We needn't worry about the Jews here. There are none."

"Listen to the magistrate, Antonio," Carmago said. "The Jews only pollute our air during the hours of commerce. Why should we fret about their useless lives after they go home to their wives and their suppers?"

"That's where your thinking goes astray," Antonio cautioned. "I'm not talking about the Jews who come and go, in and out of Alghero each day, but of the *marranos,* the *conversos* who walk among us, day and night. They may look and act like pious Christians, but beneath their Catholic disguises beats the heart of Abraham. I tell you it's true! Scratch the surface of their thin papal-loving skins and you'll find Semitic blood singing only songs of the Torah."

"So you propose to rout out those *conversos* who are really heretics, hiding among us as Christians?" the magistrate asked.

"Exactly!" Antonio replied. He sat back in his chair, pleased that his companions had finally understood his meaning. "I see them all the time at Mass, receiving Holy Communion, making the sign of the cross as if they truly believed. But I can smell the heresy on their foul breaths, read it in the depths of their muddy eyes. They go through the motions, genuflecting, saying Catholic prayers, making novenas to the Madonna. But inside their hearts they're reciting Seder prayers, counting the days until Passover, Chanukah, Yom Kippur.

"They begrudgingly carry their babies to the baptismal font, and afterward they hurry home to wash the sacrament's blessing from their children's foreheads. In Seville it was widely known that they celebrated Passover and gave oil to their synagogues. My cousin Juan told me an easy and reliable way to identify *conversos*. Climb to the top of any city tower on their Sabbath day and look out at the rooftops of the homes below. The chimneys without smoke even on the coldest days of winter belong to the *conversos*. Jews won't light a fire on the Sabbath.

"My cousin also told me of one *marrano* who pretended that his stomach became upset when he ate leavened bread so he could have an excuse for eating unleavened bread. That way he could eat it at Passover without drawing suspicions. They go to great lengths to disguise their intentions and their customs. We must sniff out their poisonous hypocrisy."

"They're the ones who've ferreted their way into our political are-
nas," Carmago said, "and wrestled a fair amount of the wealth from
native Spaniards. They're draining coffers of gold and silver that rightfully belong to us."

"Think of your children, Alonzo," Antonio continued, "of their diminished inheritance. How can you bequeath them the riches they
deserve by right of their Spanish lineage unless, and until, what's been
taken from them is rightfully returned?"

"You've convinced me, Antonio," Carmago announced.

"And I as well," Bautista asserted.

"Good!" Antonio said. "I'll work out the details. My plan will satisfy
the intentions of Almighty God."

IN THE DAYS that followed, the three conspirators met often to discuss and finalize their strategy. Should books be burned? Should a
young man be hired to spy on the houses of *conversos,* catching them
in their heathen acts? Should a boy be sent to climb the tower steps
to check if smoke emanated from all the city's chimneys on the day of
Sabbath? Should stones be tossed at their doors and windows? Or Stars
of David etched upon the stone walls of their shops and houses? So
many ways to launch their efforts! So many ways to reclaim the city of
Alghero for Christ!

As the men conspired, discussing matters of faith and morals, they
continued to meet at the café and also at Magistrate Bautista's home.
There they'd dine on fish soup and crusted bread, sip Frederico's finest
wines, and solidify their plans. Often Bautista's wife, Juliana, would
linger at the edge of their conversation, hovering in the shadows, listening, watching. From time to time she'd relieve the maidservant of her
duties and take it upon herself to refill the men's glasses, for she wanted
to be closer to hear their words of conviction, their growing desire to
rain purity down upon the streets of her beloved city.

Juliana's great-great-grandfather had been a Moor who'd been born
in Granada, in a village nestled against the foothills of the Sierra Ne-
vada mountains, near the confluence of the Beiro, the Darro and the
Genil rivers. As a young man he'd converted to Christianity, becoming
a *morisco.* He'd changed his name from Mussa-al-Amiri to Miguel de

Aliaga before moving his family to Seville, where he became a jewelry maker. In that city he was ever vigilant never to disclose his Muslim affiliations. He amassed a great fortune buying and selling gems and crafting jewelry and other finery for the court and its noblewomen. He married his eldest daughter, Constantina, to a lesser nobleman; she would one day become Juliana's great-grandmother. In time Miguel's progeny advanced in status, rising up the ranks of nobility through marriage and through the wealth Miguel earned from buying silver mines in Sardinia. By the time Juliana's father was born, Miguel de Aliaga's lineage had risen into the middle echelons of power. Juliana's father had emigrated to Alghero to oversee the family's Sardinian holdings and had married Juliana's mother, Marguerita, a woman whose family had moved to the city from Barcelona shortly after Alghero was claimed by the Aragonese. In the years between Mussa-al-Amiri's transformation to Miguel de Aliaga the family had interred all memory of its Islamic bones, severed all ties to its religious and cultural past.

Juliana knew nothing of her Moorish blood, her family's secret having long ago been entombed in its dusty genealogical grave. Her dark eyes, black hair and olive-toned complexion were attributed to her Spanish heritage, although she had an inexplicable love for marzipan that she satisfied only when she was pregnant and couldn't avoid giving into such cravings. And once, long ago as a child when she and her parents had been in Spain visiting their relatives, her grandmother had dissuaded her from having her fortune told by a turbaned palm reader at a street fair in Seville.

As Juliana circled the table, pouring wine into her husband's glass and refilling the goblets of the other men, she listened intently to their impassioned pleas for justice in the name of Christ. She smiled and Frederico reached out to touch her soft hand. She blushed then, thinking of his lips on hers, his belly nudged against her back at night when they lay together in their bed. She loved this man of great ideas and fiery eyes. His sharp intellect had won her heart as easily as his poetry, for during their courtship he'd written sonnets professing his love and devotion. She felt fortunate that the man her parents had arranged for her to marry was also a man with whom she had fallen deeply in love.

Carmago pounded the tabletop, emphasizing his opinion on how best to eradicate the heretics. "And we must also exterminate the

Moors. Those *moriscos* are as sly and evil as the *conversos*. We mustn't let them get the best of us."

"And the witches," Antonio asserted. "They're slyer than the Jews and the Muslims put together."

"There are no witches in Alghero," Bautista said, "and no sorcerers or astrologers either. I know. I monitor the city's business licenses."

"Don't be foolish, Frederico," Carmago scoffed. "Do you think a witch would apply for a license to vend her trade?"

The men laughed and Juliana joined in their merriment, giggling nervously, although the men didn't take notice. Thoughts of the herbalist she'd visited the week before crossed her mind. The woman had made a salve for a rash that had troubled Juliana for two weeks. There'd been no official shop; on the advice of a friend who knew how to contact the healer, Juliana had merely visited her home. Juliana's friend had said the woman was a *majarza*. The woman would take no money in payment, and asked merely that Juliana bring her a loaf of bread and a wedge of cheese the next time she found herself in the neighborhood. The ointment had cured the rash, and Juliana had gladly reimbursed the herbalist, carrying two loaves of bread and a small wheel of *pecorino* to her doorstep in gratitude.

"Ah, *Senora* Bautista," Antonio teased, disrupting Juliana's thoughts. "You haven't run into any old hags with warty noses of late, selling their wares on street corners, have you?"

Unaccustomed to being addressed by her husband's friends, Juliana blushed, shook her head and hurried out of the room. Antonio watched her walk away, his eyes fixed on the curve of her hips and the sway of her gate. It had been too long since he'd indulged in the caresses of a fine young woman. His mind wandered down roads too dangerous to travel until Juliana disappeared around the corner, out of his view. Without realizing it he sighed, then turned his attention back to the men. If Frederico noticed his friend's distraction he didn't let on, although Carmago, ever watchful of the wayward eyes of priests, catalogued the incident in his memory.

THE DISTURBANCES against the *marranos* and the *moriscos* were planned for the following week. It would begin with Albóndiga identifying culprits in his congregation. He'd then inform Bautista and

Carmago, providing them with details of the heathens' residences and places of business. Frederico would secure the services of local hoodlums and Carmago would pay the fee to entice them to commit the acts. The ruffians would begin by taunting the residents outside their homes and shops, calling them Christ-haters, Jew-lovers, Muslim-sympathizers. The following day the youths would return with stones and pelt the people as they exited their doors. On the third day the ante was increased and the boys would carve Stars of David on the exterior walls of the homes of *marranos* believed to be undercover heretics, and crescent moons and stars on the homes of the *moriscos*, the lapsed-Christian Moors. On the fourth and final day of the harassment, fires would be started. The youths would ignite Hebrew holy books and Muslim Korans, then set them upon the heretics' doorsteps, cheering as the sacred texts burst into flames.

The following week selected goods would be confiscated from shops run by *conversos*—*marranos* and *moriscos* alike. Precious gems, finely wrought candlesticks, legs of lamb, bushels of almonds, bolts of woolen cloth, pendants of coral and bottles of wine were to be hauled away. The targeted merchants would be harassed. Disparaging, denigrating names would be hurled at their astonished faces, causing customers to retreat and look elsewhere for their food stuffs and household goods.

The diabolical plan proved flawless in its execution and consequence. Each of its elements was carried out without exception. But, as had happened in Spain, some of the *conversos* fought back. Those among them of high government ranking protested to Bautista's superiors and sent letters to Archbishop Orozco asking for restitution, for they believed the accusations of heresy were unfounded—lacking any proof save for the deranged views of *Padre* Albóndiga.

The archbishop summoned Antonio to his office. "You've gone too far," he chastised. "There was no need to enter their shops and affect their income. Visiting their homes was sufficient."

"Andres," Antonio began, "you know in order to be fully effective, the plan had to be implemented in its entirety. Why do you feel the need to placate the whining complaints of heathens, no matter what kind of political sway they hold in this town?"

"Albóndiga! Save your impudence for others. Now isn't the time to call upon the kindness of our friendship. Within the confines of this office, and in this official capacity, you shall address me as Archbishop Orozco."

Antonio shrugged and frowned, but didn't oblige the archbishop.

"You fail to appreciate the influence of the men whom you have angered," Orozco continued. "The displeasure travels to levels higher, beyond my reach. I can't protect you. Be wary, *Padre*. Your pedigree is lacking, and there are forces at work here that could ruin all the advantages you've worked so hard to acquire in your short time in Alghero."

"What do you want me to do? Compromise my allegiance to Christ's Holy Church to appease the wounded egos of a few wealthy heretics?"

"That is precisely what I'm ordering you to do, Antonio. By the authority invested in me as your superior, you must cease and desist, at once. Stop harassing the *marranos* and *moriscos*."

"But even the King of Aragon would approve of my actions."

"You are not in Aragon, Antonio! And even though you are a subject of the realm, you answer to a higher monarch—a papal ruler, the voice of Christ Jesus on the Earth. Should you continue to disobey, be warned. You do so at grave cost."

ANTONIO INFORMED Carmago and Bautista that his hands were tied. Should they want to continue their efforts to cleanse the Christian blood of the city, the responsibility for doing so would fall squarely on their shoulders. As a magistrate and a count, they weren't beholden to the orders of the archbishop. Antonio vowed to support their actions in any way he could, as long as they swore to protect him and declare him innocent of any wrongdoing should the archbishop question them.

"As you insist," Alonzo said. "You're our friend and comrade."

"You've already identified the false Christians, Antonio. Your work's completed," Frederico added.

ALONZO CARMAGO continued to meet at Frederico Bautista's house, plotting additional ways to taunt those marked for harassment. Once or twice Antonio attended as well, under the guise of dining with his friends. On those visits he took every opportunity to address Juliana, asking her questions about the meal she served or where she obtained the sumptuous wine that flowed from the ceramic jug she held between her delicate hands. Her replies were always brief, though courteous, for she felt uneasy about the way he looked at her. His eyes betrayed his intentions, which weren't merely to seek information about their repast, but to endear her to him in order to seduce her. Of this she was certain, although she dared not mention it to her husband, lest he think she instigated or encouraged Antonio's advances. She didn't want to rouse her husband's jealous nature or come between Frederico and his friend.

Carmago took note of Antonio's bold actions, but also decided against mentioning it to Frederico. The count felt the priest to be harmless in this regard, believing that Antonio would put his allegiance to Bautista before his carnal desires.

One night, three weeks after Albóndiga had met with the archbishop, he arrived at Frederico's home for dinner thirty minutes past the appointed time. A sudden rain had overtaken him as he'd made his way through the winding streets and, since he hadn't thought to bring his cloak when he'd left his quarters, his clothes were getting soaked. Taking shelter inside a local tavern until the skies cleared, Antonio had imbibed in too much wine as he waited out the showers. With his stomach empty of food, he grew boisterous and began to brag to patrons nearby that he'd been the mastermind behind the eradication of the *conversos* from Alghero.

"You'll thank me, praise me, honor me for my efforts!" he boasted. "Perhaps not today or tomorrow, but in time and in perpetuity."

The tavern owner removed Antonio's glass from the table and tried to usher him out the door, but the priest pushed him away, grabbed the wine bottle and drank from its uncorked lip. He drained the bottle dry. With nothing left to swallow and no replacement bottle forthcoming from the barkeeper, the priest was compelled to leave.

"Frederico will serve me wine," he crowed. "My friend won't turn me away!"

DOWN THE TWISTING LANE the drunken priest stumbled, sloshing through puddles and tripping over raised stones in the pavement. He picked himself up, shook the excess water from his clothing, and moved forward toward Frederico Bautista's doorstep. He knocked twice, pounding with his fist until the servant woman opened the door and stepped aside, avoiding the priest's arm as it pushed through the vestibule. Down the hallway he trod, singing loudly, proclaiming his arrival. When Antonio reached the dining table Frederico and Alonzo both rose to catch him as he collapsed in a stupor.

"Juliana, a plate of food and a dry blanket for our friend," Frederico said.

Senora Bautista complied, bringing a woolen coverlet to her husband's friend, wrapping it around Antonio's shivering shoulders. Antonio grasped her hand and kissed her fingers. "You are as gracious as you are beautiful," he slurred.

Juliana retrieved her hand and rushed from the room, returning only to bring Antonio the plate of warm food her husband had requested. She set the meal on the table in front of the priest and placed a knife and fork beside the plate. "This should help warm you, *Padre*," Juliana remarked.

"Your lips would warm me better," Antonio replied. "And your breasts would warm me better still!" The priest cupped Juliana's breasts in the palm of his hands, squeezing them gently, rubbing his fingers over her nipples. He leaned in to kiss her cleavage, but his lips were intercepted by Frederico's fists.

"How dare you, Albóndiga! I know you're drunk, but there's no excuse for this lewd behavior!"

"There's no excuse for your selfish refusal to not share your wife's voluptuousness with a beleaguered and lonely friend."

"Enough!" Carmago shouted, stepping between Frederico and Antonio. The count placed his hands on Antonio's shoulder, nudging him back.

"Enough?" Antonio crowed. "I've only just begun!"

Antonio lunged at Juliana, knocking her to the floor. He threw his body on hers and kissed her face, her neck, her breasts. He reached beneath the layers of her dress and groped between her thighs. Juliana screamed. Frederico exploded, pulling Antonio off his wife.

Frederico slapped Albóndiga's face with a force that sent him flying. Juliana rose swiftly and ran from the room, weeping and calling for her maidservant's assistance. Antonio's eyes flared and his mouth set in a fierce scowl. He raced toward Frederico and rammed his fist into the magistrate's ribcage. Frederico howled and Carmago rushed again to separate the men.

Antonio proved too strong for the count. He pushed Alonzo aside, knocking him to the floor. Frederico lunged at Antonio, intent on tackling his adversary. Albóndiga reached for the knife beside his plate and plunged its serrated blade into Frederico's shoulder, twisting it with all the force he could muster.

Frederico gasped. Blood oozed from his wound. His eyes rolled back, and he collapsed to the floor.

As Carmago shouted, "Call the police!" Antonio fled the house. He raced down the street with Frederico's blood on his trembling hands.

IN THE DARK, moonless night Antonio Albóndiga stumbled through the wet streets. His breathing wouldn't still as he raced away, tripping over the stone roadway, falling every few steps only to pick himself up with great effort. A fire raged inside him, born of a lust he couldn't extinguish. The scent of Juliana's skin lingered in his nostrils, mingling with the acrid odor of Frederico's blood.

He hadn't meant to stab his friend, though he felt no remorse at having done so. He was a man, not simply a priest. The magistrate and the count should understand that. His desire for a woman was great— as great as theirs. If he couldn't have Juliana, he'd find another—even a lowly servant girl—to satisfy his urges.

At every turn of the lane Antonio passed houses secured tightly against the night, their inhabitants fast asleep in their beds. Servant girls slumbering, too, in cots or on straw mats upon the floors of humble rooms. In his fury the priest wandered from home to home, pounding on doors. "Open up! Open up! I'm in need of a servant girl!"

When no one heeded his plea, his ire heightened. Determined to find a wench he could defile, he ventured on. Turning a corner, he came upon a solitary figure walking in the night, bearing a bundle upon his shoulder. Hunched so, the man moved aside to allow Antonio to pass by, for he'd heard the pounding and the howling echoing down the lane and he sensed Antonio's foul mood.

"Get out of my way!" Antonio shouted, though the stranger had already done so. "Who do you think you are to impede the way of a nobleman? You swine!"

The man kept silent, turning away from Antonio.

"Don't disrespect me!" Antonio yelled. "Show me your face. Then bow to my authority!"

The man stepped back, placing one hand over his eyes as if to shield himself from Antonio's wrath. Antonio lunged at him, tearing the man's hand from his face. The stranger's sack fell, hitting the cobblestone. Even in the dark of night Antonio could see the glittering jewels that had spilled onto the stones—bracelets of gold and rings set with diamonds, rubies, and sapphires.

"Jew!" Antonio shouted. "You are a Jew! Or a *marrano!*"

The man turned to run, but Antonio grabbed his arm and pulled him to the ground. Antonio spat in the stranger's face. "You filthy heathen! What are you doing inside the city's walls at this time of night? Speak!"

"I live here, sir!" the man stuttered, frightened by the priest's rage.

"Live here? No Jews live here! No *marranos!* You're a heretic!" Antonio roared. He slapped the stranger and spat at him again.

"Please, sir," the stranger cried out. "I beg you! I have a wife, two daughters, a son!"

"Heathens, all of you!" Antonio bellowed. He wrapped his fingers around the man's neck and shook him. "Heretics!" Tightening his grip, he squeezed harder and harder, unhindered by the man's failing breath, his futile attempts to push Antonio away, prevent the assault, save his life. Anger claimed Antonio's heart, jailing his reason. Fury clouded his eyes, filling them with images of *conversos,* Jews, Moors, witches. "Death to you all!" Antonio railed, throttling the neck of the man who had the unlucky fortune of crossing the drunken priest's path that night. With one final blow Antonio crushed the man's larynx.

The stranger's taut chest grew limp, and Antonio released his trembling fingers. The stranger's limp body fell against the cold, wet stones. The priest stood, staring back at the human heap beside him. He paused a moment, wishing he had a match to set fire to the man's cloak. He gathered up the spilled jewelry and what remained of his strength, then scanned the street to ensure no one had witnessed his act. Satisfied that his deed had gone unseen, Antonio cradled the rings and bracelets in his clenched fist and hurried away.

LATER THAT EVENING, Count Alonzo Carmago recounted to Archbishop Orozco the story of how the priest had assaulted Frederico.

"No one has seen or heard of Antonio since the incident," Carmago said. "You must find him so justice can be served."

"You can rest assured that we will, Count Carmago," the archbishop replied. "I'm not surprised that it has come to this. From the moment I met Albóndiga, I sensed something was awry with him. I knew he'd be more trouble than he was worth."

Two weeks passed before Antonio could be located. Though he'd pocketed the slain merchant's jewelry, he was afraid to come out of hiding to sell it and was in dire need of money. He'd sent word to Quintanto through a street urchin, informing his assistant of his whereabouts.

After he'd wandered away from the body of the man he'd murdered that evening, he'd been taken in by an old man who'd encountered Antonio across town, near the outer limits of the city. The man had been out on a walk and had heard the priest ranting and howling unintelligibly. Thinking Antonio was delirious with fever, the kind stranger brought him home. The priest promptly passed out on the floor and the man and his old wife hauled Albóndiga to a cot, where the priest slept, without waking, for three days.

While Antonio slept he dreamt about his father and his mother. Pablo stood before him, solemn and resolute, his steely eyes revealing a hint of pride. "*Bien hecho*, Antonio!" he said. "Well done! You were right to kill that heretic! Don't listen to the naysayers. They know nothing of sacred duty. You're the son of Pablo Albóndiga! You're a patriot and a warrior! Destined for greatness. Never forget that."

In the dream, Antonio's mother sat in the corner of a dimly lit room, sobbing. "Antonio. Antonio." Her trembling voice echoed through his slumbering bones. "How could you do such a thing? Didn't I teach you to love all of God's creatures? You've broken my heart. What will become of you now?"

"Silence!" Pablo shouted at his wife. "Maria, you know nothing of the world and how it works. My son is a king among paupers. A man who knows what must be done and has the courage to do it. Let him be!"

DAYS LATER, when Antonio's eyes finally opened, the stranger and his wife were standing over him, looking down upon his ashen face.

"We thought you were going to die," the old man told him. "My wife made some soup. Come eat."

"What's your name, *senor?*" the old woman asked, ladling broth into the bowl.

Antonio stared blankly into her green eyes without replying. He didn't answer her because he didn't recall his name, or where he lived or what events had brought him to this house. He ate his soup, thanked his hosts for their kindness, then fell back to sleep for another two days.

Beside the bed his caretakers had set the bracelets and rings Antonio had brought with him, but the priest's mind was too hazy to notice the jewelry glittering on the small table. After Antonio awoke again, it took him three more days before he announced, "My name is Antonio."

The man and the woman simply smiled and said, "Welcome."

Slowly Antonio's brain began to recall details of the night he'd stabbed Frederico. At times he would weep, softly, remembering all the many times his friend had fed him, offered him the finest wines and meats. He felt bad that his actions had maimed Frederico. He'd meant him no harm; he merely wanted to share Juliana's bed for one night. He'd been surprised at Frederico's response, for Antonio had assumed that the magistrate would've gladly granted his request. They'd already shared so much in the short length of their friendship. How could Frederico have denied him one night of passion?

As Antonio continued to regain his strength, resting under the kind attention of the old man and his wife, the priest began to remember snippets of the dream he'd had about his father and his mother. The image of his mother sobbing haunted him. He preferred to focus on the certitude of his father's words. He'd always known he was destined to do more than hear confessions and dole out communion wafers to parishioners who spent their Sunday mornings praying for the salvation of their sorry, lost souls. He vowed to continue his fight against heresy—and make his father proud.

One day while his caretakers were out, he thought about the incident in the lane that had occurred the night he'd left Frederico bleeding and wounded on his dining room floor. It was then that he noticed the small pile of jewelry at his bedside. At first he thought it belonged to the old man and his wife, but then slowly the image surfaced of the dark sack falling to the wet street, the bracelets and rings tumbling to the ground.

Albóndiga knew that Alonzo Carmago would have gone to the authorities to report the incident at Frederico's home, and he expected there'd be restitution to pay—perhaps even deportation for his actions. After all, Frederico was a man with implacable political clout. The count wouldn't allow Antonio to go unpunished. As for the other event that evening, the mishap in the streets with the merchant, Antonio wasn't sure if anyone knew about it. He'd been careful to check in both directions before leaving the stranger's body in a heap that night. But he couldn't be absolutely sure the incident went unnoticed. Although he wouldn't have named it a crime, and he wouldn't have admitted to having committed one had he been hauled to jail or the confessional. The killing of heretics was a holy act, completely justified—indeed, exonerated in the eyes of the One True God.

Until he could find a way to escape back to Spain or perhaps flee into France, Antonio decided it was best to hide out in the home of his kind caretakers. His plan required money and some clothes, he realized. He might be able to sell some of the jewelry without being caught, but he doubted he'd be able to pawn all of it. He decided he'd have to disguise himself in order to evade those who would be able to recognize him. One morning he approached a lad in the street outside the old man's house and requested that the boy deliver a message to Quintanto.

In Antonio's unexpected absence, the priest's assistant had grown confident of his abilities to run the parish. He didn't want Albóndiga to return and order him around. When the scraggly boy knocked on the rectory door bearing a note with Antonio's name on it, Quintanto tucked the slip of paper into his pocket and offered the youth an apple for his efforts. Inside his personal quarters, Quintanto read Antonio's note. Albóndiga had asked for money and the clothes of a layperson. He included instructions for where to drop the items.

Suspecting an attempted escape, the assistant priest paid a visit to Archbishop Orozco.

"You've done well, my son, in bringing this information to me," Orozco assured. "*Padre* Albóndiga must pay for his sins."

Orozco arranged to have Quintanto comply with Antonio's request, ensuring that his own emissaries would follow the priest's assistant and take Albóndiga into custody.

"No need to alert the civil authorities," the archbishop instructed. "This is a Church matter, and we shall deal with it accordingly. Is that clear, Quintanto?"

The assistant priest nodded.

"I knew I could count on your impeccable sense of loyalty," the archbishop stated. "A promotion is in order, to repay your honesty and willingness to help in this matter."

ON THE APPOINTED day and hour Quintanto arrived at the house where Antonio was taking refuge to find the priest inside, waiting at the door. The old man and the old woman were away, and Albóndiga had placed a farewell note on the tabletop, informing the couple of his departure. He thanked them for their hospitality and care. Beside the note he left a golden bracelet to repay them for their efforts, for even though they were poor they'd shared their home and their food with him.

When Antonio heard the knock at the door, he placed the other jewels into a small sack and tucked it into his waistband. With his booty concealed, he opened the door and invited Quintanto inside.

"I can't stay long, *Padre*. I've obligations to attend to."

Antonio stared at his assistant, noting how his gaze jumped about the room instead of meeting his own. "No time even for a cup of water, Quintanto?"

Quintanto handed Antonio the satchel of clothes and a small bag of coins. "Here. These are the items you asked for."

"I'm indebted to you," Antonio replied. "I hope someday that I'll be able to repay your kindness."

"It won't be necessary," Quintanto remarked, then turned and exited.

Antonio changed into the lay clothes his assistant had supplied, placed the bag of coins inside the bag of jewelry, and re-tucked the small sack into his waistband. His eyes swept the small room one more time before he opened the door and stepped into the street.

A short distance down the lane, he was approached by two men who grabbed him securely by the arms. One of the men shouted, "Antonio Albóndiga! Come with us."

Unable to free himself from their grip, Antonio kicked at their legs until one of them slapped his hand against the priest's head and punched his stomach, subduing his resistance. They hauled Antonio to the archbishop's office and set him in a chair before standing sentinel at the door to prevent his escape.

Albóndiga stared into the archbishop's brown eyes and spat on the floor.

"Well, Antonio, I see you've yet to learn respect for authority. It's a pity, really. Had it been otherwise, I might have been persuaded to be more lenient with you. If I could I would've had you tossed into the dungeon and had you hanged for assaulting a nobleman. And for that other incident with the merchant."

Antonio's eyes widened. His actions hadn't been as secretive as he'd hoped. "But Your Excellency," he asserted, "that was no crime. Silencing a heathen is an act of courage. I'm a warrior of God."

"Silence, Albóndiga," the archbishop ordered. "You've got no grounds upon which to make such claims. You murdered a citizen of Alghero—"

"A Jew!" Antonio spat out. "Not a citizen. He was within the city's walls after curfew!"

"Not a Jew," the archbishop replied. "A *converso!* The man was a good Christian, Antonio. He gave generously to the Church, sponsored many important projects that wouldn't have been possible without his ample fortune and his generous nature."

"Impossible!" Antonio cried out. "What would a man of such stature have been doing out alone on such a wretched, soggy night?"

"His brother's wife had taken ill," the archbishop replied. "He'd gone out to bring her medicine. The sack he carried home with him that evening was his brother's jewelry. He'd meant to take it to his shop the next morning to sell it. The same sack, by the way, that was found emptied, lying beside his limp body."

Antonio's heart raced. "I know nothing about that."

"And what's that tucked into your waistband?"

Antonio reached for the bundle, but the archbishop's hand was swifter and the prelate grabbed hold of the small sack. Orozco opened the package and dumped the contents onto a tabletop. Among the coins lay several jeweled rings and one golden bracelet.

"I see you're a liar as well as a thief and a murderer, Antonio Albóndiga."

"I've committed no crime," the priest replied, "'except rendering poor judgment with regard to my dear friend and ally Frederico. As for the jewels, they're nothing more than the rewards of holy actions."

"Your arrogance will be your undoing, Albóndiga," the archbishop chided. "I wish that I could toss you into jail for murder. As it is, I have orders to keep this matter with the merchant within the archdiocese, as the cardinal doesn't want to incite a riot among the *conversos*. He's arranged to pay the man's family restitution for their loss of income due to the merchant's untimely and wrongful death. But the cardinal isn't pleased, as you might well expect, having to dip into the Church's holdings to clean up your mess. Even so, you won't be hanged for your deeds, although you might wish you had been once you learn of your punishment."

Albóndiga seethed. Every length of muscle tensed in his body and he ached to strangle Orozco, the man who'd feinted to be his ally, his friend, a man who had committed to being his co-conspirator in ridding the world of heathen vermin. Now his fate lay in the hands of a man as vile as the heretics, as ungodly as any pagan gypsy queen.

"Do what you must, Andres. You can't break me," Antonio snarled. "I'll write to my cousin Juan. Tell him you are mistreating me!"

"Your cousin has no authority here," the archbishop retorted. "And where I'm sending you, you won't have ink or the paper to write any damn letter. I intend to crush you, Antonio. Before I'm finished you'll curse your mother's womb for carrying you, curse her labor pains for bringing life to your lungs. Curse her milky breasts for giving you sustenance."

Orozco glanced at the guards who were safeguarding the door. "Massimo and Vidal! Take this filthy swine away. See to it that he's transported at once to the godforsaken hinterlands of the Barbagia."

Orozco sneered and pointed his finger at Antonio's defiant eyes. "*Padre* Albóndiga, I condemn you to life in the Sardinian wastelands. High in the mountains, with no hope of escape, you shall be Christ's servant in the land of the shepherds and robbers. You shall live among the barbarians until you wither and die. Never again will you set eyes upon the riches of this fair city, nor on the beloved hills and valleys of your mother country, Spain. Never again will you hold rank in the hierarchy of Holy Mother Church, reduced as you are to the insignificance of a cockroach beneath my fine leather shoes."

As the jailers hauled Albóndiga away, the priest launched a wad of spit at the archbishop's polished shoes. "You are swine, Orozco! May you rot in hell for all eternity! And may your mother be burned as a witch for copulating with the Devil, for how else to explain her giving birth to a man as vile as you?"

Archbishop Orozco shouted, "Feed this scoundrel to the dirty shepherds!"

He called for an assistant to clean the spittle from his shoes and then slammed his office door. He wiped his hands with a towel that lay beside the ewer and washbasin he kept on a table beside the window. He'd found them necessary and useful tools for occasions such as this, when he needed to clean the scum of arrogance from his tense fingers.

Chapter 7
The Omen

SHARDANA, SARDA, BASILIO AND CONSTANTINO had been friends ever since they had taken their first wobbly steps unaided by their mothers' hands. Although idle time was a rare gift, throughout their childhood the twins and the brothers enjoyed racing over the hillsides, splashing in the mountain streams, tossing small rocks into the rivers, laughing as the water cooled the sweat on their strong arms and legs. As the sisters grew older, if their duties at home permitted, they would sometimes visit the sheepfold that belonged to the boys' father, Arturo. There they would gather wild flowers into bouquets, sing songs with the young shepherds, and drink warm milk from the teats of patient ewes.

When the twin sisters turned eleven they began their *majarza* apprenticeship with their *Ayaya* Maredda, and their playful times with the brothers came to an end. By then, the brothers needed to learn a trade to earn a living, too, so they had little time for revelry. Under their father's tutelage the boys began to master the art of tending sheep. As they grew into adulthood the young men spent long hours on the hillsides, sleeping in their *pinnette* and living among the ewes and rams and their lambs. Then, the young women would only see Basilio and Constantino at village festivals or, sometimes, on Sundays, when the young shepherds were permitted the luxury of a few hours of leisure.

On those days the sisters would stroll to the *piazza* with the other young, marriageable women. Walking arm in arm or hand in hand, they'd sashay past all the young men who'd gathered at the tavern's outdoor tables with their friends to drink grappa or *mirto,* laughing, joking, playing cards until the sun set.

Each week the men took time away from their work to listen to one another play the *launeddas* and their *tumbarinu* drums. Some would sing along, and their strong basso and tenor voices would ring through the center of town. The poets among them would stand and recite the *berbos*, the teasing rhymes of their folklore that made them all laugh. Those who favored love poems recited them as well. One or two of the young men, primed by liquor and the sweet eyes of the young women lingering nearby, would stand, glass in hand, and recite *muttettus*, parceling out a two-part call and response—one man supplying the *isterria,* recounting the tale, another rejoining with the *torrada*, the ardent reply.

On those carefree afternoons Shardana and Sarda would share a smile with Basilio and Constantino, signaling their interest in courtship. The brothers would nod hello, indicating their own intentions, resolved to ask the sisters to be their brides. Shardana, the bolder of the twins, would stare as she passed the table where the brothers sat, intent on memorizing the shape of Basilio's strong jaw, the exact hue of his brown skin, weathered by the sun and the wind, his deep-set eyes, the dark curls that framed his face with its sharp, prominent nose, his full, kind lips. Sarda would sneak a more furtive glance at Constantino, studying his face, noting the ways the brothers resembled one another in stature and coloring, the way her beloved's face, though lined by the same life in the wild countryside as Basilio's, differed from his brother's. The curve of Constantino's fuller cheeks revealed a softness that reminded Sarda of the warmth of sheep's fleece and the memory of an illicit kiss she had unexpectedly shared with him one Sunday evening months before.

Constantino had asked Sarda's parents for permission to walk their daughter home from the *piazza* that night. Sarda's parents gave their consent, and then strolled a respectable four feet behind the younger couple. A short distance from Sarda's home, Constantino and Sarda turned the corner at the end of the lane and momentarily escaped the ever-vigilant eyes of Sarda's parents. In that brief interlude Constan-tino's lips brushed against Sarda's and he whispered, "I love you."

Her heart raced. "Yes, I, too, love you," she said.

The following June the sisters married the shepherd brothers. Though now the twins would live under different roofs, their cottages sat across a cobblestone lane from one another, two doors down from their parents' homes. The red tiles of their modest, three-room stone houses were covered with moss. The interior of each was plain and ser-viceable, but welcoming. On sunny days, two windows on either side of the entryway allowed sufficient light to penetrate the main room, warming the roughly laid granite floor and the basalt stone walls. Af-ter crossing the front threshold, visitors entered a large open area that contained a kitchen; its centerpiece fieldstone hearth was used to warm away the cold of winter. An oven crouched against one corner sat ready to bake the bread and, occasionally, a roasted chicken or a leg of lamb if times were fortunate and they could indulge in such luxuries. In the opposite corner stood a wooden table, carved from a fallen holm oak that Basilio had hauled back from his *tanca* one afternoon when he'd returned to town from tending his sheep on the hillside. There'd been enough oak for two sturdy tables, so he and Constantino stripped the bark, planed the wood, carved the legs and built a table for each of their young wives. The large room and the wooden table also served the sisters in their healing arts, for every day the *majarzas* cared for the villagers who were sick and infirm, whether their husbands were away tending the sheepfold or back home enjoying a brief respite from their duties.

Each home also contained two smaller rooms situated on either side of the open, common area. One room was furnished with a bed and a small table bearing a pitcher for water, a small basin for washing, and an oil lamp. The other room was left unfurnished, awaiting a bas-sinette to cradle their longed-for babies. Inside these cottages the twin sister *majarzas* plied their healing trade and birthed, nursed, raised and tended their children while their husbands communed with the lambs and the sheep in the countryside, a few miles outside the village.

A year after Shardana was married she gave birth to Grazia. Three months later Sarda gave birth to her son, Brontu. The cousins were as close as siblings, and they spent their days under the watchful care of their *ayaya*, Augustina, while their mothers cured the illnesses and mended the woes of villagers in between baking bread, feeding the hens, tending their vegetable gardens, and harvesting their medicinal herbs in the nearby forests and the hillsides. Within a year Shardana gave birth to her son, Isidoro. On that very same day Sarda gave birth to Anna-Bella.

"It's like our new babies are twins!" Basilio said as he and Constantino held their infants in their arms. Like Brontu and Grazia, Anna-Bella and Isidoro became inseparable, their lives, their destinies, and their households inextricably intertwined.

Out of all the *majarzas'* children, only Grazia had inherited the temperament and talents of a healer, although at an early age Anna-Bella demonstrated an affinity for wild bees. She learned to harvest wild honey and bee pollen, which the *majarzas* used in their healing trade. At the age of three Grazia nursed a wounded butterfly back to health and sent it on its way to tend to the flowers in the nearby meadow. By her fifth birthday she was already accompanying her mother and her aunt to the hillsides and had learned the names of every medicinal plant, along with their identifying characteristics. By age seven she'd learned their uses and how to make effective potions, tinctures, and salves. At twelve she shed her first menstrual blood and began to feel restless, spending time at the well in the middle of the *piazza* with other girls from the village, talking about boys and babies and the names she'd give the children she dreamed she'd someday have. On Sundays she'd stroll to the *piazza*, just as her mother and her aunt had done years before, to sneak glances at the boys who congregated there to sing and laugh.

"And did anyone steal your heart away?" Shardana would ask when she, Basilio and Grazia returned in the evening, her daughter's cheeks reddened from the sun and from flirting.

"No. Not yet," the young woman replied.

Shardana nodded and suppressed a grin. While she thought it good and necessary for her daughter to participate in this weekly courting ritual in the town's square, she and Sarda thought it was too soon for Grazia to take on the obligations of motherhood and housewifery. To divert her attentions a bit longer, they applied Grazia's considerable energy to more useful ends. At thirteen she began helping the *majarzas* treat their patients.

By the time Grazia was fifteen the elder *majarzas* felt secure in her deepening abilities as a healer and she was permitted to marry Giovanni, a shepherd from a village across the mountain pass, whom she'd met at a festival the year before.

"Do you love him?" Shardana asked.

"More than I can say," Grazia replied.

"And does he feel the same way about you?"

"Yes!"

"Then it's time you got married."

On the morning of Grazia's wedding, Shardana gave her daughter a dress she'd sewn, its hem and bodice embroidered with wildflowers and acorns. "For love and fertility!" she told her only daughter. Shardana and Sarda gave Grazia a set of apothecary jars. "For health and prosperity!" they said.

The day began with a wedding ceremony at the Old Mother Tree. There, under the bright blue sky and the leafy canopy, Grazia and Giovanni pledged their love for one another.

The *majarzas* wept tears of joy. Basilio and Constantino shook the hand of the family's newest shepherd, for Giovanni had entwined not only his heart, but his livelihood with the fate of this family. Brontu, Isidoro and Anna-Bella welcomed him with open arms.

"I hope you don't snore," Isidoro teased. "It'll make for long, sleepless nights at the *tanca.*"

Back home in the village they celebrated, preparing a feast of lamb roasted with rosemary and thyme, toasting the couple with ample bottles of red wine and *mirto.* They danced until the sun went down, then they went to bed, tired from the revelry, but content.

One year later Grazia gave birth to Martina. The news spread quickly throughout the village, and within a few days everyone had stopped by to greet the newest member of the *majarza's* family. They brought small gifts for the newborn and for Shardana and Sarda, as well, for everyone in the village knew that Martina's spiritual umbilical cord tethered her to both healers.

Three years later, when Grazia was nineteen, she began tending patients on her own. "You're ready," her mother and aunt agreed. "You've mastered the details of your craft. Your gifts will only ripen as you mature."

The *majarzas* looked forward to a long and fruitful partnership with Grazia. They couldn't know then that in three years Grazia would be dead.

UNTIL THAT TIME, life unfolded in rich and generous ways. Brontu and Isidoro were strong, industrious men who were eagerly drawn to their family's hillside *tanca*. Before hair sprouted on their chins they'd learned to shear the sheep, milk the ewes, tend the herds and play their *launeddas*. They also showed a remarkable talent for making *pecorino,* a skill they'd learned from their grandfather Arturo. "It must have skipped a generation," Basilio often joked. Neither he nor Constantino had been able to perfect their father's cheesemaking craft. Their meager efforts often resulted in runny mush or sour, inedible curds.

Two years after Grazia's death, Isidoro fell in love with the village baker's daughter, Teresina; Brontu became smitten with the blacksmith's daughter, Viviana. One summer morning a year later, both couples were wed under the canopy of the Old Mother Tree, just as Grazia and Giovanni had been. The *majarzas* and their families roasted a lamb and celebrated.

"We need more grandbabies in this family!" Shardana said as she raised a glass of homemade *mirto* to toast each couple.

"To health, happiness and a long, long and fruitful life!" Basilio added.

Even amid the mirth, Shardana's chest tightened when she looked at Teresina and Viviana. In their young and beautiful faces she saw vibrant life and possibilities, all the many things she could no longer see in her own daughter, whose dreams had been forever silenced.

Although Shardana loved her daughter-in-law and niece-in-law, she always shielded a small part of her heart from them. She would offer them advice or recipes, tell them stories of Brontu and Isidoro's childhood antics, laugh and joke with them as they sat around the table after a family dinner, help them tend their hens or gather their eggs, solve a problem or settle a dispute. Still, in small, barely noticeable ways, she would hesitate to love them the way she had loved her own daughter. She would open her heart only enough to let them know that she appreciated the kindnesses they showed to her and her kin. But she would never fully allow them to occupy the space in her heart where her daughter still lived.

IT WOULD TAKE several years for Teresina and Viviana to conceive, despite the *majarzas'* medicinal potions.

"Someone must have put a curse on our sons," Sarda complained.

"Don't give up yet," Shardana would tell her. "They're young. There's still time."

"True," Sarda said. "But I'm impatient. And we can't rely on Anna-Bella to bring this family any grandbabies."

"No. Anna-Bella isn't in any rush to get married, that's for certain."

"Well, someone will capture her heart one day. For now, she prefers tending to her bees rather than fussing over a husband and children."

Sarda shook her head, bewildered at her daughter's conviction. "But who'll look after her when she's old?"

"The bees and the Old Mother Tree, of course!"

Overhearing the *majarzas'* conversation, Anna-Bella stepped into the room. "Are you two worrying about me again? Don't fret. I have Brontu and Viviana and Isidoro and Teresina. As for grandchildren, you have Martina—and Teresina and Viviana will give you more, I have no doubt. I've been talking to the bees about them both, and they've recommended that I give them a certain kind of bee pollen—from a plant I've not been able to locate yet. When I do, watch out!"

Sarda nodded. There were many potent, invisible things that could transform the lives of humans. If the bees had given their word to Anna-Bella, far be it for Sarda to question their wisdom. She was happy to wait and watch it unfold, although she mused from time to time about how wonderful it would be to hold Brontu's child—or even Anna-Bella's babies—in her arms before she died.

Shardana was more vocal. She constantly reminded Isidoro that she wanted a grandbaby to fuss over and love.

"We're trying," he'd always reply. "And besides, you have Martina. Let's be happy with what we have."

She recalled similar conversations she'd once had with Grazia. "Martina needs a sister. Or a brother. A house should be filled with children."

"You and Papa only had two," Grazia had replied.

"Yes, but with Sarda's two babies both homes always felt complete."

When Grazia was unable to conceive again, the *majarzas* had asked Anna-Bella to talk to the bees about her cousin. The healers, too, tried to work their magic, using every tincture, every potion known to them to encourage conception, but still no baby for Grazia. Finally, nearly five years after Grazia had given birth to Martina, she became pregnant.

Shardana visited the water temple at *Su Tempiesu* to give thanks, then walked to the forest to lay a bouquet of flowers at the base of the Old Mother Tree. "In gratitude," she whispered as she knelt beside the aged oak. "May Grazia's pregnancy be easy."

Grazia's pregnancy had begun without even so much as a tinge of morning sickness, but by the end of her first trimester problems began to surface. She felt tired all the time and her appetite was low. Her back ached, making it difficult for her to stand for hours on end when working with her patients. The elder *majarzas* insisted that she stop treating villagers so she could give herself and her unborn child the rest they both needed to see the pregnancy to fruition. They took every precaution to ensure a good outcome.

Everyone in the family awaited the birth of the second grandchild with great expectation and hope.

"A boy, this time!" Basilio prayed. "We need a shepherd to carry on the family trade."

"Why not me?" Martina asked. "I would be a great shepherd!"

The others laughed.

"You're marked for another destiny," Shardana explained. Even then she recognized Martina's potential as a healer.

When Shardana examined Grazia the morning she went into labor, she sensed something was wrong.

"We've got to prepare for a difficult transition," she told her twin. "The baby's turned inside Grazia's womb."

"Don't worry," Sarda assured her. "She's healthy and in capable hands. You're the best midwife in all of the Barbagia."

By dawn the following morning Grazia lay dead, the linens of her marriage bed soaked with blood, her unborn son still curled, feet pointing downward, inside her silent womb.

Unrelenting sadness hung over the village in the wake of the tragic deaths of Grazia and her son. Though the traditional burial customs had been followed and the traditional mourners had presided, Shardana was inconsolable. Broken, she retreated to her cottage for six months, shuttering every window and locking her door to anyone but Sarda, Basilio, and Isidoro.

Finally one day, feeling a bit stronger, Shardana strolled to the well in the center of the *piazza* to collect a bucket of water to make soup for her husband and son. Another day she walked to *Su Tempiesu* to make offerings to the Spirit of her God. A few weeks later she ventured to the hillsides to sit beside *La Madre Vecchia*. There she wept until she could weep no more.

For months she visited the Old Tree, carrying her sorrow like a heavy stone. Months unfurled into years, and Shardana walked around her home and the village haunted by her daughter's death, her heart burdened with immoveable grief.

One morning nearly two years after Grazia's passing Shardana knocked on Sarda's front door, ready to accompany her twin into the hillsides to collect medicinals. Her presence at her twin sister's doorstep eased her family's distress. They knew that while she would always bear the scars of Grazia's death, she had decided to rejoin the living and could now begin the difficult task of releasing her daughter's ghost.

Five years after Grazia's passing, life went on for the twin sisters and their families. Basilio and the younger shepherds continued to tend the family's flock; Constantino continued to weave baskets and sell them to villagers; Anna-Bella continued to tend to her bees. Martina lived with Shardana and Basilio so she could be cared for when her father was busy with the sheep at the *tanca*. Anna-Bella's bee medicine worked its magic, and Isidoro's wife Teresina gave birth to a healthy baby boy. On the day Shardana's grandson was born she held him in her arms and wept, overcome by joy and by sorrow. In Donatello's sweet eyes danced the spark of hope that had been missing in her for so long.

The sweet, cooing murmurs of a baby filled Isidoro and Teresina's home, and Donatello grew strong and happy. Shardana visited every day, doting on her new grandson, singing silly songs to him, telling him stories about the sheep that roamed the hillsides where his father worked, laying her strong and tender hands on his head, praying for a long and fruitful life.

In the summer months pasturing the sheep was easier, and Isidoro was free to return to the village more frequently to stay with Teresina and their son. In winter he often camped with the flock for long stretches, tending them in the fields on lower ground to avoid the high country snows that fell during the most severe and coldest months. He felt comforted knowing that even though he was far from the village, his mother was just across the lane from his wife and his son, watching over them. At night, in his shepherd's hut, he dreamed of the day that their home would overflow with the laughter of more sons, more daughters.

Soon after Donatello's birth, Brontu and Viviana announced that Anna-Bella's bee potions had worked for them, too. Sarda cried out, "*Madre Dea!* At long last my prayers have been answered."

Both *majarzas* pampered Viviana during her pregnancy, preparing special foods for her and herbal concoctions to strengthen her womb and fortify the child she carried. Brontu often sneaked away from the *tanca* during the middle of the week to return home to make sure that all was well with his wife. Grazia's ghost always lingered just out of view, reminding them that life and all its sweetness was fragile, precious, easily snatched away without cause or reason. After the tenth moon Viviana's labor began, and Sarda's gentle hands ushered a healthy baby girl into the world.

Viviana and Brontu named their daughter Leda. They dressed the baby in a garment embroidered with acorns and ewes and carried her to *Su Tempiesu*. Surrounded by their family, they poured a cup of sacred water over Leda's brow and christened her. That day everyone feasted on fresh *pecorino* and newly laid eggs from the *majarzas'* hens. They ended their celebratory meal with sweet cakes made with wild honey from Anna-Bella's bees.

"You're flesh of our flesh, blood of our blood," Sarda proclaimed, holding her tiny grandbaby in her arms. "Always you'll belong to us like the bees belong to the hive."

IN THE DECADE after Grazia's death Martina had grown to be a young woman of considerable beauty. She'd inherited her mother's dark hair and eyes as well as her kind heart. The resemblance comforted Shardana. When she looked at her granddaughter she recaptured some of the sweetness that'd been abruptly stolen from her when Grazia had died. Like Grazia, Martina possessed a potent gift for healing, and that gave Shardana great satisfaction.

The twin *majarzas* wasted no time in apprenticing Martina, schooling her in the ways of their trade, teaching her all she needed to know so they could keep their medicinal lineage alive. The older women took note of Martina's quick intellect and her astute ability to discern symptoms and assess disease. To these skills she added a compassionate manner, and so the twin healers allowed Martina to serve as their apothecary assistant at a young age.

"She'll be ready to see people on her own by the time she's nineteen," Shardana said.

"Just like her mother!" Sarda replied. "Martina can use the apothecary jars we gave Grazia on her wedding day."

Shardana suppressed the urge to say no. Instead she nodded her agreement and quickly busied herself with work.

LIKE ANNA-BELLA, Martina had told everyone in the family that she had no intention of ever getting married. "I haven't got time for distractions," she announced.

No one expressed concern. They saw the tenderness she displayed with her younger cousins, Donatello and Leda; they knew her heart was good and true. Having lost her mother at such an early age had not injured her ability to love and care for others.

Although Martina was kind-hearted, from an early age she had also exhibited a tendency toward rebelliousness. No matter what task she undertook she was stubborn and fierce in her determination to succeed, which deepened her ability to be a discerning and effective healer. Those same characteristics also fueled her defiance. Shardana worried that Martina harbored a kind of melancholic anger. Sometimes when Martina watched Viviana holding Leda or Teresina kissing Donatello's cheek, sorrow would darken her face. In her granddaughter's lingering grief, Shardana recognized her own. And it broke her heart.

A DIFFERENT, unannounced purpose tugged at Martina's heart. For now that vision did not include babies, or a husband. In truth, the twin healers were relieved. While Shardana and Sarda were happy in their marriages, content and blessed to have been mothers, they also knew how difficult it was to juggle their familial duties with their obligations as *majarzas*. Martina's life as a healer would require her to mother her patients and be constantly and astutely in tune to their welfare.

"It's best that she waits until she's older," Sarda said.

"Yes. Maybe by then she'll be less prone to rebellion and melancholy," Shardana added.

ONE AFTERNOON while the *majarzas* were tidying up the room after a day of seeing patients, Martina made a pronouncement. "I have very stringent requirements for a husband."

"That's good," Shardana replied.

"He can't be a shepherd, like my daddy or grandpa or Isidoro or Brontu."

"And why is that?"

"If I marry—and I do mean *if*—I want my husband to live with me in our house every day, not just when the seasons allow it."

"Seems reasonable to me," Sarda noted.

"So, is there some young man in the village who fits that bill?" Shardana asked.

"Not yet."

"Have you been looking?"

"Not really."

"Would you like us to help you find someone?" Shardana asked. "We can ask Mira, the matchmaker, to help."

"No! I will never consent to an arranged marriage!"

"There's nothing wrong with an arranged marriage, Martina," Sarda said. "Two of your friends found good husbands like that."

"I don't care. I prefer to wait until I find someone as tethered to the village as I am. Someone I *love*."

"Love," Sarda said. "I can't think of a better reason to marry someone."

Shardana agreed. "Maybe in the future when you're ready, one of the young men of the village will capture your heart and surpass your expectations."

"And if it's your destiny to live the solitary life of a woman without a husband, like Anna-Bella," Sarda added, "you'll always find the love and care you need from your family—not to mention the villagers who love you."

"No one in the town will allow a *majarza's* welfare to go unattended."

THE LIFE of a *majarza* was a good one, a hard life lived in the shadow of towering mountains, but a happy one lived in the embrace of rolling hillsides, rushing streams, fragrant meadows, dense forests, wide, expansive skies, and windswept hamlets of industrious and loyal people. Theirs was a life sustained by the closeness of family and the fidelity of friendship, the shared hope of a community founded on centuries-old customs anchored to the granite hills, seared forever into their bones by the scorching sun.

Shardana and Sarda knew no other way and sought no other discipline. They lived in a peaceful village, and harmony reigned among their neighbors. When disputes occurred or grievances were presented, the adults of the town gathered in a building reserved by the community for such purposes and sat in a circle. Seated eye-to-eye, men and women, one across from another, weighed the severity of all claims, discussed possible ways to approach just solutions, and reached equitable decisions. They passed judgment and meted out punishment, if penalty was called for. Justice was always handed down with compassion.

The hearts and the minds of the Barbaricini turned in a circular motion. Round and round, united as one, the head and the emotions maintained the unbroken connection between action and consequence. They longed, always, to restore the circle, repair the harm, re-seal the covenant.

The ways of the Barbaricini were sacred, and these customs imbued Shardana and Sarda's lives with an unshakable sense of belonging. As rooted as a holm oak to the soil of their mountainous hill town, the twin healers endured every season of hardship, presided over every human loss, every hard-won or unexpected joy. Theirs was a marriage promise extended to the entire hamlet; they vowed to abide with each villager through sickness and in health, in times of wealth and in seasons of poverty, until death claimed them. They celebrated when merriment was called for; they grieved when mourning demanded its due. In this way, and this way alone, Shardana's bitter grief over the loss of Grazia gradually diminished to an omnipresent, palatable ache.

On days when the gnarled knot of mourning tightened Shardana's chest, draining her spirit and distracting her from her duties, she would cast a somber glance at Sarda, silently giving notice of her leave-taking. Sarda's nod released her twin from her daily obligations and, whether the sky was clear or overcast, clouded with snow or saturated with rain, Shardana would make her way to the ancient Mother Oak in the forest or stroll along the worn path through the woods to *Su Tempiesu*.

At the ancient water temple Shardana would close her eyes and allow the cadence of the babbling spring to enter her bones, easing her troubled heart. If rain fell she would cover her head and shoulders with a cloak and remain seated until her aching ceased. If snow iced the air, collecting in the boughs of the nearby oaks, she would watch the dark gray bark lighten, then fade to white. On sunlit days she would praise the warmth, thanking it for easing everything that chilled her. Windy days swept away her tears, drying her cheeks before she returned home.

Since Grazia's death a decade before, drought had parched Shardana's soul, making brittle and arid that which once was lush and full of hope. At this temple of sacred springs and precious water, Shardana found the solace she needed to replenish. She understood that the Earth's water was as holy as the Mother God's breast milk, and as sustaining. In this land of arid seasons and scant rainfall, snow and rain were the balm of life, quenching the thirsty soil and the hungry souls of the people of the Barbagia.

Age-old, abiding rites honored the waters of the sea and sky, the mountain streams and the hillside lakes. Mystical and magical, the consolation of water flowed in the memories of both young and old. Hundreds of years before, after the Christians had conquered the Barbaricini in the sixth century and converted many of the people to the new religion, they failed to convince the villagers to relinquish their devotion to water. The foundations of many Catholic churches were laid brick by brick over a stone grotto beholden to a deity other than Jesus. Those Christian churches had sprung up near a sacred well or spring, eclipsing the rites and rituals of those who had long worshiped a different, female God.

The Catholics deemed the waters miraculous, too, attributing supernatural healing powers to the saints and the Madonna, after whom the new churches were often named. As they had for eons before the Christians established their dioceses, the people of the Barbagia would travel from mountain pass to mountain pass to bless their blind eyes with the sacred healing water, leaving sighted and whole, the world alive with color. Men and women with maimed or lame legs were carried by family members to soak in the sacred springs, walking home unaided and jubilant. Young women prayed to conceive a child; old women begged for relief from arthritic limbs. Old men knelt in solicitude, asking forgiveness for youthful wrongs; young men beseeched the saints for abundant harvests to feed their families or fertile flocks to replenish their sheepfolds. And, as in centuries past, the healing waters heeded each prayer, listened to each supplication—and sometimes even answered them.

Shardana's ties to the water temple reached back in time to centuries before the arrival of the missionaries and their Catholic saints. Her faith was linked to eons long ago, when the ancient people of Sardinia had first set foot upon the island. These original inhabitants upheld the hallowed properties of water, and in times of aridity, when the ground was parched by drought, they called upon the spirit of Maimome as they prayed for rain. They constructed an effigy from four slabs of wood, covering each section with periwinkle branches until the shape resembled a scarecrow figure, which they named Maimone. Once the simulacrum was completed the people processed through the village's narrow streets, raising the image on high, imploring the heavens and the spirit of rain, who resided there, for a mighty downpour or a persistent drenching. They chanted: "*Maimone Maimone, Abba cheret su laore, Abba cheret su siccadu, Maimone Laudadu;* Maimone, Maimone, wheat needs water, the dry fields need water, Maimone be praised."

Along the procession route supplicating women sprayed water at the Maimone visage. The village *majarzas* trailed behind the Maimone bearers, pronouncing their magic formulas *sos verbos*, reciting their incantations to dispel the drought. Children from the village gathered to join the healers in their efforts. They were prepared, for the *majarzas* had taught the youngsters how to make a *sas ruchitas*. The children constructed their amulet from fresh canes intertwined and held in place with a stick. They carried these double-axe talismans through the streets, accompanying the *majarzas*, imploring God with fervent and unceasing prayer, making known their wishes for water, water, water.

After the Christians arrived and the ancient ways were adapted into new customs, the *majarza* and her eager cavalcade of *sas ruchitas*-bearing children would encircle the Catholic church thirteen times, intoning: "*Unu pro cada mese de s'annu e unu pro su Babbu Mannu!* A round for every month of the year and an extra one for the Great Father." Though in public these healers invoked the Catholic God, they never fully buried their reverence for the sacred number thirteen, the moon's yearly cycle through the sky.

Shardana held fast to the lore her *ayaya* had told her, the lode of truth that dwelt beneath the Christian stories. She honored the days when rounding a sacred place thirteen times was done in reverence to the thirteen lunar months, honoring the ebb and flow of the moon and of a woman's blood time and its chthonic link to the old menstrual rites. Shardana knelt before this ancient Divine Spirit on days when the grief from Grazia's death stung and she could scarcely breathe. At those times Shardana wept, imploring the Ancient Mother to rain down upon her the compassion of the One who had given birth to the world and all it contained, the One who, as Mother to All, could keenly feel Shardana's rawness, see that her heart had been ripped to shreds. The *majarza* begged for spiritual rain to douse the stinging, quench her sorrow, end the long drought caused by her mourning.

Tears dampened Shardana's palms, offering salty absolution. She would have sacrificed her own life to have Grazia's life be restored. She tried, but failed, to understand why Martina was not allowed to know her mother, why Giovanni was no longer allowed to embrace his beloved wife, why Isidoro was no longer allowed to sing and laugh with his sister, why she and Basilio were no longer allowed to rest their eyes on their daughter's shining face, touch her hand, feel her skin against their fingers. As Shardana wept her body shook. Her lament shattered the silence and the crows and the sparrows took wing, seeking shelter in the limbs of the surrounding oak trees. With each in-breath she sobbed. With each exhale she howled, "Grazia!"

When at last Shardana's eyes were emptied of tears, she grew quiet. She wiped her face and sat beside the gurgling spring at *Su Tempiesu* as the gentle flow of water enveloped her ears. She closed her eyes to enjoy the peaceful murmur, but the stream's melodic burbling grew more insistent, roiling and frothing until the once placid waters exploded into a fury of crashing waves. In her mind rose the image of the seafaring wolf—the same animal that had haunted her dreams so many months before. The ocean waters slammed against the belly of the ship as the wild-eyed wolf prowled the salt-stained deck.

"*Los lobo*" reverberated in Shardana's skull, though she did not understand the meaning of those words. From behind her closed eyes the fierce gray face of the hovering wolf stared back at her. Could it be that Grazia had sent the animal to devour Shardana's undying grief? Could Shardana's dream have been an omen that her time of mourning had finally ended? Had Sarda and Shardana misunderstood? Had Shardana's ability to decipher premonitions been clouded by her grief? Or did the menacing image forebode a time of peril and danger? Was a threatening predator arriving from across the sea?

Shardana was flooded with more questions than answers. Confused, she shook her head, hoping to dislodge the wolf's fierce face from her mind. She dried her eyes and sighed. A rustling in the underbrush claimed her attention. Glancing toward the trees, she spied a fox rushing through the scrub. Three crows roosting on a nearby tree limb turned their black heads toward her. In unison, they cawed. A shiver shimmied up her spine.

"Beware the sea-wolf," the crows warned. "Beware!"

Chapter 8
The Griffon

HE MORNING AFTER MARTINA'S tenth birthday Shardana roused the girl from her bed a half-hour before the rooster crowed.

"Today is the day," she told the youngster. "The woodlands and hills are calling us."

"The sun isn't even up yet," Martina complained, rubbing her sleepy eyes, preferring to stay under her bedcovers, savor what little remained of the waning darkness.

Her *ayaya* admonished. "Get up, child. Sleeping is for corpses."

On that appointed day Martina was to begin her apprenticeship in the identification of the thousands of plants, herbs, roots, and berries that Shardana and Sarda gathered, dried, and stored to stock their apothecary. Her *ayaya* and her great-aunt had often told her there'd be much for her to learn, although it would take a lifetime to master the knowledge of their trade. Martina's stomach tightened with anticipation and worry that she wouldn't be up to the task.

Although Martina was still young, she was smart and quick to learn and she'd shown an aptitude for what lay ahead. By the age of three she had started memorizing many of the poems and sayings so often recited by her mother and father and the elder members of her family, verses and adages deeply rooted in the cultural soul of her village. She was an able artist, too, having proven her sketching skills by the age of five, drawing images of the frogs and grasshoppers, the poppies and myrtle leaves, the ewes and warblers that populated the world of her outdoor adventures.

Discerning the various species of flowering and non-flowering plants that an herbalist used in her healing craft would be the first of many challenges for the youngster. What she couldn't know that initial day of her apprenticeship, but would soon discover, was that identifying the plants by sight was only part of her schooling. Many and long were the steps she'd need to master before she'd be able to bear the title of *majarza*. But she was destined to enter the realms she'd inherited by blood, by sensibility, and by the grace of talent.

Shardana and Martina ate a light breakfast of bread so as not to bog down their bodies. They'd need to stay alert and agile as they climbed the hillsides in search of their potent medicinal bounty. When the last morsel had been swallowed, Shardana motioned for Martina to follow her and the two crossed the lane to Sarda's home. The twin healers were to accompany the girl on this excursion.

Six months before, the *majarzas* had talked about this day, thoughtfully and carefully planning for it.

"Martina's time has arrived," Shardana had said one day when the sisters were taking an inventory of the herbs in their apothecary.

"Yes, she's ready," Sarda agreed. "After her birthday we should take her to the hills."

Sarda had invited her daughter Anna-Bella to join the outing. Although Anna-Bella was not a *majarza,* her skills as a master beekeeper would be of use to the group that morning. The bees, too, had much to teach the young initiate.

"Did you give Martina a basket?" Sarda asked her sister, whispering so as not to waken her husband, Constantino. In an hour he would rise, eat a slice of bread with *pecorino*, and then sit on the bench outside their home and weave his baskets in the sunshine.

"No, in my hurry to get going I forgot," Shardana replied. "I didn't even think to bring mine."

Sarda grabbed three of Constantino's finest handiwork from the shelf beside her front door. She nodded to Anna-Bella, then handed a basket to each of her companions before tucking one under her own arm. "Let's go," she said. A smile claimed her lips.

The sun was just beginning to rise as the three women and the young girl strolled through the *piazza* on their way toward the edge of Orune. They'd take the dirt road that led out of town into the countryside. The song of eager birds filled their ears, and the wind cooled their sweaty faces.

"Is it far?" Martina asked.

"It's neither near nor far, child," Shardana said, wanting to curtail the girl's whining. "We'll get there when we get there."

"It's no further than when you run off to the hills and play with your friends, Martina," Anna-Bella answered, tempering Shardana's serious tone.

"Patience lives in the breath of angels," Sarda said, gently touching her grand-niece's head.

"So much like Grazia, don't you think?" Sarda asked, tipping her head toward Martina.

At the mention of her daughter's name Shardana's chest tightened. She took a breath to ease the stiffness.

"Yes, she's her mother's daughter through and through," Shardana said. She managed a grin, in spite of her desire to retain a more somber demeanor. "Stubborn. And a bit of a rebel."

"The bees will be happy to see us," Anna-Bella said. "They've been talking to me about Martina for weeks now. Asking when I was going to formally introduce her to them."

Sarda touched her daughter's arm. "There is no one better than you to usher Martina into the secret world of bees."

Shardana nodded, pleased that the creatures of honey had been asking about her granddaughter—pleased, too that Anna-Bella had agreed to act as an emissary between the bees and Martina, for bee venom and honey were valuable medicines.

"The sun feels good on my face," Sarda replied. "It reminds me of the day we first brought Grazia to the forest to teach her about the plants. It was bright that day, too. It's a good omen."

Shardana walked on in silence, brooding about her daughter, dead five years by then. What a powerful medicine woman she'd been. The town had lost a healer of considerable wisdom when Grazia had passed on.

Shardana had lost her only daughter and had gained a granddaughter to raise as her own. The Divine had traded one for the other. Shardana thought it an unkind bargain, cruel and unnecessary. But fate had dealt her the most sorrowful of blows, and she had to endure it. Every morning her first thought was of Grazia. Every evening memories of her daughter were the last thing that lingered before she fell into her dreams. She would endure what she had to endure—that was what life exacted of humans. But the hole in her soul would forever remain, hollow and empty, waiting for Grazia's return. Martina was a wonderful gift, and Shardana loved her without reservation, but she could never be a substitute for her beloved daughter.

When at last the women and the young girl arrived at the edge of the oak forest, Sarda set down her basket and motioned for Martina to rest beside her on the ground, near the trunk of an old tree.

"Before you ever set a finger upon any plant," she told the child, "you must vow to never be rough or hurtful. Don't tear at their leaves. Don't yank out their roots. Don't pluck their flowers or their berries without first asking permission. They're living beings, as alive and full of spirit as you and Anna-Bella and your *ayaya*. If you harm the plants you show them disrespect. You also prevent them from being used in our medicines, for they won't share their healing properties if they've been dishonored. Treat them as you'd treat me or your *ayaya*. With love and kindness. Is that clear, Martina?"

The girl nodded, although she wasn't fully certain that she understood her great-aunt's meaning. How could plants be like humans? How could they have feelings? Were they like her playmates who cried if she slapped them? Or willingly offered a bite of sweet biscuit when she showed kindness instead? She tried to imagine the plants with faces like her friends—eyes brown and full of laughter, cheeks bronzed by the mountain sun, hair the color of dark figs.

"We don't own these beings," Shardana continued with the girl's lesson. "They're our relations—sister and brother healers. They grant us the privilege of using their potent essences to heal our illnesses, cool our fevers, calm our shaking nerves, mend our bones, ease the pain of giving birth."

Sarda and Shardana talked in reverential tones about the roots and herbs, the berries and bark they were to collect. "Each species has its own ways, its own healing touches," Sarda said. "Each possesses different medicinal properties. Even the essences that make up their potency change depending on when you pick them—morning or evening, spring, summer, or autumn."

Martina wondered how that could be. She didn't recognize any changes in the leaves or stems from season to season, other than the normal course of things—seedlings in April, blossoms in July, dried foliage in September—but she trusted the older women and understood they were capable of discerning things she couldn't yet see.

"Some herbs we gather in the early morning before the dew dries from their leaves," Shardana explained. "For others, we wait until the moon is full and harvest them under that guiding light."

"Whether you gather them in the forests, pasturelands, hillsides, or mountain tops," Sarda insisted, "always treat these benefactors as you would a visiting guest. Dress in fresh clothes and be sure your hands are clean before you introduce yourself to them. Before you pull any plant from the ground, or pluck its leaves or remove its flowers or berries, always ask permission. Always."

Shardana added, "You wouldn't race through Isidoro and Teresina's home tearing things off the shelves without asking, would you? It would be rude. You'd be branded a rabble-rouser, and rightfully so."

Martina nodded. "Yes, *Ayaya*. That'd be a nasty way to behave."

"And you wouldn't go punching Donatello in the nose as you walked by him, would you? Or pull your best friend's hair or pinch her leg? No, of course not. If you did, we'd have to convene a town council and decide how to reprimand you. The same is true for the plants. Their roots, their stems, their leaves, berries and flowers are parts of their bodies. And we must respect them as such."

"I wouldn't want to be a bully," the young girl replied.

Shardana continued. "Once the plant agrees to be harvested, you present an offering to pay homage to its sacrifice."

"You dig a small hole in the ground, then sprinkle in a special mixture, something you've put together that's stored in your medicine bag," Sarda said. "Sometimes I mix up a batch of shredded twigs and leaves, sometimes seeds or herbs, sometimes I tuck a nice chunk of *pecorino sardo* inside. I think the plants are especially fond of that one!"

Martina imagined the plant roots grabbing hold of the cheese and chomping into it. A giggle escaped from her mouth, but she cut it short, concerned that her elders would find her reaction disrespectful. She glanced at the women and, to her relief, noted a small smile on each of their faces.

Shardana added, "When you're ready to make your offering, you squat beside the plant and say, 'I want to pick your leaves to make a medicinal infusion to help the baker's indigestion,' or 'Your roots will ease the basketweaver's cold and chills, may I bring some to her?' or 'I have found that your flowers can alleviate much suffering—you're so kind to share your bounty with me.' When you do this, you're showing appreciation—for who doesn't like a compliment from time to time, a word or two about the ways you've been helpful? You don't have be human to benefit from a respectful tone. Let them know they may become part of a salve or a tincture. So many times I've heard them whisper 'thank you for thinking of me.' Plants are as human as you or I. They have generous hearts."

"If the plant is pleased with your offering, you'll know," Sarda added. "The wind might pick up. The sun might peek out from behind the clouds on a day that has been overcast and gray. Or the plant may begin to sing."

Singing? Martina thought that's what her great-aunt had said, but could she have been mistaken? She thought it odd that a plant would sing. "They don't have voices," she heard herself say.

"Oh, they do!" Shardana exclaimed. "Beautiful voices. And the songs! Oh, you'll be surprised at the melodies, the harmony!"

"Yes, sometimes the air rings with their voices," Anna-Bella interjected. "And the bees join in, buzzing along. Adding their own motif."

Martina giggled again. She thought it silly but sweet and lovely that someday, if she were talented enough and patient enough, she might hear a poppy's song. Or a juniper's. Will it be a tune fit for a high, clear soprano, she wondered? Or one more apt for the deep tones of her grandfather Basilio's voice when he sang his shepherds' songs on winter nights, when he was home from his *tanca* and able to sit before the fire with them, enjoying the company of his family instead of the bleating of the sheep? And what about the bees? She'd heard the drone of their buzzing many times when she'd visited the wild hives with her cousin Anna-Bella, but she had no idea such a noise might announce their desire to join the chorus of singing plants. The world of nature was mysterious and full of wonder. She absentmindedly fingered the handle of her basket and began to hum.

Noticing that Martina's attention had wandered, Sarda touched the girl's arm. "The singing is important, for it signals the plant's desire to help," the woman said, "but you must always remember never to pick the plant that's singing. Instead, choose another one, one that grows nearby. Also, if a plant refuses to budge from the ground when you tug it, choose another one. Such resistance is a sure sign that they don't want to end up in your *majarza* basket or in your potions."

"Martina," Shardana said. "These things we're saying will be told to you over and over again, until you remember them on your own. You have a keen mind, so I don't think it'll take you long to catch on, but you must pay close attention. As you begin to experience the plants and listen for their songs, you'll understand more fully the many things we've been trying to instill in you this morning. Above all else, remember this: although you're a human being, you're not better than the herbs and roots, the berries and flowers we harvest. Or the bees. They're equal to us in every way. They are blood relatives. As much a part of our family as Grandpa Basilio or Uncle Isidoro or Anna-Bella. Just because they don't look like us doesn't mean they aren't kin. And just because they can't speak Sardo doesn't mean they can't communicate."

Martina nodded. "I understand, *Ayaya*. They're like you and Sarda, wise and wild. Ready to serve and cure. But also stubborn as a mule, so you better not cross them!"

The *majarzas* laughed. So did Anna-Bella. "You know us too well, Martina," Sarda said. "We do have strong opinions, and can be pig-headed when we want to be."

"Yes, but you have soft eyes that let the world know you aren't evil," the child replied. "No one would ever mistake you for a poison weed."

"I hope not, child," Shardana said. "I surely hope not."

"It's time now to learn about the bees," Anna-Bella announced.

Martina's heart quickened. Ever since she could remember she had loved the bees, and had lingered by the wild hives all the many times she'd played in the forests and pasturelands. She'd followed the bees from flower to flower, flitting over the ground even as the insects flitted through the air immersed in their nectar gathering duties. She loved to watch the sunlight dance on their wings. The shimmering glow reminded her of the warm, sweet taste of honey on her morning breakfast bread.

Anna-Bella motioned for Martina to follow her to a nearby hive. Sarda and Shardana stayed seated by the tree, resting and waiting.

Martina did her best to keep pace with her cousin's stride. She arrived at Anna-Bella's side ready to hear more about the bees. Looking at her cousin, she noticed for the first time how much she resembled a bee. Her dark hair shone in the sun, and her dark eyes were flecked with bits of yellow, as if they'd been gently dusted with pollen. Her round body smelled of clover and her smile contained the sweetness of nectar. Perhaps all her many years of tending the hives had transformed her into one of her precious bee-friends.

As Anna-Bella stood near the tree that contained the hive, bees slowly began to emerge, a few at first, then ten, twenty, and more. They landed on Anna-Bella's head and arms, her shoulders and her face, as if greeting her. A moment later a swarm of bees, hundreds, emerged from the hive and took up residence on Anna-Bella's body.

Martina panicked, worried that the bees would sting her cousin and then come after her, but her fears were unfounded. The creatures simply traversed Anna-Bella's arms and legs, her torso and head until her entire body was swallowed in a mist of bees so that she resembled a walking hive, humming and alive with light and energy. After a few moments Anna-Bella's face emerged from the cloud of bees. All but a small band of bees began to disperse. Some flew back into the hive; others ventured off into the fields and the forest to forage the flowers.

A few of the insects that remained rested upon Anna-Bella's shoulder. A few others lingered around Martina, hovering near her face and head. Though she was worried that the bees had come to harm her, Martina stood steady. She recalled that bees could smell fear, and knew that if she succeeded in remaining calm, they wouldn't sting her.

Anna-Bella's calm face bore a wide grin. "They said to welcome you. Your heart is pure and your gifts are plentiful. And though they realize your destiny is to be a *majarza* and not a beekeeper, they bless your endeavors and invite you to learn more about their world and the benefits of the medicine they offer. They're your allies, Martina. Do you understand this?"

Martina nodded, though she didn't fully comprehend the words her cousin had spoken. Until this morning she had no idea that plants could sing or bees could talk. There were so many secrets that she'd overlooked as she'd romped through the countryside the first decade of her life. How could it be that she'd not known about all those things?

"There's a time for everything," Anna-Bella said, reading her mind. "And the time of the bees and plants has now arrived for you. They won't open to you until they're ready, until they know you're trustworthy. You must never abuse that trust, Martina. Do you understand this?"

"Yes," Martina replied. Of this the girl was certain. Especially with regard to the bees, for she knew that though their honey was delicious, their stinging was not. Respecting their power was important. And she sensed that so, too, was the need to respect their offer of friendship.

Martina suddenly recalled a time late last summer when she'd been playing in the meadow and had seen her cousin bend over a cluster of wildflowers. The sky had clouded over that afternoon, causing a momentary chill in the air, and Martina had thought nothing of it except to run on in search of berries to pick and eat. From the corner of her eye she'd noticed Anna-Bella gently picking something up and cupping it in her hands before breathing into the cup of her palm. The girl thought it a curious thing at the time, but having grown up in a family of healers, she reckoned her cousin's actions as somehow being connected to the ways of the *majarza* and quickly forgot about it—until this moment as a group of bees continued to circle her head. That day in the meadow, after the cloudy sky had chilled the air, after her cousin had retrieved something from the ground and breathed her warm breath into her palms, a bee had shot from her cousin's hands into the air. Martina had caught a glint of its wings as it raced toward a flower.

"Bees are ancient creatures," Anna-Bella said. "They've been on the Earth for eons, some say for millions of years. Like serpents, they live in small, dark places and carry venom. They live in a community, not unlike our village, with each member assigned to important tasks for the benefit of all. They have much to teach us about collaboration and industry. Without them the world would be bereft of flowers and fruit. Imagine a world without such beauty, without such food. They're skilled astronomers. And they can predict rain.

"The ways of the beekeepers are ancient as well. From the dawn of time, before humans knew how to sow and reap plants or domesticate animals, we've been in communion with the bees. They've taught much to those who know how to listen.

"The drones of the hive are hatched in early summer. They leave the hive only during the warmest part of the day. Though they have no stingers, their wings are powerful and their senses astute. They possess a finely tuned sense of smell and extraordinary powers of vision. They're the Queen's suitors, charged with insuring the biological continuation of the collective.

"The hive's workers are the female bees. From their bodies they secrete the wax that becomes the honeycomb. They build the cells, fill them with honey, feed and nurse the Queen and the worker larvae. They collect the pollen, the nectar and the propolis. They nurse bee babies. Some are sentinels. They hover near the entrance to the hive, ready to defend their colony from enemies. The worker bees bring prosperity and harmony to their bee brethren.

"The Queen is enthroned in the hive. She lives six to eight times longer than any of her children. The only bees she encounters are her daughter bees and her son bees. Solitary and revered, she devotes her life to selfless service."

Martina's eyes fell upon a single honeybee exiting the hive and flying off toward some nearby wildflowers. The bee darted from one flower to another, hovering above the petals, selecting the recipient of her pending pollen harvest. The bee landed on a petal and descended into the blue flower, disappearing from the girl's view.

Anna-Bella took note and invited Martina to look closer. The girl and her cousin watched as the bee worked. The creature dusted itself in golden pollen, the sticky sweet nectar clinging to its body. When the bee was ready, she turned toward the sun and flew off, heading back to the hive. Encumbered with pollen, the bee's flight was slow and laborious. She hovered over a bed of flowers to comb and clean herself, cramming the pollen into the basket-like spaces on her hind legs. With the pollen cleaned from her body, the bee was ready to visit another flower. She landed on a cluster of red petals this time, repeating her task, coating her body in pollen, leaving when she was sated, only to stop and transfer the bounty of her harvest into the hind leg baskets before moving on to another flower, then another.

On it went until the bee was drunk with pleasure and laden with nectar, at which time she slowly and arduously made her way back to the hive. Upon her arrival sister-bees emerged, crowded around her, ready to escort her to the honeycombs. The bee began to dance its fig-ure-eight ballet, vigorous and magical to behold. Martina's eyes grew wide and Anna-Bella watched as the bee, and her niece, took on an air of ecstasy.

"Such a beautiful marriage exists between the flower and the bee," Anna-Bella said. "In time I'll teach you about the importance of pol-len. It's to be treated with utmost respect. It's one of nature's most complete foods. It improves memory and sharpens alertness. It relieves brain fatigue and strengthens the capacity for concentration. When you use it as a remedy, you'll learn just how potent it can be. Every organ in the body, every tissue, is influenced by its curative powers. It contains many healing properties, but the secret ingredient, perhaps more potent above all others, is that which is derived from the dance of the harvest. The bee sucks and collects this nourishment from every part of the flower. Bee and flower unite as in a conjugal embrace, the bee caressing the flower, the flower yielding its most intimate longings to the bee."

Martina's head was beginning to ache, trying hard to remember all that her cousin was saying. There was much to learn about plants and bees—much more than she'd ever thought possible. How many times had she trampled through the forest or over the hillsides unaware that her feet had landed upon a living being—a flower, an herb, perhaps even a sluggish bee, its body bearing the burden of pollen back to the hive? She'd only admired the plants for their beautiful blossoms, or their sweet berries, or the sturdiness of their branches when she found herself in need of a stick to poke a hole in the ground or to chase away a rowdy boy who was bothering her and her friends. She'd seen the bees only as buzzing creatures whose honey sweetened her day.

As the weeks unfolded, Martina continued her lessons with the *ma-jarzas* and with Anna-Bella. Each day Shardana and Sarda ushered the child to the fields or forests, teaching her how to identify plants and roots. Once each week, Anna-Bella taught her more about the ways of bees.

The *majarzas* gave Martina a notebook comprised of scrap pieces of cloth they'd collected and bound together. They told her to sketch the various leaves, roots, berries and flowers and note their medicinal uses. In this way, the girl slowly began to learn.

"These fronds are helpful in reducing fevers," Sarda said, pointing to a grouping of green ferns. "When we make it into a mouthwash, it eases sore gums. Add it to a compress, and it takes the itch out of rashes."

"That over there is wild ginger," Shardana added. "It's a potent root. Great for the digestion. It also makes the other herbal remedies more potent. Like a lightning bolt. Speeds up the healing."

"And the roots that numb your gums and tongue," Sarda said. "Those are good when you come down with a cold or get the flu."

The list of plants and the remedies they offered grew longer and longer, and Martina worried that she'd never be able to remember them all or recall which worked best for which ailment. Barberry, fleabane, alum root, bilberry, goat's rue, fenugreek, prickly pear cactus, bitter melon, garlic, mulberry leaves, olive leaves, wild ginger—all these and more—rolled off the *majarzas'* tongues with ease. Martina's brow furrowed with frustration and worry. "It is too much!" she'd say. "No more for today. Tomorrow. After I've had some sleep. My mind can't collect all of this. My brain is rattling."

"Tomorrow, then," the women said in unison. They smiled at one another, recalling the days decades before when they, too, had been girls being trained by their *ayaya*. Oh, how their heads dizzied then. Oh, how they failed to believe they'd be able to remember a single plant or its potency. With diligent effort and unyielding guidance they'd grown to be *majarzas*, honored, respected, and needed by the villagers of Orune.

ANNA-BELLA initiated Martina into the hidden world of the bees, teaching her their little known role as conduits of the spirit realms. She showed Martina the pictures she'd drawn on and around the hives—the spirals and Vs, the meandering lines that resembled river waves—and told her these were demarcations of membranes, passageways into the

131

realms beyond where the Wise Ones, the Spirit Helpers, lived. They were the ones who whispered their knowledge and lore to the bees, who in turn aided every *majarza,* every sacred beekeeper. "These markings represent our honoring of the times when the ancestors reached out to the spirits and the spirits replied."

Martina learned how to douse the hives with smoke to draw out the bees. She watched as Anna-Bella lit her lantern and held it close to the entrance of one of the oldest of the wild hives. In her free hand she held an open jar, a dab of honey smeared inside. She chanted a quiet, deep, bee-drone. Responding to her voice, forty bees emerged from the hive and entered the jar, which Anna-Bella quickly covered. "We'll start a new hive with these willing colonists," she explained. "In this way the bees will remain healthy and vital. As we tend to their harmony, so they'll tend to ours."

After months had passed and Anna-Bella had determined that Martina was ready, the beekeeper taught her cousin some of what she knew about the power of bee venom. "While bothersome to children at play, shepherds tending their flocks and farmers in the fields, the bee sting is the source of a mystical substance we call bee venom. When used properly and with the knowledge passed down from generation to generation, bee venom can transform illness into wellness.

"There are pathways of energy that run along your body, Martina. Though unseen, these channels contain the flow of vital forces. When used auspiciously, the stinger of the bee can balance this flow, much in the same way as removing logs unclogs a river, enabling the water to flow unimpeded. When the bee venom enters the body in this way, mystical worlds often times open and the diseased body relinquishes its stronghold on illness. But these techniques are used only by the most advanced practitioners. Few are the people who can be entrusted with this knowledge. Your *ayaya* Shardana is one of the keepers of this way, as am I and my mother, Sarda. In time we'll know if you've been chosen by the bees as well."

BY THE END of her first year of study, Martina knew a great deal about the potent medicine of bees. She also realized she had much more to learn. She'd continue her studies with Anna-Bella, as the bees dictated. In time, she'd come to know whether the bees had chosen her as one of their bee venom practitioners. Until then she was content to listen to the bees and learn all that they felt she was ready to absorb. Slowly she was beginning to understand some of what the bees said when they spoke to Anna-Bella about her.

Through her work with her *ayaya* and great-aunt, Martina also knew the difference between infusions, tinctures, and salves, and the proper use of each, although she wasn't yet allowed to make them herself.

"For an infusion, you have to completely cover the plant—its buds, its flowers, or its leaves—in hot or cold water," she said to her *ayaya* one afternoon when the healer suddenly tested the girl's knowledge and memory. "Then you leave it sit for a couple of hours."

"Very good," Shardana replied. "And what about a salve?"

"For that, you cover the plant with olive oil and set it in the sun for two weeks, maybe longer. When it's ready, you press it through one of the finely woven cloths you've set aside just for this purpose. You squeeze the oil from the plant residue."

"Brava! And what about tinctures?"

"Those are made by stewing the plant in water and alcohol. Then you set the mixture in a cool place for a few weeks, give or take a day or two. When it's time you decant it. Then the tincture is ready to use."

"You've learned well, my child." Shardana beamed.

UNDERSTANDING the steps involved in concocting the remedies was not as difficult as deciphering the *majarzas'* herbal recipes. Neither Shardana nor Sarda used the same portions or amounts of ingredients, nor did they repeat the recipes for their remedies, twice. Duplicating the concoctions was impossible. While Shardana might toss in a handful of one herb, Sarda might choose another equally effective root, leaf, type of berry, or flower. A cup of this, a pinch of that, a teaspoon of another thing. Martina was learning the *majarzas'* craft was as much an art form as a science. The women selected ingredients based on a mixture of intuition, experience, efficacy, and something else equally unempirical, the individual needs of their patients. Sometimes their recipes even came to them at night in their dreams. Sometimes during the day while walking, the potion would suddenly become clear, its recipe whispered on the wind.

These methods baffled Martina, and she began to think she'd never be able to master their healing art. Still, she kept trotting off to the hills and forests accompanying the women; she kept introducing herself to the plants, kept seeking their permission to harvest their leaves, their roots; kept learning to discern the delicate differences between them and the powerful medicines they offered.

In time it became clear that Shardana had been right: Martina had a gift. If she continued to study and learn, continued to apprentice with her *ayaya* and her great-aunt, she'd one day be ready to see patients on her own. That time was not yet near, but it was inevitable.

The MONTH before Martina's menses began, Shardana announced, "You'll bleed with the next new moon."

The girl blushed. For nearly a year she'd sensed some change in her body, but hadn't said anything to her *ayaya*. Martina wasn't surprised that the elder woman had noticed it as well. She'd come to understand that, like the plants her *ayaya* harvested, Shardana could see beneath the surface of things and sense more than others less skilled.

"When your first blood comes, go to the woods. Listen. You might hear the song of the plants, the buzzing of the bees. Or maybe a bird will speak to you. Or a fox. Perhaps a wild horse or a *cinghiale*—I know how you love the wild boars that roam the forest. The unseen world will open to you in ways it hasn't yet been able to."

A shiver ran up Martina's spine. "What do I do if I hear an animal speak? Or a plant singing?"

"You'll listen. With your ears. But more importantly, with your heart. Your soul has more than five senses, Martina. And a healer needs access to these other ways of knowing—deeper ways. Let the animals and plants guide you."

Martina nodded, and continued working on decanting the tincture she was preparing at her *ayaya*'s request. She was to assist the *majarza* with her patients that morning, and the tincture would be needed. As Martina worked, Shardana walked toward the clay jars that held her medicinals, pulled out a root, and returned to her granddaughter's side.

"This is cohosh. Use it to ease your cramps, if you have them once you menstruate."

"Thank you," the young woman said.

Shardana nodded, then returned to her jars of herbs for a moment before laying an array of dried plant materials on her table. "Martina, come here," she called.

The granddaughter obeyed the healer. On the table Shardana had set a conglomeration of dried plants she'd stored. Over the wooden surface of the table she had spread some dried raspberries and their leaves, as well as dried chamomile flowers. "These strengthen your womb," she explained. "Gather these during the summer. Hang them to dry, then store them. Use them to make a medicinal infusion when your blood flows."

She reached inside another jar and set some ergot on the table. She held it in the palm of her hand for several minutes before speaking. The scent of it stirred memories of Grazia and of how she could no longer be a midwife to the women of Orune. To chase away the sorrow that crept into her chest, she took a breath before continuing her instruction.

"This increases contractions during birth. To purge the afterbirth, prepare a drink of red baneberry and give it to the mother right away. If the placenta stays inside too long, it could poison her and she might die. If the placenta is stubborn and won't give way, tie something sturdy to an end that's partially emerged from the womb. Something like a stone or a small branch. That way it won't be able to sneak back up inside the woman. Don't be afraid to push your thumbs into her belly, just above her pubic bone, to get that placenta all the way out. Then cut the umbilical cord."

Shardana taught her granddaughter which herbs to use to prevent blood clots, which to make a mother's milk flow, which to speed up labor, which to ease it. She told Martina to bury the afterbirth of babies born during the daylight hours under a tree. If the baby was born at night, she was to burn the afterbirth in the fire. Either method ensured that respect was paid to the Divine. "We come from the Earth, and we return to the Earth," Shardana emphasized. "We must always respect the Mother."

Sarda instructed their apprentice about what to do with the umbilical cord after it had been cut. "Have the mother dry it and keep it as an amulet," she said. "Later, when the child grows up, the remnant can be ground up and mixed with hot water, then ingested. This will enhance their fertility. I dispensed some to your mother before she conceived you.

"Remember, Martina," Shardana added. "The *majarza's* brain-knowledge of what plant to use, and why, is important and necessary. But it's not what heals our patients. Heart-knowing is what's most essential. In order to choose the proper remedies, the right herbs and concoctions, you have to know more than your brain can tell you. The patients, the plants, the healers—are all living beings. The cure resides in the alliance between the spirits of all three—the herbs, the *majarza,* the one who's ill—and added to that is the spirit of the village as well, the town in which the person, the herbalist, and the plants all reside. That's where the true power to transform resides. That's where all true and lasting healing comes from."

ONE DAY A MONTH LATER, Martina went for a walk in the hillsides, alone. She strolled along, allowing her mind to rest, letting the sun warm her face. A griffon vulture circled overhead, sweeping the sky with its wide, dark wings. She glanced at its head, clothed in white downy feathers, and its long neck, white as well. She admired the strength and beauty of its tawny body, the majesty of its dark tail, the splendor of its strong, wide wingspan. The vulture soared higher and higher, its wings brushing against the bright blue sky. "*Unturgiu,*" she said, calling the bird by its Sardinian name. She knew the bird held great magic, for it picked clean the flesh of carrion, the dead animals large and small that it found at the forest's edge or on the roadsides. This was a holy calling, she understood, for it helped rid the landscape of rotting flesh, protecting the living from all that might otherwise fester and harm it. This bird of prey was not a predator but instead a warrior of death, a reminder of the end of life, the beginning of regeneration. Its medicine was as strong and forceful as its hooked beak—and as formidable.

Suddenly the griffon swooped low, hovering close to the treetops, but still far from Martina's reach. Feeling an urge to rest, she sat on the ground next to a juniper tree, near an outcropping of myrtle. She closed her eyes for a moment, listening to the silence. The wind blew softly, brushing against her cheek. The sun warmed her face. Her breathing slowed. It was then that she heard the griffon speak.

The bird's voice didn't resemble a human's, yet it spoke in a language as clear as any that had ever danced across a human tongue. The *unturgiu* told her it had come to guide her, show her how to deepen her gifts, make them a strong and powerful ally for the people of her village. The griffon vulture called her "daughter," said that the spirits had chosen her to be their helper, the one who could facilitate regeneration, rebirth, transformation. The bird told her that years before her mother, Grazia, had once sat by that same juniper when her first blood had flowed, and had conversed with a golden eagle. The griffon told Martina that she should come to the hillside from time to time, sit down beside the myrtle bushes, beneath the shade of the juniper, and wait for him. He'd return and continue their conversation.

Martina opened her eyes and glanced at the nearby tree. The griffon had perched on one of the juniper's high limbs and sat, staring back at her. "Thank you," she called softly. The bird spread its dark wings, then took to the sky, circling up and up, away from her line of sight, away from the land and its human inhabitants.

The young woman stood, stretched her arms, flapping them as if she could follow the griffon, wishing she could sprout wings and fly.

A swarm of bees exited a nearby hive and swirled around her head, filling her ears with the drone of buzzing. Her bones vibrated with their humming as the bees danced in the air around her before dashing off to an outcropping of flowers.

The young woman rushed home to tell her *ayaya* about the encounter, about the bird's message, and about the blessing she'd received from the bees.

"Bees and an *unturgiu!*" Shardana exclaimed. "Blessed be!"

Chapter 9
The Journey to Orune

THE **ARCHBISHOP'S HENCHMEN**, Massimo and Vidal, grabbed *Padre* Albóndiga's stiff arms and dragged him to the holding cell, where a jailer kept watch while they prepared for Antonio's impending departure.

At the appointed hour Massimo tossed a woolen cloak at Antonio and told him to put it on. Vidal set scuffed leather boots near the priest's feet and ordered him to exchange them for his walking shoes. Massimo laid a wide-brimmed hat beside the prisoner and suggested that he take care not to misplace it, for the land to which he was going would require him to be endure fierce winters and scorching summers.

The archbishop had arranged for an uncovered cart to carry his henchmen and Antonio to Sassari, a town north and east of the port city of Alghero. No carriage or coach would cushion the priest's ass. From Sassari his passage would continue by horseback over the rough terrain of rocky fields and roadways. Nearing the mountains Antonio would be forced to straddle a mule in order to enter the hinterlands known as the Barbagia, for no carts or coaches could venture up the steep slopes and rugged plateaus of that region. Even if a carriage were sturdy enough to survive the trek, in those hinterlands there were no roads wide enough to accommodate such a leisurely mode of travel. Foot paths, serviceable enough for a man's boot or the steady hooves of horses, mules, goats and sheep, were the only routes between the mountain passes.

"You should be praising Christ Jesus that your exile came now, when it is nearly June," Massimo noted. "Otherwise you would surely freeze to death trying to reach your destination."

Antonio took their tales of this strange place as nothing more than their attempt to intimidate him into fear and loathing. He refused to cede to their tricks, and instead boldly proclaimed how he loved the mountain air, boasting that as a child he had worked for his grandfather, tending his family's sheepfold.

Massimo and Vidal scoffed at such nonsense. How could a mere shepherd's grandson become a learned priest in a city as opulent as Alghero? It was not possible, unless the Devil himself had a hand in such a reversal of fortune.

Sensing Antonio's anxiety, the jailors fed his weakness.

"Oh, in time, *Padre*, in time you'll understand what we're saying about this land of barbarians and bandits," Vidal insisted. "They'd rob their own grandmothers, they would. Without flinching. Stab them, too, the way you did poor Federico Bautista.

"Or that unlucky jeweler," Massimo scoffed.

"One word of advice," Vidal continued. "Watch your back while you live among those reckless, bloodthirsty villagers."

"You'll lose your mind in all that silence, too," Massimo warned. "Those folks are sparse on words. Sentences are as rare as diamonds in their tattered pockets. Say goodbye to your educated ways and manners, *Padre*. No one up there knows how to read or write, let alone converse on matters of grave importance such as how to save a city from heretics."

THE JOURNEY to Sassari was long and tiresome. The small, uncovered cart that transported Antonio bumped along the rutted road, its wheels seeking and finding every hole in the roadway. Antonio's head began to ache and his back pained him. When he complained, Massimo and Vidal laughed. "This is first-class comfort compared to what lies ahead, *Padre*."

In Sassari, Antonio's keepers picked up two horses at a local stable. Upon the back of a sturdy brown horse they packed Antonio's belongings and the gear they would need to make the journey inland. As the elder of the two jailers, Massimo won the right to choose first. He selected a black-and-white horse, leaving the chestnut-colored mare for Vidal and Antonio. "You didn't think we'd let you have your own, did you?" Vidal scoffed. "We can't have you riding off without us."

The journey lasted many days. On the first morning of their trek, the men and their prisoner rode from sunrise into the afternoon and evening before setting up camp at sunset near a grove of oak trees. Massimo and Vidal took guard shifts overnight, keeping watch over Antonio to prevent his escape. When at last they arrived at Bona, on the western edge of the Barbagia, they ate a lunch of bean soup and brown bread at a local tavern, then swapped their horses for mules before continuing.

Antonio grew restless. "This town must have an inn. Why can't we spend the night? The cold hard ground is too much for my tired bones."

"Are you a king, *Padre?*" Massimo admonished. "Do you think we are your vassals, escorting you to your summer palace?"

Into the cold wind of late May the mules advanced, their backs burdened with bundles and the bodies of their riders. Antonio didn't say another word.

The afternoon grew bleaker as the jailors and their prisoner rode on. The chilly spring wind bit the lobes of their ears and the tips of their noses. Antonio would find no palaces in his future home, no shops purveying fine wares, no aged wine to placate his thirsty palate, no sweet cakes iced with sugar to satisfy his fancy for dessert. The Barbagia held nothing that Antonio believed was essential to life, for he failed to see the value in rugged beauty. He could not appreciate the fierce red sky at sunrise, the lush purple sky at night, the luxury of a forest filled with a symphony of sparrows' singing.

In two days he would find himself in an isolated land running parallel to the Gennargentu Mountains, a region of snow-covered peaks, granite plateaus and rolling hills rising within the womb of Sardinia's ancient earth. The highest elevation towered more than six thousand feet above the sea. While rivers and streams, caves and grottos dotted the hillsides, the ocean was but a distant, salt-spray dream.

The travelers rode past vast expanses of holm oak forests, encountering herds of fallow deer and mouflon, the wily, wild mountain goat that thrived in the unkempt countryside of the Barbagia. Pairs of wild boar scurried past, scouring the forest floor for morsels to fill their bellies. Hares and foxes roamed the fields and woods. Partridges ran free among the grasses and scrub. With each clop of the mules' feet Antonio left behind the world of men and riches, the storehouses of fine wines and fancy meals, the libraries of learned theologians, the gay and wild social life of Seville, Spain and its Sardinian stepsister, Alghero. Each footfall took him deeper into the nearly impenetrable granite hills and tree-covered mountains, opulent with cork and chestnut trees, oak, wild pear, wild olive, and the curious strawberry tree, an evergreen shrub with unusual flaking bark. Hillsides rippled with wild rock roses, broom, violets, myrtle, heather, creeping honeysuckle, red corn poppies, and wild cyclamen. But Antonio was immune to the beauty. Hawks and peregrine falcons, red kites and golden eagles soared overhead, witnessing his long, wrenched journey.

The guards and their prisoner stopped to rest near an ancient oak, but quickly moved on, hounded as they were by the swarm of angry bees nested in the tree hollow whose teeming honeycomb the men had disturbed.

"It's too bad we couldn't have dipped a finger or two into that delicious pot," Vidal noted. "The best honey on God's green earth comes from these parts. And that's the truth."

Antonio shrugged, disbelieving such a possibility. He had sampled the velvety sweetness of Spanish honey—in Seville, of course!—and nothing could be finer.

"They say honey is a potent curative," Massimo added. "If you believe in folk medicine."

Antonio scoffed, and the jailers snorted. "Old wives' tales," Vidal asserted. "The stuff of witches and crazy village healers. Beware, *Padre*. The place you're going to is full of them!"

Massimo cackled, sending a shiver up Antonio's spine.

On and on the travelers continued, veering first northward, then east, each mile revealing new and strange flowers and animals, trees and birds. Endless fields of daisies and bog asphodel stretched out before them, enveloped by blue-gray mountains that pierced the sky. The high, metallic call of cuckoo birds unsettled Antonio as he and his guards descended mountainsides, entered valleys, crossed fields of thickets and broom, before climbing the rocky paths of yet another mountain on their way to still other valleys, other mountains that lay beyond. Long and winding trails led them away from civilization into a land as foreign to him as the surface of the moon.

"You know how the Barbagia got its name, don't you, *Padre?*" Massimo asked one day to pass the time, for their hours of travel were long and, every once in a while, he felt the urge to break the silence.

"No, I am not familiar with anything about this haunted wasteland."

"I shall enlighten your ignorance," Massimo said. He laughed, then began:

"Some say the inhabitants of this region are descendents of the people known as the Iolaos, who may have hailed from Asia Minor. Whether this is verifiable or not, I cannot say. Still, the term Barbagia is thought to be Roman in origin, derived from the Latin *barbaria*, or perhaps *barbaricum*."

Antonio stared at his guard, baffled that a man of such uncivilized demeanor could speak of such things as the Latin origins of words. The priest was certain that Massimo could not have been educated. At least not beyond the merest rudimentary requirements to enable him to read a bit and perhaps sign his name so he could conduct the duties of his position as a guard.

Massimo took no notice of the mild grimace that crept across Antonio's face, discounting it as a touch of gas, perhaps, or discomfort in his legs from the travel. He continued his story.

"The Romans described everyone they conquered as 'barbarian,' believing that any culture not based upon Roman civilization was wanting and woefully inadequate. No matter how the Barbagia received its name, its inhabitants came to be called Barbaricini. They speak an ancient tongue called Sardo, which is similar to Latin except it has a glottal stop—a clever ruse, if you ask me, used by the Barbaricini so the conquerors couldn't decipher their language or intercept their communication. Not that they talked much, as I mentioned before. But just in case, you see, they figured out a way to pull the sheep's skin over the eyes of the ones who were going to overthrow them. Must have been something smart about them, wouldn't you say, *Padre?*"

Antonio kept his tongue still, even though he wanted to ask Massimo how he came to know about such matters. While he believed nothing of the guard's tale, he found the story a diversion from the monotonous journey and didn't want to impede the telling.

"You see," Massimo said, "the Sardinian peoples in this region were fierce resisters of Roman rule. Resisters. You might wonder how I came to know that. Well, I'll tell ya. My great-grandfather came from these parts. His folks and their folks, and maybe even their folks before them, had been seafarers, lived near Sassari until some invading somebodies from somewhere drove them inland. Not a high price to pay for one's life, *Padre*. You ought to remember that over the next few weeks as you're trying to get situated in your new home."

Vidal and Massimo laughed, at Antonio's expense, before Massimo lapsed back into his saga.

"So, the earliest people of this whole island, the Resisters, as I was telling you, they fended off the Phoenicians, the Greeks, and the Saracens, too. That's partly how this region got occupied. The people who lived near the coasts—my kin, or a bit further inland, like Vidal's ancestors—fought against whoever invaded their cities, villages and countrysides. Each time the conquerors won, the rebels just kept moving further inland and higher and higher up into the mountains, so they wouldn't be overtaken. Every time they fought to the bitter end, resisting the invaders, refusing to be colonized. The folks in the Barbagia held off long past the rebels and resisters in other parts on the island. The Barbaricini just wouldn't be suppressed. It took the Romans four hundred years of trying before these people capitulated."

"Now, that kind of determination could be seen as an asset," Vidal offered. "That is, if you aren't the one trying to conquer those damn folks."

"Indeed," Massimo continued. "From what I've heard, they—the Barbaricini, I mean—felt the same way about Christianity. Oh, they're all Christians now—well, most of them are, anyway—rest assured, but it wasn't until the sixth century that the villagers in these parts stopped worshipping stones and trees and springs. Seems it took that long for the people and their chieftain, a man by the name of Ospiton, to be convinced that Catholicism was the way to go. One of the popes—Gregory I, I think—you'd know about this part way better than me,

Padre—sent two missionaries named Felix and Cyriacus to bring the Gospel of Christ Jesus to these heathens. That's what they called them back then. Heathens. The commander-in-chief of the army, a man called Zabarda, persuaded Ospiton to convert. Once that chieftain took up the Christian faith, he discouraged his followers from worshipping the old ways—you know, all those pagan idols, their trees, their sacred tombs of fairies, their holy springs and wells. The chieftain asked them all to toss out their superstitious rituals and centuries-old customs. Don't think many of them were happy about it, but they knew fate was against them. The time had come to strike a bargain. In the end, their souls were saved by Christ Jesus's blood. And they could go to heaven."

In unison Massimo and Vidal touched their fingertips to their foreheads, then to the center of their chests, then to their left shoulders, followed by their right, fervently making the sign of the cross. "Amen," they said.

Antonio simply shook his head in disgust.

The men and the mules crossed mountain heights dizzying to a lowland-lover's heart. Antonio prayed that the pack animal hauling him was sure-footed and keen-eyed, for the uneven path was narrow and rocky. One misstep would have plunged them into the depths of valley far, far below. Up and over and through and around they coursed, until at last they reached their destination.

Perched on the edge of a granite plateau, the village of Orune sat 2500 feet above sea level, overlooking the Isalle valley. The modest town was sparsely populated—home to only thirty shepherds and their families, a handful of merchants, a couple of basketmakers, a cobbler, and a dozen fieldworkers. A small, unadorned stone church stood at the end of the small *piazza,* its wooden door locked, the lock's hinges rusty from age and disuse.

At noon, under a blazing sun, the triad of mules clomped through the square in the center of town. A handful of villagers emerged from the houses and shops to investigate the newcomers. Constantino was the first to enter the square. He'd been sitting in the sun on the stone bench in front of his house, shaping asphodel into a wide and deep basket. From his perch he heard the clopping of the mules' hooves on the road, heard the braying of tired animals ready to be released from their packs. He set down the basket he was making and walked toward the square, curious about who might be riding into town at this hour of the day. A few of the women had set aside their task of sweeping their household steps to join him. A couple of shopkeepers did too.

Loud braying echoed off the cobblestone pavement. They knew the commotion couldn't have been caused by shepherds, who were still at work in the hills. And it was too early for the field workers to come home from their tracts of farmland. The sound was most definitely not that of boys at play or the young village girls giggling. Strangers! It had to be strangers.

The townspeople were not accustomed to uninvited travelers, for the mountains were far too high for even the most adventurous of explorers, and the trip through the high passes was much too arduous. And except for the tavern where the village men gathered to play cards and drink *mirto,* Orune had no inn to accommodate weary journeyers and no café to satisfy their need for a meal.

The villagers stared at the mules and their three riders, two men who appeared to be soldiers or guards of some kind, and another, an older man, dressed in attire that Constantino could not place as being the customary dress of any nearby town or village. When the mules and their riders stopped at the well in the center of the *piazza,* Constantino approached them.

"Who are you?" he asked in Sardo, his native tongue. "And where do you come from?"

Although Massimo and Vidal were not fluent in the language of the village, they understood enough of Sardinia's mother language to answer the rudimentary questions Constantino had posed.

Vidal responded, "We've come from Alghero on the northwestern coast, by way of Sassari, Bona, and up and over the mountains."

"Why have you come here?" Constantino continued.

"We bring a priest for your village," Vidal answered. *"Padre* Antonio Albóndiga. Sent by Archbishop Orozco to minister to your spiritual needs."

"We need no ministering," Constantino replied.

"It doesn't matter," Vidal said. "He belongs to you now."

The women and the shopkeepers listened as Constantino questioned the strangers. One of the villagers demanded to know who they were and how long the priest intended to stay in their town. Constantino shrugged. "Indefinitely, I think." He informed the women that the shorter man, the one with the bewildered face, was named Antonio. He was sent to be their new spiritual adviser. The women and the shopkeepers laughed.

Massimo tossed Antonio a cup and motioned for him to dismount his mule. "Get yourself a drink from the well."

As the priest refreshed himself, the guard untied the saddle bag containing Antonio's belongings from the pack mule's back and tossed it at the priest's feet.

"Good luck to you, *Padre*."

After Massimo and Vidal watered their mules, they remounted the animals, grabbed the lead of the mule that had carried Antonio to the village, then turned and headed out of the village, leaving on the road by which they'd just arrived. Antonio suppressed an urge to cry out, run after them, plead with them to stop and take him with them. Suddenly he preferred the dank and rat-infested dungeons of Alghero's jail—even death by hanging—to the reproachful eyes of the townswomen who now watched as his face paled with panic and consternation.

As the mules and the guards disappeared into the horizon, Antonio's hopes shattered. A sense of doom rested heavily on his chest. He turned to the women and to the lone man still standing by the well and mustered a pained smile. "Hello," he said. "My name is Antonio Albóndiga. I am your new Shepherd."

The people laughed, not because they understood his words, for he spoke Spanish and they didn't know his language. Their amusement arose from the puddle of urine that pooled at the priest's feet. He'd been so unnerved to have been tossed into the unwilling arms of these villagers, in the inhospitable outback of this Godforsaken island, that he'd wet himself without realizing it. He glanced at the urine, then at the people, then bowed his head, embarrassed and ashamed, thinking of what his father would have said had he been alive to witness his humiliation.

A woman emerged from a row of houses across the *piazza*. Her dark hair and no-nonsense stare sent a shiver through Antonio. She seemed to him to resemble a sturdy tree, one of the thousands he'd recently seen in the trek up and down and over the mountainsides. Her face was browned and weathered, not unlike the barks of the countless oaks he'd ridden past the last several days. Her arms were strong, as thick and muscular as tree limbs. With purpose she walked toward the group that had gathered near the well, and fixed her eyes upon the despairing priest. The other villagers made way for the woman, moving aside so she could approach the stranger. They watched her intently. The man who had spoken to Antonio's jailers nodded to the woman without saying a word.

The woman linked her arm in Antonio's and motioned for him to accompany her. Although he felt uneasy he obeyed, leaving the saddle pack that contained his few belongings on the cobblestones beside the well. The other women in the *piazza* scattered back to whatever it was they'd been doing before his arrival, and the man who'd first approached Antonio and his guards returned to the stone bench where he'd been sitting before he'd launched his interrogation.

The sturdy woman led Antonio down a narrow street to a house which he presumed to be hers, although he wasn't certain. She opened the door and invited him inside. In the cool, dim interior his eyes adjusted as the woman left his side for a moment. When she returned she held within her hands a clean pair of pants and a fresh shirt, which he surmised belonged to her husband, or perhaps her son. She offered the clothing to the stranger. With gestures she indicated that he should change and give his soiled garments to her. He did as she requested, grateful for her care.

As Antonio dressed, his eyes acclimated to the low light and he looked around the home's main room, a modest-sized area that contained a wooden table and several chairs, a hearth in the center of the room, and an oven set off in one corner. Peering closer, he noticed rows of stone jars, and several bundles of hanging plants drying in the hot midday air. Hundreds of bottles and containers of what looked to him like ointments cluttered the top of a small table near the hearth.

On a separate table near the entryway, three bowls and three spoons awaited. When Antonio had finished changing the woman motioned for him to join her and a young woman who'd stepped inside the doorway and now stood beside the older woman. The elder woman ladled a soup of mashed fava beans into each of the three bowls, picked up a spoon, and mimed that Antonio should eat. He obliged and joined them in their meal. The priest, the younger woman, and the elder sipped their soup in silence, savoring every drop of the creamy liquid, sopping it up with thick slices of bread.

When they'd finished their meal someone knocked on the door, then entered. Before them stood another treelike woman, one who in every way resembled the kind woman who'd attended to Antonio at the well and who'd filled his hungry belly with food. Both women shared the same dark eyes, the same thick, dark brown hair, the same brown skin and square face. The same spark of fierceness. Their visages were so uncannily alike that Antonio understood that they had to be sisters, and twins, at that.

The woman who'd just arrived walked up to Antonio and took his hand in hers. Heat rose from her fingers, which sent a tingling sensation up his arm. Startled, he pulled away. Not wanting to offend the woman, he shrugged and offered a wee smile.

The woman nodded, pointed to her heart, and said, "Sarda."

"Sarda," the priest repeated, not knowing if the woman was trying to tell him the word for chest in her language or if she was trying to tell him her name. The kindness in her eyes unexpectedly reminded him of his mother, and he swallowed hard to keep his tears at bay.

"Shardana," the other woman said, pointing to her own chest, in the same place that the other woman had touched on her own body.

"Shardana," Antonio repeated, now clear about what the women were trying to tell him.

The priest pointed to his heart and said, "Antonio."

"Antonio," the sisters said in unison. They smiled, pointed to the younger woman and said, "Martina."

"Martina!" Antonio said, bowing in her direction.

For the first time in a long time he smiled broadly and with sincerity. "So happy to meet you all," he said. "So pleased to be in your company."

Chapter 10
Istranzu
The Stranger

ANTONIO STROLLED THROUGH the narrow lanes of Orune. On either side rose one-story gray buildings, built of granite quarried from the region. Their somber countenance reminded him of the townspeople—taciturn and uncommunicative. "Silent as stone," the old saying went, and now he better understood the depth of that expression—understood as well the story Massimo had told him on the trek up the mountainside, the guard's tale about the peoples of the Barbagia and their peculiar ways, their odd customs, their stinginess with words.

In the first few weeks after his arrival, Antonio made an effort to be cordial to the residents of Orune. But with the exception of Shardana, Sarda and the members of their immediate families, no one greeted him as he walked around town, although plenty of people were outside, sweeping the cobblestones in front of their homes or their shops, gathering water at the well, hanging their wash, feeding their hens, harvesting their eggs, coaxing their mule to budge, sitting on stone steps weaving baskets out of some sort of reeds or weeds, of what type he couldn't distinguish. Antonio's gregariousness ricocheted off the somber faces, the reticent lips, the distant eyes that always averted his gaze as he approached. While he sensed that the reserved demeanors were probably nothing more than typical behavior for a town unaccustomed to outsiders, he felt slighted by their aloof indifference. As a man of the cloth he'd grown accustomed to reverential respect. He interpreted the villagers' reserved behavior as shunning, and took it as nothing less than a personal affront.

While he rarely saw any of the villagers engaged in conversation with one another, it seemed to him that the quiet gulf that separated him from the people of Orune was filled with avoidance or mistrust, as if the villagers were protecting something valuable and scarce. He was beginning to harbor resentment.

He knew part of the difficulty lay in the fact that he didn't speak Sardo. He found their language to be a strange concoction of glottal stops intermingled with vowels and consonants, and he didn't know if he'd ever be able to master it. Still, he'd visited several other towns and cities in which the common bond of language had been absent, and he'd found the inhabitants to be warm and outgoing in spite of the vernacular chasms that separated newcomers from longtime residents. That had been his experience in Alghero. But had he thought about it more, he would have realized that as a Spaniard he shared more in common with the colonizers of that grand city than he did with the few remaining Sardinian families who still lived and worked in Alghero.

The priest's assimilation into the customs and ways of Alghero had been relatively seamless, not at all the arduous task he'd feared it would be during his long voyage from Spain. It had taken him little time to make connections, affiliate with the right people—the count, the magistrate, the archbishop, and the other elites of Alghero. He'd managed to gain entry into the right circles, which had pleased him, until that unfortunate evening at the magistrate's house when he'd had a bit too much to drink and had found himself lusting after Juliana's breathtaking beauty. Antonio never allowed his mind to linger on the other incident, the encounter in the alley with the Jewish merchant that had resulted in his unfortunate relocation to Orune.

ANTONIO FELT something else was awry in Orune, with all the silence and the averted eyes—something that, although not sinister, he nonetheless found off-putting. He prided himself on his wiles, on his ability to acclimate and discern which alliances would prove fruitful, which to avoid. In Orune nothing seemed to hinge on the rules of order that had facilitated Antonio's career thus far. Something odd was at work, something that he couldn't decipher, and he didn't like it. Every day his head ached trying to puzzle out the mystery. He vowed to crack the code even if it took him the rest of the year. Like humans, every place had its vulnerability. Like a misshaped pot too long held in the kiln, under pressure and with the right amount of heat, it was bound to explode.

Shardana, the woman who'd rescued him from the well the morning of his arrival, had been courteous and kind, as had been her family—her husband, her twin sister, the younger woman, who Antonio learned was Shardana's granddaughter, Martina, and the others, her son and daughter-in-law, her son-in-law, and the other shepherds whose lives revolved around seeing to the needs of their sheep. Shardana had allowed Antonio to stay in her home until a suitable residence could be found for him. Her granddaughter, Martina, gave up her room for the priest, kindly sleeping on a straw mat on the floor near the hearth so that Antonio might have a proper bed and a bit of privacy.

On most days up to ten villagers visited the woman and her sister, seeking medical help of one sort or another. At the break of dawn the door-knocking would begin, before Antonio was awake and before he'd had his breakfast of cheese and bread. He found that especially uncivilized. How could a man begin his day in leisure with so much racket going on around him?

When the weather permitted the people waited outside the woman's home, sitting on the stone benches she'd placed there for that purpose. When it rained or the sun was too hot, those waiting to see the woman sat inside her home, on chairs set against the wall near the door. These men and women would wordlessly stare at Antonio, eyeing the priest from head to toe until he became so unnerved that he'd pick up his cup of water and walk outside—even in foul weather—to be free of their inspection.

Some of the patients arrived with festering sores that reeked of pus, causing Antonio's stomach to sour. Others carried wailing children, their howls chafing against his ears. Still others burned with fever, and he quickly left the room to avoid contagion, huffing as he sped past Shardana, Sarda and their charges. The women ignored the priest and his indignant behavior, focusing their attention on attending to the villagers in need of help.

Most every day the younger woman assisted the women, climbing on a chair, if need be, to pull down a jar from a high shelf or snip a bit of dried weeds hanging from the pegs above the hearth. Their work seemed odd and slightly mysterious to Antonio. He watched them shift through the twigs and dried bits of what appeared to him to be herbs or flowers or some other plant materials. He observed them applying poultices and dispensing tinctures. He heard the aching moans of patients quiet into soft murmurs. He heard the thank yous and noticed the kind touch of hands on shoulders as the people left, healed, or at least better off than when they'd first arrived.

While Shardana had been quite kind to him since his arrival in Orune, Antonio also sensed a bit of caution in her. From time to time a cloud of mistrust would fog her face and her eyes would tense just a bit, as if she were trying to discern whether Antonio was worthy enough to merit the friendship she offered. Even as she doctored her patients she'd glance at him from time to time to study his countenance, sizing up his reaction to all he was witnessing.

Antonio felt uneasy with their trade, thinking it backward and medically unsound, steeped in outdated lore and anecdotal trial and error. But from what he'd seen, the town had no medical doctor. He realized the villagers had no other recourse when they became ill, and so he felt a twinge of pity for them. He was also relieved that his health was sound, and although he wasn't prone to praying, he hoped that he would continue to be hale. He shuddered at the thought of being doctored with their antiquated ways.

While Shardana at times seemed suspicious of Antonio, her granddaughter, Martina, had taken a liking to the priest. Within a day of his arrival in the village she'd begun trying to teach him the name for common household things in her language—cups and hearth, bed and wash basin, spoon and bowl. He'd struggled with the words as if his brain and his tongue stubbornly clung to its Spanish rather than cede to the village's native dialect. What use could it be, he wondered? He didn't plan on staying long in this dusty town overrun with chickens and shepherds, devoid of any of the comforts of civilization to which he was accustomed. He'd found no place to enjoy a fine meal, no shops to purchase fine linens, succulent fruits, tantalizing pastries. As far as he'd been able to tell, there was no mayor or local constable, either. He found it curious, and wondered, briefly, how the day-to-day workings of the town were managed and who was in charge of the place.

AFTER THE PRIEST'S arrival the villagers had convened a town meeting, as was their custom, to discuss what to do with the stranger who'd been plopped down among them without warning or permission. The men and women sat in a circle, face to face, to talk about how best to proceed. Many avenues were suggested, not the least of which was to put the priest on a mule and send him back from where he'd come. However, that would've required that someone from the village assist in his return, and none of the men were willing to take time from their sheepfold, their fields, their shops, or their other duties to accompany the cleric.

Shardana and Sarda also felt the time had come to inform the villagers of the omen they'd had months before. It was their duty to warn them that they believed the stranger might very well be the wolf of which they'd dreamt. "The hairs on the back of my neck stood straight up when I first saw him at the well the day he arrived," Shardana explained. "I took him to my home and fed him, thinking it better to disarm him with generosity, as a way to defang him."

"Better kindness than cruelty," Sarda added.

The villagers nodded.

"Yes, there's something disquieting about that man," the baker said.

"Evil," Annica, the cobbler's wife, stated. "He's evil, I tell you. We should banish him to the countryside now, before it's too late."

"He'll die in the hillsides," Constantino cautioned. "Who among us would want his blood on our hands?"

"Better he die on the roadside than choke our village with his bile," the cobbler, Stefano, noted, affirming his wife's beliefs.

"We're stronger than any evil he could bring down upon us," Isidoro said. "And we have the potent medicine of the *majarzas* to keep us safe."

"It might not be strong enough!" the baker's wife said, shaking her head.

"Together, our community is stronger than any medicine Sarda or

I could dispense," Shardana noted. "If we pay attention, watching and noting his actions, we should be able to dissipate any sordidness he might display."

"I agree," Basilio stated. "And it's the duty of every one of us to be vigilant. If we stick together, we'll be able drown any mischief the sea-wolf has brought with him."

In the end it was decided Antonio Albóndiga could stay in the village—unless his future actions or words warranted his expulsion—but he'd have to find a way to take care of his earthly needs, for none of them could afford to feed and clothe him.

"We must be charitable and give him a chance," Giovanni concluded. "But he mustn't be a burden to us, either. He has to work like the rest of us, contribute to our village's prosperity."

AT THE MEETING the villagers had decided to allow Antonio to use the small house near the church that had sat empty ever since the last priest had died twenty years before. The archdiocese hadn't bothered to send a replacement, and the villagers hadn't demanded that one be sent.

Antonio thought the house was a hovel when he compared it to his more opulent quarters in Alghero. Still, he was relieved to have a roof over his head and to be away from Shardana's scrutinizing eyes and her busy home with its medical clinic. The tiny place was meagerly furnished, and even though he preferred its quiet and solitude over the din of Shardana's busy home, he grew agitated at night when darkness fell and he was alone.

Except for an occasional visit from Martina, he rarely had company. With little to do to occupy his waking moments, Antonio filled his days with a stroll through the village and evenings at home composing letters in his head to his cousin Juan and to the archbishop of Alghero, pleading his case for reinstatement. If he wasn't permitted to return to the city soon, he feared he'd lose his mind.

Because the town had no need of the services a priest could offer, Orune's men folk took it upon themselves to teach Antonio a useful occupation. One morning Constantino arrived at Antonio's doorstep with bundles of dried asphodel tucked under his arms and his son, Brontu, at hand. With gestures Constantino attempted to show the priest how to use the materials to weave a basket. Brontu tried, as well, to mimic the harvesting of the reeds, the myrtle, the asphodel and other plants that the basketmakers used to craft their wares. Antonio shooed them out.

Brontu and Constantino shook their heads as they walked away from the priest's door. Antonio thought he'd heard one of them laugh, or had it been a grunt? It didn't matter, for the priest had no intention of roughening his soft hands with the labor the pair had selected for him. He slammed his door, returned to his table and swallowed a cup of wine to soothe his rising temper.

Antonio would learn later that Constantino used to tend the sheep-fold with his brother-in-law, Basilio, but had suffered an ailment that had weakened his heart, preventing him from continuing in that line of work. Climbing the steep hillsides to reach their shepherd's hut and living in the wilds, at the mercy of the changing weather, was no longer good for Constantino's health. He'd taken up carpentry for a while until Ann-Bella had taught him the skills of basket weaving. The for-mer shepherd had taken to it with ease, pleased to have found a way to spend his time and contribute something of value to his family and his community—as was the Sardinian way. In order to help his father suc-ceed in his new vocation, Brontu had learned to select and uproot the ripe stems and tie them into bundles. After harvesting the materials, Brontu would leave them to dry for ten days so they would be seasoned and ready for use when Constantino needed them.

After Basilio heard that the priest had dismissed Constantino and Brontu, he paid a visit. With Giovanni and Isidoro at his side, the men tried, as best as they were able without the aid of a shared lan-guage, to inform Antonio that they'd willingly teach him the intrica-cies of shepherding. Isidoro had dropped to the floor on his hands and knees, baa-ing like a sheep and scampering about while Giovanni held a broomstick in his hand acting as if he were corralling an errant lamb. Basilio smiled, gesturing to the priest, cupping his hands and mak-ing circular motions, attempting to paint an image of his *pinnette*, the round, thatched-roofed shepherd's hut in which the men lived when they had to remain with their flock instead of returning to the village.

When the priest's eyes clouded with confusion, Basilio tried another approach. He retrieved his *sa resolza,* the prized shepherd's knife that hung from the rope belt that circled his waist. Eyes filled with pride, Basilio showed Antonio the knife's blade, pointed in the traditional way, *a foll'e murta*—like a myrtle leaf—and its sheath, carved from a ram's horn. Basilio spit on the back of his hand, rubbed it hard, then ran the sharp blade over his skin, demonstrating to Antonio that the knife produced a close, clean shave.

When the priest gasped in horror, the shepherd interpreted his reaction as disbelief, a grievous insult to the quality of Basilio's *sa resolza*. Antonio's reaction offended the men. To doubly verify the preciousness of his beloved implement, Basilio laid the blade at a flat angle across his thumbnail. With intense concentration the shepherd pulled the sharp edge lightly along its entire length, ending at its shiny point. "Pah!" he exclaimed.

The startled priest jumped; his face grew paler. "Leave!" Antonio shouted, pushing the men toward his door. "Or I will call the authorities!"

The following week Anna-Bella and Sarda returned to Antonio's cottage and prepared the soil in a small patch of ground beside the house, planted some peas and fava beans, some lettuce, eggplant, and winter squash. They hoped that the priest was smart enough to cultivate the garden. For how else would the man eat? At the priest's doorstep Anna-Bella had left a jar of honey she'd harvested from her wild bee hives. Satisfied that the honey and the vegetables would enable the priest to survive at least through the rest of the summer and into the autumn months, the people of the town eased their worries over his nutritional needs.

ANTONIO HAD BEEN living in Orune for several weeks, and the villagers were growing weary of his obstinate attitude. He'd shunned the baker's and the cobbler's offers of apprenticeship in their honorable trades. "We have done all we can," they said. "His well being is out of our hands."

Martina had extended her offer to instruct Antonio in Sardo, the native tongue of the village, or at least he thought that was the meaning of the mime act she'd performed one night after dinner when she'd visited him at his home. He'd hoped he was correct, for he couldn't envision living the rest of his days in the isolating solemnity that was the byproduct of his inability to communicate with the villagers in their native language. He'd found it impossible to discern the nonverbal antics that Constantino and the others had played out before him. What's more, the priest shuddered to think what Basilio had intended to do with that vile knife.

Antonio knew he would go mad if he couldn't have a conversation with someone soon. He longed for an invigorating discussion over good wine, good food. He missed the other delicacies of life he used to savor, experiences that were fast fading from his memory. He hadn't dined on fresh fish sautéed in lemon and olive oil since he'd left Alghero months before, and his tongue ached for the fruity, dry kiss of a good, red Spanish wine. Being cast into the wilds of Sardinia, surrounded by nothing but mountaintops and bleating sheep was bad of its own accord. Did the food have to be so meager as well? Surely Archbishop Orozco could have been more merciful by condemning him to the gallows and then simply hanging him.

ONE MORNING, with his daily morning stroll nearly complete, Antonio found himself before the front door of the *Chiesa della Nostra Signora Nera.* He shook his head. The bolted door simultaneously pained and elated him. With the church boarded up, as silent as the mouths of the villagers, he wouldn't have to restore its interior and say Mass every day in a building named in honor of a Black Madonna. To have christened it thus was indicative of the townspeople's primitiveness. He found it preposterous that they viewed the Mother of God as black. Our Savior may have been Hebrew by birth, but he was a light-skinned Hebrew—of this Antonio was certain. And why not call the church the *Chiesa di San Paolo* or *San Giovanni?* Or even *San Francesco?* The Lord Jesus would be better served had any one of those three *santos* been called upon to be the town's patron saint. It was clear to Antonio that the village sorely needed him.

The small church was modest in stature, made of the same gray stone that comprised the rest of the buildings in Orune. The exterior had held up well against the onslaught of the seasons. Its peaked roof cradled a bell tower, though from his vantage point Antonio could tell that the bell was as rusty as the lock on the entry and hadn't chimed a welcome to the hillside in decades. A small niche above the door once held a statue, he surmised, long lost to the ages. He peered inside the dusty windows, but was unable to determine if the building's interior was salvageable. He was unable to detect pews—or, for that matter, an altar—for the condition of the stained glass was too dire to offer him a clear view.

He wiped the grit from his hands and smirked. *Well, if you expect a miracle from me you're going to be disappointed*, he mumbled to God, or the wind.

"HOW DOES the *istranzu* like his new house?" Sarda asked her sister, who was busy preparing a medicinal tincture for a man in the village who had a high fever.

"The stranger! Ha!" Shardana replied. "The house isn't up to his usual standards. He frowned and grunted when Basilio unlatched the door to the cottage next to the church."

"Too many cobwebs and spiders for his tastes?"

"Better that than tarantulas," Shardana chuckled.

"What's to become of him?" Sarda pondered aloud. "He has no other skills besides his priestly ones, and our town doesn't need a priest."

"Giovanni's pleased with his arrival," Shardana said, "and hopeful that soon Mass will be said again in the village."

"Mass!" Sarda snapped. Her frown signaled her disgust, and her twin had no need to delve further.

Both understood that the priest's arrival would stir up old wounds. A few of the townspeople were still professed Catholics, though most of the others had found a way to mingle the old ways of their ancestors with the new Christian faith. But others, including the *majarzas*, followed the ancient teachings from the days before the Christian missionaries rode their mules into the Barbagia, coaxing the people into swapping their *Dea Madre* for the new god, a man named Jesus, who they were told was the son of the Father in the Sky.

Shardana had heard the conversion stories from her *ayaya*, Maredda, who had heard it from her *ayaya*. Before the Christians arrived the Barbaricini revered the Great One that lived in every tree, every rock, every hillside, plant, animal and human. They saw no separation between God and the Spirit that thrived in all living beings. There was no need for complicated rituals, or for priests dressed in finely sewn robes, interceding with God on behalf of their congregation.

The Good Shepherd, the Catholics called their Jesus. And what she knew of him, he was a man of compassion and tolerance. But his priests often times weren't. To Shardana, a good shepherd was someone like Basilio, a man who treated his sheep with kindness, nurturing them along so that they'd produce fortifying milk, ample wool, tender meat, creamy *pecorino*. Basilio didn't force his will upon his flock, like the priests of the God they called the Good Shepherd. Her husband tended the sheepfold, nursed the sick ones, fed them all—sang to them, even, and played his *launeddas*, his flute of wood, to charm their sweet ears and make them happy. No commandments. No hellfire and damnation. No sins and punishment. Just grace and goodness. Hardship, too, of course. Always hardship. But that was life. The harsh winds and the unflinching sun. The bitter snows and the sloppy rains. These things Shardana and the others understood all too well. Still, there were brilliant flowers, towering trees, air fragrant with honeysuckle, grapes and olives plump and bountiful, cheese and eggs, honey and bread—yes, always bread. And love. Always love.

The *majarzas* understood that the Christian God was not the same as the Catholic Church. The priests and the bishops had twisted Jesus's words, used them as their rod of authority, to bind the people and their communities to interests that weren't their own. These men of the cloth, and the political allies they courted, used the words of Christ to amass property and to divide the men from the women, placing some men above other men based on the volume of money and land they could amass. What about the people and the earth? What about the animals and the plants? The sky and the waters? The stones and the sea? How could these be bought and sold? Whose folly was it to declare ownership and thus cut off life and liberty? Where was the justice in that? Where was the compassion?

That was not the Barbaricini way. The Barbaricini thought in circles. Their hearts and souls were like the ancient stone buildings, the *nuraghi*, built by their ancestors centuries before. Hundreds of stones were hauled from the fields and hills to the village and laid one upon the other in a massive circle, up and up, like a beehive, a conical prayer stretching toward the sky, until the home or the community meeting place was complete. Every man in the village gave his sweat and blood to the effort, working thousands of hours over many years to complete a single *nuraghe*. Their pledge was to one another and to the rest of their villagers. Everyone shared the land. Everyone shared the burdens. Everyone shared the bounty. Everyone venerated the Ancient Mother who created all life.

On stone walls in caves and on the sides of cliffs the people inscribed their marks, remembering. They drew red ochre triangles to honor Her vulva, Her menstrual blood, the entryway to the Womb that sustains every human until birth. They drew spirals to indicate continuity and spirit, the breath, the life force. They drew meanders to honor the serpents, the shedders of skin, molting and transforming from old to new again—birthing, renewing over and over, like the Earth, like the seasons, like the wheel that turns and spins. They carved tombs into the rocks to cradle their dead, placing them in the womb of the Mother, who was once more called upon to usher Her people to their second birth in the world beyond this one, the realms where every spirit traveled once it took leave of its body.

That's why Shardana's ancestors built the sacred wells, the water temples like *Su Tempiesu*, aligned with the cycles of the moon and the sun, the solstices and the equinoxes. That's why they placed stone pillar sentinels at these sacred sites, to guard the gateway from this world to the next. And the dolmens—they were portals, stony archways to the netherworlds.

SHARDANA PONDERED all these things as she helped Sarda finish preparing a tincture and other herbal potions they'd need that day when treating their patients. "Our ancient ways are sacred," she said.

"Yes, and I hope we're able to preserve those ways," Sarda said.

"You mean the priest?"

"Yes. He's the wolf come to eat the sheepfold. I know it in my bones."

"You're right," Shardana said. "And we're doing all we can to tame him."

"But will it be enough?" Sarda asked.

"Only time will tell," Shardana replied.

"What good will we be to our village if we fail this challenge?" Sarda asked.

"We do as best as we can," Shardana said. "The rest is out of our hands."

"But Martina—"

"We've taught her well. She's got a good head as well as a kind heart. She won't be fooled by the priest-wolf."

"I hope you're right."

"We've got to trust that. Nothing else makes sense."

Shardana wiped her brow and sat back in her chair. She believed in the power of medicine and stories to transform and to heal. She was a keeper of the stories, the transmitter of long, nearly lost origins. She saw and heard, smelled and tasted the untouchable. She entered the underworld of the soul and reemerged with omens and blessings. It was a burden she sometimes found difficult to carry, but carry it she would. Even with the horrible reckoning that might lie ahead, her life held joy and beauty. Even though she'd suffered the loss of her daughter, there was much that filled her with gratitude. To live rooted to this village, to love and be loved by the people of her town, the members of her family, was medicine enough to ease whatever terrible grief might claim her, whatever ominous future might unfold.

As she cleared away the plates and bowls she'd used to concoct her medicinals, Shardana began to sing out loud. Her clear voice filled the room. She sang a *ninnia,* a lullaby, one that her mother, Augustina, used to sing to her and Sarda when they were babies. The twins, in turn, had sung it to their children to soothe their restlessness. Grazia had sung it to Martina as well. As the words sailed through the air, tears streamed down Shardana's face.

Sarda glanced at her twin and set aside her task. "Come." She reached for Shardana's hand and guided her to a chair beside the hearth.

Shardana continued to sob as Sarda chose a medicinal remedy that would ease her sister's suffering. Sarda sensed that her twin was weeping for Grazia. While she knew there was nothing she could do to erase her sister's sorrow, the proper medicine would help Shardana temper the loss and release it. Sarda held no power to determine how or when her sister would let it all go. She placed the cup of steaming liquid into her sister's hand and rested her palm upon Shardana's shoulder.

"Tomorrow is the anniversary of Grazia's passing," Shardana said through her tears.

"We'll go to *Su Tempiesu* to honor her," Sarda said.

"And we'll bring Martina, too. She must never forget her mother."

"I see Grazia in Martina's face," Sarda said. "The same eyes, the same mouth, the way she sets it with determination when she's intent on something."

Shardana wiped her eyes and blew her nose. She took a deep breath, then sipped some of the remedy her sister had prepared. She managed a half-smile.

"You've been so good to me, Sarda. Even when my sadness put an extra burden on you. I'm grateful for your kindness and your love."

"Life is hard, Shardana. We both know that. Nothing makes sense if we don't help one another."

"Yes, even the priest deserves our kindness."

"Yes. He does."

"But if he hurts Martina—"

"She has a tender heart and a capacity for compassion, but she's fierce, too. She doesn't suffer fools easily. She has no tolerance for mean-spiritedness."

"I hope you're right. You know she's taken the priest on as a project. She told me she senses a darkness in his soul that's in need of cleansing. She aims to ply her skills in the service of his redemption."

"*Madonna mia!*" Sarda said. "She's set a mighty challenge for herself. But she's got some powerful allies in her medicine bag. And the griffon will guide her. Never forget, she has us to back her up. Antonio doesn't know what he's in for."

The sisters laughed. Sarda was pleased to see a bit of joy return to Shardana's dark eyes.

Chapter 11
Shearing the Sheep

AT DAWN ON A WARM MORNING in June, Antonio was awakened from a deep sleep by a loud knock on his door. He jumped out of bed and followed the noise to the front of his small house. "I'm coming! I'm coming!" he called out. "Patience!"

He swung open the door to see Giovanni standing before him. The shepherd's face was somber and calm, and he gazed intently at the priest.

"I've come to bring you to the *tanca,*" Giovanni stated. "Get dressed immediately." The shepherd knew that the priest couldn't understand very much Sardo, so he motioned for Antonio to follow him.

The priest shook his head. In his native Spanish he announced, "I'm going nowhere at this time of day. It can't be six o'clock yet."

Giovanni didn't understand Spanish, but from Antonio's set jaw and tightly held mouth he understood that the priest wasn't going to willingly comply with his request. The shepherd stared back at the priest's adamant eyes and spoke again. "I've been instructed to bring you with me to the pasturelands."

Antonio resolutely crossed his arms over his chest. "Go away now," he insisted, thrusting his chin at Giovanni.

The shepherd didn't move. Even though the priest's words were gibberish to his ears, Antonio's gestures and posture clearly conveyed his refused to cede the ground he held. "We're going to shear the sheep this morning. You're in need of a trade," Giovanni continued. "You have to come with me so we can teach you."

For weeks Martina had been teaching Antonio to speak Sardo, but the priest had succeeded in learning only the most rudimentary of phrases and a few of the words that the young woman insisted on repeating over and over. "Sheep" and "trade" were two of the important words that Martina had insisted be part of Antonio's language lessons.

"I have a profession, you idiot," the priest scoffed in Spanish. In mangled Sardo he added, "I don't need to tend to your sheep."

Giovanni offered a wry smile. "Your trade is of no use to the villagers, *Padre*. It's best you find another way to earn your keep. Or starve."

The shepherd's face betrayed no sign of anger or disrespect. The words he spoke were merely the factual resolve of the villagers who'd met in the community council to decide what to do about the priest who'd arrived, uninvited, in their town with no identifiably sustainable skills.

Giovanni shoved his boot between the priest's threshold and door, preventing Antonio from shutting him out. "Come in if you must," the priest said, continuing to speak in his native Spanish. "But I'm not going to the hillsides with you. It's back to bed for me."

Antonio turned back into his house, Giovanni following closely at his heels. Before Antonio could reach his bedroom door the shepherd grabbed his shoulder and held it firmly. "Do as I say, *Padre*. It's for the best."

The priest needed no advanced skills in Sardo to understand the meaning of Giovanni's strong grip. Antonio possessed neither the stamina nor the strength to romp around the countryside herding ewes and rams. He'd rather die a slow death of starvation before entertaining an occupation he believed to be beneath his status. Still, he ceded his will to the pain that throbbed in his shoulder from Giovanni's vise-like fingers. He couldn't see any way to disobey the shepherd that wouldn't result in further trouble, so he decided to join him, but only to placate him and the other villagers. He hoped that he'd sufficiently fail in mastering the duties they sought to impose upon him and he'd be able to convince them to let him be.

The priest nodded, informing Giovanni that he'd oblige his request.

The shepherd released his hold on Antonio, and the priest faced him.

"Might you spare me one moment for a sip of *mirto?*" Antonio asked, lifting an invisible cup to his lips, gesturing his need for refreshment.

Giovanni shook his head. "No, *Padre*. We're late. Change out of your bedclothes, but don't eat or drink anything. There'll be food at the *tanca*."

The shepherd reached for Antonio's arm to lead him outside, but the priest drew his elbow close to his ribcage, preventing Giovanni's attempt to usher him to the door.

"I'll go with you," Antonio said in broken Sardo. "But don't handle me like one of your ewes."

ANTONIO QUICKLY changed from his bedclothes into trousers and a shirt. He cursed Archbishop Orozco for having banished him to a land where he'd have to endure countless indignities such as the one he was about to embark upon. He grew agitated thinking about his old friends in Alghero, Count Carmago and the magistrate, Frederico Bautista. He imagined them stuffing their morning mouths with fresh pastries and hot sausages, a buxom servant girl attending to their every whim—a bit of jam for Frederico, an extra piece of sausage for the count. "God damn them all to hell," Antonio seethed.

"Hurry, *Padre*," Giovanni called again. "We can't keep the sheep waiting."

The sheep! The sheep! Antonio was disgusted at the thought of it all. He longed for a savory meal prepared by *Senora* de Leon, his former housekeeper at the rectory in Alghero. He even wished he could stand at the altar at the Church of *San Francesco* watching as perfume-laden wrinkled old women dropped golden coins into his collection plate. Anything, anything but the sheep! Had his old cohort, Bautista and Carmago, been within arm's reach, he would have throttled them for the part they'd played in his exile.

To the priest's dismay, he and Giovanni walked to the pasturelands. Antonio had hoped for a mule, at least, to ease the trek and relieve him of some of the back-breaking work he assumed awaited them in the hillsides. The priest and the shepherd remained silent as they set off down the dirt road, Giovanni lost in thought but keeping a watchful eye on Antonio should the priest decide to turn and run back to the village. Giovanni couldn't know that Antonio had sense enough not to attempt such folly. The shepherd surpassed the priest in size and stature, towering over Antonio's small, compact frame. From glancing at Giovanni it was easy to discern that his forearms and legs were firm and muscular, the result of having spent his childhood and early youth working the hillsides, tending the flock. Antonio was older than Giovanni as well, so the priest, though reluctant to follow the shepherd, was sensible enough to realize that he'd surely lose if a physical altercation arose.

Antonio took some small consolation in knowing that Giovanni and the other men would never discover his secret life, for he refused to admit to them that he was no stranger to being a shepherd, having assisted his grandfather in the countryside in his Spanish homeland when he was a boy. His father, Pablo, had long ago distanced himself from his family's humble beginnings. As a magistrate he'd traded favors with his political allies to make sure that Antonio would be allowed to enter the priesthood so his son's hands would never be calloused by hard labor. On those evenings when Antonio's mother suggested that she'd rather her son become a shepherd or tend the olive trees like his grandfather instead of engaging in the sometimes disreputable politicking that was required of a city official, Pablo would raise his hand, threatening to strike her, and say, "No son of mine will dirty his clothes with the sweat of labor!"

Although Antonio had enjoyed the pasturelands as a lad, had even learned to shear sheep, his once-sharp skills were as dull as his desire to pursue that occupation. Antonio smiled smugly to himself. He was resolved that Giovanni, and the others, wouldn't prevail in their efforts to make a herder out of him. He had become a man of refinement and culture. He would never stoop to shoveling sheep shit or grabbing a ewe's teat to squeeze milk into a bucket. He was destined to savor the fruits of such labors, dining on succulent roasted lamb, filling his belly with aromatic *pecorino* cheese, and warming his loose-muscled limbs with the finest woven woolen cloth. His father's influence had made sure of that.

GIOVANNI AND ANTONIO traipsed through fields, along the leafy edges of forests, stepping on stones to ford streams, and climbing the sloping hillsides until they reached the family's *tanca*. Brontu, Isidoro and Basilio stood beside their hut, patiently waiting for Antonio and Giovanni. Seeing the men in their rightful habitat, Antonio suppressed the urge to curse them, recalling the time after he'd first arrived in Orune when the three of them had enacted a scene in his living room, Basilio brandishing his shepherd's knife, trying hard to convince Antonio of the majesty of their trade. Antonio had managed to put them off then. Now he stood at the edge of their pastureland, frowning as he scanned the field.

Antonio noticed hundreds of sheep secured in pens. Their bleating and baaing filled his ears with a terrible din, causing his temples to ache. An unpleasant mixture of lanolin from the sheep's fleece and the putrid stench of urine, feces, and soured ewe's milk overtook his nostrils. He wanted to cough to dispel the odors, but was unable to muster enough breath from his tightened lungs to accomplish that task.

He thought of his grandfather, of how he often smelled of sheep sweat, dusty dung and dried milk. The memory brought little comfort to him, even though it took him back to the only time in his life in which he'd felt truly happy and at peace, for that was a truth he'd spent the past fifteen years trying to expunge from his heart. He was destined for greater glory, he adamantly insisted. Though he'd never sit on a royal throne ruling nations, he believed himself fated to live among kings and scholars, not among shepherds, the lowliest of the low.

Basilio's dog, Mutos, ran to greet the priest with his tail wagging and a welcoming bark. Antonio shooed him away, flagging his hand at the dog's face. Mutos's bark sharpened and he stepped back, avoiding Antonio. The dog bared his teeth but returned to Basilio's side without harming the priest, content for the time being to watch the newcomer and, if needed, to defend Basilio and the others from any further display of ill manners on the part of their visitor.

"Good morning, Antonio," Basilio called. "Glad you could join us. It's a lovely day to shear the fold!"

The shepherds had spent the early morning hours corralling their herd into a grouping of pens, making sure not to overcrowd the animals so they could prevent urine and shit from smearing and staining the fleece. When the sheep were rightly situated, the men laid several large woolen blankets on the ground, preparing a way to catch the fleece as they sheared the animals. This would insure that the wool remained as clean as could be expected, given the nature of their task.

The June morning they'd chosen as their shearing day promised to be warm and sunny, which pleased the men, for the heat would tease out the grease in the fleece, making the fibers stronger. Eliciting the fleece's natural oils would lubricate their shearing implements as well, making it easier for them to cut the wool more uniformly and more easily. It was far better to shear the sheep closely and remove the fleece in one piece, paying careful attention not to tear or break it apart.

"We're ready," Isidoro announced to Basilio.

The older shepherd nodded, then handed Antonio a shearing tool. "You'll work with Brontu. He's agreed to teach you."

Reluctantly the priest took the tool and stood beside the shepherd who was to be his instructor. Giovanni manned the pen, releasing an animal to each of the shearers, confining the rest to their corral until their time to be shorn arrived. Basilio, Isidoro, and Brontu each straddled a sheep and began to cut away the thick coat.

First each grabbed the top knot, then the head and neck, cutting in swift, sure motions, releasing the dense fleece from the animal's body. With smooth movement their cutting shifted next to the shoulders, then the backs and sides, finishing with the legs, bellies, breech and tags. Within minutes the three capable shepherds stood beside their now-nude sheep, the animals shivering in the early morning breeze without their dense coats. The shorn wool lay on the woolen blankets, mounded in piles like newly fallen snow.

Antonio had straddled his sheep as well, but the animal, sensing the priest's hesitancy, had butted him off and raced away, running toward the open field, bleating wildly as it trotted off. Mutos chased after the distressed animal, herding it back to the pen and Giovanni's waiting arms. With a steady hand Giovanni ushered the ewe into the corral, careful not to allow any of the other sheep to escape.

"You've got to do better than that, *Padre!*" Giovanni chortled. "Or you'll surely starve."

The other shepherds laughed, bruising the priest's ego with friendly banter.

"Don't be so timid, *Padre,*" Brontu insisted. "Think of it as making love. You must be firm, yet gentle—let the sheep know who's in charge."

The men laughed louder, then, at Brontu's insinuation, and the priest joined them, for although the shepherds thought it amusing that a man of the cloth would understand the art of making love, Antonio knew better. Long ago, before he had become a priest, he had fallen in love with the daughter of his uncle's business partner and had savored many a sweet kiss, lying with her under the stars once after a family feast, when the others had gone to bed. Before he'd been sent off to the seminary to study, he'd nearly succeeded in seducing the young woman, robbing her of her virginity, denying her entry into the circle of civilized society. He'd undone her bodice and was nearly ready to take the next step when the woman's father caught them. Antonio, who'd received little more than a reprimand for his part in the encounter, had agreed to sign a paper attesting to the fact that he'd not deflowered the virgin, who was still chaste and fit for marriage. For his confession he'd been granted an early exit from town and an early entry into the seminary.

Being a priest didn't stop Antonio from satisfying his sexual appetite. He often disregarded his vow of celibacy, thinking it inane that God would expect such a sacrifice of a man as virile as he. He'd shared the bed of many married women in Spain while an unsuspecting husband was off tending to business or running the government.

Giovanni released the next round of restless sheep, doling an animal out to each of the waiting shearers. This time Brontu assisted Antonio in his shearing efforts. The priest hid his discomfort and succeeded in completing his task, although his work took more effort and more time than the others. Still, when the fleece he'd shorn came off nearly in a single piece, the shepherds smiled and shook their heads approvingly.

The men spent the rest of the morning focused on their tasks, stopping only to allow Giovanni to bundle the accumulated fleece, bind it with rope, then haul it off so they could continue to shear the thick coats from the rest of the waiting herd. When the sun rose higher in the sky, the men stopped and ate a lunch of bread and *pecorino*, washed down with a swig or two of red wine. They planned to save the *mirto* for later, when their chore was finished and they wouldn't have to be in full command of their wits and their talents.

While Antonio's skills were not as finely honed as those of the shepherds, he managed to shear one sheep for each ten fleeced by the others. In spite of himself he found a certain enjoyment in the labor, working his body to a satisfactory sense of fatigue. His spent muscles ached, and sweat flowed down his brow. His thirst grew fiercely, and so did his hunger. His arms and back ached as he sat beside the others, chewing his modest meal and swallowing the wine. While the conversation among the men was minimal the priest didn't mind, for the silence didn't feel odd to him as the silence in the village had, even though he preferred enlivened mealtime conversation. Instead he listened to the songbirds warble in the tree limbs and became mesmerized by the bleating of the sheep. From time to time he thought of his mother and became filled with an unexpected sense of peace. By the end of the meal Mutos sat beside him, sniffing at his fingertips, begging for scraps. Antonio tossed the dog a bit of cheese and patted the animal's head.

The shepherds observed the slight transformation that had overtaken the priest and exchanged glances with one another. A look from one to the other sufficed to say that they felt confident Antonio would master their trade, with enough practice and more days spent in their pastureland. In the priest they sensed the heart of a shepherd and they wouldn't have been surprised if Antonio had burst into song or stood to recite a poem, as often happened when the men of the sheepfold gathered together at their *tanca*.

After lunch the shepherds and Antonio resumed their duties, shearing and collecting the fleece, releasing the unclothed sheep to the pastures to feed and romp, guarded by Mutos. By six that evening all but twenty-five sheep had been relieved of their wooly coats. Eager to complete their task, the men sped up their efforts, cutting more swiftly and with great skill. Trying to match the shepherd's pace, Antonio straddled his sheep and clipped quickly, removing the top knot, cutting away the wool around the animal's head and neck. He shifted to the sheep's shoulder and, for a moment, a bee hovered near his ear, distracting his focus. He meant to swat the insect but instead nicked his own chin, slicing his face. Blood dripped down the edge of his jaw. His father's stern, disapproving face loomed in his mind. He cried out in pain and the other men ran to his side.

"The gash is deep," Basilio noted. "We've got to get him to the *majarzas* at once."

"But the sheep," Brontu insisted. "We're nearly done shearing. How can we leave now? Clot his wound with a cloth and let's continue."

Antonio lay on the ground, his hand fast against his cheek, trying to stop the bleeding. He moaned and his eyes pleaded with Basilio to disregard Brontu's suggestion.

"A man's life is more important than fleece," the older shepherd replied. "You and Giovanni can stay with the flock. Isidoro and I will take the *padre* back to the village. I'm afraid if he doesn't get care immediately, he'll lose too much blood."

THE TWO SHEPHERDS hurried down the hillside, Antonio between them, their strong hands gripping the priest's arms as they hauled him over the trail. They ushered Antonio over the rocky pasturelands, along the dirt roads, through the fields and over the streams he'd traveled earlier that day. With great haste and purpose they flew, covering ground quickly until they reached the village. At the well they met one of the townswomen, Annica, and asked her to hurry on to Shardana and announce their arrival. The woman did as they requested. By the time the shepherds appeared at Shardana's doorstep with the pale and bloodied Antonio in stride, she was ready to assist them.

"Bring him inside," the *majarza* instructed her husband and her son. "There, by the table. Set him down."

The woman pressed a clean cloth against the priest's cheek, holding it firmly to stop the bleeding. "Martina," she called to her granddaughter. "Grab a bucket of water and another cloth. We have to clean the wound before we apply salve."

Shardana shooed Basilio and Isidoro from the room. "Go back to the *tanca*. Finish your shearing. Your help here is no longer needed. Antonio will be alright. Don't worry."

The shepherds glanced at the priest's ashen face and nodded. "It's a shame," Isidoro muttered to his father as the men left the house. "The *padre* had proven he could swap in his cleric's collar for shepherd's shears. Now he'll surely return to his old ways, with a scar to nurse and mend. And a reminder of the perils of our profession."

"Don't cast him off so quickly or so easily," the elder shepherd said. "I think sheep's milk runs in his blood. His eyes glimmered when he heard the sheep bleating."

171

INSIDE, SHARDANA AND MARTINA worked diligently to stop Antonio's bleeding and dress his injury. Shardana pulled a container of pine pitch from her apothecary and unsealed the jar. She reached for another jar filled with powdered hemlock bark, which she used immediately to staunch the blood flow. With patience and deftness, she inspected the gash to determine its depth and severity.

"You're fortunate, Antonio." Shardana spoke softly as she washed the priest's wound with clean water and a cloth. "One inch higher and you'd have gouged your eye. One inch to the side and your ear would've been shorn off. One inch lower and with a bit more force and you might've cracked your cheekbone. Or who knows, even sliced the artery in your neck."

The healer continued to gently touch the priest's cheek, tending his injury. He groaned in discomfort, recoiling. With respect for the wound and compassion for the man, Shardana rested her hand upon Antonio's shoulder. "We'll take this as slowly as we need to. But you have to trust me. I mean you no harm."

The priest cautiously eyed the healer. While he was in grave need of her care, he felt unsettled by her folk magic and her potions. He felt grave distain for the woman's supposed medical ways. When he'd taken ill or required medical help in Spain or in Alghero, he would see no one but a physician, privileged as he was to have wealthy friends and acquaintances who granted him access to their medical doctors, men who'd studied the works of the Greek masters of medicine. When he needed an infirmary or a hospital, he could easily find treatment at one of the monastic clinics affiliated with local monasteries or priories. Never did he place his life in the hands of an unschooled peasant woman whose training relied on folk medicine and foolishness, not the practiced science of those he deemed more learned than Shardana. Her amateur skills might serve the needs of a pregnant villager or a sickly shepherd, but Antonio believed they were woefully lacking when it came to addressing his dire condition.

The presence of Martina eased his troubled mind a bit, for he felt affection for the young woman who'd been kindly teaching him some of the villagers' native language. He trusted Martina, but felt less sure of her *ayaya*. What if Shardana was more than a folk healer? What if she was a sorcerer and cast a spell upon him? What if she poisoned him and left him to die in this godforsaken mountain town? He'd never return to Alghero then, or Spain, as was his fervent wish.

Sensing Antonio's uneasiness, Martina took his hand in hers. "Don't be afraid, *Padre*. I wouldn't allow any harm to come to you. My *ayaya* is known far and wide for her healing skills. Many people travel over the mountains and valleys to receive her medicines."

Antonio was able to grasp only part of Martina's Sardo, but he began to feel reassured by her tender eyes and the careful way she held his palm. As his cheek ached more intensely and the throbbing pain caused his vision to blur, he had no choice but to place his trust in the *majarza*. He relaxed his shoulders, eased back into his chair, and sighed. "Yes. Okay. Proceed."

Together the *majarza* and her granddaughter prepared a salve to seal the wound, using the pine pitch she'd grabbed earlier from her medicinal pharmacy. Mixing the correct dosage in the right portions, she crafted an ointment that she'd eventually apply to Antonio's face. As Martina stirred the pine tar in a shallow cup, Shardana applied bruised oak leaves to Antonio's wound to reduce the inflammation. While the compress eased the priest's swelling, the healer searched her storehouse for last autumn's acorns. Taking a knife, she shaved thin slices of acorn skin from the nut's hard exterior, removed the bruised oak leaves from the open cut, and applied the thin layers of acorn skin. Over this application Shardana smeared the pine tar remedy, covering the gash with a thick blanket of medicine, sealing it so that it could mend.

While Shardana continued to work Martina brewed a remedy from oak leaf bud, which she gave to the priest, instructing him to sip slowly, allowing its curative effects to take hold and assist in further relieving the inflammation that puffed his cheek.

The priest's pain slowly began to subside and the spinning in his head eased. His breathing calmed and he was once more able to focus on objects in the room. Martina did her best to explain to her friend the frequency with which he was to apply the salve in order to properly care for his injury. The remedy, she instructed, should be taken every morning with breakfast to help his wound heal. She cautioned that should the wound become infected, he had to return and they'd prepare some other medicines for him to use.

"After the wound heals, you'll have a scar," Shardana told the priest. "A souvenir of your day of sheep shearing. Wear it proudly." She smiled, then motioned toward the door. "You can go home now. Rest."

The priest rose and found his knees unexpectedly wobbly. Martina took his arm and helped him to the door. "I'll take him to his house, *Ayaya,*" she announced.

"Don't be long," Shardana replied. "We've got other patients to see." The healer glanced at the men and women sitting patiently outside her front door, hoping for her help. They cared little for medical degrees or credentials. Experience had taught them the certainty of Shardana's practiced hands and ancient knowledge. They trusted the efficacy of her potent medicines and lasting cures.

"I'll come back quickly," Martina assured her. "I won't shirk my duties."

Shardana nodded, pleased that her granddaughter took her craft seriously, for since the priest's arrival in the village she'd begun to question Martina's allegiance to the old ways. Her granddaughter spent every Thursday evening instructing Antonio in Sardo so he could communicate with the villagers in their own language. While Shardana found that admirable and compassionate, she worried that her granddaughter would fall under the sway of the priest who came from the sea, the man with the untamed heart whose ways were so different from their own. What concerned Shardana more, however, was the bitter root that she sensed was buried deep within the priest's bones. He was the wolf, the very same one that she and Sarda had dreamt of, although Antonio had yet to fully bare his fangs as the animal in her dream had done. In time, Shardana knew he'd reveal his true nature. She prayed that Martina's tender kindness toward him wouldn't bring harm to her granddaughter. When the sea-wolf decided it was time to bite, Shardana knew he would bite hard.

"Who's next?" Shardana asked, glancing at the villagers awaiting her care. "Ah, Salvatore. Yes, come in. How can I help you today?"

"I'm suffering from diarrhea," the man informed her. "My wife, Johanna, sent me here for a remedy. I need to get better so I can return to the fields."

The *majarza* led her patient to her hearth, inviting him to rest in the chair beside her while she stood nearby listening as he told her all about his troubles while she concocted a mixture of ground acorns and water. She filled a cup with the tonic and handed it to her patient. "Drink this," she instructed.

As the man drank the potion, Shardana prepared several more doses of the remedy for him to carry home. "Take these as needed until your discomfort goes away."

"Thank you, Shardana!" Stefano replied. "I'm certain I'll feel better shortly. Your medicine has never failed me." He handed her a small basket of eggs in payment. "Johanna said to give you these."

The *majarza* smiled. "You're too kind, my friend. I'll think of you with great affection this evening as I savor a supper of eggs and bread."

"It's the least we can do to repay you," the man stated. "I wish we could offer more."

"What you've given is enough," the healer replied. "It's my greatest hope to help in the ways I am most able. Go now. Be well."

Chapter 12
The Festival

BY MID-JULY ANTONIO'S FACE had healed, but he scowled every morning when he washed his face and ran his hands over the raised skin of the scar that remained from the accident at the sheepfold. That disfiguration was a constant reminder that he hated being in Orune, hated the sheepfold and the shepherds who tended it, and hated the villagers with their silent ways—although he had grown fond of Martina, and he felt a tinge of gratitude toward Shardana for having tended to his wound the day his face had been slashed.

He refused to rejoin the men at the *tanca,* so, with nothing else to do to alleviate the long hours of boredom that consumed his days, Antonio asked Brontu to break the rusty lock on Orune's church, *La Chiesa di Nostra Signora Nera.* He'd decided to prepare the sacristy for proper use.

It had been months since Antonio had been exiled from his post at the church of *San Francesco* in Alghero, and he hadn't once thought about saying Mass, a rite so central to his religion and one that his fingers had been ceremoniously anointed to perform. Though he'd taken his priestly vows many years before in Spain, he lacked the conviction to carry through on his promise to God now that he'd found himself banished to this mountainous outpost. He'd never been fond of his profession. It had been thrust upon him by his father, and he didn't want to continue to live the life of a cleric. Had his expulsion from Alghero delivered him to a place larger and more sophisticated than Orune, he might have tried to pass for a count or a baron and entirely disowned his role as *padre*. But his luck hadn't proven to be fortunate.

Slowly, Antonio was beginning to cede his pride to the facts at hand. He lived in Orune now. In such a woefully wee village his options were dismal. Determined to avoid the sheepfold, or any of the other menial occupations the townspeople had suggested—each of which, he believed, was unfit for a man of his educational statue and worldly connections—Antonio was begrudgingly resigned to acquiesce to the inevitable. What else could he do? Fate had cursed him. And now it laughed in his face. Without a drop of noble blood in his veins, his dreams of a life of luxury were futile. Being a man of the cloth was his inescapable destiny, and, sadly enough, it appeared to be his duty. He decided to make the best of a sour situation. Once, when he'd suggested to Constantino and Basilio that he ought to be appointed the town's magistrate, they'd laughed and said, "What would you do? We handle all the village's business as a community, Antonio." With no higher civil office to be had in Orune, the only way he could seize a bit of authority and garner a modicum of respect from the villagers would be to wear the priest's alb and usher the heathen, lapsed Catholic townsfolk back to God Almighty.

As requested, Brontu chiseled away at the metal clasp that secured the church door. With great effort the shepherd finally cracked the lock and unbolted the entryway, allowing Antonio to step inside.

The dank interior of the small building smelled rancid from years of inattention. Some animals, perhaps mice or other small creatures, had made good use of the place, nesting and bearing their young. The odor of urine and excrement soiled the air—perhaps a remnant from generations of rodent families, perhaps irreverent deposits from prankster hooligans who'd entered surreptitiously through some of the broken windows that had never been repaired. The church's stone floor was littered with dirt. Its walls and ceiling were covered with dust and cobwebs. Its wooden pews were parched and cracked from years of festering heat. Antonio shuddered when he first laid eyes on the vestibule. By the time he made his way to the altar the stench had caused his stomach to heave and he rushed outside, vomiting his lunch beside the entryway.

Days later he coaxed the cobbler's son, Giacobbe, and several of the other village boys to clean the church, promising to teach them to read—knowing all along that he had no intention of making good on his offer. When Giacobbe and the boys finished their tasks, the church, though not pristine, was inhabitable and ready to be put to its intended use.

"When do our reading lessons begin, *Padre?*" Giacobbe asked.

"When Jesus rises again on Judgment Day," Antonio replied.

On the last Sunday in July Antonio Albóndiga performed Mass for the first time at the newly re-opened church. Though the interior was now clean and serviceable, it was devoid of ornamentation except for the lone painting of the *Nostra Signora Nera* hanging behind the altar. The image was identical to the statue housed in the grotto by the streambed outside of town. When Giacobbe's mother, Annica, heard the priest was planning to say Mass in the church, she asked her husband Stefano to bring the painting to Antonio and tell him to place it behind the altar. When Antonio scoffed at the idea Stefano explained, "Annica has been tenderly taking care of this painting in our home ever since the church was boarded up. She didn't want the cobwebs and the animals to destroy the Blessed Mother. You'd break my wife's heart if you didn't honor her request. What could it hurt?"

It dismayed Antonio that the only image of Jesus in the entire church was to be found in a painting where the Son of God was a baby cradled in the arms of His mother. There was nothing the priest could do to change that fact. The Madonna would have to suffice, unless he learned to carve a statue of Jesus out of oak or cork wood, or paint a different image to grace the altar.

Twelve townspeople, including Constantino, Brontu, Giovanni, and Martina, attended that first Mass. To offer Holy Communion Antonio had fashioned hosts out of stale bread, mere minutes before he started the service. Without bothering to wash his hands he'd pressed small chunks of bread into small circles with the heel of his palm. If one looked closely, one would have seen bits of dirt embedded in the makeshift wafers. He had no wine for the consecration. He had already consumed the weekly allotment Constantino was kind enough to set on his doorstep every Monday morning. Instead, Antonio used sheep's milk, hoping Jesus wouldn't be offended. He'd found a tattered alb and other threadbare vestments in a drawer in the priest's dressing area, a small side room behind the altar. However, he was unable to locate any small bells or candlesticks, although he'd found plenty of misshaped candles, bent and listing to one side as if intoxicated. Somehow the wax tapers had survived their entombment, tucked away as they'd been for years in a dusty, hot corner of the boarded-up church.

Antonio's prayer missal and his Bible had made the journey intact from Alghero to Orune. Still, he lacked an altar cloth and an altar assistant. He puzzled a bit about how he was going to turn the pages of the missal in the midst of enacting the rites, but scoffed at Martina when she'd offered to help. He was offended at her suggestion that a woman could perform that sacred duty.

He began his weekly peasant's Mass—for that is how he referred to it—with a blessing and a prayer, welcoming the hearty souls who knelt before him, speaking in the little bit of Sardo that Martina had taught him thus far. Though his congregation was small, the participants were attentive and polite. All twelve took communion, and none grimaced at the soiled wafers or complained about the sheep's milk communion wine.

When the last hymn was sung and the prayer books closed, Antonio felt strangely satisfied and relieved. Silently he sent a thank-you to Jesus for helping him bring the Good News to these indigent folk, many of whom were on the brink of returning to their ancient Godforsaken ways. Although Antonio's challenges were many, his religious determination was surprisingly strong. With the help of God, he trusted he would prevail.

IN EARLY AUGUST, after the priest had gotten the town boys to sweep and clean the old church named in honor of their beloved *Nostra Signora Nera,* and after he'd acquiesced and hung Annica's painting of the Black Madonna behind the altar, he'd announced to his handful of parishioners that the fifteenth of the month was nearing. They'd nodded and smiled, but their blank eyes revealed they had no idea why the priest thought that date was significant.

"It's the Feast of the Assumption," Antonio explained. "The day the Mother of Jesus was taken bodily into Heaven, to be reunited with her only child, her Holy Son." So holy was she, the priest reminded them, that though a mere mortal, her limbs were excused from decay and rot and assumed straight into the realms of the Divine.

Antonio saw the festival as an exercise in recruitment, an opportunity to gather more sheep into his fold. He'd taken it upon himself to turn the hearts of the nonbelievers away from their pagan ways and towards Catholic piety and faith. He'd concocted his ambitious goal one night after supper, sitting alone in his room, craving the conversation of his friends back in Alghero, the count and the magistrate. They'd expect nothing less of him, he'd concluded. As men of authority they'd never abide the lax habits to which these townspeople had grown accustomed. Something had to be done, and Antonio Albóndiga was the man to do it. That night he fell asleep thinking that perhaps there was some Divine Reason for his exile to this nearly Godforsaken land. Like his cousin Juan, the assistant to the Inquisitor, his righteous duty was to rid the world of heresy.

When Antonio had reminded them, those in the village who'd been baptized Catholic, lapsed though they'd become, began to recall a time when the folks in Orune had celebrated the old festival in honor of the Mother of God. It had been too many years since the archdiocese, headquartered many miles away in the provincial city of Nuoro, had failed to appoint a replacement priest to oversee the welfare of the village souls when the beloved head of their parish had died. The people of the town didn't care that Antonio hadn't been sent to them by the archbishop of Nuoro. In fact, the bishops and archbishops of the diocese knew nothing of this vagabond priest's existence, and wouldn't have sent Antonio to Orune had they been given the opportunity. The fiscal authorities in the diocese of Nuoro saw no need to plant a priest in a village as poor as Orune; tending to the salvation of people too indigent to fill a proper collection plate each week made no sense to them. With their usual collective shrug the men and women of Orune simply accepted whatever fate blew their way—ill or benevolent— and Antonio Albóndiga was no exception. Sanctioned or not, he was a priest. Catholic, or not, the townspeople welcomed the procession. They looked forward to waltzing the statue or the painting of their beloved *Nostra Signora Nera* through the streets of their village.

At first Albóndiga had refused the villagers' request to honor their

Black Madonna. "You'll have to paint her face white before I'll approve of any procession for her," the priest cautioned.

The people refused to compromise on the color of Our Lady's skin.

"St. Luke carved our beautiful statue!" the baker's wife stated, invoking the sanctity of the blessed evangelist in order to hold fast to their convictions.

"If St. Luke carved the Madonna black, then she's black," Stefano the cobbler reasoned.

"The same goes for the painting," Annica insisted. "St. Luke created that, too!"

The Catholics in the village, lapsed or not, elected Constantino as their spokesman. "You go," they told the former shepherd turned expert basketweaver. "You tell *Padre* Antonio that the statute at the sacred well—and the painting behind the altar—must remain black."

Constantino did as directed, becoming the voice of his friends and neighbors. As was the custom of the village, he abided by the decisions made by the community's council. On a warm morning in early August he visited Antonio to plead their case.

"He was St. Luke, after all," Constantine said, conjuring every ounce of persuasive power he could muster. "And St. Luke was a personal friend of Jesus's mother, a man who, before he became a saint in God's glorious realm, had sat across the dinner table from the Virgin Mary in her simple home in Nazareth. With his own eyes St. Luke beheld the face of Jesus's mother, a face of deepest ebony. For us in Orune, that's proof enough to know that the Mother of God was dark-skinned and beautiful."

Antonio stared at the basketmaker and shook his head. "No. This cannot be," he said. "St. Luke didn't have a meal with the Blessed Mother. You're mistaken. And besides, he was a doctor, not a painter. Nothing you've said has convinced me to agree to your request. The Madonna's face must be lightened. She's a Catholic, after all. Not a heathen."

"You're making a grave mistake, *Padre,*" Constantino replied. "Please reconsider. It's a small request, you know. Who cares what color Her skin is? Perhaps she stayed too long in the fields planting barley with the farmers, and her black face is merely a sign of too much exposure to God's beneficent sun. You know how fierce our Sardinian summers can be."

Antonio shrugged, pondering the possibility. But he didn't change his mind.

Constantino tried another angle. "Or perhaps the smoke from all those countless candles lit to honor Her and Her Holy Son turned her face the color of soot. How can anyone deny the sanctity of thousands of prayers? Surely a worldly and educated priest like you can understand how many thousands of candles it must have taken to turn her once-alabaster skin the color of midnight coal."

Antonio nodded. "Yes. Thousands of prayers. Perhaps even tens of thousands."

"Hundreds of thousand of prayers, *Padre*, don't you think?" Constantino offered. "And think of how many churchgoers it would take to pile up that many prayers. Your congregation could be the biggest, most influential in the diocese."

Antonio narrowed his eyes and considered Constantino's remarks. The priest thought about the statue of Our Lady of Montserrat in his homeland. That Black Madonna was enshrined in a sanctuary near Barcelona. Pilgrims traveled from every corner of the country to kneel before her statue, lay their woes at her feet, ask her to intercede on their behalf with her son, Jesus. Many believed that the statue had been carved by St. Luke and then brought to Spain. But Antonio had grave doubts that St. Luke had been such a prolific artist.

He recalled a conversation he'd had with Martina about *Nostra Signora Nera.*

"Why is the Madonna black?"

"She's black because she's black," Martina had responded.

"Is she African?"

"Long ago, yes, she came from Africa," Martina told him. "But she's ours now. She belongs to our people and we love her."

"But why, if she's not of *this* place?"

"She's of *every* place," Martina explained. "In a time long before this town ever existed, or even long before they called this island Sardinia, or the name Africa was given to that continent beyond the sea, the people who lived in caves and on mountaintops, or the ones who lived in the forests or on the plains—they all called Her *Dea Madre*. Mother God."

"But God's not female," Antonio said.

"God is female!" Martina insisted. "And male, too. Why do you think otherwise?"

"Why do you insist that God is a woman?"

"I insist only that God be revered as the Originator of everything that is, was, and ever will be. To me, the Earth and all it contains emerged from God's womb, like babies come from the womb of human mothers, like lambs come from the wombs of ewes, like sparrows from the eggs of mother-birds. The first, original principal of all life is female."

"But what about the male? It takes his seed to also create life."

"That's true," Martina agreed. "Even so, every child lives for nine months in his or her mother's uterus. It's in that darkness that we first take shape and grow. That's why my allegiance is to the *Dea Madre* and *Nostra Signora Nera*. We all arise from darkness, and into darkness we all return."

"But God the Father created the Universe and everything that lives. He gave His only begotten Son to save the world."

"That's the way *you* believe. There are other ways—more ancient ways that my people remember and uphold."

The word "blaspheme" began to form on Antonio's lips, but his affection for Martina superseded his automatic reflex to dispute her claims and spit that word into her face. He thought about the Black Madonna of Montserrat in Spain and the rabid devotion of the Catholic pilgrims there, in the country of his birth. He didn't understand the depths of the passionate love people held for that dark-skinned statue.

SOME SAY the Montserrat Black Madonna had been hidden in a cave in the ninth century so the Moors couldn't destroy it. It had been discovered hundreds of years later by shepherds who'd seen a bright light and had heard heavenly music, which drew them to the grotto where the statue had been buried. When the Bishop of Manresa suggested the Black Madonna be moved to his town, the image refused to be lifted. Though small and easily carried, it suddenly became too heavy to hoist. The Virgin Mother had made her decision. She wanted to stay on Montserrat. And so four chapels were built to honor her—and eventually a monastery.

Albóndiga had personal acquaintances—priests, bishops, and parishioners—who'd been to Montserrat. They'd spoken of the undying devotion professed by the pilgrims they'd encountered there. He'd never made the trip from Seville to Barcelona to witness these things firsthand. He had no desire to do so. The darkness of her skin allied her too closely with the Jews and the Muslims, which unsettled him. He thought her a dangerous icon, a baser form of the more pure and holy Virgin Mary, the rightfully light-skinned Mother of God.

The pilgrims to Montserrat said that statue's blackness arose from the darkness of the wood from which it had been carved. Others suggested the Madonna's skin had grown soot-black from the innumerable candle flames—just as Constantino had suggested as the reason for the skin color of the Black Madonna of Orune. Antonio didn't care for the whys and the wherefores of how the Madonna's skin had lapsed from white to black—or if it had ever been white at all. He was not devoted to Our Lady of Montserrat. Black or white or any color in-between was less of a sticking point to Antonio than the heresy of proclaiming her a demi-god—or worse yet, a god unto herself. Give her what was rightfully due her as the Mother of Jesus. But never, ever deify her!

He knew the villagers of Orune were as enamored of their Black Madonna as the Spanish pilgrims who'd made the arduous journey to Montserrat. He vowed to do whatever was necessary to weaken their allegiance to their *Signora Nera*. A thin line separated these Black-Madonna-loving Catholics from their heretical Jewish and Muslim counterparts. He wouldn't stand for such nonsense in Orune. This was *his* parish now.

Antonio understood that Constantino was playing him for a bit of a fool. All of Constantino's talk about hundreds of thousands of candle soot-stained prayers was merely the basketmaker's attempt to humor the priest. But Antonio's desire for a greater influence in the village was overtaking his anger at Constantino's finagling. He wanted the final say in all parish-related concerns. He had no desire to have a debate on articles of faith and doctrine with the basketmaker, or anyone else. How dare this peasant assume he knew better than Antonio about how to save the lapsed Catholic souls of Orune! How dare he presume to usurp a priest's authority!

Albóndiga paced the floor, thinking of how best to answer. The basketmaker sat patiently at the table, watching the priest walk from one end of the room to the other. He quietly waited for Antonio's reply, certain that his reasoning had found a way to penetrate the priest's bravado while permitting him a way to salvage his ego and retain the upper hand.

Antonio found himself at a crossroads. If he remained stubborn and denied the villagers' request, he'd be true and faithful to the Catholic Church and to his own promise to combat heresy wherever and whenever it arose. He was, after all an authority on that matter. And he sensed he was the only true and verifiable Catholic in Orune. His refusal to comply with the town's request would also send an irrefutable message to the villagers. He was the one and only Shepherd of their Faith, the sole mediator on all things religious. While that option satisfied him greatly, something else—a niggling feeling of disquietude—demanded that he consider a compromise. Though he had his suspicions that the town was teetering on the edge of heresy, he was greatly relieved to have a Catholic ritual to perform. Even if executing that ritual meant parading through the streets with a statue of a Black Madonna.

He despised their *Nostra Signora Nera*, hated that the painting of Her looked down upon him every time he said Mass in his church. He'd seen the statue of Her once before, in the grotto shrine at the place outside of town, where the people had moved it years before. He'd been out for a walk one day in late June, seeking a break from boredom he often felt in town, seeking a reprieve from the town's taciturn residents. That day he came upon the niche, situated near a stream. He'd stooped to drink from the water, and when he stood his eyes had met the statue's coal-black gaze. Her nose was as flat and broad as an African's and Her skin as dark as tree sap. Antonio was certain that the statue was no mirror image of God's mother!

Still, to establish his rightful prominence as the village's pastor it might benefit him more to give in to the townspeople's desire to carry their Black Madonna through the streets of Orune for the Feast of the Assumption. Better to humor them and encourage participation in Catholic rites than to slam an iron fist down upon the altar and refuse their request.

Though he hated to admit it, he realized it was best to wave a flag of surrender to signal the end of this skirmish and set his sights on winning the bigger war. He consoled himself, thinking that if he gave in now he could stand firm later, when their wavering souls were more firmly in his grasp. Bending now was the right way to proceed, if only because it would give the villagers a reason to trust him. They'd begun to grow used to him and his ways, and had slowly eased their view of him as the resident *istranzu*. He'd grown weary of being their stranger. He was beginning to understand that he'd have no real and lasting authority over them unless they gave that authority to him. And that would be impossible until they fully accepted him into their community.

"All right," Antonio said, finally. "I agree. You can have your Black Madonna in the festival. But you must only carry the statue—not the painting."

Constantino smiled and rose from his chair, eager to tell the villagers.

"And only for this year!" Albóndiga added. "And only because there's no other Madonna within miles of here to replace the one you have. Next year our Madonna will be white. I'll make certain of that!"

ON AUGUST 14, the evening before the procession, three men from the village took two mules and a cart and set off for the grotto shrine at *Su Tempiesu*. There they loaded the statue of *Nostra Signora Nera* onto the wooden vehicle and carried it back to town, readying it for the parade.

A week before, Constantino and Brontu had applied their considerable carpentry skills to the task of building a tabernacle to hold the blessed statue during the street procession. They'd chosen sturdy holm oak branches that had fallen after a sudden windstorm in May. They'd trimmed the bark, then planed and sanded the limbs until they were smooth and ready. Carefully they carved delicate rosettes enlaced with myrtle leaves along the length of the four handles. In the sideboards they applied a design of spirals and stars, using clay and oil to make a paint of ochre red, which they used to complete their decoration. On the center platform, where the statue would be set, the men had etched a cornucopia overflowing with pomegranates, sheaves of grain and rounds of *pecorino* cheese.

The people of the community selected ten men from the village to be the statue-bearers and shoulder the tabernacle through the twisting lands and byways of town, ushering it to its final landing place at the church. Several of the village women had thoroughly cleaned and prepared the church, getting it ready to receive their beloved statue.

Nothing in Orune was discussed or decided without first convening the town's adult residents. For generations the men and women of the village had met at the round building constructed of stone that was reserved for such matters. In a circle, facing one another, the townspeople spoke their minds and expressed their concerns. Antonio had been present at the meeting to discuss the festival as well, sitting in the circle beside Martina, although a week before the meeting some villagers had protested when they learned that Shardana and Sarda had invited the priest.

"He's not a true member of the village," they complained. At the well, in the baker's shop, at the doorsteps of neighbors, in the tavern at the edge of the *piazza* they scoffed, *"Istranzu!* A stranger!"

The twin sisters understood that Antonio's status as a newcomer was still unsettling to many of their friends and neighbors. The sisters, too, were wary of the priest, ever on the alert for signs that the wolf inside him would lunge at their throats. While Antonio's foul nature had revealed itself from time to time, he'd mostly managed to keep his anger at bay. The twin healers continued to think it best to remain lenient towards him until his actions dictated otherwise. It was a precarious dance, they knew, but if the priest agreed to the villagers' request to venerate the Black Madonna, perhaps transformation was possible. Wasn't Antonio's Jesus capable of performing miracles? Still, they accepted the dissenting villagers' arguments and let them have their say. Without criticism they tempered each disapproving comment with a more accepting point of view.

"Yes, he wasn't born here. Yes, he doesn't know our ways," Sarda said. "But this is a good way for us to teach him our traditions."

Shardana added, *"Istranzu* he is, and so he will always remain. But he lives among us now. We can't change that. He can't alter the accident of his birthplace, nor can we. Though his bones are Spanish, maybe we can transform his heart, help him learn how to make it beat to a Barbagian rhythm."

So, it came to be that the minds and hearts of the dissenting villagers softened, and all agreed that Antonio would be welcomed at the decision-making meeting. Constantino was sent to tell the priest about the meeting and invite him to join the townspeople. Everyone had eventually come to accept the fairness of the invitation. Since the gathering was to involve matters related to the church, it was only equitable that the priest had a voice in the outcome. After all, Antonio had failed in every attempt to learn a trade other than that of the clergy; it was wise to support him in continuing the only work he seemed able to do. And it was best for the village that he find some worthwhile endeavor to occupy his time.

On the appointed meeting night, Antonio Albóndiga took his place in the circle. He thought the configuration odd—no one identified as the clear leader, no one presiding, no one keeping order and maintaining the agenda. Still, this unusual way proved sufficient, as the people wasted no time in speaking their minds, settling matters and moving on. Those in attendance, in their matter-of-fact way, chose the ten tabernacle bearers, then glanced at the priest seeking his opinion before confirming the selection. Antonio didn't personally know any of the recommended men, for few villagers other than the *majarzas* and their family members had yet to make an effort to befriend him. Still, he nodded his assent, and the proceedings continued until the business at hand had been finalized and the opinions of all in attendance had been heard.

ON THE MORNING of the fifteenth of August, Orune's young and old, whether Catholic or not, rose from their beds with great anticipation. They changed quickly from their bedclothes, then consumed their breakfasts. While adults sipped wine and chewed slices of hard-crusted bread, their children swallowed mouthfuls of warm sheep's milk and munched bits of cheese their parents had set before them. With satisfied stomachs, old and young combed their bed-mussed hair and stepped into their best shoes. There would be no work that day—no tending the sheep, who had been safely penned in sheepfolds across the mountainside, no sweeping of stoops or baking of bread, no weaving of baskets, no washing of clothes, or no dosing of medicines unless someone unexpectedly became gravely ill or broke a bone, or was otherwise in need of immediate, emergency care. This day the villagers had set aside for something beyond the realms of blood and sinew. This day was reserved for matters of the Spirit, something the people of Orune cherished as much as precious grain and sheep's milk.

On that morning *Padre* Antonio Albóndiga was to lead the villagers in a procession in honor of the *Assunzione della Barbagia Vergine*. The sweltering August sun beat down on the heads of men wearing their traditional black berets, women adorned in their traditional red scarves, children prancing in the alleyways on their way to the *piazza*, their dense, dark, curly hair uncovered and wild. Some of the men brought drums, others brought tambourines. Several carried *launeddas* in their strong arms, cradling the region's traditional triple-piped flute as if it were a precious infant—for this instrument, which the uninitiated would mistake for a scrawny bagpipe devoid of a sound bladder, was as dear to their hearts as their own children. Some of the women carried wooden beaded rosaries in their folded hands, others cradled baskets brimming with red field poppies and aromatic honeysuckle.

Shardana and Sarda joined their friends and neighbors. The excitement of a festival on a cloudless summer day made them joyful, and they wanted to dance and sing, eat and laugh with the people they loved, even though they didn't venerate the Catholic Mother of Jesus. In the solemn face of the Black Madonna they recognized their beloved *Dea Madre*.

The relentless sun beat down on the *launeddas* players as they placed their lips on the mouthpieces of their triple pipes, each finger of reed varying in length, and sucked in a bellyful of breath. From the depths of their lungs emerged strange and wild tones that hovered in the air. The tambourines shook and drums reverberated, announcing the official start of the procession.

With grave concentration, the marchers began. Through the streets they processed, huddled together like herds of solemn sheep, swathed in their black and white clothing, their thoughts silently ruminating through their minds. Although a mere six souls had been at Mass the Sunday before, everyone from the town gathered to join the parade that day.

The statue-bearers lifted the Black Madonna onto the wooden tabernacle, then heaved the long carved handles onto their bony shoulders. In unison they stepped in line behind the priest, who sprinkled holy water on the street before him, behind him, to his left and to his right. Antonio had taken the water from the well in the *piazza* an hour before the festival was scheduled to begin and had blessed it in the name of the Father, the Son, and the Holy Ghost.

Most of the festival-goers saw the procession as a break from the work and the worries of daily life. The chance to come together to feast on delicious food, to listen to soothing music and maybe enjoy a laugh or two with their husbands and wives, their children, their friends and neighbors, was rare

Not even the handful of Catholics among them focused on the religious nature of the event. No matter what their spiritual affiliation, all the villagers loved *Nostra Signora Nera*. She'd seen them through the lean years of drought and near famine, the difficult years of influenza, and a host of other ailments. She alone listened to their pleas for rain to quench the parched land. She alone listened to their prayers on cold winter nights when the fuel was running low and spring was still months away. She presided over the birthing of the lambs, the shearing of the sheep, the weaving of baskets, the baking of bread, the pressing of the olives into oil, the making of the cheese, the harvesting of crops and herbs, the birthing of children, and the passage from this world to the next.

Into *Nostra Signora Nera's* arms the men and women of Orune fled for comfort and for solace. There they were free to laugh and to cry. Of this truth they had great assurance and everlasting faith. Though the priest would never comprehend their devotion, they didn't need him to. While Antonio had set his sights on saving their souls, the people didn't seek his approval or his spiritual guidance.

Catholic or not, they were Sardinians first and foremost. They believed in the sanctity of water and stone, of blood and bone, of tears and laughter, immediate and intimate. Death and life were twins hovering over the shoulders of every man, woman and child. Fate would deal them what it chose, but in the end, the womb of Earth awaited every human—whether of noble birth or of peasant stock. *That* was the mystery the townspeople celebrated on August 15, the *Festa of the Assunzione della Barbagia Vergine*. In honoring Her, they honored their own assumptions into heaven, their own rising from the ashes of despair into the promise of hope.

The parade meandered through the streets, carried along by the ee-rie lilt of the flutes and the cadence of the drums that mingled with the mumbles of prayers and the singing of children. The tabernacle-bearers proceeded, carrying the Black Madonna over the cobblestone pathways through town. Three steps forward, two steps back, the statue-bearers moved in silence, on the waves of the music that surrounded them, remembering the ancient rhythms, celebrating the spiral, the circle, the nonlinear, cyclic revolutions of their world.

When at last the men reached the church and placed the Madonna in Her throne upon the central altar, the small sanctuary was jammed with festival-goers. People crowded in, shoulder to shoulder, singing songs to their beloved *Signora Nera*. Antonio Albóndiga blessed the crowd, prayed thanks to God the Father, and dismissed them all. Men, women and children disbursed into the streets to begin the eating and the dancing.

Some of the townspeople who'd been charged with hauling tables and chairs into the center of the *piazza* rushed to fulfill their duties and prepare the area for the festival activities. Others hurried home to collect the special food they'd been preparing all week long for the occasion. They returned to the *piazza* hauling platters of exquisite cheese, handcrafted by their shepherd husbands and sons. The plates overflowed with an assortment of *caprino, fiore sardo, semicotto, caglio, casagedu, casu marzu, pepato, pecorino sardo*, and *romano*. Soft curd and hard, sheep's milk, goat, or cow, slightly acidic or mild, aromatic or piquant, the platters contained something tantalizing to please every palate.

The women had outdone themselves preparing trays of sweets as well. Delicious sponge fingers, *sa voiardi*, sat beside platefuls of the shepherds' favorite *sebada*—two circles of pan-fried pastry dipped in honey, filled with ricotta, then fried to a sumptuous golden brown. Bowls of almonds, hazelnuts, and dried figs graced each table, as did baskets of *pane carasau*, the wafer-thin, crisp bread that was the main-stay of the shepherds when they were at their sheepfolds.

Though meat seldom blessed their daily tables, no festival would be complete without roasted and grilled *arrosti*. A wild boar had been caught and dressed, and that, along with a suckling pig, had been slowly rotating on spits over open fires for hours. Aroma from the searing meat filled everyone's nostrils. Their mouths watered, rousing their appetites.

Antonio had been unprepared for such opulence. For months he'd subsisted on fava beans and bread with the occasional bowl of soup, if Shardana or Sarda had enough to spare and were willing. A wedge of *pecorino* from time to time might appear on his doorstep, and just last month Sarda's unmarried daughter, Anna-Bella, had left a hen inside the church so the priest could enjoy some fresh eggs. When Antonio looked at the fine sweets and cheeses spread out before him on the day of the festival, his eyes grew wide with greed, his belly lusty with anticipation. Not since he'd left Alghero last May had his tongue been allowed to savor such delicacies. Gleefully he filled his plate and his stomach. As Antonio savored every morsel, his eyes noticed Basilio uncorking a bottle. The priest rushed to the shepherd's side, cup in hand, eagerly awaiting the first drop of red wine, anxious for the liquid to soothe his gullet.

When at last the eating and wine drinking were completed and all the villagers had enjoyed their fill, the amusements and merrymaking began in earnest. Giacobbe, the cobbler's son, engaged in a rousing game of *morra* with some of his young friends. One lad gestured with his right hand, thrusting several fingers into the air; another followed suit. The boys raised their voices, vying as they called out numbers.

"Five!" Giacobbe crowed.

"Eight!" his competitor retorted, shouting over his friend.

"No, it's three!"

"Ah! What bad luck!"

Over and over the boys played, fingers flashing, voices rising until one fortunate youngster guessed the correct number as the others crowned him the victor.

While the boys played, Constantino and Brontu settled their overstuffed stomachs with two bottles of *aquavite*, the aromatic *grappa digestif* they favored for such occasions. Other men passed a bottle of *liquore di mirto* from table to table. They preferred the liqueur distilled from the abundant wild myrtle that grew throughout the hillsides, thriving among the basalt plateaus and rugged mountains.

As glasses of aperitif were consumed, the dancing began. In Orune, no festival could be official without its *ballu tundu*, the ancient dance handed down from generation to generation. When the *launeddas* signaled the first note, husbands took the hands of wives, fiancés clasped the hands of their beloveds to encircle the fire pit that had hours before generously roasted the meats they'd consumed. The fire circle was transformed into the hub around which this wheel of merrymakers would turn.

Clasping hands, the men and women created an unending link. As the music played, the dancers swayed and moved. The circle of people turned in rhythm to the beat of feet against cobblestone, their cadence cradled in the familiar arms of the *launeddas'* notes.

Antonio clapped his hands and leapt to his feet, wanting to join in. He rushed to the circle, attempting to shoulder his way in. The dancers quickly cast him out, for tradition reserved this circle for men and women who were betrothed or married. The unexpected shunning, and Antonio's overindulgence in wine, *aquavitae,* and *mirto* caused him to stagger and fall to the ground, bruising his knee and his pride.

The *morra*-playing boys laughed at the red-faced priest. "So, the man who failed on his promise to teach us to read has misread the *ballu tundu!*" they shouted.

Antonio cursed them as he tried to steady his spinning head in order to rise to his feet.

"*Su tropu istorpia,*" Martina said, looking down on the top of Antonio's head. Too much disturbs. She offered her hand to the priest, who grabbed hold and stood up. She led him to a chair and touched his shoulder in comfort before rejoining her *ayaya* and her great-aunt, who'd both stopped dancing.

"How is he?" Sarda asked.

"His pride is wounded," Martina explained.

"As it should be," Shardana stated. "He's ignorant of our customs, yet he still wants to impose himself on our ways. Isn't it enough that we've opened our homes to him, cultivated a garden, re-instated this Catholic festival so he can feel useful and appreciated?"

"You're too hard on him, *Ayaya*," Martina said. "He's lost and can't find his way home."

"He's wandered too far from his Mother," Shardana snapped. "That's his problem!"

"Surely his heart will soften in time," Sarda appeased. "Once he learns our language and can understand our ways better. Surely, then, his heart will rein in his goat-strong head."

"I have every hope of that," Martina noted.

"Child, you're as gentle as your mother," Sarda said, smiling and stroking her grandniece's cheek. "You see good where others smell only shit."

Shardana replied, "The good in shit is revealed only in how well it composts."

"*Gemella*, have patience with the child," Sarda soothed. "She'll make you and her mother proud, you'll see."

"Grazia was no fool," Shardana insisted. "*Bona commenti su pani—* she was as good as bread. And she could decipher the twisted logic of evil as skillfully as our *Ayaya* Maredda. She'd have held no tolerance for his arrogant, vile disregard for the ways of others. Remember the sea-wolf, Martina. I can't warn you enough. There's something evil in Antonio."

"Maybe we're supposed to be the searing sun and burn the foul clouds away from his soul," Martina offered. "Maybe his bite is more dog than wolf."

"Maybe we're to be the thunderbolt that singes his considerable ego, the storm cloud that washes away the ill-will he harbors," Shardana replied. "*Furat chi benit dae su mare*. He who comes from across the sea is a thief. I warn you, Martina. Be wary of the priest. A scar on his face doesn't make him a shepherd any more than a festival makes him a tender of souls. Be kind to him, but be cautious."

Chapter 13

Ubuntu

"GOOD AFTERNOON," MARTINA SAID, smiling at the priest as he opened the door of his home.

Without returning the young woman's smile, Antonio nodded and ushered her inside. "*Recepción*," he said in his native Spanish.

"*Benénnidu!*" she corrected, pronouncing the greeting as it was spoken in her native Sardo.

Antonio shrugged. In spite of himself, he grinned. "I'm afraid old habits die hard."

"All the more reason for my visits," the young woman said. "Today, you must shuttle your mother tongue to the back of your brain, at least for a while, so we can continue your Sardo lessons."

"You're a fierce taskmaster," the priest joked, his typically cool countenance thawing in the presence of Martina's infectious warmth. "Are we allowed a cup of wine first?"

She set a basket on the table in Antonio's kitchen and took a seat. "If you'd like," she said.

The priest poured some wine for himself and his guest. "Cheese?" he asked, offering her slices of the *pecorino sardo* he'd arranged on a plate with several slices of bread.

"No, thank you," Martina said. "I've already eaten."

"What's inside your basket?" Antonio asked. "It's not my supper, I presume."

Martina laughed. "No. Not at all. Nor is it a slice of cake to sweeten your wine. I've brought some things to show you so when I teach you Sardo you can match the words to the objects they define."

She took a sip of wine, then reached inside the basket, removing what looked to Antonio like tangled weeds and gnarled roots from her garden.

"*Arbutu*," Martina said, pointing to a reedy plant that Antonio vaguely recognized from having seen clumps of it heaped beside Constantino's doorstep. "Asphodel. That's how you might know it. It's the plant the basketmakers gather, dry and use when they weave their baskets. Just like this one here. Constantino made this basket for me."

"*Arbutu*," the priest repeated.

"Good!" the young woman replied.

She pointed next to a small red flower. "*Atzagndda*. Red poppy."

"*Atzagndda*," Antonio said. "*Amapolas rojas*."

"Not Spanish," Martina scolded. "Use Sardo! How else are you going to be able to communicate with us?"

Antonio raised his eyebrows and grimaced. "I'm sorry, but it's difficult to stay focused. The flowers are so lovely."

"Don't tease with me, Antonio," Martina insisted. "I don't have time to play. This is a serious matter. If you aren't up to learning today, I'll come back some other day. I've many other things I need to do besides instructing you."

"I understand. Continue."

Martina held up a spring of rosemary. "*Tzípari*," she said.

Antonio sniffed the air, savoring the aroma of the herb. "*Tzipari*," he echoed.

Grabbing hold of a fennel frond, she announced, "*Tzichiría*." Pointing to a sprig of rue, she said, "*Curma*."

Removing a piece of paper and a bit of coal from her basket, she began to draw. Antonio moved closer to see the results of her artwork. "*Gròdde*. Fox."

"You're an artist as well as a linguist," the priest noted.

"In my work with Shardana and Sarda I must draw the herbs and roots we gather to make our medicines. But you distract me, *Padre.*"

The priest smiled, pleased he'd been able to derail her. He glanced at her hair, enjoying the way it lay softly around the edges of her face. He thought about reaching out to touch it, take one of the thick, dense tresses in his fingers. Instead he wrapped his fingers around the cup.

"*Bidduri*," she continued, moving her hand over the paper to render an image of another plant. "Hemlock."

Next she drew a wing, then the body of a bird. "*Irbírru*. Marten." Her hand continued to move swiftly over another section of the paper, sculpting lines until the image of a grasshopper emerged. "*Tilipírke*," she said.

Each time Martina spoke a word in Sardo Antonio repeated it, sometimes two or three times, hoping to etch the cadence of the consonants and vowels into his memory. The drawings helped him visualize the words, aligning the sounds to a picture of the thing itself so he could embed it into his brain. The dried plants she'd laid upon his table worked the same magic. He was beginning to be impressed by her facility for teaching. He hadn't expected this beautiful young woman to be so intelligent and creative, having lived her entire life in the hinterlands of the Barbagia, far from the hallowed halls of a university. Still, had she been a city dwelling girl she wouldn't have been admitted to an institute of higher education anyway. He found himself thinking that was a pity, even though he hadn't thought women capable of the discernment and analysis required of men like him, who had studied with learned professors.

"What would Orozco say?" the priest muttered, unaware that he'd spoken those words aloud.

"Who?" Martina asked, setting aside a bit of charred coal she'd been using to sketch her drawings.

"Oh, nothing," Antonio replied. "Just someone I knew in Alghero." "A friend?"

"Yes. He used to be—" Antonio averted her gaze, setting his sights on the plate of cheese sitting at the end of his table. He reached for a slice of *pecorino sardo* and placed it in his mouth. He let the creamy, pungent flavor melt onto his tongue before chewing.

"You must miss him," the young woman said, noting the glint of sadness that lingered over the priest's face.

He did miss Orozco—or, more rightly, he missed the collegiality of his time with the men he'd befriended in Alghero. The suppers of roasted meat and tawny wine. The sweet desserts of honey cakes. The robust Spanish wine, so pleasing to his palate, unlike the homemade version he was forced to slug in Orune.

"That was a lifetime ago," Antonio replied.

"It's only been since June," Martina responded. "What do you miss most about the city?"

"You've never been outside of Orune—"

"I've been to Nuoro twice!" she asserted. "And I often roam the countryside beyond the village with my *ayaya* harvesting herbs and roots for her pharmacy."

"Nuoro!" he laughed. "That's a sorry excuse for a city. Seville! Now that's a gem of a metropolis! Cultured, alive, full of beautiful women and intelligent men! Oh, and the air on a summer night. So fragrant— so seductive!" He paused, gazing out the window, dreaming of some other time and place. "Alghero isn't bad, as such places go," he continued. "It has a modicum of culture—all of it imported from Spain, of course. So the city isn't without its charms. Although there are too many *conversos,* if you ask me. They soil the air with their false faith. But as a child of the dusty mountaintops and a berg as sleepy as Orune, you wouldn't understand the vitality and allure of a city."

She frowned at his dismissal. "So what's a *converso?* And what's so great about Seville or Alghero that makes you pine for those places?"

He glanced at her and sighed. "You are naïve, aren't you. *Conversos* are Jews who've been baptized Catholic but lapse back into their heathen ways. In Spain, they know how to deal with heretics. They burn them. Or confiscate their property, unless they amend their ways."

"They burn people?" Martina asked, horror overtaking her voice. "How could they do such a thing?"

"To purify the blood of the faithful," the priest explained. "Only one true apostolic faith will unite Spain, and that faith is Catholic."

"But there are many ways to know God," the young woman asserted. "Surely as a priest you realize that."

"As a priest, I know there is only one Faith. Catholicism. Anything else is heresy."

Martina stared at Antonio's face, which had grown sour and tense. His eyes shone with a meanness she'd never before seen in him, or anyone else. The purple-red hue of the scar on his face underscored the foulness of his tone. It scared her, and she decided it was best to turn the conversation back to talk of the cities he'd mentioned. "And the cities, Seville and Alghero? What do you miss about them?"

"The night life," Antonio said, sighing. The tension in his face gave way to melancholy.

"You mean strolling around the streets after dark?"

He laughed. "No. Well, sort of. It's a term used to describe revelry. Things like parties, dinner with friends, dancing, you know."

"Like our *festas* here in Orune?" the young woman asked, trying to fashion an image in her mind that would satisfy her need to understand the world Antonio came from.

"Oh, grander than that!" Antonio asserted. "And not just on special occasions. I'd dine with my friends four or five evenings every week. Platefuls of roasted lamb, boar, sometimes chicken. And oh, the wine—" The priest's voice trailed off as if lost, trying to find its way back to Alghero.

"Every week!" Martina exclaimed. "What an extravagance. What a waste!"

"No! What life! What jubilation!" Antonio interjected. "Every day a celebration of the bounty of God's providence."

"You must have been very rich," the young woman noted.

"Not I," the priest replied. "But my friends. Yes! I knew many men in important circles. Men of grace and high social standing. Men of means. And taste. Men of wealth whose every word was heeded. People who could buy and sell all the villagers of Orune thousands of times over."

Martina's eyes grew wide. "What would that profit them?"

Antonio chuckled. "Oh, you're such a naïve girl. Money. Power. Authority. These are the things that keep the world spinning, my friend."

"*Su tropu istorpiat,*" Martina replied.

"You'll have to translate that for me," the priest said, smirking. He'd grown bored with his Sardo lesson and impatient with her insistence.

"Too much disturbs. That's what we say here in Orune. Too much is not always a good thing. In fact, it can be a vice. It can corrupt the senses, make one's mind and heart foggy. It can poison the soul."

"Hogwash!" the priest said. "Too much is paradise. God wants His children to be opulently blessed. In food. In wine. In romance!"

"And your priestly duties?" Martina asked. "In the city, did these revolve around feasts and revelry as well?"

"No, of course not. Occasionally we held a *festa* or two, but not every week. The life of a priest is not a royal adventure, Martina. It didn't suit me well. I would've fared better as a nobleman, a count or a viscount. A baron at the very least. But fate had other plans for me."

"And romance? Was that part of your ill-fated priestly life as well?"

"I'm still a man," Antonio asserted. "A cleric's collar doesn't erase that fact. There've been women, from time to time—" His eyes grew bright and he touched his fingers to his lips, remembering a kiss or the scent of a long-lost lover's perfume.

"And how did you end up here in Orune? So far from your feasts and your friends and your women?"

The sparkle dulled in Antonio's irises. His mouth tensed. He pursed his lips. "That's none of your business," he snapped.

"I think you're wrong," Martina said. "We deserve some explanation for your arrival. The guards, the mules. They dropped you off. Stranded you. Doesn't seem like the entrance of a nobleman."

Antonio slapped his hand against the tabletop. "Enough!" he yelled.

Martina gathered her drawings and the remnants of the herbs and roots she'd brought along for the language lesson. "It's time for me to go," she said.

"That's best," the priest noted. "Take your basket and your insolence and leave."

MARTINA'S HEART raced as she hurried through the *piazza* heading back to her home. Antonio's sudden, violent eruption disturbed her. She wasn't accustomed to someone being unable to rein in his anger. She would speak to Shardana about the priest's outbursts, find a way to better understand them, or at least learn how to avoid them. Perhaps this is what her *ayaya* had meant about Antonio and the sea-wolf.

Martina didn't like being the brunt of Antonio's ire. He repaid her offer of friendship with rudeness. He was such a surly man. What had happened to him in Alghero, or earlier still, in Spain, where he told her he'd grown up? What could have happened that would have soured his spirit, caused him to turn against her offer of friendship? She only wanted to lend him support, teach him how to speak the language of the people with whom his destiny was now linked. Why did that disturb him? Was it because she wasn't wealthy like his city friends? She couldn't offer him parties and fine foods, but she didn't want to. More and more she was beginning to understand that his heart was deeply troubled. He wore his gruffness like a cloak, protecting him from inclement weather. What would it take for him to surrender his heart, trust in her beneficence?

"*Subisonzu a connosches sos amigos,*" she muttered over and over, trying to calm her ruffled spirit. "A friend in need is a friend indeed. I'm his friend. Even if he can't return that gift yet."

Nearing her *ayaya*'s doorstep Martina recalled a word she'd often heard Shardana use when talking about people who presented a façade to the world that resembled a chestnut burr—all gnarly and spiked—in order to protect their softer interior from harm. "*Ubuntu.*" That was it! That was the word that often fell from Shardana's lips. "It means 'the point,'" her *ayaya* had explained. "The converging of all disparate things into a single essence. From humanity to others, my sweet child. That's how one must always live one's life. Giving love from one's center point. It's the only way to crack open the protective shell and savor the fruit of the chestnut that waits inside."

Ubuntu. Martina resolved to apply that term, and all it meant, to her interactions with the priest. If Antonio was too pig-headed, or if his soul was too eviscerated to receive her humble kindness, her actions wouldn't be in vain. Approaching him with compassion would strengthen her resolve to be a better person, one committed to the values her *ayaya* embodied. And, she prayed, it would melt some of the resistance in Antonio's heart, perhaps make him begin to dream of things other than city women with their succulent feasts and their men of power. Perhaps it might even tame his feral heart.

Chapter 14
The Punishment

IN THE WEE HOURS OF THE MORNING Giacobbe, the cobbler's son, crept into the church through an open window and landed feet first on the stone floor. He stared into the inky darkness, allowing his eyes to adjust. In the stillness he listened to hear if anyone else was in the sanctuary—*Padre* Albóndiga, perhaps, in the back room, where the priest dressed before Mass, or maybe a villager steeled away in the corner of one of the pews, kneeling fervently in prayer, or sleeping—though of course no one would be huddled in the church at that hour of night. All the townspeople were fast asleep in their beds, of this Giacobbe was certain. He'd heard several of them snoring as he'd walked past their houses just minutes before as he'd made his way along the narrow lane from his home to the *piazza*, then to the church. Still, the lad knew he must take every precaution so he wouldn't get caught.

With his eyes accustomed to the interior dimness, Giacobbe glanced quickly around the church, satisfied that he was wholly alone. To orient himself toward the altar he walked down the aisle between the pews, touching their rounded wooden edges. When he reached his destination he climbed on top of the altar and planted his dirty shoes on the woven cloth that ran the length of the stone tabletop—the very same woolen runner the boy's mother had made and presented to the priest the week before.

The lad recalled accompanying his mother, Annica, the morning she'd given that small gift to the priest. It was her way of thanking Albóndiga for re-opening the church after the long years of disuse. Even though she'd already donated the painting of the Black Madonna, she wanted to give the priest something that she'd made herself. "I didn't paint the Madonna," she explained to her son when he asked her why she was being so nice to the priest.

Although she didn't consider herself to be a staunch Catholic, she'd told the prelate that she loved the ceremonies and the singing. "I like the way the bells tinkle just before you raise the Host during the consecration," she'd said. "It's been a long time since I've been able to hear that sweet sound. Sort of reminds me of the ewes up on the hillside. That tiny tinkle—so friendly, so soothing."

Antonio had nodded, politely at first, but when the boy's mother had continued on about missing the smell of candle wax and the aroma of incense the priest's patience wore thin. Sensing his irritation, Annica recalled her original feeling about the priest, when he'd arrived in the village a few months before. She'd noted the twinge of anger in his heart back then, at the well that morning he'd arrived. And she'd been frightened by the omen the *majarzas* had told the villagers when they'd gathered in the community building to decide what to do about the uninvited visitor. What if he really was the evil wolf, sent to destroy them all?

Still, Albóndiga's temperament had mellowed since his arrival, and he seemed to be adjusting to the village and its ways. Thanks to Martina, he was trying to learn Sardo so he could talk to the villagers. That had to count for something. Instead of turning away from him that morning in the church, she decided to corral her mistrust and extend kindness toward Antonio, just as she'd seen Shardana and Sarda do many times before.

Annica had thanked the priest for allowing her son to be one of the boys selected to remove the debris and clean out the cobwebs, making the church building serviceable once more. The priest nodded, accepting the weaving as if a gift were expected. He didn't pause to note the fine handiwork; he'd failed to pay even a small tribute to the skill and artistry of the woman who stood before him, a wife and mother who, after long hours of tending to the needs of her son and her husband, had spent many evenings selecting the wool, then spinning the yarn for the weaving, creating a dye for the fibers with plant pigments and oils, choosing a design that she thought would please the priest. Annica had settled on an ochre-yellow hue for cloth's background. Black was the color she'd chosen for foreground design, weaving a cross into the center of the fabric.

When Antonio glanced at the woolen cloth Annica had set in his hands, he saw only a rudimentary rag. He thought the weaving lacked the finer, flaxen edges of linen, a material he was more accustomed to using to dress and finish the altars of the churches in Seville and Alghero over which he'd presided.

That day the boy had accompanied his mother to the church and had noted the slight downturn of the priest's mouth; had noticed, too, the way the priest's eyes never met his mother's. He remembered that the priest had failed to fulfill his part of the bargain to teach Giacobbe—and the other village boys who'd toiled to clear the church of dirt, scrub the building's stone floor to make it shine again—to read.

The boy's heart raced, thinking of the many ways this man looked upon the people of Orune with disdain. This man who'd been plopped into the center of their town, tossed away by two mule-riding disheveled guards one afternoon, was supposed to be the holy guardian of their souls. Though Albóndiga had lived among the people of Orune for months, he hadn't made even the slightest effort to befriend any of the villagers, except for Shardana's granddaughter, Martina. The boy thought it rude that the priest repeatedly turned down the villagers' offers to teach him a trade. He found it odd that the priest walked through the lanes and byways of the village mumbling to himself, as if he were possessed by some spirit—perhaps even the Devil himself, the horned god of evil the priest often spoke about from the pulpit on Sunday mornings during his weekly sermon.

One thing was clear to Giacobbe—Albóndiga kept his distance because he didn't want to become like them. Even at the festival honoring the Assumption of the Virgin the boy had noticed the way Antonio watched and stood back, snickering at the stories the villagers told of their ancient ways, trying to muscle his way into the *ballu tundu* when any fool could see by glancing at the dancers that the circle was open to only those who were already married or engaged to be wed.

Standing on top of the altar table, Giacobbe stomped his feet, then with his toe he nudged his mother's weaving to the cold floor. He held back the urge to howl, knowing that doing so would awaken the villagers and alert them to his plan. Instead he urinated on the bare, granite surface of the altar.

With his bladder emptied, he jumped to the floor and glanced at the painting of *Nostra Signora Nera*. He bent his head in supplication. "I'm doing this for you," he whispered to the Madonna's unflinching eyes. "For you and for all of us in Orune."

The lad made his way to the back room where the priest stored his vestments. Groping for the cabinets, he rummaged through drawers until he found what he was looking for. He grabbed the tattered alb and tore at the fabric, dropping its dismembered panels to the floor. "You shall pay for your disrespect," he said, his voice low and iced with anger. He squatted over the damaged garment and defecated, wiping his filthy anus with the edge of the priest's alb. When he was finished, he went searching for the Holy Communion hosts. Unable to locate the sacramental bread, he found the cup the priest used as his makeshift chalice. The boy grabbed it and spit into the chalice before smashing it to the floor, shards of clay splintering in every direction. No longer able to contain his glee, he laughed and let loose a howl of victory.

"Who's there?" A voice rose out of the darkness. It was a man's voice as fierce as the bandits who filled the stories his grandfather often told him during long nights around the pit fire as they huddled together for warmth in the small shepherd's hut on his uncle's *tanca*.

A figure approached, shielding his eyes with one hand and holding a lantern in the other, the light from the lamp illuminating the floor where the boy stood. Giacobbe turned to go, hoping to escape capture, but strong fingers gripped his shoulder, nailing him in place. The lantern's flame flickered, revealing the identity of his captor. Giacobbe stared into the man's searing eyes and trembled.

The priest's face smoldered with an intensity that scared the youth. He recognized the boy—he'd been one of the lads playing that game of *morra* at the festival, one of the youths who'd snorted and laughed at him when he'd fallen to the ground. Impudent brat!

Clutching the boy's shoulder, the priest used the lamp to spread circles of light around the area, revealing the boy's deeds. The stench of shit assaulted his nostrils.

"You filthy swine!" Antonio Albóndiga roared. "How dare you desecrate the house of God!"

"*Padre*—" the boy whimpered, "I—"

Antonio set the lamp on the floor, a thud echoing through the darkened church. Before another word could escape the lad's frightened lips the priest raised his freed hand, slamming it hard against the flushed cheeks of the young outlaw. Although the boy cried out in pain, the priest was determined to exact his revenge. Inside Antonio's head rang a rapacious hammering, shooting searing pain into his temples. The gnawing headache that often preceded his bouts of rage had returned. He raised his hand again, shoving his palm against the boy's head, slapping the lad's face, bruising his chin, bloodying his nose. He tossed the boy against the stone floor, kicking him without concern for his life. The youth curled into a ball, instinctively protecting his face and his belly, absorbing the priest's blows with his back and his buttocks.

With his rage spent, Antonio spat at the boy and cried out, "Go home to your mother and father, you ill-mannered weasel! And let them see what becomes of a fool who disrespects the House of the Lord."

Battered and bloodied, the boy crept along the cold stone floor, dragging his injured body as best as he could. Exhausted, he was unable to stand or run away. He trembled on the floor beside the door to the priest's dressing area and cried.

"Stay here and die for all I care," the angered priest seethed. "The world's better off without the likes of heathens such as you!"

WHEN THE ROOSTER crowed later that morning, Annica roused her husband, Stefano, so he could begin his day's work as the town's cobbler. She stoked the fire in their hearth and set a pot of water to boil to make the soup that would be their evening meal. "Giacobbe," she called to her son, "it's time to feed the chickens." When Giacobbe failed to reply the woman grew angry, thinking her son was being lazy, refusing to toss off his bedcovers to begin the day. "Giacobbe," she called once more. "Get up, now!"

Irritated at her only child's disobedience, Annica walked to the straw mat on the floor near the far corner of the room where her son slept. His blanket was pulled back and the mat was empty. Perhaps he's already feeding the hens, she thought, smiling at her son's initiative, chiding herself for having doubted his work habits. She went to the door and glanced outside to thank him, but he wasn't among the hens that pecked the dirt in her modest courtyard. "Giacobbe!" she shouted, loudly, insistently this time.

"Madonna, Annica!" Stefano declared. "You're going to wake the dead with your yelling. Let the boy be."

"He's gone!" the woman cried out.

"Gone?" Stefano grunted. "Where could he have run off to? Orune isn't so vast a place that we could lose our son, Annica. Maybe he decided to spend the night up at the *tanca* with his grandfather. You know how much he loves the shepherd's life."

"No, it's not that. He's in trouble," she said. "I can feel it in my bones." She made the sign of the cross, touching her fingers to her forehead, her heart, her right shoulder, then her left. "*Madonna mia!*" she cried.

"Relax, Annica," Stefano said. "If he hasn't come home in an hour to help me with the cobbling, then we'll send Martina to the hills to look for him. Most likely he's taken off with the shepherds, if not last evening then early this morning. You know how he longs to be one of them."

"I pray that he's with your father and your brother," Annica said. "I pray my intuition is wrong this morning."

GIACOBBE WOKE with a stabbing pain. His face was caked with dried blood, his body heavy with aching. When he opened his swollen eyes he saw the cold stone floor of the church. Slowly he recalled the priest's harsh hands on his face and back, the sharp words he used to disgrace the boy in the middle of the night when he'd snuck up behind him and caught him in the middle of his acts of mischief.

Giacobbe was unable to move, and he knew his parents must be worried about him. He was only eleven and not used to spending the night away from home, except when his parents gave him permission to stay at the sheepfold with his relatives. He wanted to call out, but his ribs hurt, preventing him from inhaling deeply. How was he to get home, he wondered? How was anyone to find him? It wasn't Sunday; no one would be coming to the church for Mass.

He glanced at the image of *Nostra Signora Nera* and sent a prayer toward her staring gaze. *"Madre mia,* oh Most Holy One, help me find my way home."

"Your prayers are futile."

The voice that addressed him belonged to the man who'd beaten him. The boy closed his eyes and silently shouted at the Madonna, *You who are the protector of the weak and the oppressed! Save me now and I will forever be your willing and faithful servant.*

"I'd hoped you'd died," the priest said. "But I see that I have to deal with you more rigorously now. Your crimes are brutal. Your punishment should be brutal, too."

He straddled the boy, a broomstick in his hand, intent on flogging him again. He raised his arm and whacked the stick across the youth's arm. The boy howled. The priest swung the stick high into the air, concentrating all his might into continuing his gruesome task. He dropped his arm to hit the lad, landing the butt of the broom across the boy's legs. A terrifying cry raced from the boy's twisted mouth.

From the back of the church a voice rang out. "Stop! Don't harm the child!"

Antonio turned to face Constantino. The priest had forgotten that it was the basketmaker's habit to visit the church every morning at seven for a half-hour of prayer before he began his day. Had the circumstances of this morning been different, Antonio might have invited Constantino over for a bite of bread and a slice of cheese after the basketweaver's early morning meditation, which the priest occasionally did, for he'd taken a liking to Constantino. His aim was to gain the basketmaker's confidence, perhaps even befriend him. He was always in search of allies, should a time arrive when he might need one in town. But this day Constantino was an interloper, a damn nuisance, not a friend whose loyalty the priest had hoped to cultivate.

"Get out of here, Constantino," Albóndiga warned. "This is a church matter, and it shall be handled by the church."

"You've beaten the boy severely. Whatever retribution you sought is satisfied by now."

"I've only just begun," the priest scowled.

"I'll have to stop you, then," Constantino replied. "That's not how we mete out justice in our village. If the boy has done you wrong, he'll be tried by the community and a proper and fair punishment will be leveled against him."

"Oh, he's indeed done something wrong!" the priest roared. "Take a look around you, Constantino. He's urinated on the altar, he's smashed my chalice, he's torn my vestments and shit on them as well. He's blasphemed the Lord Jesus, and I will not tolerate that!"

Constantino's eyes scanned the evidence the priest had offered, then glanced at the boy, huddled against the cold stone trembling in pain and fear. "Yes, he's wronged you, *Padre*. And I can assure you he'll be made to atone. But not in your way. It has to proceed in our way."

The basketmaker heaved the wounded boy into his strong arms. "I'll take him to Shardana and Sarda so they can fix him up," he told the priest. "Then the villagers will gather to determine his punishment."

The priest blocked Constantino's exit.

"Step aside, *Padre*. You've done enough harm."

In Constantino's dark eyes Antonio saw a fierceness he didn't recognize, a boldness that the basketmaker had never before revealed. The priest had thought him to be harmless, a man more at ease with reeds and lambs than with humans, and more gentle and passive than the animals he used to tend. On that day the priest discovered that beneath Constantino's calm exterior lay a wild allegiance to his people and their customs. Though modest and humble, Constantino wasn't timid. Though age had stolen much of his youthful beauty, he could be as ferocious as any of the outlaw bandits that roamed the untamed landscape of Sardinia. He was *belli, feroci*, and *prodi*. Beautiful, fierce, and proud.

SHARDANA AND SARDA wept when Constantino set Giacobbe on their table. The boy's bruised body was purple and swollen; blood stained his face. He cried out when the women tried to gently wash his cuts, apply salve to his injuries.

"I don't care what the lad did," Shardana said. "No one deserves to be treated so savagely."

"What if he'd desecrated the water temple at *Su Tempiesu* in such a disrespectful manner?" Sarda asked. "What would you've done?"

"I would have taken it up with the community council and demanded restitution," Shardana replied. "He would have suffered the consequences of his actions. But he wouldn't have been violently harmed as he's been."

When the boy was cleaned and his wounds cared for he rested and slept, exhausted from the ordeal. The *marjazas* sent Martina to Annica and Stefano's home to tell them that Giacobbe was at Shardana's house.

Martina raced through the lane until she reached the cobbler's house. She knocked quickly, loudly. Annica opened the door, Stefano at her side.

"Come quickly," she told them. "Giacobbe's been injured."

"Was there an accident at the *tanca?*" Stefano asked, his heart pounding with fear.

"No, at the church," Martina replied. "An incident—a problem—come, you'll see—"

"What kind of problem?" Annica asked, her eyes tight with worry.

"Antonio—" Martina stammered. "His headaches—he gets blinded by the pain—"

"The priest? He's harmed our son?" Stefano asked. He clenched his fists.

Martina nodded. "Come. Hurry. My *ayaya's* waiting."

They ran back through the streets, arriving at Shardana's doorstep out of breath and frantic. Annica flew to her son's side, weeping when she saw how badly he'd been injured. "I'll rip out that demon-priest's eyes!" she yelled, trembling.

"You'd be no better than he," Stefano reminded her, reaching out to comfort his wife.

"He's nearly killed our Giacobbe. How could I forgive such evil?"

"With the compassionate heart you're known for, Annica," her husband soothed.

"No! My heart can't forgive this," she said, sobbing. "He's just a boy. I don't care what kind of harm he did to the priest or to the church. Antonio's an animal. He's got to be punished for this! Where's your outrage? He's your son, Stefano! Your only child!"

"I'm as furious as you are," Stefano assured. "But tearing the priest limb from limb will serve nothing. Revenge is ugly. Our boy will live and be well again. The *majarzas* will see to that. As for Antonio, we'll have our justice. The community will deal with him. Swiftly and firmly."

LATER THAT DAY Shardana, Sarda and Constantino called an emergency town meeting to tell the villagers about the incident at the church. Wives and mothers set aside their chores to attend, leaving their younger children in the care of their older siblings and cousins. Shopkeepers closed their stores for the duration of the gathering. Shepherds were summoned from their *tancas*. Brontu and Basilio left their sheepfold in the capable hands of Giovanni and Isidoro so they could represent their families in this urgent matter. Annica had stayed home to tend to Giacobbe, but Stefano was there to represent his family. So was Antonio Albóndiga.

After the people gathered and settled into the community circle, Constantino began. He described the scene he'd witnessed that morning, described, too, how he'd carried the boy to his wife and sister-in-law for mending. The villagers listened to the basketweaver's tale and noted the anguish on Stefano's face.

"We're sorry for your family's pain, Stefano," Constantino said, speaking on behalf of the rest of the villagers. Turning to Antonio, he said, "What do you have to say in your defense, *Padre?*"

Antonio rose from his seat as if preparing to deliver a sermon at the lectern during Mass. Resolutely, he gestured with his hand, still swollen and bruised from the beating he'd give the boy hours before. With urgency and vigor he described in vivid detail each of Giacobbe's vile deeds. The group listened to Antonio's outrage at the boy's behavior. "It is a sacrilege!" he declared. "A despicable, heathen action that deserved a heavy hand."

Some of the villagers nodded in agreement. Others shook their heads in disbelief that Giacobbe could have done such a thing. All the villagers empathized with the priest's anger over the disrespectful manner in which the boy had destroyed the sacred things. They listened, also, as Shardana and Sarda talked about the boy's condition when Constantino brought him to them.

The *majarzas* detailed the wounds the priest had inflicted. Constantino reaffirmed the state he'd found Giacobbe in when he'd happened upon the boy and the priest in the church earlier that morning.

Finally, Giacobbe's father spoke in his son's defense. "The punishment was too harsh!" Stefano exclaimed. "His actions were unacceptable, I agree. But it was mischief, not evil, that caused him to behave in that way. He's just a boy. He should be reprimanded. But not beaten nearly to death!"

One by one the villagers agreed that the youth's actions were wrong and harmful and that he should atone for them, set right all the things he'd disrupted. They thanked Antonio for his input, expressed their sorrow at the priest's loss and humiliation, then dismissed him to confer among themselves as to the appropriate punishment they'd levy upon Giacobbe.

"I should have a say in the sentencing," the priest insisted.

"You've already passed judgment and meted out punishment," the villagers told him. "The rest is for our community to decide."

In the priest's absence the townspeople voted to conscript the boy into being the priest's assistant for six months. Giacobbe would stand at the altar, serving Antonio when he said Mass. The priest had been complaining about not having anyone to help during the consecration, and so the villagers thought it fitting to appease him in this way. They also reasoned that if Antonio had to work beside Giacobbe, he'd come to see that the lad was not vile and unredeemable, as the priest had presumed. The boy was merely lacking in proper judgment, unable to rein in his impulses.

Some of the villagers voiced concern that the priest would turn against Giacobbe, if the lad was required to serve the man who'd beaten him.

"The boy, at all times, should be accompanied by Stefano when he goes to the church to assist at Mass," Constantino suggested. "That way, when he's in the presence of the priest he'll be under his father's protection."

"What about the priest?" Shardana asked. "What punishment does he receive? He should be reprimanded for his heinous actions against Giacobbe."

Murmurs raced across the room. Many of the others had wondered the same thing, but they'd been afraid to broach the topic.

"He should pay for his actions as surely as Giacobbe," Shardana insisted. "What example do we set for the boy if we allow the priest to go unchastised?"

"You raise a valid point, Shardana," Brontu agreed. "The priest should atone for his actions, too."

The others concurred, and talk began of how best to proceed, for the villagers knew Antonio would be furious once he learned about their decision. He'd already proven he could be violent, using his fists rather than his reason to solve problems. They debated for an hour until they finally arrived at a resolution. Antonio Albóndiga would be sentenced to clean the chicken coops of all the townspeople for the next six months. "Shit begets shit," they pronounced. Satisfied, they summoned the priest back into the room.

The assembled council informed Antonio of Giacobbe's assignment. As they suspected, his desire for vengeance was raw and uncontained.

"That's no punishment! That's an insult to me and to Christ Jesus," the priest scoffed. "Throw the bugger in jail, or at least flog him in public. You're being too lenient!"

"He's already been flogged, Antonio," Sarda stated. "You've seen to that."

"This is our communal decision, *Padre*," Basilio added. "You have to live with it."

"What's more, *Padre*," Constantino said, "we believe your actions against the boy also warrant a reprimand."

"That's outrageous!" the priest shouted. "I've done nothing but defend the House of the Lord. What that lad did was blasphemous!"

"Nonetheless, your actions were abhorrent," Brontu stated. "You nearly killed the boy. We can't allow you to live among us if you don't pay for your crime in some way."

"Crime? I've committed no crime!"

"Silence!" Shardana stated. She rose. Standing face to face with Antonio, she stared into his furious eyes.

"You came into this community uninvited," she began. "We opened our hearts and our homes to you. Even when it was difficult to do so. You show no respect for our customs and our ways. And you would have murdered that child had Constantino not interceded. We live by a moral code here, Antonio. A code of justice with compassion; a code of human equality and of the belief that we're all tied, one to the other, as oxen are yoked together. Either you abide by the council's decision, or you leave Orune immediately."

The priest clenched his fists. He was unaccustomed to being spoken to in such a tone and manner, especially by a woman. He narrowed his eyes and glared at her. When he opened his mouth, ready to spew vile, slanderous words, she pointed her finger at his nose. He stopped, suddenly fearful that she might cast a spell upon him, for he'd secretly thought all along that she was a witch, not a healer. For all he knew she'd sent a demon to possess him that morning, igniting a fire inside him that burst into the headache and marched across his temples, throwing him into a fit of rage. For all he knew, it was Shardana's heathen spirit, not he, who'd beaten the boy.

"The choice is yours, Antonio. Go or stay."

"If you stay, you must clean the chicken coops for six months," Constantino said, reaffirming Antonio's punishment.

Antonio let loose a crazed laugh. "How dare you insult my dignity! Such a crass assignment for a man of my birth and standing!" He turned and swiftly left the room, calling out, "You've not heard the last from Antonio Albóndiga."

Fuming all the way back to the church, Antonio vowed to find a way to persuade his former friend, Archbishop Orozco, to reinstate him at the Church of *San Francesco* in Alghero. Surely he'd served long enough in this Godforsaken hinterland to warrant an absolution for whatever sins the archbishop thought he'd committed. Not even Andres Orozco could hold onto his grudge in the face of the depth of audacity that Antonio was now encountering. Surely by now that incident with the magistrate, Frederico Bautista, had blown over. The knife wounds Antonio had inflicted were undoubtedly healed, and if a scar remained it would have faded to a mere crooked line by now. If he could only dine on a bowl of fish stew and a plate of roasted wild boar with the archbishop, the magistrate, and Count Carmago like he'd done on countless nights when he lived in Alghero. He fervently believed that his former allies would come to his aid and liberate him from his current prison.

He resolved to write to the archbishop, detailing Giacobbe's vandalism of the church, the lame punishment exacted against the boy in payment, and the inane sentence the villagers had placed on the priest. He'd describe Shardana's sorcery, too. He'd inform them that the spell she had cast on him had instigated the entire episode. Armed with this irrefutable evidence of heresy, Antonio knew Orozco and the others would intervene. Without hesitation Orozco would heed his request—he'd understand the severity of the priest's situation and do all that he could to allow Antonio to return to Alghero—and if not Alghero, then perhaps his beloved Spain.

To guarantee the success of his petition and to ensure his swift exit from Orune, Antonio decided to also request a reprieve from the archdiocese in Nuoro, just in case Orozco refused his plea. It was best to have a backup plan. If Antonio could convince someone in a position of authority at Nuoro, someone higher up in the hierarchical ranks than Orozco—a cardinal, perhaps—to have a letter delivered to Alghero on Antonio's behalf, Orozco would have to rescind the exile he'd inflicted on Antonio.

Perhaps, he reasoned, it would be prudent to plead his case in person. If he traveled to Nuoro, the authorities there would see he was a reasonable man, sentenced to a life beneath his considerable talents. He decided to take short trip to Nuoro and discuss his situation with the archbishop's prelate. That was the best way to begin his exit from this Satan-loving region.

Barbarians! The Romans were right! The Barbaricini are all barbarians! The God-fearing Catholic leaders in Nuoro would surely heed the dire circumstances of his plight—and his request to be relocated would be granted, thus ending his confinement in the hellish mountains of Sardinia.

Chapter 15
Limpieza de Sangre

IN SEPTEMBER, THE MOUNTAINSIDES and forests near Orune were blanketed in gold and red and green. The dense, dark leathery leaves of the majestic holm oaks tumbled to the ground, coasting on the autumn breeze. Some landed on the thick, bristly-haired backs of wild *cinghiali* that rooted the woodlands in search of food, their sturdy hooves trampling the undergrowth of the carpeted forest floor as sparrow hawks, partridges and goshawks circled the blue sky above them. Below, wild hares hopped among the grasses, going about their business. Small, sable-colored Sardinian deer foraged on the leaves of strawberry trees and the needlelike tips of rosemary hedges. Other animals scurried through thick patches of lentisk, myrtle, pink cistus, heather, holly, and hawthorn. The hillsides blazed with red poppies, oleander, and yellow broom signaling their final glory before the impending winter. Eternally green stands of juniper and cypress presided over the burst of autumnal color that would all too soon turn a dull wintry brown.

Two weeks before the mid-September autumn equinox, on an early Sunday morning, Sarda and Martina walked the hills and forests harvesting medicinal herbs and plants to restock their apothecary before the snowy season settled in.

Earlier that morning when Sarda asked if Shardana was ready to go on their harvesting expedition, she'd snapped, "No! Not today. Go by yourself. Or take Martina with you."

Sarda frowned and nodded. The mood inside her sister's small house had grown too uncomfortable to accommodate the three women, so without a word Sarda motioned to Martina to grab her basket. The younger woman complied and the pair set off, neither one mentioning Shardana's dourness.

Martina had never seen her *ayaya* so irritable—not even when she was deeply mourning Grazia. Lately Shardana had been snapping at Martina's slightest missteps, impatient with her when she couldn't re-call the recipes for their tinctures and ointments, even though Mar-tina's memory lapses were infrequent. She only made mistakes when she was tired from having worked a long day tending to their patients followed by an evening spent tutoring the priest in Sardo.

Sarda and Martina walked to the hillsides in silence. From time to time they'd stop and expertly identify and select the specimens they needed, filling the baskets Constantino had crafted for them from the wild, long-stemmed asphodel that flourished in the upland pastures. Once in a while one of the women would pause and glance into the watchful eyes of a deer or a fox before continuing on. Around them hummed bands of industrious bees flying to and from their woodland hives.

The women absorbed the beauty, soaking up the scents of autumn, allowing the forest's earthy aromas and its rustic palette to soothe their worried hearts, for in addition to adjusting their temperaments to ac-commodate Shardana's recent erratic moods, they had both spent many days and nights pondering the meaning of the events that had trans-pired in the village since the priest's arrival in June. Both wondered if the priest's latest behavior towards Giacobbe had triggered Shardana's moodiness. Martina didn't want to upset her great-aunt or speak poor-ly of her *ayaya*, but she needed to settle her heart about it all, so she overcame her hesitancy.

"*Ayaya* seems preoccupied," she said. "Do you think she could be fretting about Antonio and all that's happened since his arrival?"

"There are many things on her mind these days, Martina. Don't fret. She'll work it all out. She always does. Eventually. Until then, let's just give her some room and time to see her way clear of it all."

Martina nodded, then asked, "On Sunday, would you join me at Mass? I know that isn't anything that interests you, but I'd be grateful if you'd come with me anyway. I know *Ayaya* doesn't approve. But you understand how much I love the ritual. The lyrical, magical tones of the Mass said in Latin. I love the singing, too. And besides, I'd like you to see that Antonio isn't a complete ogre, although how he treated Giacobbe was unforgivable. He is trying to fit in here."

Sarda nodded. A slight smile crossed her lips. Although she knew Shardana wouldn't want her to encourage Martina's growing interest in Catholicism, she also understood that Shardana would never prevent her granddaughter from following her heart, even when doing so contradicted everything that Shardana believed. While Sarda shared some of her twin's concerns about Martina's growing devotion to the priest, her great-niece's request about accompanying her to Mass seemed harmless. Sarda did appreciate the music, and admired the ceremony evoked during the Catholic ritual, even though she would never adopt the Christian ways.

She thought it a good idea to observe the priest's actions with his new altar assistant, Giacobbe. She wanted to ensure that the boy wasn't being harmed under Antonio's tutelage.

WHAT MARTINA didn't tell her great-aunt was that she also attended Mass because she held an inexplicable, growing fondness for the priest, although she knew his actions were often gruff and sometimes violent. She certainly was horrified by his treatment of Giacobbe, and had she been old enough to participate in the village vote on the matter, she would have thrown her support for the punishment inflicted. She knew something festered inside Antonio. Still, sometimes, when he was caught off-guard smiling at the song of a bird or gazing off into the hills, Martina noted that a content, almost gentle countenance claimed his face. At those times of surreptitious glimpsing she knew his spirit wasn't devoid of goodness, and she hoped through kindness to coax more of that tenderness to the surface.

Shardana's estimation of Antonio had permanently soured after his brutal actions against Giacobbe. Until then she'd exhibited more patience, cautioning others in the village against ostracizing the priest, urging compassion, asking them to give Antonio a chance to fit in.

"He's doing the best he can," she had emphasized. "Think of how strange you'd feel if you'd been taken from your home and plopped down in the middle of an unfamiliar place, filled with faces you didn't know, a language you couldn't comprehend. Give him time. He'll come around."

Even though the image of the ominous sea-wolf from her dream always lingered at the back of her mind, she had believed her own words until the priest's actions had eroded her convictions. His cruelty toward Giacobbe erupted from something more sinister than the excruciating headaches Martina was quick to point to as a reason for Antonio's vile behavior. It was true that of all the villagers, Martina knew the priest the best. She spent more time with Albóndiga, teaching him Sardo, taking walks with him in the hillsides, concocting medicines to ease the culprit headaches when they flared. Still, Shardana couldn't shake the feeling that gnawed the pit of her stomach every time she thought of Antonio Albóndiga. If he'd been so vicious toward Giacobbe, when would his ire rain down upon her granddaughter?

SHARDANA TOOK some comfort in knowing that Martina had more insight and better judgment than Giacobbe. She was both older and less prone to excitable behavior than the boy. Antonio would have less cause to react violently towards Martina, even though Shardana knew that hostility rarely had anything to do with the actions of the one being victimized and everything to do with the aggression of the abuser.

In some ways Antonio and Giacobbe were alike. The lad had always been mischievous, pulling pranks on the other children, sometimes stealing eggs from his neighbor's hens. He harbored a restlessness that wasn't yet tamed by the love and attention of his parents or the other members of the town, for each villager looked after the needs of their friends and neighbors in their own ways, as best as they could.

Everyone in the village knew that Giacobbe longed to be a shepherd, live in the hills with his uncle and his grandfather, but the boy's father, Stefano, had refused to allow his son to take up the trade. He wanted Giacobbe to apprentice with him, learn to repair shoes so he could become the village's cobbler after Stefano passed away. Giacobbe didn't want to be a shoemaker. He often sneaked off to the *tanca*, staying days on end in the mountain pasturelands beside the sheep, shirking his household chores. Annica had tried to persuade Stefano that sheep's milk was in the boy's blood, but her husband wouldn't listen. "He is my son! He will carry on my trade."

Time and again Shardana had tried to help Giacobbe focus his considerable energy on useful matters, asking him to help her with chores around her house, sweeping the stoop, washing off the tables, rinsing out her medicinal jars, fetching water for her from the village well. Sometimes he'd agree and she'd reward him with a slice of *pecorino sardo* and a bowl of soup or a piece of *pane frattau*. Over time the boy had learned to subdue his cravings for tomfoolery, although he didn't entirely quell his love of wreaking a bit of havoc. A few days before he'd desecrated the priest's sanctuary Sarda said she'd seen Giacobbe tossing pebbles at the church windows, trying to nick the glass. Antonio had intercepted the lad, scolding him and sending him on his way. The interaction must have triggered Giacobbe's desire for revenge. Two nights later he defiled the place.

Before Antonio's arrival, life in the village had not always been idyllic, but for the most part people had lived in peace with one another, trusting that when conflict arose it would be resolved quickly and with kindness. Antonio had stirred up a squall of uneasiness in the villagers that wasn't readily calmed. Factions were beginning to form. Neighbors bickered with one another about whose eggs were the freshest, whose sheep the hardiest, whose baskets the strongest. Mistrust was beginning to surface. And everyone felt a growing undercurrent of discontent.

"It's the priest," the baker's wife asserted one day at the well with other village women. "He's brought bad blood to our town. It's a wonder the water is still drinkable. It's only a matter of time before the grain withers in the fields and the ewes' milk dries up. I'd bet they'll be no birthing of lambs next February. He's a poison that kills everything."

INSIDE THE DIMLY LIT church, Sarda and Martina sat in the first row of pews on the right side of the altar. Watching the priest recite the prayers and incantations of his sacrament, Sarda noted that the ceremony was not unlike the rituals she and the others performed at solstices and equinoxes and the cross-quarter holy days in between—although when the weather permitted Sarda and Shardana would praise their God outdoors, not inside a stone building. They preferred to celebrate beside a stream, an outcropping of rocks, or a grove of trees, sometimes in a cave or near the water temple at *Su Tempiesu*. In those places the women most strongly felt the presence of their God, the *Dea Madre*.

As the priest raised his voice and lifted the small circle of bread into the air, Sarda wondered why he faced the congregation with his back, not his eyes. She found it peculiar and sad that he turned away from the people gathered to witness his rite. Like a door shut against them, Albóndiga stood sentinel between the villagers and God; only he could unlatch the gate, allowing entry into the sacred realms where Jesus resided. Sarda believed that God resided in the soul of every living being. One didn't need an interpreter to commune with Her. Perhaps, Sarda reasoned, this cloistered, cordoned-off Catholic God was as lonely as Antonio, equally separated from the blessed mysteries of all He had created.

Martina began to whisper prayers, genuflecting, bowing her head in reverence. Sarda tried to follow her grand-niece's lead, but failed. Her body refused to cooperate. Instead she sat back in the pew and curiously observed the young woman's actions. Should Martina choose to follow the Christian way, Sarda realized that Shardana's heart would most likely break, unless Martina found a way to merge the ancient ways with the Christian rites as Grazia and others in their family had done. Still, Sarda trusted in the deep love and respect her twin held for Martina. She trusted that the bond between *ayaya* and granddaughter would prevail. Sarda breathed more easily remembering that blood and Spirit were too strong to sever that ancient and holy link.

DURING THE MASS Giacobbe excelled in his service to the priest. The boy held the cloth Antonio used to wash his hands before he began his communion rite, folding it neatly and with great care when the priest no longer needed it. He stood attentively throughout the service, glancing from time to time at his father, Stefano, who sat in the second pew. Each time Giacobbe caught Stefano's eye relief washed over his face, his shoulders relaxed, and the surety of safety sunk into his bones.

For his part, the priest had unexpectedly taken a liking to the lad, seeing in him traces of his own unbridled, youthful self. The pair possessed identical willfulness and a penchant to be contrary, which Antonio took for a sign of intelligence in the youth. The priest concluded that Giacobbe must be woefully underserved by this village, isolated in the mountains since birth, with no chance of seeing the world or exploring its remarkable cities. Faced with nothing but shoemaking or sheepherding in the hillsides and the daft customs of a near-primitive people, the lad must surely be aching to break free, just as Antonio had been when he was eleven. Where he'd dreamed of a future in the realms of great men and great ideas, coffers of silver and gold, a beautiful wife on his arm, perhaps a seat in the government, he'd been consigned to the sphere of baptisms and funerals, weddings and confirmations. He felt condemned to a life not of his choosing. Perhaps Giacobbe could flourish under Antonio's direction. Perhaps he might induce the boy to run off to Nuoro in a few years and get an education—although the priest wasn't sure if that was possible, as neither the boy's parents nor Antonio had the means to finance that extravagance.

While the lad endured his penalty without complaint, some days even displaying an affinity for the tasks, the same could not be said of the priest and his community-induced penance. Although Antonio had complied, cleaning out the hen coops throughout the village, he did so begrudgingly and with a great deal of complaining. He squawked as much as the chickens whose roosts he cleaned, until the women he was consigned to assist could no longer endure his complaining or tolerate his sour attitude. One by one they granted him amnesty, offering him a slice of bread and a chunk of cheese in exchange for his silence. In this roundabout way Antonio wended his way into the hearts of some of the villagers, who began to see him as more than a crusty curmudgeon, in spite of the contrary viewpoint expressed by the baker's wife at the well.

As his language lessons with Martina progressed the priest grew better at holding brief conversations with the townspeople—when they deigned to speak to anyone, for they remained a solidly reserved lot. Still, he was beginning to understand that reticence was innate in them and not a reflection of how they might regard—or disregard—him.

Even though Antonio began to feel a sort of affection for the town and its people, he didn't want to remain in Orune. He still pursued his decision to approach Archbishop Orozco requesting to be reinstated at the parish in Alghero. Albóndiga wrote a long and detailed letter to Archbishop Andres Orozco, taking care to be respectful, even acquiescent. He penned an identical missive to the prelate in Nuoro, reaffirming his decision to investigate every avenue that might hasten his departure from the Barbagia. Finally, he wrote a letter to his cousin Juan, hoping he could get the Grand Inquisitor himself to intervene on Antonio's behalf.

For weeks he queried villagers, asking if anyone would be willing to carry a letter for him back to Alghero or even to Nuoro. Each man he approached stared blankly back at him, shrugged, and shook his head. "Too far," most said. "Too arduous," others added. "This is my home," another insisted. "Why would I want to leave it, even if only for a short time?" In a pique of desperation the priest thought to ask Giacobbe, but finally came to realize the folly of his logic. The lad was too young to attempt the journey alone, and if Antonio were to suggest that he accompany the boy the villagers would certainly deny his request— perhaps fearing that the priest would harm the boy if he misbehaved on the journey.

With his exit plans stalled, Antonio did his best to continue to acclimate to life in Orune. In September he suggested that the village hold another festival, this one in honor of the Blessed Virgin Mother's birthday on September 8. Fondly recalling the fine food and the drinking of the *festa* they'd held in August, the priest planted his request for a repeat gathering into the ears of everyone who'd listen. What he failed to understand was that the townspeople couldn't afford to dip into their precious storehouses only six weeks later to provide sustenance for another Feast Day celebration. Doing so would exhaust their supplies. With winter fast approaching, a birthday party for the Virgin would have to wait until next year.

Melancholy and dissatisfaction set in, and soon Antonio began to wake with a searing pain in his temples. The aching was so intense it blurred his vision and soured his already vinegary mood. Day slipped into night and into day once more and still his cranium refused to stop pounding.

On the fifth day of sleeplessness and constant head-hammering, Martina arrived at his door in the early morning, ready to conduct their weekly language lesson. Although she normally delivered those lessons in the evening after she'd finished her tasks for the day, that morning she woke up missing Antonio, and had asked her *ayaya* if she could be dismissed from her healing duties to go visit the priest. She knocked three times before Antonio opened the door. He stood before her, squinting with intense effort, a grimace on his lips.

Martina cried out, "Antonio!" She reached for the priest's hand and immediately ordered him to follow her. "We've got to go to the *majarzas*. They've got to concoct a medicine to give you relief. The potions I've been making for you aren't working."

She placed her kerchief over Antonio's eyes to shield him from the bright morning light as she led him to her *ayaya*'s doorstep. They scurried across the *piazza,* drawing curious stares from the women at the well and the others at their windows.

"Eh, Martina, who's the bandit you're dancing with?" one teased. The others laughed, but Martina ignored them.

The young woman and the priest found the *majarzas* in Shardana's kitchen, brewing a remedy. The twin healers were resting, having already seen three townspeople that morning for various ailments. They were taking a break to quench their thirsts and talk a bit. When Martina entered with Antonio's face sheathed, the sisters set down their cups and walked toward them.

"What's wrong?" Sarda asked.

"His head rattles. The aching is intense," Martina explained. "He needs your help."

Shardana led the priest to a chair. No matter what spiritual or temporal disagreements might separate them, she set aside all past arguments and attended to his ailment. Martina closed the window shutters to dim the sunlight and lit a candle. Sarda removed the scarf from the priest's eyes. The sisters worked diligently, asking him about his condition, how long and how severe. Was he nauseous as well? Thirsty? Dizzy? Were his ears ringing? Was light flashing before his eyes? Fever? Sweating?

On and on it went until the priest, in his exhaustion and discomfort, sighed. "Enough with your questions! If you can give me something to ease the terrible throbbing, I'd be most grateful. If not, let me go home and get back into my bed."

"Yes, we can help," Sarda replied. "But first we have to concoct a tincture. Give us a moment."

While the older women prepared the medicine, Martina offered her friend a cup of cool water, then sat beside him, waiting. "Remember, they don't expect any payment for their services," she told the priest. "It's not their way."

Antonio nodded, slightly, careful not to move his head too much. "But later, you should repay them in some way. A basket of eggs. A loaf of bread. A wheel of cheese. If you don't, you'll have insulted them."

"Yes, I understand," the priest whispered. "It was the same that time they fixed my face after the injury at the sheepfold. Today, as well, I'll do it. If their medicines work."

"Repay them whether their medicines work or not. To show your respect," Martina explained, although she had no doubt the priest's ailment would soon be under control and quickly eased.

Sarda returned with a vial and placed it in Antonio's hand. "Take three drops of this directly on your tongue or with a cup of wine, three times daily. The pounding in your head will stop."

Shardana refilled the water in the cup Martina had given the priest. "Take your first dose now. Then go home and rest. In an hour, you'll be able to sleep. When you wake up, your head pain will be gone."

Antonio swallowed the cup's contents. Tears gathered in his grateful eyes. "How can I thank you?"

"Be well, Antonio," Sarda said.

"Go now. Rest. Let the medicine work," Shardana added.

As the priest rose to leave, Martina followed.

"Stay here," Shardana told her granddaughter. "We have a lot of patients to see today. We need your help."

The young woman nodded. "Go home and rest, Antonio. I'll visit you later to see how you're doing."

The priest walked back across the *piazza* toward his house, holding Martina's kerchief over his eyes to shield them from the sun. At home he lay on his bed and quickly fell asleep. When he awoke four hours later his pain had eased considerably, although a dull ache was still present. He took his medicine as the *majarzas* had recommended, and in a few days the piercing headaches that had ravaged him were silenced.

Astonished, he almost called it a miracle, but resisted. He remembered to pay his respects to his caregivers, returning to Shardana's home two days later with a basket of vegetables from his garden. "For you and your kind sister," he said, sincerely grateful for their help.

Had Antonio had access to their potent medicine back in Spain he might never had been exiled to Alghero, for the incident that led to his reassignment was rooted in his inability to find relief from his migraines. Although Antonio didn't suffer from the blinding head pain very often, when he did the unbearable intensity drove him to regrettable actions.

In Spain his career had been advancing well. Those with clout in the Catholic echelons of Seville had remarked about his keen intellect and his astute understanding of the Gospels. He'd also heard rumors that the archbishop was considering him as a possible future candidate for bishop. Then one fateful day, the wheel turned. While living in the priests' quarters in Seville, where he'd been assigned the position of assistant pastor, he'd come down with a raging headache one evening and had been unable to sleep the entire night. The next morning the cardinal, who'd been sent from Rome to review the actions of the local inquisitor, was in Seville, and Antonio was sent to escort him to a meeting with the bishop and the archbishop. When Antonio awoke with a blinding headache he approached his superior, explaining his situation, and asked to be relieved of his duty. "There's no one else to fulfill this obligation, *Padre*. You must endure the headache and proceed."

That morning the bright sun glinted off the stone buildings with uncommon fierceness as Antonio opened the carriage door for the visiting dignitary, a man who talked incessantly in a high, shrill voice, which only added to the din ricocheting inside Antonio's skull. The priest did his best to smile and be cordial, although nausea set in soon after the carriage progressed down the street.

With the cardinal oblivious to his discomfort, Antonio began to sweat profusely. He was overcome with dizziness. The small bit of bread he'd eaten for breakfast propelled itself up his esophagus, spewing a gastric mess over the prelate's garments. Aghast, the cardinal signaled for the driver to stop. He opened the door and with one swift movement of his polished boot he shoved Antonio into the street, causing him to bump his head on the cobblestones. Enraged and sickened, Albóndiga lunged at the prelate, wrapping his hands around the visiting cardinal's throat. Antonio squeezed with all his might. Although he felt weak due to his headache, he might have strangled the dignitary if the coachman hadn't intervened.

The Archbishop of Seville did not take kindly to Antonio's misdeed or the disrespectful and violent manner in which he'd mistreated the visitor, who in addition to being an important member of the Catholic hierarchy happened also to be his closest friend. The archbishop sentenced Antonio to service in Alghero, far from the inner circle of the Catholic hierarchy in Seville. "Since you've behaved like a barbarian," the archbishop had said, "you shall be sent to Sardinia to live with them."

The offended colleague whose throat had suffered the vise of Antonio's hands wasn't entirely pleased at the leniency of the sentence. He'd envisioned a jail term for the priest, but had been dissuaded from pressing civil charges when he learned of Antonio's malady. He was persuaded that banishment to Alghero would suffice. Although the city was under Aragon rule and thus was more civilized than other areas of the island, the city's location on the western shore of Sardinia qualified it as a remote outpost. Alghero was sure to feel like punishment to Antonio Albóndiga, who harbored aspirations of greatness.

THE POTION the *majarzas* had given Antonio erased all traces of his foul head pain. For days after he walked around town in a jovial manner, sending greetings to all, singing, and once, according to Sarda, even dancing a little jig in the *piazza* when he thought no one was looking. Shardana set aside her grievance against him, deciding that perhaps, just as Martina had suggested, it had been the insufferable malady, after all, that had caused the priest to so frequently be in such a foul mood.

For a time all was well in the village, and early autumn eased into late fall. Antonio's urgency to petition the archbishop in Nuoro for reassignment had abated. By the end of October, before the first snow fell, the priest decided to take a stroll outside of town. He set off for the water temple, *Su Tempiesu*, having heard that the view was especially lovely in that area that time of the year, despite the fact that the gray eyes of November were peering around every corner. He'd also heard stories of the temple's finely-crafted cut-stone architecture, although he questioned how artisan-wrought stonework could have found its way into the primitive Barbagia. He'd wanted to ask Martina to join him on the stroll, but he couldn't find her anywhere in the village. With the morning fast slipping away, the priest set off alone.

SU TEMPIESU was a masterpiece of craftsmanship, just as the villagers had related. Antonio had scoffed when Martina had told him months before that the water temple had been built sometime in the 1200s—twelve centuries *before* the birth of Christ! At the site that day the priest's mouth dropped open as he gazed at the stunning array of perfectly cut limestone and lava rocks. Graced by small, monolithic trachyte arches, the place had a decidedly sacred air. Martina had told him of the great reverence for water that had inspired the original builders to craft the temple. With his own eyes he could see that glory. Its refined design and artistic rendering belied its ancient beginnings. Although Antonio couldn't have identified the structure's resemblance to ancient Etruscan burial buildings, those who knew of such matters could've told him that the origins of the water temple at *Su Tempiesu* reached farther back in time than the days of the Etruscans. It reached all the way back to the Mycenaean culture of Cyprus—perhaps even further, if the stones could only break their silence and share their innate truth.

Whatever ancient hands designed and built *Su Tempiesu*, its perfection was unquestionable, even to someone as disbelieving as Antonio Albóndiga. The place exuded a spiritual magnetism that even he recognized. Throughout the ages the site had drawn visits from devoted people from far off places. Many and varied had been the pilgrims who'd gathered to celebrate beside its succulent springs. Ancient worshippers of water and stones had proclaimed it sacred, as had people who venerated Carthage's Tanit, Rome's Ceres, and Greece's Demeter. Even baptized Catholics, such as the Christians in Orune and nearby towns, honored and understood the holiness of that place. If one listened closely to the rustling of the wind, one could decipher three-thousand-year-old prayers whispered by multitudes—and the lilting merriment of festival-goers rejoicing with food and wine, song and dance—for the site had been sacred from the beginning, when only the stream wended its way through the countryside, eons before the temple had been built.

Antonio looked upon the wondrous structure, the likes of which he'd never before seen. The water temple receded into the earth. Its finely cut stone steps descended to a small well above which rose a conical, beehive-shaped aperture not unlike a smaller version of the curious stone ruins the priest had seen dotted here and there across the landscape. "The *Nuraghi,*" villagers had said when he'd asked about the ruins. But true to their brevity of speech, when questioned further all they'd say was, "Our ancestors."

From the base of the water temple's stone steps, at the foot of the well, Antonio looked upward, through the tapering spiral stone beehive. At its apex an opening allowed light to filter down on his face. Serenity filled his bones and he closed his eyes, breathing calming, letting his eyes drift gently back into their sockets. His mind wandered far back to his childhood. Inside his head he heard his mother's voice humming a lullaby, singing to him softly as she cradled him close to her heart. He recalled falling asleep to its rhythms, wanting never to be released from her secure embrace.

His ears tingled with the sound of women's voices, and he smiled until he realized he was no longer strolling the terrain of his memory. The voices he now heard came from the field not far from the well where he stood. He left the water temple to investigate, first dipping his finger into the well water and making the sign of the cross.

When he reached the top of the stone stairway he glanced around, trying to determine from which direction the singing voices had come. Across the field he spied a grove of chestnut trees nestled among a group of tall rocks, massive structures of basalt which, from his vantage point, seemed as strong and sturdy as henchmen. He set off toward that stretch of land.

As he drew nearer, the voices rose in song again. Sweet, high, clear tones filled his heart with an unexpected yearning. He walked quietly, not wanting to disturb the women or to disclose his presence. He wanted nothing more than to bask in the beauty of their music on this bright and crisp late October afternoon. He drew closer and saw that the stone mounds he'd mistaken for henchmen actually resembled monolithic sentinels. He also noticed a circle of seven women: Shardana, Martina, Sarda, Anna-Bella, Teresina, Viviana, and Annica.

Within the center of the ring a pit of stones cradled a small fire. The women held hands, chanting words that were unintelligible to him, for they weren't spoken in Sardo, Spanish or Latin. He watched and waited, listening.

When the women's song ended, Shardana spoke first.

"We give praise to our Great Mother, She who grants life and sustains us. She who oversees death, and carries us home."

"*Ave, Dea Madre*," the women replied. "*Ave,* Isis; *Ave,* Ceres. *Ave,* Tanit. *Ave,* Cybele. *Ave,* Maria Nera."

The priest's ears began to burn. As he continued to spy on the women, the quietude he'd previously experienced evaporated.

Sarda spoke next. "Today we honor the coming of the mid-time between the autumn equinox and the winter solstice, the night when the veil between the living world and the world of the spirits dissolves and we experience the liminal immanence of all creation."

In unison the women replied, "Blessed be."

Annica's voice rose now. "May the coming winter be kind to our sheep and our men."

"May we have ample provisions to fill our hungry bellies," Viviana added.

"May we have enough fuel to warm our bodies. May the spring return with haste," Teresina prayed.

"This we ask in the name of the Maiden, the Mother, and the Crone," the chorus of voices responded.

"All things begin and end in you, O Mother of Us All," Anna-Bella proclaimed.

"May the Mother's grace and compassion shine down upon us," Martina prayed. "May Her justice prevail and may peace reign in the hearts of all Her people."

"Blessed be," the women resounded.

Antonio's chest tightened. His eyes began to itch and burn. He felt the familiar tension in his temples returning, although it was less biting than it had been before he'd benefited from the mercy of the *majarzas'* medicine. He tried to still his tongue, indebted as he was to the medicinal skills of the *majarzas*, but he couldn't abide the heresy he was witnessing. It pained him doubly to see his friend Martina entrapped in servitude to a heathen god. When the women broke the circle and began to dance among the stone sentinels beside a babbling spring, he could no longer contain his outrage.

Antonio jumped out from behind the stand of trees he'd used to conceal his presence. "Heathens!" the priest shouted. "Heretics! You shall burn in the fires of hell!"

Startled, the women faced Antonio, his cheeks scarlet with anger, his eyes puffed and swollen. He pointed his finger and shouted, "I shall put an end to this pagan worship. As God as my Holy Judge!"

Shardana stood unyielding, her icy stare locked in battle with Antonio's raging irises. Martina's impulse was to quell her friend's fears, but she fell silent, unable to find the words she felt would reach his resistant mind. Sarda touched Anna-Bella's shoulders, for her daughter trembled at the priest's angry outburst. Teresina gripped Viviana's shaking hand.

Annica spoke in their defense. "You can't harm us, Antonio. Our God is as powerful as yours. And our belief is as strong and as eternal."

"*Limpieza de sangre!*" the priest retorted. "Your heathen blood must be cleansed! And I'm the man to do it!"

Chapter 16
The Attidadoras

WORD SPREAD THROUGHOUT THE VILLAGE that the priest had spied on the seven townswomen who'd gathered near *Su Tempiesu*. From lips to ears, all across the *piazza* and down every winding lane the air buzzed with talk of the horrid accusations Albóndiga had heaped upon Shardana, Sarda and the others.

Even those in the town who were Christians never paid any mind to the rituals these women frequently enacted at the water temple. Had anyone asked, they would've shrugged, "It's just their way." It wasn't merely that they'd learned to avert their eyes to the women's unorthodox ceremonies. Most of the town's Catholics had grown up believing there were many ways to venerate the Great Mystery. Many could recite cherished familial lore about great-grandmothers and great-grandfathers who'd dearly held to the old ways before they'd been forced to pledge their allegiance to the Christian god.

To that generation, transferring the outward signs of their spiritual beliefs had seemed easy at first, since the Christians often built their churches on or near the ancient sites where the old ones intoned their gods, sometimes female, sometimes male. Some of the Christian rites even felt familiar to those of the townsfolk who'd newly converted, especially when the early missionaries enthroned the statue of *Nostra Signora Nera* behind the altar at the temple to Tanit that had been turned into a Catholic church named in honor of Jesus's dark-skinned mother. Even the revered temple at *Su Tempiesu* had been built to resemble the sacred body of the Goddess Tanit. The keepers of the old ways felt at home in *Nostra Signora Nera's* sturdy arms because her face resembled the Mother God they'd venerated for centuries. As long as they could worship the Christian's *La Signora* without trouble, they felt comfortable embracing the Catholic baptism and Mass, as well as that religion's other sacraments.

To the newly converted, the Mystery was still the Mystery, no matter what name the priests chose to call it. What the old ones didn't like was being threatened and denigrated for choosing to hold onto some, or all, of their ancient customs and beliefs. They thought it was sacrilegious that the priests of the religion of Jesus didn't appreciate the beauty and sanctity of the multitudinous ways to celebrate and honor the Sacred. Whether God was male or female, or both, the Divine didn't reside in a stone building—and never would. Once in a while the Divine might stop at a church to visit, just as a good friend stops by for a cup of wine and a slice of *pecorino sardo*. But God didn't live in the churches. God preferred the air and the soil, the water and the trees, the souls of the rocks and hillsides, and the breath of every living being.

IN THE VILLAGE Antonio did his best to garner support for his attack against the women, but none of the townsfolk would listen. He knocked at their doors, stating his impassioned plea, but the people shut their doors in his face. From house to house he traveled until his fists were raw from rapping and his voice was hoarse from ranting. He returned to his cottage even more convinced of the righteousness of his mission.

He stopped allowing Martina to visit him, even for Sardo lessons. "Go away, witch!" he cursed. "You are a heretic and I will not have you darken my doorstep!"

His migraines returned. Day and night his head throbbed without relief, for he'd nearly run out of the medicine Shardana and Sarda had concocted for him and he refused to ask them for more. "Heathens!" he shouted to the walls as he placed shirts and pants over the windows of his home to block out the sunlight that caused his eyes to ache and his temples to burn. Even though the light of early November had grown dim and dull, the day hours were painfully bright to him. He ate little. He slept fitfully at night. He stopped shaving and bathing. Wild and wooly, he began to resemble an errant ram, one who'd strayed from the *tanca* and had lost its footing trying to find the path back to the pastureland.

Antonio's first act of aggression was to harvest from the early November hillsides what little remained of the reeds and stems that had been so abundant in August. He gathered the spent plants and set them in a corner of his house to fully dry. The priest had watched Brontu do this once, when the shepherd had gathered asphodel for Constantino's basketwork. But Antonio's intentions had a more sinister aim. In the solitude of his rooms he bundled the cut sheaths into makeshift bodies until they resembled seven unkempt scarecrows. With his task complete, the priest secured the effigies with rope and hauled them to the center of the *piazza* one windless, overcast November morning. He placed them in a circle, situating the bundles as if they were the women he'd encountered on that late October afternoon, on All Hallows Eve.

With his makeshift coven in place, he raised his voice, proclaiming, "Today the purging begins! I light these bodies to cleanse the blood of the heathen swine that lives among us. May they embrace the salvation of God Jesus before their human bodies are buried in the cold clay of death."

On that cold and solemn November morning, Antonio lit the first body of reeds and sticks, then the next and the next until all seven effigies burned with a brilliance that lit up the square, spewing smoke and ash into the sky. From the safety of their windows, the villagers peered at the priest.

"He's lost his mind!" the baker's wife suggested.

"He'll incur the wrath of the *majarzas*," Stefano the cobbler declared.

"He's gone to his Devil," the butcher said.

The seven women whose straw images now blazed in the center of town watched with caution and disdain.

"His lunacy will pass," Sarda said, hoping her words would prove true.

When the last ember smoldered on the charred cobblestones, the priest let loose an eerie laugh and returned home to plot his next steps.

The following morning Antonio marched through the streets of Orune reading a list of grievances against the women.

"They've sold their souls to the Devil," he announced, walking from lane to lane, pausing at every doorstep. "They've cavorted with Satan," he said, "and they've eaten the flesh of unborn babies. They've pledged their allegiance to pagan idols, and they've danced in the woods praying to false gods. Theirs is the way of evil and sin. They must be washed clean of their sins."

Over and over, all day long until the evening light occluded his sight, the priest marched from one end of town to the other, repeating his litany of grievances. At each home the occupants tossed buckets of foul water or peelings of rotting vegetables out their doors and windows on Antonio as he passed by. Nothing deterred the priest from his mission; the villagers' actions served only to further incite his passion to persist and rid the town of the vermin women.

The following day the priest rose before the rooster crowed and set a table and chair in the center of the *piazza,* although the wind was cold and the air smelled of impending rain. As the village women came to the well with the first light of dawn to draw water for their households, Antonio began to rant about the torturous methods he planned to use against the seven women he was accusing of witchcraft.

"To enact their confessions and redeem their souls," Antonio stated, "I'll first apply the *strappado.* Now, those of you ignorant peasants who don't know what a *strappado* is, pay attention and I'll instruct you. The *strappado* is the invention of angels in the service of God. This ingenious roping device is strapped around the vile arms and legs of the evil witch. Then it's duly tied so she can't wiggle her way to freedom. We Avengers of Heaven then place weighted stones on the ropes' ends. And you good people of Orune have plenty of granite for such holy purposes! Once the heathen witch is pinned in place, the ropes are raised on high! Stretching and arching her body to its breaking point! And when she can bear no more, when she's on the verge of swooning, the Mighty Keepers of Truth release her writhing bag of bones to the pavement. Oh, how her limbs will smolder with pain! Oh, how she will wail, to no avail!"

Some of the village women at the well cast their fierce and angry eyes at Antonio. Others spat at him, warning him to stop his contemptible monologue or they would silence his tongue for him. They all wanted to toss the contents of their wooden buckets at him to douse his ire, but they didn't want to waste precious water on such a louse.

"Your disrespect is wicked, *Padre,*" the baker's wife said. "All my life I've known the women you're accusing. Never have any of them harmed a fly."

The women hastily collected their water pails and hurried home, whispering among themselves, "He's gone mad!"

"Should this application not suffice to induce confession," the priest continued, unfazed by the villagers' taunting, "I shall perform the next phase of persuasion—the *aselli!* Oh, it's a delicious torture, the perfect water torment for women who gather water from the well each day to quench their heathen thirst!"

Antonio continued his rant even after his audience had rushed away, returned home, and shut their doors. The cold wind slapped the priest's face and he shivered, but he kept going, not even pausing to pull his coat collar around his exposed neck to ward off the chill.

"I shall lay each offending witch down on a trestle with sharp-edged rungs and secure her limbs with an iron band. Shardana will be the first! Then Sarda. Then that despicable Annica. And if these vermin haven't confessed their abhorrent crimes by then, Anna-Bella's turn will follow. Then Teresina's and Viviana's. And last will be Martina!"

The priest paused after speaking his friend's name. For a brief moment the syllables caught in his throat and he felt an urge to cry. He steeled himself, forcing back his tears, then continued.

"Into Shardana's blasphemous mouth I'll force a wad of linen. Then I'll raise her feet above her head and pour a jar of water into her mouth and nose until I snuff the breath out of her stinking body. She'll gasp! She'll cry! But I won't heed her pleas for leniency. Over and over I will drown her gullet, tighten the cords that bind her arms and her legs until her veins explode! When I grow tired of her wailing, I'll turn to Sarda and the others and repeat the punishment. If after all this the witches don't repent, if they still refuse to confess their heresy, each shall meet the same fate as the reed-and-straw bodies I burned in the square days ago."

As the words of vengeance rolled off Antonio's parched lips, he thought of his father, Pablo, and of his cousin Juan de San Martin, a loyal servant of the Grand Inquisitor, Tomás de Torquemada, a man the Spanish crown entrusted with eliminating heretics from every nook and cranny of every town and city throughout that great and honored country. Antonio wished that Torquemada, Juan, and Pablo could see him doing the work of the Lord in Orune with such righteous fury. Antonio wished Archbishop Orozco would witness his act of faithfulness to his beloved Church. Then they would have no further reason to wait a moment longer to pluck him from the hell of his isolation, return him to Alghero, maybe even permit him to sail back to his beloved Seville.

He would write another letter to Orozco that evening, and perhaps one to his cousin Juan as well, telling them of what he'd witnessed at the well. He'd provide details of his testament against the heretics of Orune. They'd see his purity, understand his allegiance, forgive his wrongdoings—and set him free.

He'd grown lax since the *majarzas* had cast their spell on him, plying him with elixirs, falsely telling him it was medicine for his migraines when in fact it was a potion to poison his soul, turn his heart away from Christ Jesus and the Catholic Church. How foolish of him to think he could make a life for himself in Orune. What folly to think that Martina's friendship would be enough. That she-devil had duped him, tempted him with kindness, when all the while she wanted only the corruption of his immortal soul.

"HIS RANTING continues," Martina announced to her *ayaya* and great-aunt after she'd strolled through the *piazza* several times that day, the autumn winds whirling around her ears, hoping to catch her friend's eye and convince him to stop his malevolent spewing.

Antonio had refused to acknowledge her presence. He turned his back to her each time she drew near. "Go away, witch!" he had yelled.

"What does he hope to accomplish?" Sarda wondered aloud. "No one in the town will stand behind him and support his insane accusations."

"He's a troubled man," Shardana stated. "The tirade he discharges is his attempt to eradicate his own demons."

"Someone has to help release him from his tomb," Martina replied. "He'll catch pneumonia. He's just out there in the middle of the *piazza,* exposed to the wind and the damp air."

"You've gone too far, being a nursemaid to that raving priest," Shardana snapped.

"I've done nothing but show him kindness, *Ayaya*," Martina said. "That's what my mother would have done. Nothing else would have been acceptable."

"You could have used your intelligence to see the man for who he truly is. Not the man you hoped he was," the older woman said. "He's a vile, angry wolf. His actions and his words attest to that. Have you no sense, child?"

"I'm no longer a child, *Ayaya*," Martina asserted.

"How else can you explain why you champion this man who'd have you and your kinfolk burned in the *piazza* for nothing more than reciting some prayers by the water temple?"

"He wants to kill us," Sarda interjected. "Your *ayaya's* right about this, Martina."

"But he has no authority to do so—surely you can see that. He's pitiful," the young woman stated.

"Yes," Sarda replied. "But even though he won't succeed in murdering our bodies, his words harm our spirits."

"My mother would say lies have no power over the Truth."

With trembling hands and a shaken voice Shardana replied, "Your mother would've said, 'This man is dangerous to us and our community. We have to find a way to silence him, or we have to banish him from our town.'"

"How do you know what she would say?" Martina challenged. "You're not my mother."

"No! I'm not your mother!" Shardana shouted. "But I carried your mother in my womb, nursed her at my breast. Buried her in the earth. Grieved her loss every day of my life. I'm the one who raised you, taught you everything you know about being a compassionate healer, about being a good and honorable woman. After your mother died, I was the one who tended your illnesses and your sorrows. Wiped your tears. Rejoiced at your happiness. Kept you safe and warm. Put food in your belly and love in your home. I did everything your mother asked me to do to bring you up properly. After all that, how dare you choose the maniacal priest over your own flesh and blood!"

"Then help me keep my mother's memory alive," Martina said. "Help me put her ways into the world so she can live again through me."

Sarda touched her twin's shoulder. "*Gemella*, Martina isn't turning against us. Remember, the priest has condemned her, too. We have to band together. We need to pool our potent power to combat his evil outbursts. Remember the sea-wolf and the sea-serpent. It's time to coil our bodies, hiss and strike back."

Shardana nodded. She held her sister's hand. "Last night I dreamt of Grazia. She hovered above the ocean waves and told me we needed our strongest medicine to defeat Antonio. She said the wolf was mighty and fierce, but not as powerful as the serpent. She vowed to help us."

"I dreamt of her, too," Sarda replied.

"And me as well," Martina said. "My mother has never left us, *Aya-ya*. She's here right now, to guide us through this ordeal."

UNTIL THE SUN SET that chilly November evening, Antonio raged and ranted in the square, proclaiming his intentions to threaten the *majarzas* and their allies. The pounding in his head rose with each acrid syllable. Later at home the hammering exploded into unbearable piercing, but nothing remained of the medicine that Shardana and Sarda had prepared for him. Had the vial contained even the tiniest of drops, he would have refused to allow their elixir of Satan into his body. With great effort he found a pen and some scraps of paper and wrote to his cousin and to Orozco, even though he knew he had no way of delivering the letters. He tossed and turned all night, unable to sleep; the tension in his temples kept him awake. Several times he thought he heard his father's voice calling, "Kill the heretics, Antonio!" Once he thought he heard his mother weeping. At dawn, as he prepared his breakfast, someone knocked on his door.

Isidoro, Brontu, and Giovanni had come down from the sheepfold to coax some sense into the priest's rattled brain. Antonio's merciless attempts to persecute their kin were sending the entire town into a frenzy of fear and anger. The harassment must end, they informed him.

"You've gone too far, *Padre*," Giovanni stated.

"I've only begun," the priest asserted.

"We Barbaricini are a fierce and determined people, *Padre*," Brontu

239

stated. "You've lived among us long enough to know that. We're loyal to our blood relatives, our neighbors and friends, the sheep, and the Earth and the sky. Be warned. It'll not go well if you persist in attacking all that we cherish."

"I answer to a higher authority," the priest boasted. "The King of Aragon and the Lord God Jesus."

"Nothing is higher than what we hold most dear," Isidoro stated.

"Blaspheme!" the priest shouted. "I will have you all excommuni-cated and all your souls will burn in hell."

"If that's so," Giovanni said, "then we'll see you in hell too, *Padre*, for surely Satan's flames will kiss your face as well."

"Heretics!"

For two weeks the priest's rampage continued, through rain and snow, through windy gusts and chilly days of waning sun. Nothing de-terred him; his ire was fueled by thoughts of how proud his father and his cousin Juan would be if they could only see him battling against all odds for their holy cause. The townspeople did their best to ignore him, going about their business as best as they could against the back-drop of his endless ranting. Some took to stuffing bits of cloth into their ears to quell his insufferable orations.

The priest refused to stop even though his voice grew more hoarse and unintelligible as time went on. When finally it was clear that An-tonio was not going to end his vigil without the townspeople interven-ing, the frazzled villagers met to decide how to stop his hateful harass-ment.

In the community circle, Basilio spoke first. "It's obvious that the man has gone insane. And although I don't want to inflict harm upon a feeble-minded person, I don't want the persecution to continue. He's defiling my wife, my granddaughter, my sister-in-law, my grand-niece, our daughters-in-law, and our beloved neighbor Annica. His actions are bloodying the hearts of every villager."

"We've tried to reason with him," Giovanni added. "We've done our best."

"But his mind's reeling beyond reason," Anna-Bella insisted. "How else can he explain his inability to relinquish his futile crusade?"

"He's troubled," Martina said, hoping to instill a sense of compas-sion into the proceedings.

"Without a doubt that's true," Sarda agreed. "Still, our village has been disrupted by his behavior for far too long. We have to find a solution."

"But what do we do with a madman?" asked Annica. "He's stopped caring for himself. He hasn't bathed in weeks, and the stench from his body makes the air all around the well putrid and un-breathable."

"The man's worse than a bandit," Stefano said. "Giacobbe can't stand to see Albóndiga so riled up. It reminds him of the beating he received at the priest's hands this summer. He's relieved he hasn't had to serve beside Antonio at Mass. Not that the priest has even been fulfilling those duties. He's so fully absorbed with his present mission."

"He has offended our beloved *majarzas*," Isidoro stated. "He doesn't understand that their ways aren't the ways of his Devil."

"I say we cast him out, like the Christians cast out Satan," Brontu interjected.

At last Shardana spoke. "Exorcism. That's what the Catholics call it. He seems to be possessed. Perhaps we can try to undo the spell first. If that fails, we can then talk about exiling him from our town."

AND SO THE COMMUNITY decided that the *majarzas* would enact a rite to dispel the demons from Antonio. The twin sisters worked day and night scouring their apothecary for the right mixture of herbs to concoct the necessary potion, diving into their memories to recall the right recipe and the perfect incantation that would free Antonio from the fiendish spirit that owned his soul.

"We need to add some of Anna-Bella's honey and some bee venom," Sarda said.

"Yes!" Shardana agreed. "That sacred medicine can cure just about any illness. With bee venom, mystical worlds can open and the body— and the spirit—can relinquish its disease."

They figured that the priest wouldn't allow them to come close enough to him to get him to ingest a curative potion, so they opted for a combination of chants and the sprinkling of hallowed tincture in the vicinity of the chair on which the priest sat the middle of the *piazza*. A week after the villagers met to discuss the matter, the twins had compounded the right formula and announced to the townspeople that they were ready to proceed.

The next morning when the rooster crowed, the sisters left their houses. They marched toward the square in the center of town, joined by their family members and their friends. All the adults in the village marched toward the square. Two of the strongest men stopped at the church to take down the painting of *Nostra Signora Nera* that hung behind the altar and carry it with them to the place where the others were waiting near the well.

As expected, the villagers saw Antonio already at work, spouting his vile accusations and proscriptions for persecution. When he noticed the crowd of townspeople heading his way, he stood, brandished a crucifix, and cried out, "I call upon the name of Christ Jesus to protect me from all you heretics!"

Without a word the villagers formed a circle around the perimeter of the square so that the priest couldn't escape, and also so he would not feel entrapped. In the sky above them two griffons soared above the crowd. A swarm of bees hovered nearby, ready to lend their help, if necessary.

The birds, the bees, the people, and their painting of the Black Madonna waited for Shardana and Sarda to begin their work. With their medicine pouches securely wrapped around their waists, the twin sister healers stepped into the center of the circle and faced Antonio. Both sisters held vials of the precious compounds in their steady hands.

The priest spat at them. "Don't come near me, or I'll call upon Christ Jesus to rain fire down upon your heathen heads."

"We intend you no harm, Antonio," Sarda explained. "We've come as friends, to help you."

"Then confess your sins and rise to glory in the Sacred Blood of Christ Jesus."

Shardana sprinkled the air with some of the potion, chanting a prayer as she worked. A handful of bees circled her head; the vibration of their wings cradled the sacred words the healer intoned.

"Don't call upon your She-Devil false idol!" the priest cried out.

"She's calling upon the Spirit of healing, Antonio," Sarda explained. "Nothing else."

Sarda joined her sister in sprinkling the potion around the *piazza*, taking care to douse the ground inside the circle.

As the women worked, the priest watched every move they made.

The women wended their way around the circle, drawing closer and closer to Antonio in tighter, concentric circles, anointing the space between them and him with the liquid they carried in their mysterious vials.

"May peace prevail in your heart, Antonio," Shardana said.

"May peace prevail in your soul," Sarda added.

"My heart and soul reside in the Peace of the Kingdom of God," the priest shouted, brandishing his crucifix. "May God Almighty condemn you all to the fires of Hell where you belong!"

"May you remember the tender touch of your mother's hand," Shardana called out.

"May you remember you entered the world in purity and light," Sarda said.

"She-devils. Be gone!" Antonio ranted, holding his hand in front of his body, attempting to hold the sisters at bay. "Oh, Almighty Father, give me strength!"

The griffons flew lower, circling around the crowd before spreading their wings and soaring higher above the square. On and on again they swooped low, then flew high, casting their blessings on the events that transpired below them. The swarm of buzzing bees was so loud that the vibrations of their wings filled the air of the *piazza* with a mystical humming.

Shardana nodded to the birds and the bees. She felt their power flow through her body and return to the Earth. She closed her eyes and breathed deeply, shoring up her strength. She nodded at Sarda, signaling their next step. She turned to Antonio and said, "May you remember the kindnesses shown to you by those in our village."

Sarda intoned, "May you remember the sheep's milk left on your doorstep."

"The fresh eggs left on your doorstep," Shardana added. "The sweet honey from the wild bees."

"The garden cultivated for you, the fresh vegetables for your table," Sarda said. "The work our village boys did to clean and prepare your church. The patience and kindness shown to you by your friend Martina, who taught you to speak our language."

Antonio stood and held the crucifix over his chest. "Lies! Heathen lies! You poisoned me with your Devil's work! Your heathen tongue!"

he shouted, staring at Martina, who stood in the crowd of villagers who encircled the *piazza*.

"May you remember all the good things you've done in your lifetime," Shardana said.

"May you remember all the kindnesses that others have shown you," Sarda said.

Antonio's eyes darted from one twin to the other. His mouth tensed, and his brow became bathed in sweat. His knees threatened to collapse, but he somehow found the strength to stand his ground.

"May you know that you are part of the One Great Mystery that sustains every living thing," Shardana said. "Humans and animals, birds and bees, plants and trees, sky and earth, air and water."

"May you remember and may you be blessed by them," Sarda added.

Antonio spit at the women. Trying to muster his rage, he said, "Heretics—" in a voice that was nearly inaudible.

"Blessed be," Shardana answered.

"Blessed be," Sarda concurred.

With their ritual completed, the women rejoined the outer circle of villagers. The griffons swooped down and perched on the stone ledge of the well, watching and waiting. The cloud of bees circled the well, then flew back to dance around Antonio's head before the priest swatted them away. In unison, and without hesitation, every one of the villagers became an *attidadora*, those faithful dirge-singers who selflessly accompanied mourning families at all the village funerals. Their loud, clear, eerie voices rang out, interceding on behalf of Antonio's soul.

"Let Antonio's spirit die to the anger that possesses it," they sang. "Let it rise again to a life of glory and kindness."

They sang for the man he used to be before the terrible demon of hate had entered his skin. They sang for the man he was yet to become, born anew in a baptism of community and care.

Befuddled by the circle of bodies, overcome by the chanting, dizzied by the words Shardana and Sarda had recited, overwhelmed by the singing that rose from the men and women who surrounded him, Antonio stood motionless, his hands at his side, his mouth silently open. With one final effort he raised his crucifix, trying to muster the strength to call down the wrath of God upon the heads of these people he knew to be heretics. Two of the bravest bees from the swarm swooped in close to the priest and stung his hands, his neck, and the scar on his face that marked the day back in June when he'd tried, and failed, to sheer the sheep.

Welts began to rise on his skin, and his weary arms fell flaccid at his side. He could have sworn he saw the contorted face of the young Jewish boy whose hanging he'd witnessed long ago when he had been a boy himself. Antonio's stomach tightened and his chest clenched. He rested his precious crucifix on the ground at his feet. And began to sob.

In the dim light of the November dawn, the priest's legs collapsed under the burden of his hatred. With trembling knees he sat in the chair in the middle of the *piazza*. Unable to speak, he stared at the villagers who encircled him. Though each of the faces had grown familiar to him, there was something about them he no longer recognized. Had the sun burned through the cloudy haze to shine on their heads? Was that the reason their bodies seemed to shimmer? Was he going mad? Were the weeks of sleep deprivation catching up to him at last? Or was it that insufferable migraine that refused to abate? Maybe it was the lack of food that made him feel so sick, so woozy. Was the bile that had collected in his liver eating away at him? Perhaps it was the *majarzas*! They'd cast another spell on him, preventing his tongue from expressing the truth of his heart. And what was that truth? That the souls of the seven women were lost beyond repair? That he would burn them alive if he only had the strength, raining God's wrath down upon their barbarian heads?

He closed his eyes, hoping to shut out the faces of the villagers. Their mouths were somber, yet it wasn't anger he felt rising from their chests, although he couldn't determine the exact quality of the feeling that emanated from them. Something about the tenor of their mood reminded him of his boyhood. And his mother. The lullabies she used to sing to him. The soft sound of her voice as it floated through the room when she prayed her rosary every evening before the small statue of the Blessed Mother. His heart ached, thinking of how her soft hands used to gently brush back the stray strands of hair that fell over his forehead before she kissed his cheek every morning when she served him his breakfast. He thought, too, of the gentle strength he used to feel as he ran across the pasturelands outside of Seville. Oh, how he would fly! His feet fast, his legs keeping up with his exuberance. Then, every step had felt so unencumbered. What had happened in the intervening years to change that? How had he come to this foreign place, this land of sheep and mountains, this town perched between heaven and hell? What kind of limbo did he now inhabit? And how could he be freed?

He inhaled deeply, releasing a long out-breath of air with a resonant sigh. He became aware that the unending din in his head had ceased howling. Opening his eyes, he stared into his hands and wept again. Waves of sorrow roiled his chest. He sobbed, unable to dam the torrent he'd unleashed. Tears coated his cheeks, his chin, collected in the palms of his hands. Snot ran from his nose, but he lacked the strength to wipe it away. He longed to compose himself, but couldn't. He longed to rush back to his house, to allow his cleaved heart to erupt in solitude, but he was unable to do so.

For nearly an hour Antonio sat in the middle of Orune's *piazza* and wept wordlessly. The villagers stood in silent witness until the furious edicts he'd been issuing for weeks were finally stilled.

When at last his tears had been spent and his weeping hushed, Antonio rose from his chair. He made his way to the circle's perimeter, walking toward Martina with open arms. His friend reached out to him. As she gathered him to her chest, Shardana and Sarda widened the circle, making room for the priest. Martina wept as she held Antonio close. The townspeople continued to sing, their songs sailing through the cold November air, alto voices sending good wishes, soprano voices lifting the priest's hopes, basso voices echoing in his bones, tenor voices showing Antonio Albóndiga the way home.

Chapter 17
Reconciliation

AT DAWN THE FOLLOWING MORNING the *piazza* remained empty. Its only occupant was the sun that slowly inched its way over the stone pavement while the skulking clouds retreated down the mountain. The priest's chair no longer occupied its ominous place in the center of the plaza, as it had for weeks. The prior evening, after the villagers had performed the exorcism, one of the farmers had returned the chair, along with Antonio's crucifix, to the priest's home. On the morning after that day of atonement, no women gathered at the well to fill their water buckets. No shepherds strolled by on their way to their *tancas* and their ewes. No bleary-eyed baker ambled over the cobblestone streets to open his shop. Except for Orune's vigilant rooster, every soul was fast asleep, exhausted from the work of saving Antonio Albóndiga.

Antonio rose at ten, his spirit refreshed, his body calm and relaxed. He bathed and shaved, washing away the residue of dirt and sweat that coated his hair, his torso and his limbs. He put on a clean shirt and a fresh pair of pants before preparing his breakfast. He removed the makeshift drapes he'd placed over his windows weeks before to block the bright sun that had aggravated his headaches. He stared at the tabletop as he ate a crust of stale bread. Hearing a knock on his door, he opened it to find an egg in a small basket sitting on his doorstep. He scanned the lane looking for who might have delivered the gift, but saw no one. The egg had been laid by Shardana's hen earlier that morning, and Martina had placed it on the priest's threshold, rushing off so he wouldn't see her.

The priest took the basket inside. He placed the egg in his hand and reached for a knife. Lightly he tapped a tiny hole in the top of the fragile shell, then sucked down the yolk and albumin in a single swallow.

When he finished his breakfast the priest searched for and found the letters he'd written to his Spanish cousin Juan and to Archbishop Orozco in Alghero. Thinking about all that had happened since his arrival in Orune last June, Antonio lit a candle, even though the sunlight streamed through the windows. Slowly he let the flame lick the corners of the notes he held in his hand, setting the letters on fire. The ashes fell into his half-empty wine cup, where they landed in the small pool of liquid that he'd failed to drain. Fire and water mingled to form a muddy stew, less fierce and less intolerant than scorching flames or torrential rivers, but more forgiving of failings, more eager to meld into mutable clay, a substance capable of making something that saves and sustains.

Antonio stood to stretch. His muscles relaxed and unknotted as he reached toward the ceiling. It had been a long while since his body had felt limber enough to flex and bend. He'd blamed it on the damp mountain air, the vile food he'd eaten since his arrival in Orune, but his stiffness was nothing more than a residue of the hate he'd carried in his joints, a fact that escaped his dull awareness. He thought about walking to the church, saying Mass to celebrate the lightness that unexpectedly filled his heart, but he changed his mind. He wanted to visit Martina, to thank her for her kindness towards him in the square the evening before—and if he could muster the courage, he wanted to ask for her forgiveness. He was beginning to realize that he had a lot to learn about these Barbaricini, things that had nothing to do with mastering their odd language. Perhaps, if Martina were willing, she could tutor him to be more fluent in the cultural language of her people, as well as their mother tongue.

At eleven that morning he grabbed his coat and headed out the door, strolling through the *piazza* on his way to the house in which his friend lived with her grandmother Shardana and the shepherds Basilio and Giovanni. The wind had lessened and the late November air had been warmed a bit by the sun, so the priest didn't secure the belt of his cloak or turn up his collar. He glanced at the blue sky and smiled. As he passed by the church a griffin circled the roof of the building, a sign of goodwill to those, unlike Antonio, who would have understood such an omen.

With the morning nearly spent, all the villagers were finally awake and going about their daily tasks, gathering water from the well in the *piazza*, harvesting eggs from the hens in their back yards, making baskets, baking bread, mending shoes, preparing meals. When Antonio walked past the baker's wife, she greeted him with a nod. Did he detect a slight smile on her lips? Surprised at the woman's friendliness, he said, "Good morning," and hurried along.

Across the lane from Martina's home Antonio saw Constantino sitting on a stone bench, weaving a basket. "Hello, *Padre*," he called out. "Did you sleep well?"

"Yes, thank you," Antonio said, surprised by the man's congeniality. "And you?"

"Oh, yes!" Constantino remarked. "Like my days at the *tanca*. Deep and full of dreams."

Before knocking on Martina's door Antonio asked the man, "Are Shardana and your wife seeing patients today?"

"Yes, yes, of course. Every day someone's ill, in some way or another. But they're both away right now. The wife of one of the shepherds is giving birth today. She started her labor an hour ago."

"Is Martina with them?" the priest asked.

"No," Constantino replied. "She stayed behind, in case another villager needed tending to. She's inside."

Antonio nodded, then walked the few steps from Constantino's home to knock on Martina's door.

Martina appeared, her long brown hair fastened behind her neck, an apron covering her dress signaling she was prepared to accept patients, should the visitor be one.

"Antonio, what brings you here?" the young woman asked, surprised to see the priest on her doorstep.

"I came to visit," he said. "Can I come in for a moment?"

"Yes, of course," Martina replied. "But I have work to do today, so you can't stay long."

"I understand," Antonio said. "I won't keep you."

She glanced at the places on the priest's skin that were still swollen from the bee stings he'd received yesterday in the *piazza*. She considered what kind of salve she could offer that would ease the welts, but she decided that the venom the bees had injected still needed time to work its magic. "Sit down," she said. "Tell me what's troubling you."

The last time the priest had been outside Shardana's house he'd accused the *majarzas* and Martina of being witches. Now an unfamiliar pang of remorse stabbed his chest. He glanced around the room, eyeing the apothecary that had been his salvation several times. That medicinal storehouse had remedied the woes of every one of the residents of Orune, and some of the sheep in the hillsides as well. Antonio looked at Martina's face, already beginning to show signs of undue sorrow even though she was only sixteen, and he wondered why life was meant to be such a burden.

"Did you have something you wanted to say to me, Antonio?" Martina's question disrupted his thoughts.

"Oh, yes. Sorry. Yes, I—" Unable to retrieve the words he'd practiced, the priest uncharacteristically stammered.

Martina allowed him to stumble, holding back her instinct to rescue him. She'd been pondering her *ayaya*'s words about Antonio and her own actions towards him. Though Shardana wasn't correct on every count, the young woman couldn't deny that her motives hadn't been completely altruistic. There was something about this man that she felt drawn to, although he was nearly ten years her senior and unlike anyone she'd ever known.

"You see—I wanted to say—I mean—" Antonio continued to stumble, and Martina continued to give him ample room to trip and fall.

"Oh! What use is it?" Antonio finally blurted out. "I can't say what's on my mind. I'll try some other time."

"Suit yourself, *Padre,*" Martina replied, the edges of her mouth turning up slightly. "Another time."

Antonio turned to leave, then spun around to face the young woman again. "Tonight," he said. "Can you come to my house? After dinner? Another Sardo lesson, maybe? If you aren't too tired by then, after your day of work." His eyes briefly met Martina's before he quickly glanced at the window.

"Yes," the young woman said. "I'll stop by around eight."

"Good," the priest said. "I'll be waiting for you."

THAT EVENING Martina arrived at Antonio's doorstep at the appointed time. She paused before knocking, looking over her shoulder to see if any of the other villagers were watching. She felt as if she were sneaking off to visit a lover, although she knew this wasn't true. Still, she couldn't erase the nagging that filled her heart, telling her that she wanted more from the priest than she sensed was right.

Antonio opened his door, holding a lit candle in his hand. He smiled. "I wasn't sure you'd actually come," he said.

"Why wouldn't I?" the young woman replied. Had the candle been able to provide more ample light, the priest would've seen a slight blush on Martina's cheeks.

"I thought you might need to rest after a long day of seeing patients."

"Can I come in?" Martina asked. "It's cold outside."

"Forgive me," Antonio replied. "Of course. Come in."

The two sat quietly at Antonio's table. All around the room the priest had lit candles and several oil lamps. The light cast an aura that felt church-like to Martina. The scar on Antonio's face softened in the soft light. The room was solemn. She'd hoped for a more jovial atmosphere. Her work day had been tiring, and she didn't have the strength for a somber conversation that evening. The priest sat silently, avoiding eye contact with her.

"So," the young woman began, "are you ready to tell me what you stopped by my house to say earlier today?"

"What?" He said, feigning ignorance. "I don't know what you mean."

"Don't be coy, Antonio," Martina said. "Something is troubling you. I can see it in your eyes. If you're not ready to tell me that's fine, but I have to go, then. I'm tired and I want to go to bed."

The priest sucked in a breath of air. He could no longer avoid what weighed on his heart.

"I meant to tell you," he began, then paused, finally looking into

Martina's eyes. "I meant to say that you've been most generous towards me."

Martina nodded, returning the priest's gaze with her own intent stare.

"When not many in the village offered me kindness," he continued, shifting his tone from appreciation to blame. "So often the silences, the cold stares, the outright hostility." His voice rose in anger.

Martina glanced away, not wanting to engage his ire. She stood to leave, but he reached for her hand.

"Please," he said. "I'm sorry. I shouldn't nurse such animosity. Please, stay. Let me finish."

The young woman sat back down and spoke. "I'll stay, Antonio, so long as you speak the truth. From your heart, not the bruised places in your bones, the old worn out places that no longer serve you. I've had enough of your anger, my friend. It's time to choose a different way."

Antonio pursed his lips, closed his eyes. He inhaled deeply, trying to quell the rage that flared inside him. It wasn't Martina's words that evoked his fury, but still he wanted to lash out at his friend, scream, rant, tell her she knew nothing about his soul, his heart, or his mind. She was nothing more than a silly young woman, certainly uneducated and unsophisticated. How dare she presume that she could see inside his mind, discern his most intimate thoughts, and dismiss him!

At the creases of his brow the familiar tightness began to bite his temples. He placed his fingertips there and pressed against the pain. A single tear slipped down his cheek. He swiftly wiped it away. But he hadn't moved fast enough to conceal his sorrow. Martina watched the anguish wash across his face.

"Why are you so upset?" she asked.

The priest opened his eyes. He stood and began to pace the room. "You come here under the guise of friendship and insult me!" he seethed.

"Antonio, I meant no harm. You misread my intentions."

"Every time I think you're extending your heart to me, you slap me like a whip, smarting me to the core."

"That can't be true," the young woman asserted. "I've nothing but affection for you."

"Affection?" the priest shouted. "That's not what I'd call the spiteful things you've said."

"Spiteful?" Martina said, her voice rising in anger. "How dare you! If anyone's full of piss and vinegar it's you, Antonio. Not me! My *ayaya's* right about you!"

"Shardana? What possible insights could she have about a man like me?"

"She may not have studied at a university like you, Antonio, but that doesn't mean she's stupid. She's wise beyond any of the things you learned from your fancy books and your narrow education."

"How dare you!" Antonio said, charging at his friend, his hand open, ready to slap her.

Martina stepped aside, averting the swing of the priest's arm. She'd hoped the *majarzas'* exorcism and the villagers' songs would've taken hold by now, but she could clearly see that the priest had much further to go before he was ready to release all the bile that poisoned him. He'd need more time, and perhaps some more medicine for his headaches. It seemed to her the migraines were at least partly responsible for the tirade he was now unleashing at her.

"I won't talk to you when you're like this, Antonio. I'm going to leave now. We can meet again when you're calmer. Then perhaps you'll be ready to tell me what you're really so upset about."

"No!" the priest shouted. "If you leave now, never come back."

"As you wish," she replied, turning toward the door.

Antonio rushed pass her, blocking her departure. "Martina, give me a chance to explain."

"You've run out of chances, Antonio," she told him. "Speak to me civilly. Now. Or never speak to me again."

Antonio clenched his fists and shut his eyes. "My head," he whispered. "The pounding—"

When Martina touched his arm Antonio began to weep. Tears fell from his eyes, and he let them. His fists relaxed, and he reached for his friend's hand, clasping her fingers between his sweaty palms. "I'm so sorry—" he said, grasping for words and air. "Please forgive me—"

His legs buckled and he collapsed to the stone floor, continuing to sob. Martina knelt beside him, placing her arm around his shoulder, offering comfort. When at least Antonio's sorrow had emptied, he spoke.

"I'm an old fool," he began. "A dog who bites its devoted master.

You've been nothing but kind to me, Martina, since the first day I arrived in Orune. Your language lessons, your laughter, the small, un-expected gifts of bread and cheese, the medicine for my headaches. The way you opened your arms to me in the *piazza* yesterday, with the entire village watching. You didn't care what they thought, you befriending the priest who'd rained fire down on you, who'd called for your death and destruction. Your tenderness was the only thing that kept me from lunacy all these many months. And I've been pitiful and slow in repaying you with the respect and homage you deserve."

"It isn't homage I want from you, Antonio," the young woman said. "From the first moment I saw you I felt drawn to you, as if you held a piece of my heart that I'd lost in the hillsides when I was a girl, there among the myrtle bushes and the asphodel reeds. I didn't understand it at first, and I understood it even less as you revealed your surly nature. When you condemned me and the other women I cried, thinking I'd been wrong to have hoped your heart was pure beneath all those layers of hate. Was I wrong, Antonio? Is my *ayaya* right about you? Are you a wolf, sent to destroy everything she and I hold dear?"

"I don't know, Martina. I think there's great truth in your *ayaya*'s words. Although I want to believe I can be a different kind of man. Up until now, my life has fit the picture Shardana has of it. I'm not the soft-hearted fellow you want me to be. Maybe in time I might become that. But for now, I'm what I am. A bit worse for wear from the ways my life has unfolded these past few years. But I'm less harsh than before the singing in the square. The eyes and faces of you villagers pierced something in me. And I don't know yet if I have the courage to mend it in the ways you offered. I only know I can't go on the way I've been."

Martina looked gently into Antonio's sad eyes. She wiped the wet tears that remained on his cheeks and ran her fingers over the purple-red scar. She softly kissed his lips. "I love you, Antonio Albóndiga," she said. "I shouldn't, but I do."

The priest gently returned her kiss, then pressed his lips to hers more firmly, his sadness changing to passion. "I love you too, Mar-tina," he said. "More than I've ever loved anyone."

He gathered her into his arms and kissed her neck, her hands, her face. He untied the belt around her waist, loosening the bodice of her dress. He kissed her bare breasts, her nipples, her belly. She ran her hands along the length of his arms, over his buttocks, down the back of his thighs. She loosened his shirt and the belt that held his pants in place. She placed her hands at his waist, then opened her legs to him.

"Are you sure?" he asked.

"Yes," she said. "I've wanted this for a long, long time."

Chapter 18
As Good As Bread

DURING THE REST OF NOVEMBER Martina visited Antonio under the guise of continuing his Sardo instructions, so she wouldn't draw attention to their budding romance. In mid-December, just before the Feast of Santa Lucia and the winter solstice, she told her *ayaya* and her great-aunt about her love affair with the priest.

"What have you done?" Shardana asked. Her mouth fell open and she slapped her palm against the tabletop.

"Stay calm," Sarda said, reaching for her twin sister's arm. "Let her explain herself."

"It just happened," Martina said. "He's more gentle and loving than you would've expected. Believe me."

"How can you be so sure?" Shardana replied. "It's only been a month since the exorcism. I don't trust that wolf!"

"Our potions were potent," Sarda said. "You know that. And so was the bee venom and the medicine circle the villagers created. Remember, he broke down in the *piazza*. Completely undone. You saw that with your own eyes."

"I know what I saw! And I still don't like this!"

"*Ayaya*—I—I—love him."

"You're only a child, Martina! What can you know what love is?"

"She's sixteen, Shardana. Already a woman. You and I were married with babies when we were her age."

"But he's ten years older than her!"

"The heart doesn't see age, *Ayaya!*"

"No, but it does see cruelty and evil, Martina. I fear for your safety. He's proven himself to be a vile man."

"Give it time, Shardana," Sarda said. "Let the exorcism take hold. Let's see if we were able to coax real and lasting kindness out of Antonio's shriveled heart."

"He better not hurt you, Martina. If he so much as harms one hair on your head, I will see to it that he's exiled from our village. Even if you do love him.

"Don't worry, *Ayaya*. I'll leave him on my own if he's cruel or violent. I promise."

THREE NIGHTS LATER Shardana had a dream.

Two griffons soared over the *piazza* as Martina and Antonio were strolling through the square, hand-in-hand on their way to the woodlands to enjoy a beautiful spring afternoon. Shardana stood by the well and watched them walk by. Her chest tightened at the sight of the priest touching her granddaughter. She stooped to pick up a rock, ready to throw it at Antonio's head when she felt a hand touch her arm.

"Put the rock down, Mama," Grazia said. "Don't worry. You've taught her well and she's chosen wisely. He's not the wolf he was when he first came to Orune. Your medicine took care of that. Give her your blessing. I've given her mine."

"No, Grazia," Shardana said. "I don't trust him."

"Then trust me. Trust her."

THE NEXT MORNING Shardana made Martina a cup of her favorite soothing tonic and set it on the table beside her usual breakfast of bread and cheese.

"Thank you, *Ayaya*. Why the special treatment? It's not my birthday."

"Your mother visited me last night."

"And what did she say?"

"She told me she'd given you and Antonio her blessing. She asked me to give you mine as well."

Martina reached for Shardana's hand. "What have you decided to do?"

"Child, he is not what I want for you. But I won't intervene. I'm not ready to fully bless this union. He still has to prove to me that he will always respect you and treat you well. If he shows himself to be honorable, I think I could come around to it—eventually."

"So be it, then," Martina said.

Shardana kissed her granddaughter's cheek. "Don't rush to marriage, though. Give it time."

"He's a priest, *Ayaya*. He can't marry me."

"Ah, yes. Maybe that's for the best," Shardana replied.

SINCE THAT November day in the *piazza* when the people gathered to dispel the demons that claimed him, the priest's myopia had broadened to encompass a different way of viewing the world. Slowly the community's exorcism was taking hold. Antonio didn't relinquish his belief in Jesus, but he no longer summarily dismissed the views of the others or felt the need to cleanse the blood of those who disagreed with his religion.

Martina's friendship had worked its alchemy, transforming Antonio's vile temperament into a pleasantness that none would've suspected he was capable of. Her acceptance of him proved to be potent. And he was most astonished by how she'd opened her heart to him, becoming his lover. That felt like grace to him, and that, he knew, was no small gift.

Over time and with great patience she schooled him in the ways her people had lived for countless centuries, teaching him about their curious form of conflict resolution, the ways they always thought in circles. "Nothing is linear," she explained. "We think in spirals and circles. Like the seasons, one turning into another, like the wheel rotating round and round, like eyes and mouths, wide and ovate, willing to see and taste the possibilities."

He was surprised by her uncommon wisdom. He hadn't expected such sagacity in a young woman nearing her seventeenth birthday. Slowly the ways of the villagers came to seem natural to him, until at last he, too, began to think that life resembled—if not a circle, then a pendulum, swinging out, then swinging back. Even Jesus had said, "As ye sow, so shall ye reap." Antonio had come to realize that the unbroken arc of the circle held within its strong arms the power of forgiveness.

By early February the cold and long days of darkness settled in, and Antonio found himself with ample idle time. His vegetable garden lay fallow under the frozen, silent ground, and though much of his days were spent at Constantino's side learning to weave baskets, he had also begun to learn the art of whittling. Basilio had given Antonio a prized shepherd's knife, which the priest used to carve small bits of wood as he sat in front of the fire on long winter evenings. At first he sculpted small animals—ewes, hares and foxes. Over time, and without realizing it, his artistic renderings began to resemble the statue of *Nostra Signora Nera* at *Su Tempiesu*. The similarity was lost on him until Martina noted it one day when she visited.

"She's beautiful, Antonio."

"Ah," the priest said. "Her eyes remind me of my mother's."

"And *Nostra Signora Nera's*," the young woman pointed out.

The priest examined the small wooden carving he held in his hands, and saw instantly that both he and his friend were right. The carving's eyes were identical to the eyes of the townspeople's beloved statue—and peering back at him he also saw his mother's eyes. He smiled broadly and chuckled. In the weeks that followed he began to search the woodpile for larger pieces of holm oak and cedar branches to create bigger statues. By early March he'd sculpted a four-foot image of *Nostra Signora*.

"For the altar," he informed Martina and Constantino one afternoon over a cup of wine.

"She's beautiful, *Padre,*" Constantino said. "I only wish I could craft baskets with as much elegance."

"You do, Constantino," Antonio told him. "You do!"

SLOWLY ANTONIO'S once stern façade began to transform. Like wind and water, life in Orune eroded Antonio's rock-hard countenance. In some ways he now resembled the kind-hearted *Santo Francesco,* the rich man who disinherited himself from his father's fortune to live a humble life of servitude in the countryside. Villagers had seen Antonio talking to the sparrows in the chestnut trees outside his home, thinking no one could see or hear him. He frequently spent his mornings walking the hillsides. From time to time he even visited Basilio and the other shepherds in their *tanca*.

Twice a week he began to fulfill the promise he'd made to Giacobbe months before about teaching the boy to speak and read Spanish. One afternoon Giacobbe confided in Antonio. "My father wants me to be a cobbler. But I always refused. I told him I wanted to be a shepherd. But now, I want to be a priest."

Antonio talked to Stefano and Annica, convincing them to send their son to school in Nuoro so he could get the education he needed to pursue his avocation. The boy's parents had seen how Antonio's friendship had helped Giacobbe set aside his rascally ways—and that fact alone pleased them. The boy's newfound focus was a miracle to which every villager could happily attest.

SPRING CAME LATE that year in the Barbagia.

On the first warm day Shardana and Sarda took to the hills and forests, scrounging for fresh herbs to replenish their medicinal pharmacy.

"*Bona commenti su pani.* You're as good as bread," Shardana said, smiling at her twin.

"And more sustaining," Sarda replied.

The women laughed as they trudged through the wildflowers. The winter had been difficult, and it felt good to be walking among the budding flowers and the early shoots of the season. The air cooled their cheeks, but the sun warmed away their cares. After the snowy days and the dark, frigid nights, their supplies had run low from having treated so many colds during the months when summer seemed a distant memory and spring refused to blossom.

A nasty bout of influenza had struck nearly everyone in the village that winter. Even Giacobbe had caught it, and that lad was rarely sick. Constantino missed three days of basketweaving, though he swore it was only two. Stefano recovered quickly, but Annica did not. The twin sisters nearly lost their dear friend, and they fretted and fussed over her, finding the right medicinal combination and the correct dosage until she revived her strength and fully recovered.

Diarrhea weakened Basilio for a full week, and Giovanni, Brontu and Isidoro had to shoulder more responsibility at the sheepfold. When Antonio offered to help, they gladly accepted.

Even after Basilio got better and returned to work, Antonio continued to visit the *tanca*. Once or twice a week Antonio would sit on the ground near the *pinnette* and whittle on small branches he'd collected during his walk up the hillsides. He frequently spent whole afternoons there, watching the shepherds work. From time to time he'd toss small bits of cheese to Basilio's dog, Mutos, who no longer barked at the priest. One late March morning Giovanni and Isidoro were trying to urge a group of stubborn ewes into a pen and Antonio unexpectedly set down his carving knife to help.

That night Antonio had a dream about his great-grandfather, Marco.

Marco was talking to his olive trees, telling them about his great-grandson Antonio. "He used to love the olive groves. I was a very, very old man, but I remember him especially loving the pasturelands. Every year he'd ask his grandfather Jose if he could help shear the sheep. Of course, that was before his father Pablo corrupted his head and his heart with stories of conquests and glory. Pablo thought his son was too good for the land. He sent him off to become a priest. Bah! What good did that come to? He was meant to be a shepherd. Tending to ewes and rams—not the souls of congregations."

The following morning Antonio woke early, dressed, and walked to the *tanca*.

When he reached the pastureland he was surprised to see Shardana and Sarda. The women had brought their shepherds some supplies—a basket of *carasau* flat bread and a couple bottles of *mirto*—to replenish their food and drink.

He nodded at the *majarzas* and the shepherds, who stared at him with curiosity.

"What brings you here today, *Padre?* Time for more whittling?" Isidoro asked.

"Call me Antonio. Not *Padre*. Just Antonio."

Isidoro shrugged. "What about your congregation?'

Antonio walked towards the shepherds and rolled up his sleeves. "Isn't it time to milk the ewes?" he asked.

Giovanni nodded and glanced at the scar on Antonio's face, remembering the time back in June when the priest had cut himself as he tried to help the shepherds shear their sheep. "Be careful, so you don't get hurt."

"The *majarzas* are close at hand if he does," Basilio noted.

Brontu handed Antonio a pail. Mutos barked. Isidoro shook his head in disbelief. "So you're ready to be a shepherd now?"

Antonio nodded. He crouched low and began to milk the ewe. He squirted some of the warm liquid into his mouth, swallowed, then smiled. "Ah! The elixir of life!" he said.

Sarda smiled, and Shardana shook her head.

"The exorcism," Sarda whispered to her twin. "It has finally taken hold."

Antonio pulled on the ewe's teat, letting a steady stream of warm milk hit the bottom of his pail. "Have you ever heard a more beautiful sound?" he asked.

Giovanni and Brontu slapped their knees and laughed.

"Welcome to our *tanca*," Isidoro said.

"We'd better get you some warmer clothes," Shardana said. "The spring nights are still cold in these hills."

"And a sleeping mat," Sarda added. "You'll need something to cushion the dirt floor of the *pinnette*."

"I hope you don't snore," Brontu said.

"Only when I'm dreaming," Antonio replied. A wide grin claimed his face.

"Perhaps the sea-wolf no longer needs to bare his teeth," Sarda said.

"Yes, it seems his heart has let go of its ambition for conquest," Shardana noted.

With one hand on the ewe's teat, Antonio paused to momentarily eye the *majarzas* and the shepherds who were watching him. He shrugged and, without a word, continued milking.

"*Bona commenti su pani,*" Basilio said. "Antonio, you're as good as bread."

"But is he as sustaining?" Isidoro added.

"Only time will tell," Shardana said. "Only time will tell."

Epilogue

IN MID-DECEMBER, NEARLY A MONTH after Antonio's ranting and raving in the town *piazza*, the long unmarried Anna-Bella met Stefano's nephew, Tommaso, who was a cobbler like his uncle. Tommaso had learned the trade from his father, Natale, Stefano's brother. Natale had passed away unexpectedly that November, and Stefano and Annica had gone to his funeral, reuniting with Stefano's family, who lived in a village across the mountain pass. While he was there, Stefano invited Tommaso to visit Orune. One evening during Tommaso's stay, Annica asked the *majarzas* and their families over to meet Stefano's nephew. She served them flat bread with honey and introduced Tommaso to Anna-Bella.

"She's a masterful beekeeper and a skilled basketmaker," Stefano said. Nodding at Sarda, he added, "And the daughter of one of Orune's *majarzas*."

"She's not married," Annica whispered in her nephew's ear as she refilled his cup. "Can you image one so beautiful without a husband? You should do something about that."

Tommaso discretely glanced at Anna-Bella, and she discretely returned his glances. Throughout the rest of the evening they exchanged knowing smiles, silently indicating their interest in one another.

Before Tommaso left for home the next morning, he stopped at

Sarda and Constantino's home, to ask the healer and her husband if he could court their daughter.

"You'll have to ask her," Sarda said. "She's a grown woman."

Overhearing the conversation, Anna-Bella entered the room and smiled. "I would like that very much, indeed."

Anna-Bella and Tommaso were married on the first of January. Sarda tried to convince them to plan a spring wedding so they could have a proper celebration with a feast outside in the warm spring sunshine, but her daughter refused. "I've waited long enough, Mama. I want to marry now."

The bride and her groom exchanged rings to the sound of their loved ones' New Year's well wishes, "*Saludi e trigu!*" Good health and wheat!

Tommaso moved to Orune to work alongside Stefano. The cobbler was pleased to have someone he could pass the family business on to, since Giacobbe, who had never showed interest in learning that trade, was off in Nuoro studying to become a priest.

In February Teresina became pregnant with her second child. Isidoro was unable to conceal his joy. He didn't stop grinning for weeks. He wept when the ewes began birthing in the sheepfold that spring, thinking of the new child that would soon bless his own home the coming autumn. In November their daughter, Valentina, was born.

"She's got Basilio's eyes," Shardana said as she held her granddaughter close to her heart. "And Isidoro's nose!"

Valentina's older brother, Donatello, disagreed. "I think she looks like a wrinkly old ewe!" He poked his baby sister's belly before running outside. Although generally a kind-hearted boy, Donatello had a mischievous streak. His favorite pastime was to chase the hens in the yard. Shardana sometimes worried that her grandson would follow in Giacobbe's foolish footsteps. "Don't fret," Sarda said. "Donatello doesn't show the slightest trace of the sourness that sometimes takes hold of the cobbler's son."

In late spring Giovanni fell in love with Teresina's cousin, Minnia, who lived in a town across the valley. The two had met at the winter holiday celebrations when Minnia's family had travelled to Orune to see Teresina and Brontu. Though the heavy snow had prevented Giovanni from seeing Minnia very often after she returned home with her mother and her father, after the lambs were birthed in February he was able to spend a few of his rare days off with her in her village, and their courtship blossomed. They were married that June, and Minnia moved to Orune to live with her new husband and his family.

During their courtship, it pained Shardana to see Giovanni with someone other than Grazia. But Martina took a strong liking to Minnia, and Sarda and the rest of Shardana's family felt great affection for Giovanni's new love. What finally won Shardana over was Minnia's interest in preparing the tinctures, poultices, and salves that the healers used to treat their patients. While Minnia didn't have Grazia's innate gifts as a healer, she had a kind and generous heart and was eager to work beside them, helping in the ways she could.

By then Martina had moved in with Antonio. One day she had mentioned to Shardana and Sarda, "Since Minnia married my father and came to live with us, our house is too crowded. Antonio has his whole house to himself."

"It makes sense," Sarda agreed.

Shardana frowned, without saying a word.

"You'll see me every day, *Ayaya*, when we treat patients."

"I suppose you're right," Shardana said, her lips softening. "Go ahead. Live with the priest. But know you have a home here if you need. Always."

"He's not a priest any more, *Ayaya*. He's a shepherd."

"Well, he's got a long way to go before he masters that trade," Shardana said. "Until he does, he's still a priest in my mind."

When it came to all things related to Antonio, Martina was used to her *ayaya's* grumpiness. She smiled and touched Shardana's hand. "I'll tell Antonio tonight. He'll be so pleased. For months, he's been asking me to move in with him."

DURING THE FIRST YEAR of Anna-Bella's new marriage, she'd tried twice to conceive and had miscarried both times. She was so inconsolable that she'd stop visiting the wild hives to tend to her beloved bees. She'd all but given up hope of holding a child of her own in her arms until her mother and her aunt approached her one day, with a special concoction they'd distilled.

"The bees told us exactly what was needed," Shardana told her.

"And the plants we selected happily obliged," Sarda added.

By the end of her third year of marriage Anna-Bella found herself carrying not one, but two fetuses. Sustained throughout her pregnancy by the medicinal herbs prepared by the *majarzas* and the love and devotion of her husband, Anna-Bella gave birth to a son and a daughter, whom she named Mario and Maria. Sarda wept for joy as the babies' heads emerged from her daughter's body gleefully sucking air into their lungs. Both children were healthy and grew strong and quickly, nursing at their jubilant mother's breasts.

Two months later Isidoro's wife, Teresina, gave birth to her third child, another son, whom they named Bonfiglio. As Shardana cradled the new babe in her strong arms her heart beat fiercely. "Bonfiglio has Grazia's eyes!" she exclaimed. "Isidoro's nose. And Teresina's lips."

"The perfect combination," Sarda agreed. "He's also got your fiery spirit. When he's hungry, his howling rattles the walls of Isidoro's house. The hens cluck and race off down the street, filling the *piazza* with so much clatter the women at the well cover their ears and shake their heads."

The sisters laughed. "I remember when Grazia was a baby, oh so long ago," Shardana reminisced. "How fragile she seemed, how tender her soul. Everyone in the village loved her, even when she was only a small child. She'd visit the neighbors and return home with small gifts tucked tightly into her pudgy fists. A piece of bread. An almond. A slice of cheese. Sometimes only a kiss, which she'd show me with great relish before safeguarding it dearly, storing each kiss in a jar right next to my herbs and tinctures. 'Like medicine,' she'd always say. 'A kiss is as good as your medicines, Mama.'"

"Such an unbearable loss!" Sarda said. "She was taken from us too early."

Shardana nodded, wiping tears from her damp eyes. "Yes, but the *Dea Madre* sent Teresina to Isidoro and more grandbabies to fill my arms. She sent Viviana to Brontu and grandbabies for you. And Minnia, of course. Giovanni is so happy! Who would have guessed Minnia would so quickly learn how to apply the salves and poultices we make for our patients. Grazia would be so proud of her family."

"And especially of Martina," Sarda added. "She'll carry on Grazia's legacy, and ours. Thanks to her and Minnia, our bloodlines and our medicinal secrets will survive into the future."

"Grazie is very proud of Martina," Shardana agreed. "And I am, too. As long as she doesn't marry that priest."

"He's a shepherd now," Sarda teased. "Besides, priests can't get married."

"When have rules and regulations ever prevented Martina from doing what she wanted to do?" Shardana asked. "She lives through her heart, which is a wise and precarious way to live. In time we'll see how well her life unfolds. For now, I'm content to grow old and watch her discover what fate has in store for her. She tells me she wants to have babies with Antonio. No marriage, but babies. She's always been a rebel."

"Maybe she's more like you than you think," Sarda said.

Shardana nodded. "I think you're right."

"Well, if she does decide to have children, may she be blessed with many healthy ones," Sarda said. "And may one of them be born a *majarza!*"

THE FOLLOWING WINTER Constantino took ill a month after the birth of Anna-Bella's twins. His face grew pale and his eyes dimmed. He developed a rattling cough, and nothing Sarda and Shardana concocted was able to ease his discomfort. Aches spiraled into fever and stabbing pain. He lost his appetite and slept most days. On the night he died, Sarda held his hand and sang to him songs about fields of asphodel and reeds, describing intricately made baskets of exquisite design created from the bounty of the hillsides. She comforted the man who'd blessed her life, giving her two strong children and decades of companionship and devoted love. When her husband breathed his final breath, Sarda kissed his forehead and then his lips. "Go well, my love," she whispered. "I'll meet up with you in time." She placed her wrinkled hands over her face and wept.

The twin sisters prepared Constantino's body for burial. They washed his cold limbs and anointed his hands, feet and brow with sacred, scented oil. They dressed him in woolen pants and a white shirt. They combed his thinning gray hair and placed his favorite black beret on his head. Beside him they set the last basket he'd completed, its center emblazoned with a red star. They sang the songs of his childhood and prepared the foods of his youth. They toasted the man they both held dear, and celebrated the wisdom and kindness he'd shared with them during his living.

At Constantino's burial the *majarzas* and their family members bowed their heads in silent prayer. The widow Sarda asked the *Dea Madre* to cradle Constantino in her dark womb, and birth him into the world that waited beyond one he'd so newly left. Basilio's chest tightened with grief and he wept for his brother. Shardana and the others—Anna-Bella, her husband and children, Brontu, Teresina and their children, Giovanni, Minnia and Martina, Isidoro, Viviana and their young ones, and Antonio—sang the mournful dirge of the *attitadoras*, blessing Constantino's life as was the Barbaricini custom. As their dirge filled the air Sarda wailed, lifting her face toward the sky, tears streaming down her sallow cheeks.

Shardana wrapped her arm around her sister's shuddering shoulders, whispering, "Ah, *mia sorella*, ah, ah, ah—" The residue of her own longing for her departed daughter, Grazia, gnawed at her bones. With all her heart she wished she could erase Sarda's misery, though she knew nothing in her apothecary was potent enough to do so. Time and kindness were the necessary antidote to Sarda's despair. Time and kindness she'd have—Shardana would see to it, as her sister had done for her so many times before.

Sarda lived another twenty years, long enough to see Anna-Bella's twins grow into young adults with families of their own; long enough to see Martina grow into the fullness of her *majarza* skills and give birth to a daughter, Grazia-Maria; long enough to see Giovanni and Minnia give Martina a half-brother, whom they named Matteo; long enough, too, to help Shardana bury her beloved Basilio and to watch Brontu and Isidoro—and even Antonio—deepen their skills as seasoned shepherds and makers of exquisite cheese.

With Sarda's passing, Shardana spiraled into a deep despair, the likes of which she'd not experienced since Grazia's death decades before. Shardana felt as if half of her heart had been ripped from her chest, half her lungs dismembered, half her soul tossed into thin air. Life without her twin held little joy for the old woman Shardana had become.

Though in time her gloom dissipated, she was never quite the same. She went about her daily duties, providing consultations with Martina regarding her patients, continuing to treat a few of her own as well, as her energy allowed. Every spring she trucked through the hillsides with Martina and Minnia to harvest the fresh crop of medicinal herbs. On the mountainside she'd rest against the sturdy branches of the ancient holm oaks and dream of her sister, of Basilio, and of Grazia. On long dark nights, alone in her home sitting by the hearth, she'd review the events of the evening of Grazia's death, second-guessing the decisions she'd made, the medicines she'd used, the treatments that had failed to save her daughter, and she'd cry, wrapping her arms around her waist, rocking in grief.

One evening Antonio paid her a visit, bearing a gift in his arms.

"*Buona sera*, Shardana," he said when the wise woman opened her door. "May I come in?"

"As you wish," Shardana replied.

Antonio set the wrapped bundle beside a chair and sat down. Shardana set a crust of fresh-baked bread, a slice of *pecorino sardo*, and a small bowl of figs on the table for her guest.

"*Grazie*," the priest said. "You've been too kind to me. Kinder than I often deserved."

"Kindness is the truest religion, Antonio. In my long life that's the one thing I've learned the most. The Divine breathes kindness into our hearts, and it's our charge to kindle it amd share it with others. Nothing more complicated than that. Nothing more difficult, as well."

"Indeed," Antonio said, before motioning to the bundle he had set beside his chair. "I've brought you something."

He stood and unveiled the gift, revealing a four-foot sculpture he'd carved for her from the darkest wood he'd collected from the deep heart of the forest. From out of the dimming light the olive-colored eyes of *Nostra Signora Nera* stared kindly at the old woman's stunned face and Antonio's shy smile.

"She's magnificent, Antonio. Thank you!"

"A gift for you from the Mother," the priest replied. "And from Grazia's granddaughter, our daughter Grazia-Maria."

Shardana touched the Mother's blue-black cheek. "Grazia loved *Nostra Signora Nera*. So deeply."

"Yes. Martina has told me this many, many times," Antonio said. "I dreamt of Grazia and Martina one night a few months ago. They walked hand in hand in a field of red poppies and dark wheat, singing songs and laughing. They spoke of the Dark Mother. They kept calling Her the Sacred One. Grazia-Maria was there, too, running through the fields, picking herbs and talking to the bees. They all spoke of you. They said no one surpassed your skills at midwifery. Grazia wanted you to know that her dying wasn't your fault. She asked Martina to have me sculpt this statue for you, so you would hear your daughter's message and know that she harbored no ill will toward you for that night so long ago when you weren't able to save her."

Shardana wept. "Grazia!" she called out. "I'm sorry!"

Antonio took Shardana's hand in his and held fast. "There's only kindness, Shardana. Remember, there's only kindness. And abiding forgiveness."

SHARDANA WOULD LIVE to be very, very old, simply falling asleep in her bed before dawn on a mid-summer morning, never to awaken. Martina and Minnia attended to her body, anointing her with sacred oil, dressing her in the traditional woolen garment of her village, placing a black woolen scarf on her head. They kissed her closed eyelids and chanted prayers to the *Dea Madre*, beseeching Her to accept Shardana into Her loving embrace. They wept at her passing, but took comfort knowing that she'd lived a long and fruitful life and she was now at home, once more, with Sarda, Basilio, Constantino. And Grazia.

Antonio attended the burial service, not in any priestly capacity, but as one of the many villagers in mourning, sounding out the *atti-itidus* for the loss of their beloved friend and the town's revered senior *majarza*. Into the wind they released their song of lamentation, their voices joining together in one singular dirge.

Beside the stream next to the sacred water temple at *Su Tempiesu* the people placed Shardana's body into the ground. The sun shone brightly that day, though the hearts of each mourner wore a cloak of gloom. The sparrows sang, the bees buzzed, the crows cawed, and above Shardana's gravesite a pair of griffon hawks circled. Beside her *ayaya*'s coffin Martina set a handful of acorns from the ancient *Madre Vecchia*, the oldest holm oak in the forest. Then Martina sprinkled the earth with water from the sacred well and covered her *ayaya*'s coffin with a red cloth.

"Into the womb of the Mother, we place Shardana today," Isidoro intoned.

"Into the womb of the Mother, we return our mother back to Your most holy arms," Martina added, choking back tears.

"Into the womb of the Mother, she shall rest and restore, making ready for her return," Minnia said, eyes gazing intently at Shardana's coffin of holm oak.

"Into the womb of the Mother, we weep tears of sadness at her passing," Anna-Bella proclaimed.

"Into the womb of the Mother, we release our sorrow," Giovanni whispered.

"Into the womb of the Mother, my mother is laid to rest," Isidoro said, wiping tears from his cheeks. She was as good as bread."

"And more sustaining," Antonio added.

"It is finished in beauty," Martina announced.

"Blessed be," Viviana and Teresina replied.

"Blessed be," the others said, in unison. "Blessed be."

Acknowledgements

THIS NOVEL WAS INSPIRED BY a trip I took to Sardinia in 2004 as part of a Dark Mother Study tour led by Lucia Chiavola Birnbaum. We visited ancient ruins left by the island's earliest inhabitants, archeological museums that contained countless cultural and material artifacts, and Catholic churches in which the Black Madonna was venerated. I was deeply moved by the island's prehistoric memory of a time when the Divine Female, whom the Sardinians call *La Dea Madre* (God the Mother) was venerated. I was also struck by the culture's matrifocal sensibility and the ways in which members of the island's earliest communities would come together to collectively resolve issues.

I am grateful to Norcroft, a writing retreat center for women (now defunct) for the gift of time and space and creative support. The first drafts of many of this novel's chapters were written there, in my writing room by the shores of Lake Superior. I am also grateful to Nancy Caronia and Sandy Shwayder Sanchez for reading early drafts of the novel and providing their insightful feedback.

I would like to thank my partner/spouse, Jane Butz, for her ongoing love and unwavering support. She has always been the most avid champion of my work. I am grateful to my sisters, Teresa and Peg, and their spouses, Linda and Steve, as well as my brothers, Stefano,

Michael, Peter, and David, and their spouses, Eileen, Maggie, Jo, and Mary Alice, for their loving support and their encouragement of my creative efforts. Thanks are also due to my mother, Margaret Malley, and my father, Frank Saracino, and his wife, Rose, for their love and support. I am grateful to my dear friends Mary Beth Moser, Cheryl Hagen, and Judy Maselli for the many ways that they have supported my creative efforts and my spiritual journey.

I would like to thank my publisher, Peggy Elam, for believing in me and publishing my work. Working with her is a writer's dream come true.

I would like to thank all the people who have read my work and bought my books over the many years since my first novel was published in 1993. Your votes of confidence (and your patience) have helped sustain me through the long process of writing a novel.

Lastly, as always, I would like to thank my grandmothers, Fiora Lazzuri Vergamini and Immacolata Patella Saracino, who bequeathed to me a genetic memory of the ancient times, which I carry in my soul. I am listening, and I remember too.

MARY SARACINO

About the Author

MARY SARACINO IS A NOVELIST, POET, and memoir writer who lives in Denver, Colorado. Her novel *The Singing of Swans* (Pearlsong Press, 2006) was a 2007 Lambda Literary Awards finalist. She is the co-editor (with Mary Beth Moser) of *She Is Everywhere! Volume 3: An Anthology of Writings in Womanist/Feminist Spirituality* (iUniverse 2012), which earned the 2013 Enheduanna Award for Excellence in Women-Centered Literature from Sofia University. Mary's short story "Vicky's Secret" earned the 2007 Glass Woman Prize.

Mary's other book-length work includes the novels *No Matter What* (Spinsters Ink, 1993) and *Finding Grace* (Spinsters Ink, 1999) and the memoir *Voices of the Soft-bellied Warrior* (Spinsters Ink Books, 2001). Her poetry and stories (creative nonfiction and fiction) have been published in a variety of literary and cultural journals and anthologies, both online and in print.

Mary is a member of the editorial board for *Return to Mago: Magoism, the Way of S/HE* (http://magoism.net). She is also a writing coach/teacher/editor and the founder of MOTHEROOT, which offers embodied art-making and creative writing workshops and classes centered on the Dark Mother/Divine Female.

For more information, email or visit

MARY@MARYSARACINO.COM

WWW.MARYSARACINO.COM

Words of Praise

The Singing of Swans

"Women who fly through the night skies, priestesses who receive initiations, and girls who do vision quests in ancient sacred caves—all this wonderful pagan lore Mary Saracino juxtaposes against an all-too-modern heroine's chaotic awakening to the deeper purpose of her life. This well-researched page-turner is packed with herbal knowledge, her-story lessons, and a genuine understanding of ancient and contemporary women's spirituality. Rich and powerful—I hope it will become a movie!"

Vicki Noble
co-creator of *Motherpeace,* author of *Shakti Woman: Feeling Our Fire, Healing Our World* & *The Double Goddess: Women Sharing Power*

"*The Singing of Swans* is more than a novel. It combines an immense amount of learning, a great novelist's ability to weave the present, the past, the far past, and the future into a spell-binding story... and to transmute all this into an offer of life to all of us trapped in contemporary deadening cultures."

Lucia Chiavola Birnbaum
author of *Dark Mother: African Origins and Godmothers*

"*The Singing of Swans* lives up to the promise of its title in every imaginable way. The author's evocations of the natural world are exquisite, as are her descriptions of a history so ancient it blends into myth. The author has combined a great deal of historical research with a soaring imagination, a passion for nature and a gift for drawing believable characters to create a truly masterful work that includes and transcends actual history, myth and epic poetry. Its theme is the age old conflict between the respectful nurturance of the earth and its gifts, and the rapacious exploitation of nature motivated by greed....[It] will appeal to serious readers interested in magical realist literature, feminist spirituality, religious history, mythology and herbal lore, as well as those who just love a good story brilliantly told. Highly recommended!"

Sandra Shwayder Sanchez
Front Street Reviews

"Saracino's mythology gives a voice to women while also providing social commentary about oppressive forces throughout history. Woven through Madalene's story are the stories of other Streghe: Rosalina, Josephina, Ibla, and Magda, and their struggles to maintain their voice and their connections to the Divine Mother. Using the physical connection of blood ties—to our ancestors and Mother Earth—as well as spiritual ties, Saracino illustrated our sacred connection to the divine in nature and each other, woven as thread through a tapestry, to the past and the future. While I occasionally enjoy a fun story in a nice, neat package, I truly appreciate those stories that leave me asking questions and searching within myself. How am I connected to all that has happened in the past and all that will happen in the future? We are not islands unto ourselves and Saracino shows our connections—how our pasts have shaped our world today and how we shape the future."

JEANNE WINSLOW
Feminist Review

NO MATTER WHAT

"Unflinching, insightful, beautifully written..."

DOROTHY ALLISON
author, *Bastard Out of Carolina*

"In this strong first novel, Mary Saracino creates a strong narrator who quickly engages our sympathy. Saracino excels at creating the inner turmoil of the child with an adult burden and the powerful emotions at work in this dysfunctional family. The book is absorbing..."

ROCKY MOUNTAIN NEWS

FINDING GRACE

"A timeless narrative so beautifully written it was hard to put down. Finding Grace left nothing to be desired, a gut wrenching story where things truly end for the best."

JUDGE'S COMMENTS
*1999 Colorado Authors League "Top Hand" Award
for Mainstream Fiction*

Voices of the Soft-bellied Warrior

"As much an intimate story about the art of writing as it is about her struggle to literally gain back her voice, Mary Saracino's memoir is a brave and intricately drawn map of her long journey from trauma to recovery."

JUDITH KATZ
author of *Running Fiercely Toward a High Thin Sound*
& *The Escape Artist*

"This is the book that I've been waiting to read. This is the book that I will read and reread. This is the book that shows the pain. But this is the book that shows the possibility, too. A stupendous achievement. Saracino speaks here as she has never spoken before; as no one has ever spoken before."

LOUISE DESALVO
author of *Vertigo* & *We Begin with Food: Italian American Women Write About Identity, Ethnicity, and Sustenance*

She is Everywhere! Volume 3: An Anthology of Writings in Womanist/Feminist Spirituality

"Filled with essays, stories, poetry, and works of art...a huge cauldron filled with a nourishing stew of Goddess spirituality. No matter if you've been devoted to the Goddess for twenty years or you're a newbie just meeting her, this is a book worth reading and savoring. But it's not fast food! You need to carefully chew and savor what you're reading and seeing. When you do, you'll be nourished for a long time."

BARBARA ARDINGER, PH.D., WWW.BARBARAARDINGER.COM
author of *Secret Lives* & *Pagan Every Day*

"I propose that this volume, an important addition to college courses in women's spirituality, women's and gender studies, philosophy, and religion, is also comari. As we, the readers, move within this laboratory, we are encouraged to bring forth from within our bodies, hearts and minds the values of justice with compassion, equality for all people and transformation that characterize the world/s where She is Everywhere."

LOUISE M. PARÉ, PH.D.

About Pearlsong Press

PEARLSONG **P**RESS **IS AN INDEPENDENT** publishing company dedicated to providing books and resources that entertain while expanding perspectives on the self and the world. The company was founded by Peggy Elam, Ph.D., a psychologist and journalist, in 2003.

We encourage you to enjoy other Pearlsong Press books, which you can purchase at www.pearlsong.com or your favorite bookstore. Keep up with us through our blog at www.pearlsongpress.com as we promote health, happiness and social justice at every size.

Healing the World One Book at a Time

Fiction

Judith—an historical novel by Leslie Moïse
Fatropolis—a paranormal adventure by Tracey L. Thompson
The Falstaff Vampire Files, Bride of the Living Dead, Larger Than Death,
Large Target, At Large & A Ton of Trouble—paranormal adventure, romantic
comedy & Josephine Fuller mysteries by Lynne Murray
The Season of Lost Children—a novel by Karen Blomain
Fallen Embers & Blowing Embers—Books 1 & 2 of The Embers Series,
paranormal romance by Lauri J Owen
The Program & The Fat Lady Sings—suspense novel & young adult novels
by Charlie Lovett
Syd Arthur—a novel by Ellen Frankel
Measure By Measure—a romantic romp with the fabulously fat
by Rebecca Fox & William Sherman
FatLand & FatLand: The Early Days—Books 1 & 2 of The FatLand Trilogy
by Frannie Zellman
The Singing of Swans—a novel about the Divine Feminine
by Mary Saracino

Romance Novels & Short Stories Featuring Big Beautiful Heroines

by Pat Ballard, the Queen of Rubenesque Romances:
ASAP Nanny | *Dangerous Love* | *The Best Man* | *Abigail's Revenge*
Dangerous Curves Ahead: Short Stories | *Wanted: One Groom* | *Nobody's Perfect*
His Brother's Child | *A Worthy Heir*
by Rebecca Brock—*The Giving Season*
& by Judy Bagshaw—*Kiss Me, Nate!* & *At Long Last, Love*

Nonfiction

Acceptable Prejudice? Fat, Rhetoric & Social Justice
& *Talking Fat: Health vs. Persuasion in the War on Our Bodies*
by Lonie McMichael, Ph.D.
Hiking the Pack Line: Moving from Grief to a Joyful Life
by Bonnie Shapbell
A Life Interrupted: Living with Brain Injury—
poetry by Louise Mathewson
ExtraOrdinary: An End of Life Story Without End—
memoir by Michele Tamaren & Michael Wittner
Love is the Thread: A Knitting Friendship by Leslie Moïse, Ph.D.
Fat Poets Speak: Voices of the Fat Poets' Society &
Fat Poets Speak 2: Living and Loving Fatly—Frannie Zellman, Ed.
Ten Steps to Loving Your Body (No Matter What Size You Are)
by Pat Ballard
Beyond Measure: A Memoir About Short Stature & Inner Growth
by Ellen Frankel
*Taking Up Space: How Eating Well & Exercising Regularly Changed My
Life* by Pattie Thomas, Ph.D. with Carl Wilkerson, M.B.A. (foreword by
Paul Campos, author of *The Obesity Myth*)
*Off Kilter: A Woman's Journey to Peace with Scoliosis, Her Mother & Her
Polish Heritage*—a memoir by Linda C. Wisniewski
Unconventional Means: The Dream Down Under—
a spiritual travelogue by Anne Richardson Williams
Splendid Seniors: Great Lives, Great Deeds—
inspirational biographies by Jack Adler

www.ingramcontent.com/pod-product-compliance
Lightning Source LLC
Chambersburg PA
CBHW021059030726
47496CB00006B/1906